P9-EMJ-530

50

The Loyalist's Wife

Elaine A. Cougler

Peache House Press

Peache House Press

Certain characters in this work are historical figures, and certain events portrayed did take place. However, this is a work of fiction. All of the other characters, names and events as well as all places, incidents, organizations, and dialogue in this novel are either the products of the author's imagination or are used fictitiously.

Copyright © 2013 by Elaine Cougler

All rights reserved.

No part of this book may be reproduced or re-transmitted without the express written consent of the author.

Cover by Spica Book Design. Cover artwork from a painting by Pietro Antonio Rovari, 1701-1762.

Text layout and design by To The Letter Word Processing Inc.

The back cover photo of the author was taken by Paula Tizzard.

Printed and bound with www.createspace.com

ISBN-13:
978-1490414898

Acknowledgements

THESE PARAGRAPHS ARE TO THANK the numbers of knowledgeable and helpful people whose work for and belief in my project have contributed in large measure to its success. Museum and historical site curators, as well as a number of librarians, have pointed me toward books which I might not have found but for their interest in my project and their thorough understanding of the resources they have.

A number of readers, Wayne Caslick, Karen McSpadden, Kevin Cougler, Marie Avey, John Cook, Millie Gremonprez, Urve Tamberg, and Alva Forsyth, kindly read my rough draft and offered helpful suggestions. Some of them gave unstintingly of their time to read and comment on subsequent revisions. To all of these, I offer my sincere thanks for their generosity and their knowledge.

For unwavering support in answering questions and encouraging me over and over again, I thank my friend, Sharon Clare, whom I met in an excellent writing class. And I thank the writers, critique partners, and workshop presenters whose comments have frustrated, puzzled, and ultimately helped me to get to publication. One of those whom I met along the way is Terry Fallis, winner of the Stephen Leacock Medal for Humour for *The Best Laid Plans*. Terry's unstinting generosity and kind encouragement have culminated in his testimonial on my book cover, for which I am deeply grateful.

My sister, Linda, has been the keeper of my offsite manuscript for several years, through many updates and revisions and even through two moves, mine and hers. My son, Kevin, recognized that I could and should write this novel, and my daughter, Beth, always gave me excellent and honest advice, even when it might hurt. My husband Ron, has been my partner on the research trips, has respected the closed door of my office, and has helped me through the occasional lows that accompany the writing process on a journey of this magnitude. These are the wonderful people closest to me who have believed in me. Without them, I truly could not have completed this work. Thank you, all.

For Ron, Kevin, and Beth,
my personal Loyalists

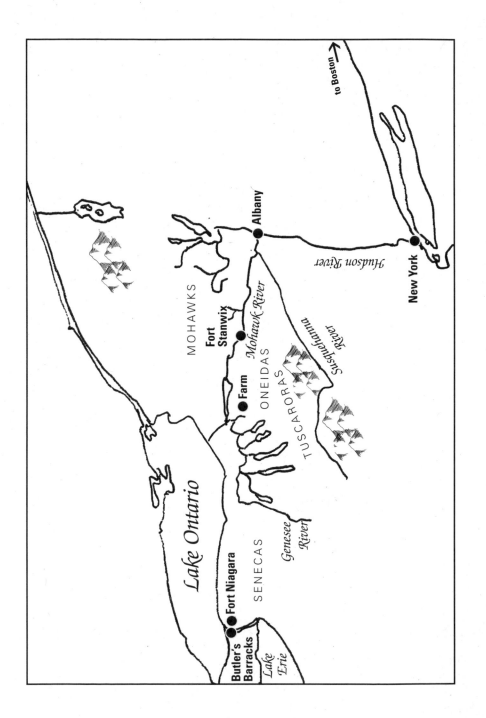

Chapter One

New York State
April, 1778

JOHN WATCHED HIS SMILING LUCINDA carry the pail of water into the cabin and thought how lucky he was to have fallen for her. She hefted the bucket to the sideboard and began filling the kettle. In the last two years she had learned to milk the cow, yoke the oxen, and chop wood for their stove. She barely reached his shoulder and was so slight he could wrap his arms around her until they touched his own sides again.

From his chair at the table he watched her. White apron ties streamed over her grey homespun skirt which swept back and forth over plain dark shoes darting across the bare plank floor. She hummed a sprightly tune and he smiled to hear its joy, a reflection of his own since they married. He wanted to reach out for the flaming red-gold tendrils cascading down her back, sparkling in the morning sun which streamed in their one window. He longed to stretch out the happy moment.

"Lucy."

She flashed him a wide smile and brushed an errant curl behind her ear.

"You should let me carry the water," he said.

"Honestly, I don't mind. I can carry it just fine." Two spots of brilliant blue sparkled his way and she winked at him before swishing her skirts around back to her task.

He chuckled and reached for the red-hot axe head on the stove top. The broken handle bits needed to be chipped out and replaced with the new handle he had made before he could cut more wood. He should be out in the field finishing the planting but Lucy would need the axe. "Stand back. Away from this axe head." With his hammer and chisel, he pried out the bits of burned wood. "There. The rough part's done."

Lucy moved to his side and set the kettle on the stove. "Why are you doing that just now? Shouldn't you be finishing the planting?" She laid her hand on his arm a moment before carrying on with her chores.

He set the axe head to cool on the metal shelf above the stove. Already its red heat was dissipating but John felt his own temperature rising. He took a long, lingering breath, held it a moment, and sat again at the table.

"I have something to tell you, Lucinda."

"Lucinda! Only my father ever called me that." She looked at him again and set the water dipper on the dry sink. She wiped her hands on her apron and sat at the table facing him. "What's wrong, John?"

He cleared his throat, swallowed, and spoke. "You know what's been happening with the militia and the British? I mean the fights and the tension everywhere?" *Of course she knew. Why did he start with that?*

"Yes," she said. "That rider last week spoke of ruffians in Boston again and the King's men leaving entirely." Her brows twisted into a frown. "But what does it all have to do with us so far away?'

"That rider, Hilton Cross, was looking for men to ride with Butler's Rangers, a group of soldiers who support the King, and..." he reached for her hands across the rough-hewn table worn smooth with daily living, "I am going with them."

He held his breath and watched his reflection shrink in her narrowing eyes. Her hands jerked out of his.

"You're going where?" Her voice rose with each word. "You're leaving me here alone?" She stared, right into his soul, it seemed. "You're not joking?"

"No, I'm not joking. Lucy, we have to fight for what we have. We cannot just sit back and hope the British will do it for us."

"But…you need to be here. To do the planting. And…and clear the next three acres."

"I'm sure you can do the chores, and the clearing can wait until I get back."

"But when will that be, John?" She had tears in her eyes now. She sat back in her chair and stared at him. "You might never come back."

"Now, now. Of course I will," he said, but a slight tremor took hold of him and he sat silent a moment. "I've thought and thought about what is best to do." He straightened his shoulders. "We must stand up and fight for our land. It's the only way to get rid of these ruffians once and for all." He reached again for her hands but she pulled away.

"How long have you been preparing that speech?"

"Lucy. That's not how it is. Please listen to me!"

She pushed out of the chair and stormed through the curtain into the bedroom. He could hear her slamming drawers and muttering. And then she stomped back into the room.

He faced her. "The crops are almost planted. It will be months before harvest. Don't you see? I have to go now!" He slammed back from the table and glared at her, his fingers clenched into tight fists. "I thought you would understand. I thought you'd want me to fight for our land."

"I don't understand why you've taken sides with the British. There must be something you're not telling me."

John flinched but held his tongue. She didn't need to know.

"Can you really be leaving me to do all of this work myself? I, I…" She twisted back and forth before him, for once at a loss for words. And then she reached for his arm. "But, John, the land stealers we heard about…"

He swallowed but sat silent, watching her, wishing he might wipe away her worry, wanting to hold her to him and keep out the warring world. *Why can't she see?*

She slumped into a chair and dropped her face into her crossed arms. Her shoulders heaved. Her breath came in great gasps and he watched her hands tighten and whiten on her arms. He knew she was trying to hold back tears and his own eyes were blinking fast. He stomped to the door, opened it, and crashed outside.

AS LUCY SOBBED OUT HER MISERY, thoughts of blue-coated soldiers and haggard men straggling through thick trees flooded her brain. Threatening strangers smashing at her door, long nights alone in the cabin, and longer days afraid of every sound—all these possibilities assailed her. But what really scared her was the thought that while she was here carrying on as best she could, John would be fighting and maybe getting hurt or worse. She couldn't quite bring herself to think of what that 'worse' could be as John was her life, her whole life.

As her breakfast pitched back and forth in her belly, tossing like the small boat they took up the Hudson in the fierce wind those two years back, she looked around their two-room cabin. His rocking chair sat near the stove, a treasure they had brought with them from Boston. What a trip. John had spent the summer before on the farm, felling trees, clearing the land and working a forty foot square for a garden, building the log cabin with not one but two rooms, and counting the days, he had written her, until it was time to take the long journey back to Boston, get married, and bring her here to start their life together.

She closed her eyes and saw again her father's stern face—he hadn't wanted to trust this stranger from the back woods—as he handed her to John in the parlor before a very few witnesses. John's fresh shave had revealed for the first time that morning the dimple on his chin and she had watched it waffle and wiggle as he repeated the wedding vows. She had raised her smiling face to his for the kiss that sealed their marriage. And, in a whirl, they had supped with the wedding guests, said their good-byes, and set off on the boat from Boston to the mouth of the great river the Mahican Indians called Muhhekunnetuk.

She had been shocked when she saw the cramped riverboat on which John had booked passage. Their many belongings caused quite a stir and the captain had refused to take the large stove until John coaxed him with an extra shilling. When they changed to an even smaller boat for the trip on the Mohawk River, she had stood in the wet grass content now to trust John with the unloading, the bargaining, and the reloading of their possessions.

The final two days had been along the forest and mountain tracks. She had met Frank Smyth, John's bachelor friend and his widowed father whose land was ten miles from their own. Staying the night with John's friends, Lucy had first felt she was Mrs. John Garner.

They had reached the cabin the next day. It was all so quaint and pretty in the waning sunlight that she had cried out and wiped tears from her eyes. Concerned, John had reached for her and she had explained her joy at seeing her new home for the first time. They had cleaned the cabin, set out their treasures from Boston, and eaten their first meal at home.

They were completely alone as they prepared for sleep that night. No neighbors nearby, nor friends, nor fellow travelers marred the woodsy silence. Lucy heard John come into the cabin and bar the door. In the tiny bedroom she hung her dress on the hook beside the rope-slung bed and slipped under the patchwork quilt. Even though the night was warm she pulled it up to her neck. The last rays of evening sun lit the pine logs above the dresser she had insisted on bringing from Boston. As the light faded she wished her heart would stop racing. John's hand pulled back the black curtain. His face appeared, beard grown in again with red-brown whiskers out of which shone his shy grin, and he stepped into the tiny room. The curtain dropped behind him.

"Your clothes look wet," she said.

"I had a good wash at the well pump." He slipped his suspenders off, pulled his drab shirt over his head, and lowered his trousers before sitting on the creaky bed to remove them. He, too, slid under the patchwork quilt and turned toward her. "All alone." His fingers found her hand and slid up her bare arm. "Finally. Only the two of us."

"I love our cabin, John."

He moved closer and raised up on one elbow. His rough hand touched her cheek and brushed back over her hair, all loose around her face. He drew back, nodded his head, and looked her in the eye as he answered in a throaty voice. "I'm glad, Lucy."

"And I can hardly wait to start work in the morning to make it as beautiful as I can. I know just where to hang that engraving of the two—"

His lips found hers, a lovely softness tingling between them, and he gathered her to him. She slid her arms around his taut body, fingers kneading his skin, and kissed back with an intensity born of sudden desire. Her petticoat bunched up as he slid his hands around her smooth thigh to her bottom and he inched the garment higher.

"Wait," Lucy whispered. In a trice she had it off and tossed on the floor. "Will that do?"

SINCE THEN, EACH DAY HAD BEEN a study for her as she learned the ways of both the farm and John's person, and reveled in it all. He had chuckled at her first attempt to milk the cow and showed her over and over until she learned. In fact, raccoon skinning, corn planting, haying, all of it he taught her with patience and smiles. She had thought she knew him. Until today. That he could have been planning to leave her behind, alone, while he went off to fight a war was unimaginable. And to leave the farm, which he loved almost as much as he loved her—she just couldn't believe he was the same man.

Lucy's eyes came back to the door and John's abrupt departure played again in her mind. She willed him to come back inside and say he wasn't leaving, but the door remained shut and no noise filtered through. What was he doing? She went to the window. He stood chopping wood by the barn. Even at this distance she saw that he swung the axe with a vengeance surely meant to assuage his guilt, and her heart softened.

Enough of this worrying. She had work to do, the fire to feed, that stew to cook for their noon meal. She hoisted up her pail of water again and filled the pot on the stove. She pulled chunks of dried deer meat from their larder at the end of the cabin, dumped some sad-looking potatoes into her apron, decided the one squash left from last fall was fit to eat and moved to the table carrying her load. She sat down and went to work.

Just as she was putting the stew pot on the stove, a horse whinnied outside. She rushed to the window, saw John rest his axe, and look to the edge of the forest trail. The rider from last week was back. She dropped the curtain and hugged herself as she felt the tears come. Hilton Cross was here already. And John was leaving. Too soon. She had so much to say to him. And now she wouldn't get the chance. She wiped her eyes with her apron and again peered out at the talking men. They seemed in no hurry. Perhaps today was not the day. A flicker of hope fanned in her chest.

Lucy busied herself with tidying the cabin, sweeping the floor, fluffing the pillows on the bed, straightening the patchwork quilt— she held it to her face for a soft memory of Boston—and attending to her many other daily chores, as the simmering stew gradually filled the cabin with a soothing and enticing aroma. When the sun was high in the sky, she could stand the suspense no longer and stepped out into the spring sunlight to study the two men near the wood pile. John stood deep in conversation with his hands on his hips, his head nodding from time to time. Mr. Cross gestured as he talked, shifting from one foot to the other. They must be ready to eat. John turned, saw her, and motioned Mr. Cross to follow him.

At least she had made lots of stew. Usually she reveled in visitors, rare as they were out here in the woods. Today, however, she was wary as the men walked the well-worn path to the cabin, the wiry Mr. Cross, in the first heat of spring still wearing his worn woolen coat and a dark cloth cap pulled low over his brow. He tied his horse to the railing and followed John to the porch. A whiff of stale sweat assailed her nostrils as the man doffed his cap and dipped his head in her direction. John stared hard at her, his teeth clenched tight and taut. He expected her to be hospitable.

"Welcome." Lucy forced out the words and the smile that went with them and was rewarded by the grin on John's face.

"Thank ye, ma'am. I've been riding quite a piece and am very glad of yer hospitality."

"Hilton Cross, you remember Lucinda?"

"Charmed, I'm sure, ma'am." Mr. Cross' eyes met hers briefly as he smiled a yellow-toothed grin. "Sure 'tis fine to get off my horse for a real dinner. Thank ye, ma'am."

"We're pleased to have you, Mr. Cross, and you are welcome to share what food we have. It's spring, though, and the larder is almost empty, but we're doing well enough." She led them into the cabin.

As the men sat to eat, Lucy quickly lifted the stew to the plates, worrying the whole time about John leaving with Mr. Cross, about how lonely and lost she would be without him, and whether she would even be able to survive on her own. She set the plates before the men and turned back for hers, trying to still her shaking hands. A deep breath. She forced a smile to her face and sat. The men were already making short work of their stew.

"Hilton, I need a couple more days here before I go. How long will you be in the area?"

"I been ordered to be with Butler by the end of next week." He looked up from his plate and studied John. "I'm guessin' we could wait until day after tomorrow but that's about all. We'll be ridin' hard to make it at that."

"I do appreciate that, Hilton." John's eyes flicked toward Lucy before settling again on Mr. Cross. "What is it I need to take with me? My musket, I know, but you'll give me a uniform?"

"Nae, no uniform. You'll be wearing your own things. Bring a warm blanket. Ye might be sleepin' rough a fair bit. Yer musket, that rifle," he pointed to the gun standing by the door, "and yer knife, too, be mighty handy."

"No. Lucy's rifle stays here. She might need it."

Cross glanced at Lucy and hastened to add, "Ah, it'll be no time and ye'll be back to yer farm again."

And then, like a man who had seen the pearly gates open wide for him, Mr. Cross stood, fixed his hat to his head and strode to the door. "Thank ye, ma'am," he called. "I'll be through early Friday with the rest of 'em. Mind yer ready at the turnoff, John."

Lucy sat staring at the door, her brain in turmoil. Today was Wednesday. Early Friday John was leaving. She felt his eyes on her but didn't respond. How would she cope alone in the wilderness? She sighed. Maybe she could go back to Boston to her father's house. But, no, she would not embarrass John that way. Her father was sure to think John had failed her and that he had been right to oppose their marriage. She wouldn't think of her father. Besides, John needed her to look after their farm and their future. Their farm depended on her. She would just have to cope. Whether she liked it or not, he was counting on her. She shifted in the chair, bringing her red, rough hands to the table, but scowled at John as she stood. She pushed her chair against the table.

"What do you expect from me?"

"I expect you to abide by my wishes. You are my wife." He glared at her. "And I will have your help." He shoved his chair away from the table so hard it clattered over onto the pine floor and, like an angry bear whose territory had been invaded, he charged towards her.

She stumbled backwards and grabbed at the bedroom curtain for balance, afraid of John for the first time since she'd known him. He stopped. His mouth dropped open as if to speak, but nothing came out. Her muscles froze and, for a long glaring moment, she clung to the curtain as though it might protect her. He swept a lock of hair from his face, backed off a step, and tore his eyes away, as though he couldn't bear to look. Then he stumbled around the table toward the door.

"You never want to settle things. You just go. Always. And this time, you're actually leaving me here all alone, forever. Do you not care about me at all?"

He whirled around. "Oh, I care. But one of us must face facts. Look to our future."

"You'll be killed." She shouted it. Her biggest fear. Yet John's hand closed on the door latch and pulled it open.

"I have no choice, woman!"

The slam shook the floorboards under her feet. She stared after him.

THAT NIGHT SHE WAS STILL FURIOUS. John had spent his day mending the chicken fence and mucking out the oxen. He was trying to do as many chores as he could so she wouldn't have to, but still she fumed. While he was building a fence to make a small pen for the oxen and the cow, she had beaten her braided rugs and washed John's spare clothes, hanging them on the bushes to dry in the spring sunshine.

When evening came and she sat in the low light of the candle waiting for John, her eyelids drooped. Presently he came in, barred the door, and went straight to the bedroom where she could hear him now, rustling about. He had not even looked at her. The bed creaked as he climbed in and rolled on his side, facing the window, she thought, as he always did. She should go to him but couldn't. Instead she sat in the silence holding her tears at bay.

When his breathing slowed, she snuffed out her candle and felt her way to the bedroom. She dropped her outer clothing to the floor and slipped into bed where, for the first time since their marriage, she turned away from her husband.

....

Chapter Two

IN THE SMALL HOURS OF THE MORNING the rooster crowed. Lucy felt John shift to his back. She cracked open her eyes and John's sad news slammed back into her conscious mind. Her thoughts muddled like her clothes strewn on the plank floor. *I should get up, away.* She inched her feet towards the edge.

"The two shillings a day the Rangers give will pay off our land if I stay till fall."

He was awake. Knew she was, too.

"Did you hear me, Lucy?"

She rolled over onto her back, careful not to touch him. "Do you think the money will make me agree to this madness?"

"No, but it will help." He cleared his throat. "I didn't tell you about Sir John Johnson's wife and Mrs. Butler."

"Who?"

"Johnson supports the King, you remember. He had to flee for his life to Montreal. Leave his family behind. The Continentals have Lady Johnson and Mrs. Butler as hostages. In Albany. The locals even threatened to do violence to them and to their families if Johnson and Butler dared to act against the Continentals."

"Butler? Who's he?"

"Another King's man. He's the colonel forming Butler's Rangers." His voice softened and he turned to her. "The force I'm joining," he whispered.

"His wife is a hostage and he's still fighting? Recruiting more soldiers?" She faced the wall again. "Isn't danger to your family enough reason not to go?"

"But that's just it, Lucy. The danger. We have to keep these upstarts from coming any closer. Butler has to fight and so must I." Just the barest hint of excitement accompanied his hurried words.

A strip of sun flashed on the log wall before her. "You want the adventure! You're excited to go off and fight a war!" She jerked around and caught the surprise on John's face. "You are. Don't try to hide it." She bounded out of bed, grabbed her clothes and left the bedroom.

BY SUPPER HIS BUNDLE STOOD TIED BY THE DOOR and he had finished the last rows of seeding and shoveled out the stable. Not a word had passed between them the whole day, a situation new and nasty for Lucy. The latch slipped quietly and John stepped into the cabin.

She put their plates on the table and sat to eat. Neither spoke. She smelled the musky odor of dung on his clothes and wished he had cleaned up. On their last night, why hadn't he? Surely his leaving her was less important to him than to her. She lifted the dirty dishes to the dry sink and poured water to wash them.

"I'll dry."

"No. I can do them myself." She turned her back and moments later heard the door.

Long after she had fallen asleep alone in their bed, Lucy wakened to the shifting of the rope-slung mattress. Would he speak to her? He didn't. As she listened, his breathing slowed and he fell asleep. He wasn't about to apologize, she realized, or change his mind. Staring into the darkness she felt the tears start, but stifled them as best she could, the brute force of her pride beating down any urge to talk.

....

SHE WOKE TO POUNDING ON THE CABIN DOOR.

"Anybody home?"

John threw off the patchwork quilt and jumped to the floor.

"What is it?" whispered Lucy, in her fear forgetting her anger . "Who's there? Is it Mr. Cross?"

"No, it's Frank. He's coming with me," John said. He stumbled about the bedroom pulling on his trousers. "I'm coming, Frank," he called.

Lucy grabbed her dress. "He is? And you didn't tell me?"

"I didn't think it mattered." He pulled the curtain aside and glanced back at her. His face was screwed up in that confused grimace she had come to know so well.

"Our nearest neighbor is leaving, too, and you didn't think it mattered?" She sat on the edge of the bed, glaring at him.

"Lucy. His father will still be there..." His voice trailed off.

"An old man. And so far away."

John shrugged his shoulders and backed out of the tiny room. She tried to breathe slowly in and out, in and out, as she pulled on her skirt. *Keep calm, keep calm.* She heard John take the bar from the door. As she crept up behind him, he let in the grey light of dawn, an enveloping mist whose tendrils touched her feet, bare and cold on the hard floor. And Frank, a shadowy outline, stood beside his horse, not ten feet away. "You're early," John said. "Come inside and get warm."

To the stove he added wood, poking it into place until the banked fire sprang to life. She pointed Frank to his chair at the table, and turned to the stove.

Usually Frank Smyth was a welcome visitor. He and John had helped each other often since John's arrival four years earlier. Periodically, Frank appeared and John and Lucy enjoyed his easy nature and ready wit. Today her anger with John swept across the room to include Frank, too.

"Did you ride half the night to get here?" John sat opposite his friend, avoiding her.

"Well, you might say that, although I did spend time napping in the saddle. Old Jackie knows the way as well as I do and she just loped along." Frank chuckled. "And what about you? Everything ready to go?"

She turned to John, her furious fear choking off the words she longed to say. Their eyes met and she thought he almost understood her fearsome worry, but he looked away and spoke to Frank.

"Almost. I just need to saddle up and tie on my bundle. Shouldn't take long." He glanced her way again, but she went back to hacking the cold meat against the board. Each slice cut across the growing chill in the still room, a lonely, bereft kind of chill, which had nothing to do with the temperature. He turned to Frank. "I need time to feed the stock and fill the water up once more for Lucy."

By this time they were pushing food into their mouths and she joined them at the table with her own plate. She looked at Frank. "How long do you think this Ranger thing will last?"

"Oh, I'm sure it won't be more than the summer. These militia boys just need to feel the might of our King's forces against them and they'll give up this America nonsense soon enough. Right, John?"

"That's what I think." John faced her and took a deep breath. "This is the British we're talking about. The King has more armies than the Continentals have men. We'll crush these brigands in no time and be home here again on our farms, safe and happy. You'll see."

She didn't answer. She studied the empty cup in her hands. How could they believe what they were saying? There was so much unrest in the Americas that tales of stolen farms and fighting seemed to ride on the wind all the way out here to their isolated wilderness. Settling it would be a hard task. The Indians were all mixed up, some siding with the British and others with the local militia. And they changed sides like the breeze changed direction.

"Lucy?" John's loud voice startled her.

She squeezed her eyes shut and forced them open again, focusing on his dipped eyebrows, his lengthening beard and half-open lips that seemed to be weaving words.

"I said, are you sure you'll be all right?"

"I'll have to be, won't I?" She pushed back from the table and looked him straight in the eye. "The chickens will keep me company. Why, we'll be cackling together all day and I'll hardly notice you're gone." Her voice cracked but she held his gaze.

"There. That's the spirit, Lucy," said Frank. His eyes shifted back and forth from her to John. "You'll, ah, be glad, yes glad, of a little peace and quiet. You'll, ah, have time to gather your plants in the woods and…" Worrying his hat in his hands he studied the floor boards.

John, too, stared at the floor. "Time to pack up." He grabbed his coat and hurried out the door, Frank right behind.

She gathered the food and tied the odds and ends in a piece of oilcloth then sank into John's rocker where she clutched the package against her as though it was John and she could keep him there. But it wasn't and she couldn't. And there was no comfort to be found in the chair's rhythmic rock, rock, rock, rock on the hard, pitted pine underfoot.

And then the men were back inside, John with his hat and musket as he shifted from one foot to the other. Frank stood by the door, suddenly quiet. Softly he opened it and disappeared. John moved to Lucy.

"Time to go. Take care…you hear?"

His voice caught, and his arms tightened around her but she was afraid to look at him or even breathe. She couldn't let down her guard for a second for fear she would just fall weeping to the floor. She wouldn't lean against him for even a moment. Instead, she straightened and, in the hardest voice she had ever used, said, "I'll be fine. You'll be home before I even miss you, right?"

He dropped his arms to his sides. "Yes. I'll send a message when I can."

"Well, you'd best be off, then." She pushed him away, pulled open the door and went outside. John stomped onto the porch, brushed past her and hurried to his horse. He swung up and headed for the forest. Frank fell in behind.

As they reached the trees, both looked back but only Frank waved. Lucy's hand flew up partway as she ran a few steps toward them and then stopped. She saw John kick his boots into his horse's side and turn swiftly away from her.

And pull the horse up short.

She stiffened, caught her breath. He left Frank and galloped towards her, hat waving, past the woodpile, past the open barn door, and by the newly ploughed garden plot. He pulled Maudie up short at the porch, his features fixed in such a pained grimace as she had never seen. Off the horse he came and up onto the porch, into her outstretched arms.

The tears came then, and she let them. Her face against his homespun shirt, she clung to him and breathed in his woodsy scent. All her pent-up feelings poured forth in a frenzied river of emotion. "John, John," she moaned, and he held her tighter in a vise-like grip such as she had never felt before.

Presently his hands moved to stroke her hair and she looked up at him. As her own must be, his face was red-blotched and wet. His eyes were full but he smiled.

"I am sorry, Lucy."

"Sh, I'm sorry, as well," she whispered. "Don't worry about me. I'll be…safe, I know I will." And fresh tears welled up but she took a deep breath, swallowed, and stepped back.

John reached for her curls. "I need one, Lucy," he said and quickly pulled. She barely felt it. He wrapped the long glistening strand around his finger and slipped it into his pocket. He took her in his arms once more, this time softly and gently, his kiss a last goodbye. He pulled away and she watched him remount and slowly ride off. His back was stiff and straight, his hat slightly atilt, and his body rocked with the horse's gait, as he trotted slowly but steadily away from her, into the trees.

Chapter Three

ALREADY SHE MISSED HIM. The little cabin was so utterly silent that the falling chunks of ash in the stove seemed like thunderclaps. From the barn, Molly bawled, needing to be milked. Tears brimmed but Lucy wiped them away and pushed back the curls that had slipped out of her cap.

But outside, the sun shone only for her, it seemed, and she smiled in spite of herself. Sitting on the stool in the barn she rested her head against Molly's warm belly, happy to feel the cow's reassuring girth.

"You and I are becoming friends, aren't we, Molly?" Her two hands worked smoothly as she grasped the teats, rhythmically closing gradually from her index fingers down to the little ones, as John had taught her, pulling the milk out in a steady stream. The whoosh, whoosh of the milk into the pail lulled Lucy's thoughts. Soon she moved her stool to the other side and repeated the process.

Molly shifted her feet and edged away. "Co boss. Steady, girl. We've got a little more to go. Co boss," soothed Lucy with John's words, and they relaxed into their duet once more.

Next she scattered seed to the busily pecking chickens and their resident rooster. She gathered two fresh eggs for her breakfast but left the others for the hens to hatch. Soon she would have a lot of little chicks running around and her job would be to keep them alive and raise them for food, but the best part would be holding their soft yellow down against her cheek.

Even though spring meant lots of work on the farm, there were special joys. John would miss them this year. "His own fault," she whispered, but immediately swallowed the thought.

The oxen munched hay. The chicken fencing was torn. She glanced around but saw no wild animals; nevertheless, she quickly found some wire and mended the hole, then headed for the cabin and breakfast.

The eggs tasted wonderful fried in a little grease and accompanied by a glass of fresh milk. Later she would go look for the green shoots she had seen on their walk in the forest and bring some back. Already she missed John and didn't really feel like making a meal for only herself. She would have to get used to being alone. *Why did he have to go? Why?*

That sound. A soft shuffle in the dirt. What was it? As she started up from the table, her ears straining, all was suddenly quiet. Very quiet. Probably nothing but she would check outside. Lucy lifted the latch and pulled open the door.

Air rushed into her mouth like the wind sweeping into the cabin on a cold white day in winter, taking the breath away from all in its path. Her mouth closed and she swallowed once, twice, desperately trying to moisten her tongue.

A group of Indians, seated and silent on their lathered horses, stared at her as though they could see right through her, and knew she was alone, fair game for anything they wished. But they moved not a muscle.

Best not to provoke them or show fear. John's words popped into her head. She squared her shoulders, grabbed her rifle from beside the door, and strode onto the porch. There was not a sound, save her swishing skirts and hollow steps striking the wooden porch floor.

What tribe they were from? Friendly? They wore a wide assortment of clothing, from beaded Indian jackets and vests to faded red soldier coats. Their moccasined feet protruded from leather breeches which had seen many days riding. One wore a headdress of several feathers, the leader. His black eyes darted all around but always came back to stare at her. She held still, in spite of her shaking hands and thudding heart in her hollow chest. In a gradually growing monotone of unintelligible sounds, the Indians muttered among themselves and pointed at the cow grazing by the barn, the chickens pecking in the dirt and the rooster strutting around his hens as though keeping them safe. Then they looked back at her.

She didn't move but held tight to her rifle. She wasn't sure what these men wanted but so far she and John had never had problems with any of the Indians. One of the horses snuffled out a torrent of noisy air, spooking her. Its rider gripped the reins with one hand and stroked the horse's neck with the other. The man wore a necklace of huge bear claws strung on a leather thong around his neck. His red-streaked face harbored those hard black eyes. He pointed to the oxen and the cow. Were these men simply hungry?

The leader scowled at her, glanced back at the brave, and gave a quick shake of his head. He dug his knees into the horse, and jerked it around. Away into the trees he rode, the others following.

Taut as a bowstring, she continued to watch the path and listen, but all was silent. Her strange visitors had gone and in the hot sun she breathed again. Then she swayed, her knees collapsed and she toppled over.

Sunlight streamed down on Molly as she munched on bright bits of grass, flicking her tail periodically at worrisome flies, while the oxen had found the shade and rested happily. Chickens cackled and bees buzzed. Presently, Lucy groaned, opened her eyes, and pushed up off the porch. She rubbed her elbow, spotted her rifle in the grass, and leapt to her feet. Her blinking eyes scanned the empty yard, before focusing on the trail into the trees. It was bare and empty, like the stage at the theater in Boston after the curtain came down.

I must have fainted. Thank the Lord they were gone. She stared around at the familiar little world she and John had created and, with every breath she took, sucked in its utter loneliness without him.

The days went by in a monotony of chores and meals, sleeping and pondering as Lucy adapted to being alone. She thought often of John and his whereabouts and of her vulnerability should anyone sinister come near. She had to have a plan for the future and, standing near the barn, began sketching one out in her mind.

The Indians were bound to come back. They knew she was vulnerable. That could be a problem although she and John had lived quite peaceably with most of the tribes so far. Most of the Iroquois nation tribes sided with the British but the Oneida and Tuscarora were more inclined to see what they could get from the revolutionaries. And various individual bands changed sides as often as she did the milking. She could never be sure which way the wind blew if they appeared again.

What did she have to defend herself? Her rifle, certainly, and a good supply of ammunition. She would keep it loaded and near at hand whatever she was doing. She also had her kitchen knives and John's skinning knife but she doubted she'd be much good at protecting herself with them. Nevertheless, she'd keep them handy, especially when she went outside the cabin. She paused beside the barn. "I could put an emergency package out here…right by the wall where that dip is."

By supper time she had buried her package beside the barn. "Really, I'm sure I'm being a little paranoid but it's better to be prepared, isn't it, Molly?" Molly mooed. "You're the only one who talks to me." Laughing, Lucy headed for the cabin.

As the days turned into weeks and no one came to bother her or her farm, Lucy grew calmer. She still felt strangely exposed when out in the yard but no one ever came her way. She had reduced her meals now to two, one midmorning and the other at night because she had so much to do and, besides, eating alone just gave her time to miss John. Often she would walk in the woods looking for diversion and, as the days lengthened, relief from the heat of the afternoon. She was adept at recognizing many plants and certain barks with medicinal qualities. Fortunately she had had little need to test her knowledge since joining John on their remote farm.

On one such foray into the forest Lucy was busy digging the roots of some rhubarb for transplanting when the forest became suddenly quiet. The birds were silent, there was no wind, and the hairs on her neck rose up. Carefully she stood and peered in every direction but saw or heard nothing.

"John," she called, pretending he was close by. "John. Have you come to meet me?" Silence.

She heard a soft rustling to her right and jerked around. A magnificent stag stood still and alert in the distance. She whispered, "Ah, it's only you, is it? I won't hurt you." But she looked away for her rifle. Could she get to it? Should she shoot the deer for meat? When she glanced back it was gone. She gathered up her sack of plants and roots as well as the rifle and made her way back to the farm.

As Lucy walked by, Molly's big brown eyes followed her but she went on chewing her cud. The hens cackled their off-key nonsense as they pecked in the dirt. "Never give up looking, do you?" Lucy smiled, "even though it's hours since I put out any grain."

The cabin was as she had left it, a shady respite from the afternoon sun. She took the pail out to the well and filled it to the brim with lovely cool water. Hurrying, she stepped back inside and dipped a cup of the refreshing nectar. She sat down to drink at the table. "Where are you, John? Are you still angry? Why haven't I heard from you?" She glanced at his work shoes by the door. He had left them behind, taking only the boots on his feet. He couldn't take that much on the horse, he had explained, and she had agreed. "I wonder if you are hot, too, today. Oh, where are you?"

Resting her tired head on her arms, Lucy sagged onto the table. Breaths came in short bursts as she felt her face heat up and her eyes overflow with tears which dripped hot on her arms. From somewhere within, though, the thought gradually took form. This was pointless. She sat up. *I'm not going to cry. I know he's doing very well and he would not want me to be worrying.* She dragged herself out the door to see that the animals were secure for the fast approaching night.

Immediately she backed up into the cabin again. A man stood looking at Molly. Lucy was sure he hadn't seen her but she had seen him and the horse standing near him. She grabbed the rifle, made sure it was loaded and turned the door handle. No one was going to take her cow.

"What are you doing?" She raised her voice, the rifle at her side, ready to aim at a moment's notice.

"Well, hello there, ma'am. Just having a look at your fine cow here." The man turned to face her and continued. "It's been a long time since I've seen one so healthy."

He appeared friendly but Lucy was wary. At this distance she couldn't see his eyes. She stood and waited.

"I'm riding to Fort Stanwix, ma'am. Need to rest my horse a bit." He took a few steps towards her and stopped. "Might I have a drop of water? If it's not too much trouble?" He took off his tattered brim hat and his smile lit up his whole weathered face.

She smiled back. "Yes, certainly. Wait just a moment."

She stepped into the cabin for the dipper wondering what to do. Here it was almost nightfall and she should offer the man hospitality for the night but the thought of that was just too scary. He should ride on, she thought, as she opened the door again. He hadn't moved but now came forward. He took the dipper from her, stared a moment into her face, and turned to the well. "You all alone out here, ma'am?"

Her insides tightened just for a moment. "No. John is just late getting back from the neighbor's but I expect him any time."

"Would that be John Garner? Is this his place?"

"Yes. Do you know him?" Lucy stepped off the porch towards the man.

"I guess I do. He gave me a message for you." The stranger walked back to his tethered horse and rummaged in his pack. "Here it is, ma'am." He held in his hand a wrinkled and worn bit of grayed paper. Its edges looked frayed and dirty but Lucy stepped forward to grab it from his outstretched hand.

"Is he alright? When did you see him?" *At last, some word.*

"Oh, it's some time now I've been on the trail. Must have seen him a couple of weeks back. He gave me this for you. He looked so anxious, I said I'd come this way, on my journey. It was his eyes. Pleading like. He surely misses you."

"Thank you for bringing the letter, sir." Lucy looked suddenly at the trail-weary man. "What's your name?"

"Oh, ma'am, these days I don't usually tell people," he said, but seeing her frown went on, "It's Maycock, ma'am. Niles Maycock, at your service." He swept his hat from his head and bowed low before her.

"Would you like to wash up at the pump and join me for supper, Mr. Maycock? It's not much but you're welcome to share it."

Mr. Maycock nodded. "I'll just see to my horse a moment, ma'am."

Lucy went inside as the stranger brought his horse up to the cabin. Through the window she watched him fill the pail at the well and then splash his face while the horse drank. She dropped the curtain and smoothed open the letter in her hand.

> *Dearest Lucy*
>
> *I have much to tell you about our travels thus far but want you to know I am thinking of you and miss you. Our road has been hard at times but also tedious. We spent many days and nights riding to meet Colonel Butler, the weather keeping us moving so that we would not freeze at night. Frank continues to be a pleasant companion and I would be sorely remiss if I did not mention his help. He shoots well and killed a rabbit for our supper the first day out, which meat lasted us for some time and allowed us to save our dried meat. Mr. Maycock is passing through and has agreed to take this to you so that I must write quickly before he leaves. He is a good man and you may feel safe with him. I trust all is well on our farm. I think often of its pleasant situation. My time is up for Mr. Maycock is here and I must end.*
>
> *Affectionately, John*

Hungrily Lucy read the words again. John was alive. *Thank the heavens above.* She smiled as she slipped the letter into her dress and hurried to prepare supper for herself and her guest. She would use some of the greens she had found in the forest to liven up today's stew. She jumped at the knock on the door but quickly opened it.

"Oh, come in, please, Mr. Maycock. The supper is almost ready. Please sit." She indicated the chair at the table.

"I'm very grateful to you, ma'am. Not often I get to sit to a meal. Pretty lonely out on the trail."

"Just what do you do?" Lucy looked curiously at him as she sat.

"Most of what I do is travelling. My bones get saddle weary and just plain tired. I travel between the forts. Taking letters and small packages from home for the settlers out this way. I've never been so far from Boston before this trip. Seems folks want to send things to their fightin' men way out here. I.. ah…" his voice drifted as his eyes settled on the stewpot on the stove.

Lucy jumped to her feet. "Would you like more, sir?"

"Thank you, ma'am, I would."

By the time the stew was gone, the day was, too, and Lucy had lit the candles for the washing up. Mr. Maycock remained seated while she tidied.

"I am wonderin' if 'twould be too much trouble…" He took a deep breath, "…if I stayed in the barn overnight, ma'am? Don't want to be an inconvenience, but I'd welcome the shelter for a night."

"That would be fine, Mr. Maycock. I'm sure it's no trouble." Lucy had been wondering if he would stay in the barn, but didn't know how to ask. She was glad of someone else on the place for one night. Maybe she would sleep better.

Sidling to the door, Mr. Maycock took his hat from the hook and stepped to the porch. "I do appreciate that food, ma'am. Thank you."

"I am thankful that you brought me the letter, Mr. Maycock. I hope you will be comfortable in the barn."

"Good night then, ma'am."

As Mr. Maycock stepped away, Lucy closed the door and bolted it. With a last glance out the window, she turned to the rifle her father had given her, checked it and carried it into the bedroom for the night. She was used to this ritual now and, even though she felt safer with Mr. Maycock in the barn, she would keep the rifle handy.

As she brought the fire to life next morning, Lucy heard the axe splitting wood. She rushed out into the fresh morning air to gather eggs and slipped back inside to fry them and some pan bread. Since John left she hadn't cooked for anyone but herself. She hummed a tune while setting out the plates and cups and smiled to hear her own quick feet on the floor. Moving the curtain aside she saw Mr. Maycock was now checking the animals. *How kind.* She stepped out the door into the sun. "Good morning," she called. "Breakfast is almost ready."

"Thank you, ma'am. I'll be right along."

Back in the cabin, Lucy soon heard boots on the porch. Mr. Maycock tiptoed in and hung his hat before pulling out his chair. She filled both their plates and sat opposite him. "I hope you'll stop by again if you come this way, Mr. Maycock."

"I'd be pleased to, ma'am. It's always a welcome change from sleeping out. 'Specially if there's rain about. Don't know when I'll be back, though."

"And I thank you for chopping wood this morning. I heard the axe first thing."

"The very least I could do," he mumbled. "Wish I had time to do more. Long day ahead, though."

He was almost finished and Lucy suspected his thoughts drifted to the road ahead. "How long will it take to reach the Fort?" she asked.

"The Fort? He glanced at her. "Oh, the Fort. Fort Stanwix. It's a good long ride from here. Hope to be there by tomorrow night." He studied his plate as he swallowed the last of the eggs. He stood up, lifted his plate to the dry sink, and grabbed his hat from the hook. "I do thank you for your hospitality, ma'am. But I must be going. For sure that sun won't wait. I've a long road to cover before nightfall."

She followed him outside. "I do appreciate your taking the time and trouble to bring the letter from John. To know he is safe... Thank you."

"Happy to do it, ma'am. If I see him again I'll bring you another."

"I should have written one for him!" Lucy cried. "Could you take him something for me?"

"What would that be, ma'am?"

Lucy was already running for the cabin. In just a few seconds she returned swinging a raccoon tail. "Give him this, please. You know, for luck. I know it's not a rabbit's foot but he skinned this raccoon a few days before he left and he'll recognize it. He'll remember and think of home." She dropped her eyes lest he think she was too forward.

Smiling, Mr. Maycock reached for the tail and tucked it into his pack.

"I'll be leaving now, Mrs. Garner, and I wish you good day."

"Good day. Thank you, Mr. Maycock. Have a safe journey." She watched as he rode towards the trail, her hands shading her eyes from the rising sun. As he disappeared into the trees, she heard Molly's mooing and the cackling hens. *Seems I'm always watching people leave on that trail.* She watched a moment longer, retied her drooping apron strings, and turned towards her chores. Today she needed to check the planted corn for weeds and get the hoe working if she wanted to have any corn to harvest. The stalks were up to her knees and growing furiously. Last year she had helped John hoe and they had laughed and laughed, holding contests to see who could hoe the fastest. Of course she always lost but that didn't matter. This year she was on her own and the happy remembrance did not ease her heart. She drifted toward Molly with the milk pail.

Chapter Four

June, 1778

THE SUN BLAZED FROM HIGH OVERHEAD when Lucy stopped hoeing long enough to take a breath and look around. She'd covered quite a distance but still had a fortnight's work to do.

The soft black earth worked easily and her pace was good but that stiffness in her back was getting annoying. "I'm not as strong as I thought I was." She straightened up. As she took a long cooling gulp of water, she looked toward the cabin.

What a lovely farmstead they had here in the wilds. The rows of corn and wheat, the sturdy barn, cosy cabin with two rooms, the oxen, the cow, her chickens, that little peaked roof over the well—all of it pleased her. For a few seconds she almost forgot her longing for John.

She rested on the hoe and wiped her sleeve across her face. She did miss him but was coping. Her father would never have believed she could do this. He had made plain his feelings on the matter, as she and John told him their plans. 'Taking my daughter to the backwoods?' he had said. 'She was not raised for that. I'll never see her again. I'll not allow it. See here, I won't allow it." And he had stomped out of the room.

But John had followed outside, strong and adamant as he argued their case, and she had stood beside him, for once keeping silent. Father, watching her face as John talked, had finally given his blessing.

She missed his gruff voice almost as much as she missed John.

Lucy hoed the afternoon away until Molly's mooing told her the time to milk had come again. She had worked her way back close to the cabin, a good place to quit. At the well she dipped fresh water. "Coming, Molly," she hollered. "Just need to get my breath."

She glanced at the overgrown path into the darkened woods. Two tall sun-streaked maples marked the narrow opening where last she had seen John. One day he would come galloping out of those woods. He would be riding Maudie, his hat would be stuck to his head on that amusing tilt, he would call her name, and she would come running. Their world would start again as he jumped from the horse and caught her in his arms. Robins would call to their mates and bees would buzz in the hollyhocks up the barn wall. And his earthy scent would fill her nostrils as she pressed against his whiskery face for a million kisses. Oh, she could see it all so clearly. She looked again. Today was not the day.

In the cabin she poked the fire, set the coffee to boil, and heated the stew. The same stew every day was monotonous, but it was fast. When finally she finished hoeing the last row she'd sit on the porch and just watch the wheat and the corn stretch to the sky. For now, she gulped her food and rushed out to the animals. She'd sleep well tonight.

"YOU'VE BEEN GONE OVER TWO MONTHS, JOHN. When are you coming back?" She clutched his pillow and sniffed it but his scent had long since leached out. Like her mind's eye picture of him, his essence had washed away. As she drifted off she thought of all the things that had happened in those two months she had been here alone and how their life together had been rent asunder, their days now separate and foreign.

She jerked up in the bed. "I haven't had my monthly courses in all that time. I'm sure I haven't." She fell back and stared at the darkness above. Were they finally going to have a baby? What a lovely surprise for John when he came back. Smiling, Lucy closed her eyes and pictured his face at the news. His green eyes would grow as wide as his smile and he would pull her into his arms. He would let her go quickly, then, and hold her away, afraid to hurt her or the baby. Or, if he came later, she would be showing and he could see immediately. Oh, so much the better!

POUNDING RAIN WOKE HER AT DAWN and she pulled up the quilt she had discarded during the night. *I'm going to have a child.* She ran her hands over her belly. Still taut but maybe, just maybe there was a bit of a swelling there. Now she felt even more anxious for John to come riding out of those woods.

Today she needed a little fire to take away the damp of the heavy rain so she added wood to the embers and stirred them. They blazed immediately and she shut the flames in and stood the poker against the wall. She pulled on her heavy coat and went out into the rain.

Molly bawled in the barn but she gathered the eggs first while the hens pecked for food. Anxious to get back into the house, Lucy milked as quickly as she could and then checked the oxen. They would need some mucking out but not today. She opened the barn door to let them all into the paddock. Finally, she lifted the milk pail and hurried through the downpour once again toward the cabin's safe warmth.

This would be an inside day and she could catch up on some of her chores. She'd mend her other dress which she had ripped on a tree branch in the woods and write a letter to John that she could send if anyone came by to take it. She'd be ready this time. Yes, the rainy day would be just fine, although she hoped John was not out in the downpour. She was warm and dry, safe in her cabin.

By late afternoon the grey clouds had moved off to the east but the rain still sputtered and spilled off the trees. In the barn, Lucy squatted on the three-legged stool, her head pressed into Molly's warm hide, and pulled first one teat, then the other, so quickly that a whooshing white stream shot into the bucket below. The milk frothed and bubbled like the wild strawberry jam she had cooked this day on her great stove in the cabin.

Molly shifted and shunted and her hoof shot toward the pail.

"Steady, girl. We're almost done," Lucy said, and twisted her head from side to side against her hide to ease her own aching muscles and settle the cow once more. Hair fell into her eyes. If only she had not left her cap in the cabin. Sometimes the curly hair John called her crowning glory was such a bother.

Two years ago he had brought her, a Boston city girl, to this beautiful but quite isolated land and she had become a farmer. He had taken her hand to lead her to the porch, pushed open the door, and stood back to let her enter her new home. His green eyes had danced with bright specks of light, his smile all white teeth and whiskers.

Now he was gone and she was alone. A soft rain dripped just a few feet away, outside the open door of the barn, as she wondered yet again just how long John would be gone. Molly's impatient hoofs shifted again. Lucy stopped. The pail was three quarters full. Molly had given all she had to give. She leaned back and swept at her hair once again.

"That fresh milk looks good." The man's loud voice filled the small barn.

Lucy jumped off the stool and turned toward the sound. The milk stool clattered against the pail, almost tipping it, but she saved it, then glared at the shadowy outline a few feet away in the early evening light of the open doorway. He moved closer. Shorter than John but at least a head taller than she, he had not washed himself or his clothes in a very long while. Straggly hair hung to his shoulders, framing his gaunt face, and tiny eyes glinted black in the feeble light of the lantern hanging from a nail in the wall of the log barn.

"Who are you?" Her voice sounded thin and throaty, even to her.

"Sorry to startle you," he stepped closer, "ma'am," and stroked his grey-streaked face. He looked her up and down.

....

Her stomach muscles clenched as she drew her arms across her chest.

"I'm just looking for a dry place to get in out of the wet night."

He smelled. She wanted to move back but didn't want to appear weak. Or inhospitable. Perhaps he was harmless. "Never mind," she said, "you surprised me is all." Her knees wobbled as she turned to grab the lantern. She held it in her outstretched arm to get a better look. No, he was no one she had ever seen before. His battered, dripping cap remained perched on his oversized head, but his eyes, tiny black dots hard as coal, held her so that she could hardly look away. But she did. And realized the rifle was still in the cabin.

"Are you, ah, alone here…ma'am?" He inched another step closer.

"No, my husband's inside," she lied. In one continuous motion she hung the lantern again and grabbed the pitchfork leaning against the wall. She faced him, both hands grasping the fork in front of her, hoping that thin round pole with the worn tines sticking out one end was some protection. He held his ground. She swallowed and forced herself to speak. "I asked who you are."

"I'm just travellin' to Boston. Need a fine place," he said, and quickly added, "to spend the night. I knocked at the cabin door. No one answered. Saw your light out here."

"Oh? You're lucky he didn't hear you. My man doesn't like strangers much."

"No matter." He studied her a long moment. "Is he off with the Continentals then?

"Beg pardon? I…" She looked down at the hardened earth floor and the milk stains on her grey homespun skirt. "Of course not. He wants no part of…" She stopped. John would say she was talking too much.

"No part of what?"

"Of…of war, and killing."

The man's black eyebrows lifted, and she felt like she was facing down a skunk ready to spray at any moment.

He took another step toward her and shook his grimy fist. "Maybe you're one of those damnable King George lovers."

"No. You're wrong." She raised the pitchfork along with her voice. "And what's more you're on our property. Best you ride on."

He backed away and stared a long moment at both her face and the pitchfork. "I'll just be leaving then." He turned away but immediately faced her again. Indicating the full pail of milk, he spoke. "Could I have some to take on my way, please… ma'am?"

"I suppose I could do that much." Lucy held the pitchfork in one hand and clattered the dipper into the pail with the other. She filled the leather flask he held out, in her haste spilling fresh milk in the dirt.

"Thank you…ma'am."

He was so close she could almost touch the yellow ooze in the corner of his eye. It sickened her but she held the pitchfork steady and he backed toward the barn door. The crack of his mouth widened into a black-toothed grin. He gave a little wave, and sauntered into the wet night.

She rushed out and watched him, a dark specter riding slowly toward the darker forest. From the barn she grabbed her lantern and the milk pail, fastened the barn door and, with a glance over her shoulder, hurried to the cabin, oblivious to the slopping milk and the slippery grass. Inside she bolted the door and stood against it, shaking.

She tried to tell herself the man was just what he said he was, but realized he didn't even give his name, let alone state his business. With shaking fingers, she unbuttoned the coat and hung it on the door. She wrapped her arms across her chest and held tight. What if he came back? She listened at the door. Nothing. Just a little peek out the window. Pitch black now. He could be out there. She dropped the curtain.

The forest sounds filtered into the cabin but the farm animals were quiet and calm and, gradually, she was, too. She drank some of the morning's coffee and took up her sewing by the candle. There was no point in trying to sleep.

…………

Hours later, a piece of wood in the fire fell and Lucy jerked upright, her wild eyes darting about the dark cabin. The candle had died. By the dim light from the stove she could see she was alone, but outside Molly bawled and the chickens were clucking in a dreadful cacophony of frightening sounds. What was out there? She bumped against the table on the way to the window.

Solid black was all she saw through the running raindrops on the glass, except for a faint patch of limpid light, not even light, just a silver lightening in the grass, the window's weak reflection. The animals settled and she breathed more slowly. They could wait till daylight.

The fire fixed, she went to the bedroom where she lay under the patchwork quilt, fully clothed, eyes wide open, the loaded rifle scant inches from her hand.

Chapter Five

July, 1778

HORSE SWEAT AND LATHERED STEAM swept into John's open mouth as he and Frank followed along in a drowsing line of Rangers and Indians almost beaten by the heat, the loneliness, and the dusty fatigue of their constant marching through the thick forest growth. He pursed his lips against the foul air and tried not to breathe too deeply. Dry as tinder the grass underfoot snapped into beaten dust which drifted upwards and caked his face. His hand rose, unbidden, to swat a fly which had left off buzzing around Maudie's head and found his own reeking skin.

Beside him, Frank rode in a similar stench and steamy cloud of tepid air. And John had talked him into this wretched misery. His best friend had come because of him. And Lucy. He had left her behind in a different kind of hell. She had not understood and he couldn't tell her his most private reason. Yet he left her alone to cope with the whole farm and any of a hundred dangers that might assail her. In spite of the air around him, he took a deep breath to clear his head.

He spoke. "I wonder if Lucy got my letter? And if she's all right?"

"Aw, she's fine. She knows how to look after the animals and herself. She's a crack shot with that rifle of hers," he replied.

"Besides, we'll be back in no time. Butler says this will be a short skirmish."

"I keep thinking of her there, all alone. She knows a lot about the farm but it's the accidents that might happen that keep me awake at night."

"Well, there are things to worry about, no doubt, but worrying won't help her or you. Put it out of your mind." He raised his arm to point at the trees lined up beside them. "These pines would make splendid logs for a cabin. Look at how big they are."

"It's fine for you. You have no wife back home." John glanced at Frank in his new uniform. "I guess you're right, though. I'll try to be better company."

Frank laughed. "I'll look forward to that."

The trail narrowed and John, alone again with his thoughts, edged forward while Frank dropped back to follow him. Once or twice John pulled up on the reins so as not to overtake the horse ahead. He wished they were all riding and didn't have to keep this slow pace for the foot soldiers.

He and Frank were lucky to have horses. Most of the Rangers had lost theirs in skirmishes before they ever joined Butler, forced off their own land by common thugs. Thieves could take what they wished and, for Loyalists, no help was forthcoming from the local governments. The few remaining rightful owners who were loyal to the King held their property by force of arms alone.

Frank's shout from behind roused John and he turned in the saddle. "What's___?"

"Attack! Attack!" The call reverberated in the shadowed woods. The forest seemed to rise up around him and musket shot whizzed by his ears. He slid from Maudie's back and stumbled into the trees, clutching his musket.

"Over here," Frank hollered. John ran for the huge downed tree trunk. He slid over and dug in, dropping his musket to the ground while he grabbed his cartridge box. Frank was already firing. John bit off the end of a cartridge, poured a little powder into the pan, closed it, dropped the rest of the opened cartridge into the barrel, and rammed the thing tight. Replacing the rammer, he cocked his lock and fired at one of the attackers. The ball missed its mark. He reloaded.

They worked as a team. When one was firing the other was loading, but soon the attackers were too close for muskets. A shape came at him but he had no space to maneuver his bayonet.

His knife was in his hand. He felt the hot breath of the huge man and saw his club towering above, the strike coming. He lunged against the man and plunged the knife into his soft flesh. The club hit John's back but had lost its force. He yanked his knife out and stabbed, again and again. He pushed, he screamed, he twisted the knife until he felt his enemy stagger and sag to the forest floor.

"Are you all right?" Frank shouted.

Slowly John dropped his arms and stood, still as a Scots pine, the red-gouted knife clenched in his right hand. He turned.

"I'm fine," he said softly, and then lifted his head to call out. "And you? Are you hurt?"

"Not at all. They've gone as quickly as they came." He shook his head, and picked up his fallen musket. "Let's check on the others."

The trail was a scene of devastation. A few men struggled to their feet clutching bloodied arms and legs while others tied grayed strips of cloth to stop the bleeding or to cover wounds. The enemy had struck in the middle of the long column and run before the rest of the Rangers were able to get there. John could not believe the damage this small skirmish, involving only a few of the Rangers, had caused.

"Here. I found one," someone hollered, and all eyes turned to see the soldier standing with his foot on the back of a downed man. "Lucky for him, he's already dead."

"Here's another. Who got him?" The red-faced Ranger pointed to the body near the tree.

John turned away, brushing the grass and bits of dirt from his trousers. Frank looked his way and then called, "John did. Saved our lives, too. That big bugger like to have killed us, for sure."

Several Rangers were pursuing the fleeing attackers but they wouldn't go far. They all had orders to stick together and, woodsmen that they were, they knew the dangers of being cut off from the main body. The officers reined in their stragglers to get back on the trail.

A shot came from the woods. Then a shout.

"Sergeant! Get those men back here now! We've got to move on."

"Yessir!" Sergeant Newbury signaled the bugler to blow assembly.

Meanwhile John and Frank looked for their horses. John whistled his whee-ah-wheet several times before the leaves parted and Maudie ambled toward him. And there, right behind, was Frank's horse. The men mounted and headed down the trail with the rest of the Rangers, but they watched and listened just a little more than usual the whole way back to the camp at Unadilla.

As John and Frank brushed and fed their hobbled horses, all around was bedlam. In the last knives of daylight flashing across the sky, Rangers rushed to pitch their tents. The cook gonged supper. Skittish horses neighed their hunger, and the surgeon tended to moaning men.

John stood by Maudie, brushing and brushing, talking softly. "There's a good girl. Soon we'll be home to the farm, away from this rot. You did well today, didn't you? Came right back when I called you." He moved to the horse's head, looked her in the eye, and stroked the long white line down her face.

"Aren't you finished yet, John? It's time for food." Frank waited while John stowed his brush and joined him.

"Did you see those fellows over there with the surgeon? They're not all wounded. Some of them are puking their guts out and they look hot as the devil. You don't think it's the pox, do you?"

"Don't be starting that rumor, Frank."

"If we get sick, we'll be dead. Not many live to tell that tale." Frank took his elbow and steered him away from the surgeon's tent. "Best to keep back."

The throng of men rushing for food had grown thick. He turned toward a whispering voice on his other side.

"I c'n help ya keep that pox away."

He jerked around to find Nat's smiling eyes on him. The man was shorter than John by a hand and his homespun shirt glowed white against his black neck and face. His smile shone with white, uneven teeth but dark spaces showed some were missing. John relaxed. "Yes?"

"I knows how to keep the pox away," Nat said.

By this time Frank was ahead in the line, holding out his cup and his plate for rum and stew.

"Move along there, move along," the cook shouted, and John turned back to the food. "We'll talk later." He got his rations, and joined Frank, already eating, as he walked back to their tent.

"Hungry, eh?"

"I never thought this slop could taste so good. I still long for a plate of my Da's beans, though, all cooked up with a mess of greens and a hunk of fresh bread."

"I try not to think about Lucy's cooking. Makes me homesick. Say, did you hear what Nat said?" His voice rose as he searched Frank's face.

"Nope. I was too busy keeping my spot in line." Frank's eyes were still on his tin plate. "I could eat more but I guess that's all we're getting tonight." He held his plate up and licked it clean. "There, that's as good as a wash."

"Will you pay attention, Frank? I'm trying to tell you something."

"Beg pardon."

"Nat says he knows how to keep the pox away," he whispered.

"Sure, I heard a little about that from a prisoner we had here. He was wishing he had taken the cure, he said, but I just figured he was out of his mind. I didn't want to get too close to him. There's no cure for the pox."

"Listen, you know how many people have sickened, puking their innards out. If there is some way to stay clear of that, I want to know about it, don't you?"

In the fading light Frank peered at him. "I know you want to get back to Lucy. Who could blame you?"

"Yes. I do," John replied.

"All right, let's go and hear what Nat has to say, but I'm not interested in any African voodoo nonsense. You got that?"

"We'll just listen to him. And then we can decide. That's the smartest thing, right?"

Frank was already on his feet and heading toward the group of black men where Nat was sitting.

As the pair approached, Nat rose. "Evening. You two lookin' for a bit of a walk?"

By this time the camp was settling, burning fires dotted the darkness and shadowy figures lounged in the dimness of the flickering light, putting off the time till they would try once again to sleep on the hard ground. At least the night was warm. Not like the many they had endured in the late winter as they escaped the rebels who chased them off their own lands with nothing but their lives. On a night like this, people could almost forget they were at war and how much they had lost.

Nat found a quiet place well away from the Rangers and the three stood in a tight triangle.

"You mean you take pus from a poxed man's blister and put it right into a cut on my arm? You're not serious, are you?"

"Frank. Keep your voice down." He grabbed Nat's arm. "Is that what you do?"

"My people been doin' this for years. Ya don't see us getting the pox, do ya? Course that's what we do. And I heared the British army do, too."

"Well, I can't speak for the regular British army. And I never noticed who had it, black or white, only that lots of people get it." John hesitated. "Can you give us the treatment?"

"Wait a minute," Frank said. "I never said I was doing this, did I?" He turned away.

John grabbed his arm. "You don't want to get the pox, do you? And I don't want you to get it. Do it for me. And for your father."

Frank stopped, and glared back at Nat. "You're sure it works?"

"I tell you I heared the British inoculated all their soldiers."

"If they do, it's the first I've heard of it," said Frank.

"Me, too. Maybe we Rangers just don't count." John gazed off toward the camp fires lighting up the night.

"Don't you worry. Nat'll look after you. It's yer best chance, although some as have taken it have died and that's a fact. Had it myself, though, and ya see I'm healthy." He looked at John. "We can do it tonight if ya want."

John jerked his head up. "Has somebody got the blisters, then?"

"They're not sayin' much, but see that tent over by the surgeon's? I saw 'em send one of the fellows in. He was lookin' close to dyin' with the spots all over his face and hands. And staggerin' so bad, took two men to hold him up." He paused. "I c'n get in there once the camp dies down. And get us some pus."

"We're agreed then. Frank and I'll wait by our fire. Should be enough light there, don't you think?" He gulped at the sudden phlegm in his throat.

"Fine. Won' be long." Nat ambled back to his tent.

The camp rhythm diminished to the soft thrum of whispers in the night. Dark shadows loomed against the sides of tents and disappeared within. Flaps were lowered and laces were tied from the inside as the Rangers sought sleep. Most of the fires were banked but one or two still flamed high. Some late watchers peered into the flames, and, like John, most likely thought of home, of comfort, of loved ones.

Nat's voice cut into the stillness. "I've got it."

"Just a scratch with the knife is all we need?" Frank whispered.

"Ya. Quick now." Nat knelt between the two men. With the point of his knife he pricked first John's arm and then Frank's. Carefully he opened a large leaf and dipped his knife into it. "Hope I got it. Hard to see in the dark."

"Hey! What are you men doing there?" The voice was loud and challenging.

"Just checking our knives for sharpness, Sergeant." John replied and shoved his arm out of sight.

"Don't be cutting yourselves, men. You'll have plenty of enemies to hack up in a day or two." He moved off.

Nat smeared his knife into the bloody cuts on both their arms, and stood up again. "You be good now. Trust Nat." His head cocked to the right and to the left. He melted into the night.

"I hope this works," Frank muttered. "Too late if it doesn't."

John was on his feet. "Time to sleep."

OVER THE NEXT FEW DAYS Frank and John stole glances at their arms, noticing redness around the scratch and soreness when they bumped the spot. Frank was convinced he had agreed to some bit of African witchcraft and whenever he saw Nat, he glared his displeasure. John had his qualms, too, but kept them to himself. The other soldiers would not be happy to find smallpox among them, especially if they learned that John and Frank infected themselves on purpose.

Soon enough the order came to march and the men gathered their pitifully small packs. John checked his musket for the hundredth time, saddled Maudie, strapped on his pack and swung up.

Frank mounted beside him and sat, ready. "Don't know where we're going but I'm glad we're off. I get so tired of idling in the camp, thinking of the work to be done back home, and watching the burial boys digging another grave."

"You're right. Better to move and do something, even if we don't know where we're going." He guided Maudie into line. Frank fell in beside him.

After several days of tortuous travel the Rangers reached the banks of the Susquehanna River and Colonel Butler procured enough boats and rafts to take them downriver. He then hurried his two hundred Rangers and three hundred Indians to a spot where they camped on a high hill overlooking the greater part of the valley below. News came that the enemy was waiting in the forts along the valley.

John and Frank had traveled the distance on horseback, making camp and striking it in the wee hours so often that they could do it blindfolded. A new kind of monotony was waging war on them now, and the heat of the summer threatened them all.

"At least on this high ridge we'll get a breeze at night." John ran his fingers through hair that had grown long and unruly.

"We'll have more than enough heat if we attack all of those forts strung along this valley. Going to be a busy summer."

"Ah, Frank, you're never happy." John chuckled to himself.

Just then Sergeant Newbury raised his voice. "Gather round, boys. We'll be marching early in the morning. Lights out." Newbury moved on to his next group.

"You heard the man, Frank. Time to sleep."

"Time for sweet dreams, you mean. I've got a date with a lovely lady from last night and I suppose you've got your Lucy. 'Night."

Chapter Six

DAWN FILTERED THROUGH THE BLACK OF NIGHT, lighting the sky inch by inch. The bugle sounded and the bustle began. Shouted orders roused the men. Dreams and nightmares were left behind with the dark.

John chomped on his ration of dried beef. A hot gulp of coffee helped wash the stale bread down. He was used to the poor fare and didn't even think of it. Food was a means to live, fuel for the battle as much as muskets and knives. The lines formed behind Colonel Butler's mounted figure and the Rangers marched toward Wintemute's fort where they hoped to engage the enemy.

"Seems there's no one waiting for us," Frank said, as the Rangers on horseback spread across the crest of a barren outcropping of rock overlooking the valley. Smoke spiraled from one lone chimney behind the palisade, the only movement in the fort. Through the sweaty stillness of the morning, muffled hoof beats pounded into the dirt.

For a scant second, John's heart leapt at the thought of an ambush, until he saw the horse. "There goes the Lieutenant with a message for them," he said.

Almost immediately the rider was back and the word went down the line that the fort had surrendered. The Rangers marched to the next one which surrendered as well.

But a day later, while they were lying at some distance from Forty Fort, Lieutenant Turney returned after long deliberations. Forty Fort would not surrender. The Continentals were preparing for battle.

"This isn't going to be so easy, Frank. We're in for a fight."

"Well, that's what we came for. I'd just like to get it over with. Put these Continentals and militia and rough upstarts—whatever they call themselves—back in their places. We need to be home in time to bring in the crops."

"That's right. Let's get it done." He and Frank watched the action over by the trees where Colonel Butler stood holding the reins of his horse. Rangers and Indians were coming and going but all was relatively calm. Suddenly the Indians began whooping and hollering.

"Guess they got the word to attack." John glanced toward the sound.

Frank pointed. "Look at those fellows go. They are just as tired of waiting as we are."

They had their horses saddled, their muskets loaded, extra paper tubes securely stowed in their cartridge boxes. John pulled his hat askew, mounted and fell into step behind the marchers. Seeing Nat pacing among them, he glanced at his arm. The spot was almost gone. "Hey, Frank. How's your arm?"

"What arm? No problem there." He laughed. "Don't know what you're talking about."

They had reached their ambush spot in the woods when Frank sniffed the air. "The fort's on fire behind us."

John turned in his saddle. "Looks like Wintemute." Quietly he got off his horse and led her to the tree cover. The colonel was planning an ambush and would use those on horseback when they were needed to break a line in the enemy defenses. Meanwhile they waited. He could never decide which was worse, marching in the front lines or waiting and watching until they were needed.

The Indians were ranged in six separate groups on his right, although he could hardly see any sign of them, so well hidden were they. Colonel Butler removed his hat and wrapped a handkerchief around his head, preparing for the fight. He moved in among his Rangers and took his place in the centre.

The enemy opened fire from about two hundred yards away. *They've seen us,* John thought. But no one fired back and the oncoming soldiers edged forward until they were as close as a hundred yards.

"Whee-oo-ahh-whee-oo-ah." Sangerachta screamed his war cry. The air was alive with successive echoes from each band of Indians. The Rangers' guns fired. John's breath caught as he strained to see what was happening. He and Frank and the rest of the men with horses were mounted now, and ready.

"Steady, Maudie, steady. We'll go soon enough." The Indians had broken through the enemy's left flank. The signal came and he galloped right at the militia, who bolted toward the river.

He soon reached their line, broken as it was, and shouted at the fleeing men. "Halt! Halt!" A short but stocky lad turned in the tall grass, arms raised but still holding his musket, and John could see the terror in his young eyes. "Drop it!" he screamed, and the boy threw the gun down, then stretched his arms as high as they could go. Just as John jumped to the ground the boy collapsed, shot, in a bloody heap right at his feet. Maudie bolted.

He knelt beside the boy, who was still alive, his eyes two rivers of terror. "I'll be back." He patted the boy's arm as he scanned the field.

The fight was all but over. Occasional shots sounded toward the river. Rangers and Indians drove the enemy into the water and he ran to join his brothers lined up on the riverbank, aiming at the desperate, fleeing soldiers. Many couldn't swim and drowned. Others were shot by the ranks on the shore. Soon enough it was over.

John turned back to the wounded boy, but was stopped by Indians raging over the field before him. The bloodlust was on them as they screamed their discoveries of wounded enemy lying helpless on the ground. They tore from one body to the next, yanking treasure off corpses, slitting throats and slicing tomahawks into enemy flesh. John was still forty feet away when he saw the brave who scalped the boy.

He heard the screams, first of the boy and then of the Indian who jerked up his left arm holding a bloody mass of hair. Falling to his knees, John dropped his musket, scrambled to grab it, load and fire. He felled the Indian with one shot. He had shot one of their own and jerked around to see if anyone had noticed.

"John! John! Where are you?"

He whirled.

"Are you all right?" Frank ran across the desolation toward him.

"Yes."

"You don't look so good."

"No wounds. You?"

"I got a few good shots off but the fight was over almost before it began. We sent them running, didn't we?"

John straightened his coat, and picked up his hat. Grabbing his gun he turned his back on the dead boy and, with Frank, headed across the field to the trees. "Maudie. Maudie," he called and then whistled. Frank did the same.

"There she is." Frank pointed to the left where Maudie grazed in the grass as though nothing had happened. "And there's my old Jackie."

AROUND THE RANGER CAMPFIRES that night many stories were told, some of bravery and some of death, but none were more shocking than the stories about the bloodthirst that had seized the Indians after the battle. They had taken only five prisoners. But they had scalped two hundred and twenty-seven men, in retribution, they said, for their losses the previous year at Fort Stanwix.

"Many of us here have relatives on the other side." Frank was cleaning his musket by the light of the fire. "The Indians could be killing our cousins or brothers."

"I know. They're good warriors and we need them, but they can be most fearsome when they go wild like that. It makes me wonder what is in store for us."

"What do you mean?" Frank asked.

"The Colonel ordered us to stop them but we couldn't. They were out of control. What if they turn on us that way?" He stared into the fire Frank had built to ward off the mosquitoes. As the bits and twigs burned faster and faster, the larger branches caught, smoldered, and burst into flames until the heat forced him to step back.

"There goes the Colonel now. Over by the doctor's tent." Frank pointed his finger. "Wonder where he's going?"

"He probably needs to clear his head just like we do. I heard he was not too pleased with the blood bath today."

"We shouldn't get too upset, John. Only soldiers were killed. It's not as though we massacred women and children."

"That's true, but I saw a young boy killed for no reason, as he lay helpless in the grass." John looked into the fire and saw the scene again. He heard the screams, smelled the blood, watched the boy's bloody scalp swing in midair.

"John. John!" Frank's voice was urgent. "You have to let it go. It's war. Not pretty. You have to let it go." He rose and kicked at the fire. "I'm for sleep."

IN THE MORNING the Rangers were marching again. They intimidated the three forts on the other side of the river into surrendering immediately. Many of the few surviving regulars had fled in the night and the settlers remaining were defenseless. The Rangers spent the day organizing the burning of the forts, except for Forty Fort, which Butler ordered to be left as shelter for the women and children, and as a storage place for the herds of cattle and wagonloads of supplies they plundered from the enemy.

John and Frank were ordered there. Riding through the open gates, John saw women and children mostly, whose glares and sullen glances left no mistake about their thoughts. Only the six of them on horseback had the task of dealing with all of these people.

"Bring your grain and your goods here, to the center of the square," John shouted. "We'll not take all that you have, but bring it here to be counted. We'll leave some for you to feed your children."

"How can we trust you?" A shout from the back of the crowd.

"We have families, too. We won't see you starve." John's voice took on a note of sincerity as, fleetingly, he thought of Lucy. "We won't see you starve."

Slowly the women moved off, holding tightly to the hands of their young children and watching the older ones carefully. John noticed a boy, maybe twelve years old, who seemed alone but for the little child he tugged along beside him. Where was the mother? The wee one was crying and, pulling back, plopped himself in the dirt. His face was smeared with tears that he vainly tried to rub away. John couldn't hear what he said. Suddenly the older boy reached down and picked up the toddler. He struggled under the dead weight and almost lost his footing. He teetered and then turned away to follow the others. The bare arms finally stole around the boy's neck.

Little children, dirty and in tatters, tagged along hiding behind their mothers' skirts, their large wide eyes peeking at the soldiers, as the women lugged their goods to the center of the yard. Gradually, the pile of foodstuffs and prized possessions, the accumulations of entire lifetimes, grew before John.

"Bring me any spirits you have," John shouted. As the bottles came he opened them and poured the liquid on the ground.

"That's a real shame." Frank shook his head.

"Butler's orders. He doesn't want the Indians to have it."

"But still it's a shame to waste good liquor. I can think of lots of better things to do with it."

"Would you take two of the men and just check the cabins? We need to be sure we haven't missed anything."

"That we do." Frank and the others trotted off leaving him presiding over the mountain of goods.

"Gather some wagons and load this stuff up," he directed the other Rangers with him. "We need to get on the move."

Whoops and hollers came from outside the gates. John yanked his horse toward the noise. Two Indians raced through the gates, heading for the pile of goods beside him. He kicked Maudie into action and rode toward the pair. "Hold up there! Hold up!"

The Indians reined in and stopped, inches away.

"What are you doing?" He kept his voice steady as he took in the glaring eyes before him.

"Gonna make them pay," the tall one shouted.

"No, you're not. There's been enough killing. Get out of here. Now."

"We make up for Stanwix last year. These settlers pay." The second Indian was moving past John.

"Stop!" He aimed at the man. By this time Frank's group had returned and stationed themselves behind John.

"Best to follow orders, men." John's low voice pierced the stillness.

The two Indians stared back. They were close enough that John felt the hot puffs of their rapid breathing and saw their hands whiten and tighten on their reins as they struggled with his words. He could almost taste their hate in his dry mouth. The silence stretched.

The two edged back, but not before giving John and the others killing looks. They turned and cantered out of the fort. He breathed again.

In short order the wagons were loaded and the cattle grouped for travel. The people had drifted back to their homes. The Rangers rode out of Forty Fort with their plunder.

At headquarters he and Frank found a hive of activity.

"Bring those wagons over here."

"Cattle this way."

Shouts were everywhere in the dusty camp as the soldiers organized the spoils. He and Frank learned that a new deal had been worked out with the enemy and Forty Fort was going to be demolished along with all the others. Where would all of the people go? The prisoners on both sides were all to be set free. Furthermore, none of the inhabitants were to bear arms again.

"Those terms are pretty easy." Frank and John were brushing their horses after the rush of the day. "How do we know they won't ever bear arms again?"

"Seems a mite lenient, I'll grant you," John said.

"We've even agreed to let those enemy settlers up river keep their properties."

John shook his head. "There's only one reason for Butler to do that."

Frank stopped his brushing and studied John. "What?"

"Maybe he's thinking about the end of this war. We all have to live together."

"Could be. People have family on the other side. That's the shame of this whole mess." Shaking his head Frank went back to his brushing.

As he lay in his blanket that night, John reviewed the events of the day. It was good to be on the winning side but he really didn't have any sense of joy. He thought of the boy with his little brother. Of the young soldier he had seen scalped. Of his quick shot at the Indian.

Something pricked at the corner of his mind. That young soldier was familiar. Where had he seen him before? And then he remembered. Frank's cousin had come to help clear his land the year before his marriage to Lucy. Visiting Frank for the whole summer, the thirteen-year-old had trotted after both of them as they chopped trees, dragged logs, burned stumps, always in the way. But he had a laugh and a pair of mischievous eyes that made the men forgive him everything. Just a boy. And now that boy was dead.

Back in England the boy he had been lost everything, too.

He twisted in his blanket and wondered how the mothers and children were faring this first night without the fort to protect them. Then he thought of Lucy. He thought of her reddish hair and her sparkling eyes, of the soft curves of her body as she lay in their rope bed with the fluffy feather mattress. He could almost forget his damp hard place on the ground as he pictured her, under the patchwork quilt, and envied her.

Chapter Seven

SHE JERKED UPRIGHT and grabbed the rifle. What was that sound? All was quiet. Must have imagined it. The room was still shadowy but dawn pushed its streaks under the curtains and through the lopsided gap between them, faintly lighting the colours of the patchwork quilt.

The gun felt cold but comforting in her hands as she strained to hear again what had startled her. The rooster crowed. She jumped, then relaxed. That must be what woke her. Still she listened hard. Was someone in the cabin? She remembered the stranger of the night before and shuddered.

For what seemed hours she sat rigid in bed and pushed her senses to feel what was in the next room, on the porch, in the yard, and in the barn. And there it was. A soft clicking in the other room. The door latch. Someone was trying to open it. She edged back the quilt and slipped to the floor. Clutching the gun she moved to the curtain at the bedroom door. She inched it back just enough to see the room. All was well there. She crept to the side of the window and forced herself to look out.

She jerked back. Someone was on the porch. The door latch rattled again. She was glad of the heavy bar across. Heart pounding she lifted the window curtain. It was the man from last night back again.

She checked her rifle. Her father had given her this and made sure she knew how to use it. She moved to the door. "Who's there?"

Her voice was as loud as she could make it but she realized how shaky she was. She called louder. "Who's there?"

"I was, ah, just wondering if I could have some food, ma'am. You gave me milk last night." His voice was plaintive but she didn't trust that sound at all. He had tried the door, after all.

"We have no food for you. You had best get on your way."

"Can you please open the door and give me something to eat. I'm terrible hungry, ma'am."

"Who are you?" Lucy didn't know what to do. She hated to leave a man hungry but she had seen his cruel eyes and she didn't like his habit of sneaking up on her. He had done it twice now.

"Jacob Daeger, ma'am. On my way back to Boston."

"What are you doing away out here?"

"Well, ah, ma'am, a man's business is his own. If you could just give me some food, I'll be on my way."

"Wait in the yard and I'll bring some out and then you can leave." What else could she do? She gathered some dried beef and a chunk of yesterday's loaf. When she had the small bundle ready she looked out and saw Daeger staring back at her from his place about ten paces away in the yard.

She dropped the curtain and lifted the bolt. The gun in one hand and the packet in the other, she stepped onto the porch.

"Here's your food." She set the packet on the ground, stepped back and gripped the gun with both hands, not exactly pointing at him but, if need be, she was ready to shoot.

"Thank you, ma'am." Daeger's words were soft but he glared through her as he stepped forward to retrieve the package. "This will sure help me on my way."

"You are welcome."

Daeger turned his back and walked toward his horse. He stuffed the package into a pouch and mounted. He paused. His eyes bit into Lucy. Hard, cold eyes, not wanting to be bested. Abruptly, he pulled back on the reins and turned away.

When he reached the trees, he turned again and stopped. Lucy stood steady. The rifle inched upwards. She narrowed her eyes. Daeger stared a long moment and then was gone.

She watched the woods until, gradually, she became aware of the world around her. Molly mooed, the chickens squawked and cackled, and the rifle became heavy in her arms. She lowered it and sank to the porch steps where she stayed until her heart stopped thumping and she relaxed.

The rest of the day was uneventful but Lucy's fatigue slowed her down in the field. She knew that Daeger was evil and the thought terrified her. For the thousandth time, she halted the hoe and looked back at the buildings, checking for anything amiss.

Daeger knew she was alone. Would he come back? She hacked at a large thistle, took a breath, and hacked again. Finally, it came loose and she moved on to the next weed. Dandelions. They were rampant throughout the patch. She struggled to get the whole root. She put her heel on the hoe and pushed, sinking it deep, then twisted the handle under the weed. Gotcha! She smiled and by reflex glanced toward the cabin. She choked back a scream.

Ranged at the edge of the corn was a group of Indians, about eight or ten at least, sitting rigid on their horses, staring at her. She tightened her grip on the hoe and walked up the row toward them. Ten. There were ten. They looked peaceful enough but her heart thumped all the same. This was the group that had been here before. She recognized the leader. Same mangy feathers, flopping lopsided from his head, and, as she got closer, she could see the same steely eyes. She carried the hoe like a staff, hitting the ground and steadying herself with every step.

"What do you want?" She called out when she was close enough to be heard. She saw that they were carrying a man over one of the horses. He looked dead. By this time she could see his necklace of huge bear claws strung on some kind of leather thong which hung down against the horse's flank. She had seen it before.

This was the angry-eyed brave who was so threatening when they had scared her a few weeks earlier. He had the same red-streaked face. She couldn't see his eyes but remembered them all the same. Hard, pin-point eyes. She shuddered.

"Can you help?" The leader nodded toward the wounded man.

"Is he alive?" Lucy noted the streaked faces of the other braves and glanced twice at a couple whose war paint seemed more like dried blood.

"Yes. He needs help. We must go."

"Bring him inside." She led the way to the cabin where the Indians dismounted and carried the injured man inside, dumping him on the floor. She knelt beside him and leaned down to listen for his heart, her cheek against the bear claw necklace. He was alive, but unconscious. Could she help him? She stood to get water.

The Indians had crowded around and she motioned them out of her way. They parted instantly, eyes on her as she lifted a basin of warm water to the floor and began to clean the head wound. She tried not to notice the swinging scalps at their waists but fixed all her attention on the injured man on the floor.

The cut was not too deep, but she washed it carefully. And that flap of skin. Maybe she could sew that back once she got everything clean. Lucky he had no hair. He must have shaved it off before the battle. She worked carefully and tenderly, willing the man not to wake up until she finished. Eventually she had the wound clean, ready for some thread to sew the flap in place. Glancing up, she was amazed to see that she was alone with the wounded man. The others had disappeared.

"So they just left you with me, did they?" she muttered. "Guess they had more pressing affairs to attend to than looking after one of their own." She shook her head and fetched her needle from the cupboard. The stitches went in more easily than she had expected and she finished in no time.

"I've never done that before, but it looks good enough. Hopefully you'll be happy with me when you recover, and not take my scalp off." She glanced at his eyes but they were still closed. He didn't look like he'd be waking up any time soon.

She stood and stretched her tired limbs. From her medicine box she took out some pine gum gathered from the large white pine on the edge of the forest. A poultice would help to draw any poison from the wound. With deft hands she prepared the medicine, found some clean ragged material and bandaged the man's head.

She sat back on her heels and studied the Indian. His red-streaked face and his bear tooth necklace made him fierce, although without the stare of his black eyes which she remembered so well, she was not frightened. She would have to wash away all that war paint.

Sweat streaked his bare arms, along with dirt and paint and the smears of something which could only be blood. His arms and chest were heavily muscled. He must be strong.

And heavy. How could she move him? He lay on the bare floor, right across her path around the table to her chair by the fire and the bedroom beyond. She would have to lift him. She stood up and started for the door to throw out the dirty water in the basin. He groaned. She froze, but slowly turned back. His eyes were still closed. She inched the door open and went out.

The sun had sunk below the trees, leaving the grass bathed in stripes of gold. She dumped the bloody water off the end of the porch and set the basin near the door. She just had time to finish up with the animals before dark. She grabbed her rifle and headed for the barn, scanning the yard. All was peaceful. Her thoughts whirled as she tended the animals. She had done this for so many nights now, but this time she was even more skittish.

Finally, she carried the evening's milk pail across the yard and stepped quietly up onto the porch. She put her ear against the door. *I must be crazy, listening at my own cabin door.* She straightened up, opened it and slipped inside.

The Indian was still unconscious, although his body had shifted slightly on the floor. Lucy lifted the milk to the sideboard, grabbed the basin, and went outside for cold water.

....

She knelt and gently washed the man's perspiring face. "I'm not sure I can save you, my friend, but I'll do my best. We have to get this fever down." She lifted the bear claw necklace to swab the sweat away from his skin. "The more I wash you, the cooler you'll be. I hope you don't mind."

She talked soothingly as she washed his skin, rinsed the cloth, wrung it out over the basin, and put it to his hot flesh again. As she worked, the war paint gradually disappeared and the frightening Indian became just a man who needed help.

By the time she finished she had an idea. If she could get the buffalo robe underneath the man he would be more comfortable and she could shift him to the side of the cabin.

She laid the robe on the floor and tipped the man to one side, ignoring his guttural groans. She held his weight, her foot against his back, and tugged the buffalo robe as close as she could. When she removed her foot, the man rolled onto his back, a choked-off scream escaping from deep inside, but at least now the robe cushioned him from the hard floor.

She lifted his legs fully onto the robe and gently pulled him and the robe the rest of the way. He was heavy but she kept going. After much tugging on her part and groaning on his, the man lay along one side of the table leaving the other side free. Lucy collapsed in John's chair.

She could see that this Indian was going to be a lot of work. She didn't know how she could add extra chores to her day but she was lonely and having another person there, even though he was unconscious, gave her hope. She would care for him. If Daeger came back she wouldn't be alone.

Her hand caressed her stomach and the baby growing inside. She felt a definite bump now and smiled. John would be happy.

After her own soup supper, she tried to force open the Indian's mouth to give him some as well, but the liquid just slipped down his chin. She was afraid of choking him. Could unconscious people swallow? She didn't know, and soon gave up. In John's chair again, she sat, watching the Indian.

....

John. What would he think of this? Would he worry about her if he knew? She wondered where he was, if he was cold at night, or had enough to eat. She thought of his steady strong arms around her in the bed at night. The one thing she wouldn't allow herself to think about was the fighting. There were just too many dangers in those kinds of thoughts.

She wished she'd been more sympathetic toward him. They had to keep their land safely under the King's rule. John had to go. Those ruffians calling themselves Americans were just not the sort to be tolerated. She and John might be poor, they might work with their hands, they might even have come from nothing, but they were British subjects. "And proud of it," she muttered aloud. Surely John was right. They had to fight.

Presently her thoughts returned to the room and she bathed the man's face and arms again, cooling him as best she could. It was full dark now. She might as well go to bed. She would rise in the night to check her patient.

Surprisingly she went right to sleep, waking in the dark to tend the Indian. She lit a candle, took the water basin and cloth and washed his body once again. She could feel the heat right through the cloth. If only he would wake up she could give him something to help cool him inside. She went back to bed and slept till the rooster's raucous call sounded before dawn.

Lucy checked the patient, bathed his fevered brow, his arms and chest and his hard hands. He seemed a little cooler now but maybe that was just that he had lain on the floor all night. Gingerly she lifted the bandage on his head. The wound looked clear. No bleeding. Good. She would change the bandage later. She noticed an odor. *Oh, my. You've wet yourself. What can I do about that?*

The question puzzled her as she did her milking and feeding. She had nothing to put on the Indian. Could she even get his breeches off to wash? She would have to try. And the buffalo robe would have to be cleaned, too. Maybe she should have left him on the bare floor.

Soon she was back in the cabin with her pail of milk. It wasn't full by any means. Molly gave less and less every day. Lucy strained the milk into a pitcher and covered it with a cloth to keep the flies out. She would eat later. Just now she had to tend to the Indian.

Taking the basin of cool water to the floor beside the man, she knelt by his head, wrung out the cloth, and touched his face softly. She swabbed his cheeks, his still-closed eyes, and his fore-head. Again she wrung the cloth, removed the bandage exposing the wound, and touched the cloth to the reddened skin. This looks very good, she thought. The area was hardly puffy at all. Ever so lightly she drew the cloth over her stitches, cooling and cleaning at the same time.

"Awwwrh."

She dropped the cloth. Was he waking? His eyes remained closed. Presently, she stood to get clean bandaging materials and more pine gum, then knelt again to apply them. The man slept on.

Now the time had come to solve the breeches problem. Quickly she unlaced the thongs holding the britches together at the waist. Then she pulled them down, lifting, pushing, pulling and tugging until she had them off. She took the basin of water and swabbed the man's lower body, trying to keep her mind on the animals outside, the crop in the field, the hoeing she still had to finish, the color of the buffalo robe, the need for more stew to be made— anything to take her mind off her task.

And then she was done. Looking around for something to put over the man she spied her coat. Hmm. No choice, she thought, and grabbed it from the hook and covered him. She took the breeches outside to clean them and lay them in the sun to dry.

Chapter Eight

July, 1778

TODAY SHE WOULD FINISH THE HOEING. Not a moment too soon. The corn was fairly flying out of the field. The weeds had to go or its growth would soon be stunted. Lucy stood and looked around, proud of the job she had done. John would be pleased. Everything was growing well here on the farm.

The baby. Her belly swelled more every day. She must be about three and a half months by now, she thought, but she wasn't really sure. *Are you a boy or a girl, little one?* She held the hoe in one hand while her other slid over her belly. "I love to hold you already. I can hardly wait to cuddle you in my arms, sweet thing." She grabbed the hoe and poked at yet another thistle.

The sun was high in the sky when Lucy returned to the cabin for some food. She hadn't even remembered to eat breakfast with all her work on the Indian. She picked up the dry breeches and stepped into the cabin. As her eyes adjusted from the bright sunlight to the dim room she realized something was different. Immediately she looked toward the buffalo robe. Oh! Two dark eyes stared back.

"You're awake."

Silence.

She moved closer. "I washed your breeches for you." She held them up. "Are you feeling better?"

More silence.

"Can you hear me?" Lucy knelt beside the man. He shrank back and she jumped a little.

"You're going to have to trust me. You were wounded in the battle and your friends brought you here for me to help." She laid the breeches on the floor beside her patient. "I washed these for you." Standing up again, she moved to the sideboard and poured a mug of milk. Quickly she knelt again beside the Indian and offered him some. He struggled to raise his head and drink. "Pthwah!" He spat out the milk.

"What are you doing?" Lucy jerked away from him, taking the mug with her. "Don't you like milk?" His dark eyes cut into her. "I'll get you something else."

In a moment she returned with a crust of bread which she dipped into some cold stew. She looked at him once more. "You need to eat," she said as she held it to his mouth.

He sniffed. His eyes bored into Lucy's. Slowly, his lips parted and he accepted the food. This time all was well. Lucy talked softly as she fed the man lying on her floor. He took all the food in the bowl. "Very good," she said and rose to put the bowl back on the sideboard. The Indian reached for his breeches. He glanced at his lower body and grimaced. Apparently the coat was not suitable. He struggled to sit up but fell back.

"You may need some help."

"No. No help." He spoke at last. He tried to sit again, his eyes scrunching with the effort but to no avail. Lucy moved beside him.

"Would you like me to help?" She gestured toward the breeches. He grunted.

She wasn't sure what that meant but reached for the breeches. Reluctantly, the Indian loosened his grip on them and she moved to his feet to put them on for him. Leaving the coat over his body she inched the breeches up his legs. He shifted to help. Avoiding his eyes, she removed the coat cover and fixed the thong at his waist. She hung the coat on the door.

"Good." The Indian clipped the word but at least he was communicating.

Lucy prepared her food at the sideboard. She would drink the milk even if he wouldn't. The baby needed it and she needed it. She sat at the table and spooned in the cold stew which tasted like a banquet, so hungry was she. She glanced at the man, fearing those piercing eyes, but he slept again. She let out a breath. He might just make it.

After eating, Lucy went out to the corn again and spent the rest of the afternoon hoeing and pulling weeds. She took water breaks when her row neared the cabin but kept at the job until the sun was sinking. She hoed the last row and was finally back to the cabin. Her back ached as she stood straight to survey the lovely rows of clean corn stretching from the cabin to the forest. She was tired and achy but it was a good tired. She had finished the whole thing. John would be so proud of her.

She entered the cabin and looked toward the Indian. Those coal eyes stared back at her.

"How are you feeling? Can you sit up?" Lucy took his arm and pulled to help him. "What is your name?"

The man let out a groan and jerked his hand to his head.

"Your wound probably hurts but you'll have to leave it to heal. Don't touch it." She shook her head. "What is your name?"

"Black Bear Claw." He looked around the room and then back at her. "Water."

"You want water? Just a moment." She jumped to get a mug and brought it to him.

He drank deeply, and thrust the cup back at her. "Water." His voice was urgent.

"I just gave you water."

"Make water. I make water."

Lucy understood. She rose and disappeared into her bedroom, returning with the chamber pot. "You can use this. I'll just go outside and see to the animals."

Darkness was falling and Lucy rushed to get the cow milked, the oxen penned for the night and the chickens cooped up. As she approached the cabin she stole another glance at the corn in the field but couldn't see too far. Still, she was happy. Her homestead was in good shape and she was doing it all by herself. And growing a baby as well. She held her belly and pictured the tiny being inside her. Would John ever see their child? The thought surfaced for a split second, but she pushed it away and stomped onto the porch.

Over the next few days Lucy and the Indian got into a routine. She cooked and helped him to eat. He gradually gained strength and, after his first wobbly attempts to stand and walk, got his balance back. Now he sat at the table to eat and went to the outhouse to relieve himself. Each time Lucy changed his bandage, the wound had healed a little more until it was completely covered with scabbing around the edges of the flap. He didn't talk much but that terrifying black-eyed stare had gone, and in its place were sidelong glances at her as she worked. Even though he was quiet Lucy talked to him anyhow.

"You're doing very well now. Soon you'll be ready to ride a horse again. I wonder when your friends will come back for you." She glanced over at him, sitting at the table, finishing his stew.

"Soon. I hope soon." He didn't look up.

Lucy hoped not too soon. She felt safer with him here. She hadn't seen any more of Jacob Daeger but she feared he would be back. With taking care of the Indian, she hadn't thought much about his scary person but now her back stiffened and her pulse raced as she recalled his last visit. Oh, he would be back, she was sure. She had seen the look in his eyes.

As she sat in the chair that night, the Indian resting on the buffalo robe across the room, she let her mind wander once again to what John might be doing. She tried to imagine where he might be and what was happening to him. She dozed.

....

John called her but she couldn't reach him. She could hear him but couldn't see him. Where was he? She saw the soldiers running with upraised guns and she heard their wild hollering. Colonel Butler rode furiously at the trees. Indians howled and horses screamed. She saw John just as Maudie neighed and bucked high in the air, knocking him off. He was falling, falling, slowly, brushing a branch, his arms pumping in slow motion as though trying to grab hold of something, anything, before he smacked to the ground.

She jumped from the chair, startling the Indian, who knocked over the table. He had his knife in his hand and was circling, shifting from one foot to the other as his head jerked from her to the door and back again. Slowly his hand relaxed and lowered the knife. He grunted with the strain of leaning over to right the table and chair.

"I must have been dreaming. I'm so sorry." Her hands covered her cheeks. "It's all right. Everything's all right." He must have dozed, too.

"Sleep. I sleep now." The Indian turned and pulled his buffalo robe off the box, spreading it deftly on the floor. She checked the door, peeked outside the window and slipped into her bedroom. She needed to move him to the barn.

The next day she woke to scuffling in the other room and knew her guest was up. At the heavy thud of the door bar and the soft click of the door closing, she relaxed. He had gone to relieve himself. She rose and dressed, tidying the bed with a speedy pull of the patchwork quilt. Today she would move him to the barn. His wound was almost all healed and he could take the buffalo robe out there. They would both have some privacy.

THE HENS CACKLED LOUDLY as she released the coop door and they pushed out to their pen. The rooster had already crowed but, in his excitement, let out another cock-a-doodle-do behind Lucy. "Aren't you having a grand day of it?" She spread the seed and then hurried to release Molly and the oxen. Her pail was waiting and

Molly was willing so the milking took no time at all. "Not much here, Molly. I'm afraid you're drying up."

If John were here he would take Molly to visit the bull over at Frank's place but that would take a few days and Lucy couldn't leave her chores for that long. Besides she wasn't too sure of the way. She had only visited Frank and his father on her way to the farm almost two years ago. Since then John had made the trip a couple of times and she had been the one to stay behind. "I'll just keep milking you as long as I can."

Lucy carried her pail to the porch, thinking she would see the Indian somewhere around. But she was alone. Maybe he went back inside. She lifted the latch and stepped in. The cabin was empty. She set the pail on the sideboard and covered it with a cloth. "Where are you, my friend?" She went back outside.

The chickens peck-pecked in the dirt. The two oxen and Molly nosed the grass, tasting and biting. When they liked what they found, they chewed forever on each mouthful. Everything was calm and quiet, just what it should be on a warm July morning.

"Hello-o-o-o-o! Where are you?" Lucy shouted from the porch but got no answer. Had the Indian just left? Was he well enough? She turned and went back inside to her breakfast.

With all her hoeing and caring for the Indian, Lucy had been neglecting the cabin. Today she would wash the bedding, sweep out the whole place and go hunting in the woods for something tasty to liven up her stew. The season was getting on but maybe she could find something wild and green, and, if not, her garden was bursting. Truth be told she longed for a walk in the cool woods. She would take the gun in case she found anything to kill. Some fresh meat would be most welcome.

Lucy dragged the big tub into the yard and made several trips to fill it with hot water from the reservoir on the stove. She knelt on the grass to scrub the sheets, her small clothes, towels, and the cloths she had been using to minister to her patient. As each item was done she wrung it out and made a pile beside her on the chair she had brought out.

The wash tub was too heavy for her to lift and dump so she dipped out a lot of the dirty water and then tipped the tub over to empty it. She was tired and the sun felt hot on her neck as she knelt to rinse the clothing in fresh water. This time she wrung out each rinsed item, rose and walked to the bushes to spread the clean wash. In this sun it would dry in no time.

She still had not seen anything of the Indian. By now he should have come back but he had not. She might as well get used to being alone again. Lucy looked toward the trail, but this time she wasn't looking for John. She hoped the Indian was all right.

Wait. Someone was coming through the trees. He was on horseback. Daeger? She raced for the cabin. When she stepped back onto the porch, her rifle in hand, the horseman was much closer.

"Hello, Mrs. Garner," he called. "Hello."

Niles Maycock. Lucy dropped the rifle to her side and sagged to the step.

"Are you all right, ma'am?" Mr. Maycock was off his horse and running toward her.

"I'm fine. Just…a little…tired."

"I thought I'd check back in on you since I was pretty near. Are you sure you're all right?" Mr. Maycock leaned over Lucy and offered his hand to help her up.

"I am. Of course I am." She forced a smile. "I was afraid you were someone else. Please, come inside and have some cool water."

"Just let me look after my horse, ma'am."

Sitting at the table Lucy sipped at her water. Mr. Maycock gulped his.

"I am just that thirsty, ma'am, and this water tastes like nectar from the gods. May I have some more?" He was already out of his chair and helping himself to the water on the sideboard.

"Please. Drink as much as you want. Water is one thing I have," Lucy laughed.

"It is most appreciated, ma'am." Carefully he set the mug on the table and looked at Lucy. "You said you thought I was someone else. Who would you be greetin' with a loaded rifle?"

"Oh, it's nothing." Seeing his raised eyebrows, she added, "A man was by here a couple of weeks ago and I had to chase him off with the rifle. He was not pleased."

"You out here all alone. Not good. What did the man look like? Do you know his name?"

"The second time he came back he told me his name. Jacob Daeger." Lucy shuddered as she remembered how his eyes had filled with hate as he stared at the rifle she pointed at him.

"Now, there's a nasty man, ma'am. I don't take kindly to him. You were right to chase him off."

"What could I do? I'm here all by myself, I don't know when John is coming back, and anyone can come through those trees and find me here, defenseless." She jumped up. "What am I to do?"

"Let's think on that for a bit, ma'am. Meanwhile, could I bed down in your barn for the night again? I wouldn't mind some home cookin' and I could sure help you with some chores around the place before nightfall."

"Oh, of course you can stay, Mr. Maycock. I'm pleased to have you. But you must tell me what you know about Daeger."

"That old skinflint?" He let out a breath of air and turned for the door.

"Wait. I need to know."

Again Maycroft faced her. "He's a slippery character, with a bad reputation. I heard about him on the boat coming up from New York. Folks said he killed a man for his land but the neighbors ran him off."

Lucy sat up straight. "In cold blood? He killed a man for his land?"

"Said the man threatened him, but no one believed him. Had to run for his life." He sat down again and looked straight at her. "This is the first I've heard of him way out here. You're right to keep a watch."

"Maybe he'll find someone else to rob," Lucy said. Mr. Maycock nodded and headed out the door.

When Lucy went to bed that night she felt safe. Mr. Maycock was in the barn, her larder held a freshly killed rabbit and the

Indian was well, and gone on his way. Her thoughts were random as she moved her hand back and forth over her bulging tummy. Funny Mr. Maycock didn't notice. Maybe he did but just wouldn't say anything.

John. She wished she could see his face when he heard the news but she had decided to write it in a letter. She tried to remember exactly how he looked that day when he had ridden out but the image was fading. Would she forget what he looked like? Surely not.

Maybe if she thought of that she would see him more clearly. She pictured him riding Maudie through the trees and disappearing. She thought of him coming back, of his arms around her, touching her here in their bed, so soft, so tender, so… John.

Her dreams that night were pleasant, at first, but then took a sharp turn and she saw Indians stalking the trees. The oxen pulled the cabin over and she was suffocating, struggling to breathe, pounding with her hands on the wall, trying to get out of the cabin, screaming "John! John! Help me, John!" She flew up in the dark.

Someone was in the room.

Chapter Nine

September, 1778

SUMMER SLIPPED INTO FALL and still the war raged. John's hopes of being home by September were dashed by the ever-changing see-saw of battles won and lost and, lately, sitting in camp waiting for something to happen. In the Wyoming Valley they had thought the end was in sight, so successful were their attacks on the forts there. But the militia and the Continental Army had fought back and the Rangers had, themselves, run and then settled in this backwater camp.

The worst part of all this was the idleness and the thoughts that came when the men were bored, lonely and homesick. John had watched Frank's good humor slip into sarcastic jibes at anyone close, although he, himself, had not as yet been the target. On this cool, clear morning he brushed Maudie with a steady hand, keeping his eye on a group of Rangers off to his right.

"You keep your hands off my kit!"

"Your kit? It's mine. I brought it all the way from Boston two years back." First one, then the other Ranger yanked at the small leather pouch.

"You're a bloody liar. You've never even been to Boston."

"Who you calling a liar?" The man released the kit and lashed out, his fist finding cheekbone.

"Cut that out. Save your fighting for the enemy." Sergeant Newbury, on horseback, had appeared out of nowhere. He settled the fight and sent the men off to hunt for food, then rode over to John. "I swear these fellas'll kill each other if we don't soon get them some real fighting to do."

"Any news on that, sir?"

"Nope. Everything is quiet here although Walter Butler has been cutting quite a swath over near Cherry Valley. There's a big one coming there soon."

John hesitated. "Any chance we'll be going home then, sir?"

"There's always a chance, Garner, but the Colonel doesn't want to break up the Rangers until we've finished our job. We've got to defeat Washington's upstarts once and for all."

"The men are edgy and bored, sir. Anything you can do?"

"I don't know. But we are going to be marching soon. The Colonel wants to root out some local militia who've been a problem up north. Best get your things ready for that order. Should be coming in a day or so." Sergeant Newbury flicked the reins and squeezed his boots into his horse's belly, and rode on.

"What did he want?" Frank came up behind John and stroked Maudie's head.

"Not much. We might be marching soon, though."

"Where to now?" Frank's voice was flat.

"Maybe up north, as far as Niagara. I don't know for sure."

"Well, anything will be better than sitting in this camp."

Within a few days, Butler's Rangers were on the move northward as the sergeant had said. Frank regained his humor and, with every step closer to home, his smile broadened. Maybe he thinks he's going to see his father, John thought, but he knew they were heading northwest, and would not be turning toward their farms. Seeing their families was very unlikely. Still, they were on the move and doing something. They didn't seem to be bringing much in the way of provisions, though. Usually a couple of supply wagons and some cattle would accompany them, but not this time. Hopefully Butler had another plan.

The Rangers and about two hundred Indians with them followed the trail along the Susquehanna River, stopping at night to make camp and sending scouts ahead for safety. The nights were colder now and his blanket seemed to be getting thinner as he lay on the hard ground trying to sleep.

Frank muttered in his sleep and John strained to hear but it was all a jumble. He wondered if Lucy had done the reaping and even if she remembered how. They had harvested together last year, swinging the scythe to cut the stalks and then stooking them. How could she do it alone? Was she even still there?

He hadn't heard from her for a long time and no one had been along to take messages back. The trails were getting harder for anyone to travel, but especially for the King's supporters. Stories floated in of more and more farms seized and Loyalists driven off or even murdered. *I should not have left her alone.*

Would he ever get back? What would he find? Lucy was alone in the cabin. For the millionth time he hoped she was well. His eyes were wet and he swiped at them in the darkness.

MORNING RATIONS WERE CUT IN HALF, with only a dollop of hot coffee and a small bit of dried meat. The men grumbled but accepted the food and ate quickly before falling in line once again. Toward midday the call came to halt.

"Good. I'm surely ready to eat." Frank grumbled, as he swung down.

"That short ration didn't last long, did it?" John asked.

"No. I hope we're not running low on food."

"Didn't you notice when we started this march? Hardly any supply wagons and no cows coming along. If we weren't so low on powder I'd be looking for rabbits along the way." John lifted his hat and ran his hand through his hair. "I'll be glad to find a camp and stay there for a bit. Being bored doesn't seem so bad now."

"Mount up! March on!" The call came down the line.

"No food? Or drink?" Frank shouted his surprise.

"Lucky we filled up on water last time we saw the river." John tipped his water skin to his mouth, sipped, and swung up, clucking Maudie ahead.

THE LATE AFTERNOON SUN was streaking through the trees when next the line stopped and the word came back to make camp. Methodically the men pitched their thin tents, gathered wood and twigs for fires, and settled for the night. This time food appeared and the Rangers rushed to join the line. No thoughts of Lucy's cooking or any food from home now, only the push forward to the food.

John gobbled his ration and licked his plate clean, then licked it again in case he had missed anything. Frank did the same. There was no coffee, no tea, nothing to wash it down but water, and even that was in short supply.

"At least the horses can eat grass when they find it." Frank stuffed his plate back into his pack.

"Never mind. A few more days of marching and we'll be at Niagara. There'll be lots of food there."

"You're always the optimist, aren't you? Don't you ever get tired? Or angry?" Frank kicked at the fire and the sparks flew upward in a brief burst of hot air.

"Yes. And you don't want to see it." He watched the fire and lapsed into silence as his mind played scenes of killing and blood. He heard the screams of the Indian as he scalped the terrified boy. He remembered dropping his musket, then reloading and shooting that Indian. He felt the breath of the huge man he had knifed to death a few months ago. Countless like images plagued his vision as the flames spit and flew upwards, only to burn out and float lifeless to the ground.

Darkness had covered the camp and the fires were burning down once again. Like an old married couple who had their night rituals ingrained after years of repetition, John and Frank banked the fire, checked the horses, and crawled into the tent.

....

AS THE EARLY STREAKS OF DAWN shot across the sky the lonely bugle called the men to life for one more day. Stiff with cold, John groaned and shifted his body, stretching out each joint. Near him Frank did the same. Shouts came from outside the tent. John looked out. More shouting. People ran back and forth.

"Come on. Something's happened." John slipped through the tent flap with Frank right behind.

"What's going on? Why is everybody running?"

"Check your horses," Nat called as he ran by.

He and Frank turned to look. Their horses were gone. They had been tethered just a few feet away from the tent and they were gone.

"Indians," Frank shouted.

"No one else could have stolen them right from under our noses."

John and Frank joined the frenzy of men planning what to do. When had the horses been stolen? More importantly where had the thieves taken them? They quickly learned that not all of the horses were gone, only those belonging to the eighteen soldiers who had acted as cavalry. Luckily Butler's horse and the other officers' horses had been tethered together near the cook's wagon where he slept out in the open, too much of a risk for the thieves.

"Now what do we do?" John spit out the words.

"Well. I guess we walk like the other fellows."

"And carry all this stuff? The tent, the guns, the packs? It's going to be heavy." John stopped and pulled Frank's arm. "We could leave the tent behind...if you want to freeze."

"You're right. Winter's coming. We'll have to carry it."
John and Frank packed up, making two bundles to carry. After a half ration breakfast the Rangers were marching again, this time with eighteen more men on the ground.

Spirits were low as they trod the forest path, each man's eyes fixed on the back of the one before him. The cold of the morning gave way to streaks of warming sun filtering through the leaves which seemed to have colored overnight. When they broke into a clearing beside the river, the opposite bank glowed with vibrant reds, deep oranges and sunny yellows, interspersed with the solid dark green of the pines.

"Beautiful." John stood in awe.

"What?" Frank looked to see what John saw. "Yes, beautiful. Until someone decides to set it all on fire to burn out a settler or an army."

"Look, water. Do you think we could catch some fish?" Frank was already dropping his pack to look for a line. With a length of cord tied to a branch he headed for the water a few hundred feet away. John was right behind with his own makeshift fishing pole. They worked their way through the cattails and cast their lines in the water.

"We'll never get anything without some bait. At least we've got those hooks in our packs. We've been carrying them for more than five months."

"Time we put them to use." John had been scrabbling in the wet ground at his feet. "Aha! A worm." He threaded the worm up the hook then flicked the line out over the water where it settled and sank.

Soon Frank had done the same and they fished silently, throwing the line out and gradually pulling it back toward them, then flicking again. "I've got one." Frank pulled carefully on his line. "Keep it steady. Don't lose the bugger," he muttered to himself.

John stepped on his pole and leaned over to help. "A big one. Look at that. Hang on, I've got him." John took the hook out and laid the flopping fish on the ground.

"We'll eat well now, my friend." Frank jumped up and down, his hands flailing the pole all around.

"Careful. You'll snag me."

"Let's try again. I could eat a whole fish myself." Frank scrabbled for another worm, threaded it, and tried his luck once more.

Almost immediately John landed a good-sized fish. Soon they had a string of four beauties, plenty to fill up their hungry bellies.

"Come on, Frank. We had better get back to the others." John shouldered his pack and led back to the trees. His stomach heaved and he thought of the wonderful fish supper to come. He noticed the stillness. In the bright sun he squinted, looking for the Rangers. He ran, struggling under his heavy load, searching for someone, anyone. But there was no one.

Chapter Ten

October, 1778

"MUST HAVE GONE AHEAD WITHOUT US."

John nodded. "Didn't know we were gone, I expect. We'd best pack up and catch them."

"Don't you want to eat first? I'm really hungry and these fellows will just start to smell if we don't eat them."

"We do have enough to carry as it is." He put his pack down again, took out his knife and sat down to gut the fish. "You get the fire going. I don't fancy eating this stuff raw."

Frank was already gathering twigs and branches. "Won't take long. We can be back with the rest in an hour or so."

"Let's hope so."

A half-hour later they had eaten their fill, wrapped and packed the rest, and stamped out the fire. They set out on the trail with renewed energy, walking quickly to overtake the Rangers.

The afternoon sun beat down on them and its golden rays lit the falling leaves. Birds sang overhead. John wished he could identify them all. He could hear the bobwhite's rising tweet. And the cardinal's peew, peew descending and then starting high again.

He thought of Lucy and their last walk in the woods together. To the waterfall. He would like to head home to her. Maybe that's what he should do. No. He couldn't. The hoot of an owl broke his reverie. An owl? He turned to Frank, behind him, and stopped. Too early for an owl.

"Someone's signal," Frank whispered. He nodded back and pointed in the direction the sound had come. They stepped off the trail and were lost in the trees. Moving ever so slowly and soundlessly John led the way to a dense thicket and pointed.

"Can we fit in there?" Frank asked but John was already on his hands and knees crawling between the thorny branches. Frank followed. "Ouch."

"Sh." The space was so tight he couldn't even turn to Frank but he stopped when he thought they were hidden. Frank pushed close behind. No birds sang now. John wondered who was out there and how close they were.

For several long minutes the two held their positions on hands and knees in the dense foliage unable to sit or even turn. John's knees were screaming and he was about to suggest they crawl back out. Maybe this wasn't such a good hiding place.

Hoot. Hoot. The owl sound came again, this time very near. A sharp intake of air behind him. Frank. John willed him to be silent.

"We've lost them." The voice was a whisper in the forest beyond.

A deeper whisper. "They must be hiding. Keep looking."

"There are so many trees to hide behind we'll never find them. Maybe they headed for the river."

"Good. We'll look there and then come back to…" The words were lost as the men moved on.

John and Frank waited a few minutes more and then crawled painfully backwards out of their hiding place. "Next time I'll pick the spot." Frank was pulling thorns out of his clothes.

"They didn't find us, did they? Let's go."

This time the two friends moved as fast as possible down the trail, stopping to listen as they went. They needed to put a lot of distance between themselves and whoever had been following them in the forest. When they reached a fork in the path they debated for a few seconds and then took the path which led closer to the river. Surely Butler would have gone this way.

....

NIGHT WAS FALLING and they had not found their unit. They were tired. When John stopped and looked at Frank, his own anxiety was mirrored in Frank's eyes.

"Did we take the wrong trail? We should have caught up to them by now."

"I don't know. The sun is almost gone. We have to find somewhere to spend the night."

"Shouldn't we just keep going?" Frank peered into the gloom of the dark path ahead.

"The trees are too thick. No moonlight. We wouldn't see a thing. Who knows where we'd end up?"

"There'll be no fire, you realize?"

"You're right. Hopefully the night will be as fine as this day."

"Pity we don't have any more of that dried meat. I'm getting hungry."

"Or the fish. Seems forever since we finished that." John cast his eyes around.

"Did you hear something?" Frank asked.

"No. I'm looking for fruit trees or berries or something."

"Good idea. Maybe we can find something before it's too dark."

A quick search turned up only a few dried up berries and some windfall apples. Sad fare but they made the best of it and then cut some cedar boughs to sleep on. There would be no fire, so the rapidly cooling air was a concern.

"Care to put your back up to mine, John?"

"What?" John jerked his head around to where Frank was laying out his blanket.

"The only way to keep warm. We can't chance the tent or a fire."

"You're right." He put his blanket next to Frank's.

THIS NIGHT JOHN'S THOUGHTS were of fires and heat and warm beds, of being snuggled in close to Lucy with the patchwork quilt tucked around them. Many times he woke and pulled his blanket tighter, pushing instinctively against Frank and feeling some respite from the cold there.

He felt rather than heard Frank doing the same thing so that the soft thumping in the ground did not startle him. He thought he was dreaming when he heard the neighing of horses, but Frank stiffened against him.

"John." The merest whisper of his name.

"I'm awake. What's that noise?" They were sitting up now, flicking at the light frost coating their blankets.

"Someone's on the trail. With horses." Frank stuffed his blanket into the pack and John did the same. Shouldering their loads they crept toward the trail, careful not to move too quickly. Silently they shadowed the trees.

The horses were galloping and he could feel the thump of the hooves under his feet. He looked at Frank and held his forefinger to his lips. Horses. Moving so slowly that his motion was like the swaying of the tree, John sneaked a look.

Indians. Were they friendly or not? He signaled to Frank. Slowly and silently they prepared their muskets. Maybe they could get a couple of horses, but they had nothing to barter and no idea which side these Indians were on. Holding his musket upright beside him John peeked again.

"Whee-aa-waa-waa-waa-waa! Whee-aa-waa-waa-waa-waa!" The nearest Indian yanked back on his horse and stopped, forcing the whole line to hold up and look toward the woods. John and Frank jerked back behind their trees but too late. The Indians had seen them.

Frank looked at John as the horses galloped closer. "What now?"

"Too many to fight. Maybe they're friendly." John stepped out and pointed his musket. Facing him were six staring Indians mounted on dark horses and holding weapons—knives, toma-hawks, and at least one gun—at the ready. John and Frank met stony looks from them all, but the eyes of the one in the centre held them transfixed. Hostile, mean, killing eyes.

"Good day." Frank stepped forward. Immediately the braves pushed their horses closer. The weapons went higher. The eyes narrowed. Frank stepped back.

"Can you speak English?" John's voice was calm, belying his racing heart.

Immediately the braves circled the pair and dropped to the ground, then edged closer. Their leader motioned to John's gun.

"Fine. I'll put it down."

"Shouldn't we fight for it?" Frank still held his musket.

"Hopefully they're friendly. Put your gun down, Frank."

The Indians took their weapons and pushed the pair through the brush to the path. There they tied them onto a horse, one behind the other, giving the reins to a brave who led them behind his horse. The whole group galloped up the trail.

John had plenty of time to wonder where they were going and, most of all, who they were going with. As the sun gradually cleared the trees, the horses galloped on and on, sometimes slowing to a trot or walk where the path narrowed but then speeding up again.

Toward midday they reached a bend in the river and the Indians took the path to the north east. By this time John and Frank were barely holding on, so hungry and thirsty were they. Their worries about their captors receded with the growing pangs from their bodies.

Frank spoke softly to John. "We've turned. We're going further and further away from Butler."

"I know, but the colonel's son and his Rangers are somewhere in this direction, I think."

"Like finding a needle in a haystack. Who are these Indians?"

"I've been wondering if they are part of the Iroquois Confederacy. They haven't tried to hurt us so maybe we're on the same side."

"Huh," Frank grunted, "Let's hope when we stop they don't use us as dinner."

By the water's edge, the horses slowed. In a smooth leap the brave ahead swung his leg over and jumped to the ground. He turned toward them still holding the lead in his left hand. With his right he easily loosed their binding rope and motioned John and Frank off their horse.

Frank slid off the back of the animal; then John swung down. The ground felt good but his body was stiff. He needed a good stretch and a few moments in the bushes.

John studied the brave whose back he had been watching all morning. High cheekbones gave his face a rugged look and his large nose was oddly crooked. His leggings were slit in the sides and tied at the knee and ankle with strips of leather. A coat of tanned deerskin covered the man's upper body. He wore intricate beading on his chest and a thong around his neck with just one bear claw. He must be young, thought John.

Someone pushed from behind.

"Food," another Indian barked. He tugged both John and Frank along with him. In front were two braves now and two more behind. They had no chance to escape.

In a small clearing they stood and ate dried meat and something that tasted like hardened bread. At this point the captives were so hungry they would have eaten bugs under stones. John motioned to his guard that he wanted to drink. A quick nod of the head toward the water and he and Frank were pulling out their water pouches and heading for the river.

"At least they're feeding us." Frank gulped his water and then refilled the pouch.

"Signs are good, I think. Wonder why they don't speak English. Most Indians have a few words."

"Maybe they speak more than they let on." Frank glanced back to the group. "We could try to escape."

"I think not. There are too many. Besides they have our packs. We'd have a tough time in the woods with nothing."

"Come!" The shout was meant for them. Sighing, the two friends turned back. They started to shoulder their packs but the Indians stopped them, jerking the packs away.

"We need those," Frank shouted. But he was pushed to his horse where he mounted behind John. "Now we really can't escape."

"Yes. We're captives. Those packs have our muskets." He winced as Frank grabbed his middle and the horse lurched. They were on their way again.

They had many eyes on them over the next few days as the band gradually made its way east along the Susquehanna River. Both excitement and despair plagued John and Frank as they moved closer and closer to their own homes. They had ample time to talk and the Indians didn't seem to mind, but as the hours droned on they had less and less to say.

Thoughts of Lucy and the farm occupied John. It was nearing the middle of October. Was she able to get the crops harvested? He pictured her working in the fields, using the huge scythe to cut the grain, picking the dried corn, and then cutting down the stalks to chop for the winter feed. It was all just too much work for one person, let alone one as small as Lucy.

Where were the Indians taking them? Could he get away and see her? He should never have left. Uh! A deep pain seemed to rise from his innards.

"You all right?" Frank asked.

"Just thinking about Lucy."

"What about her?"

"Nothing." John closed his mouth and white-knuckled the saddle horn.

THAT NIGHT THEY CAMPED as they had on previous nights, on the ground and near the fire, but not near enough. Their packs reappeared, minus the muskets and knives, but John and Frank were glad of their blankets and water pouches. Tomorrow they would keep the water with them in case the packs were taken again.

Daybreak came with grey streaks across an angry sky. The men shook the frost off their blankets, preparing to ride again. A little food was passed out before the band moved on down the trail. They had not gone far when the brave ahead raised his hand, and stopped like those ahead of him. Silence.

"What's this?" Frank hardly had the words from his mouth when a lonely shot shattered the stillness. The horses skittered, more shots came, the Indians whooped and John and Frank clung to their charging horse.

"We have no weapons!" John called to the Indian leading their horse. "Give us our guns!" But the Indian jerked ahead, pulling them with him.

Suddenly, they stopped. Horses bucked back down the line in a horrifying cascade as shots and screams—horses' and men's—rent the air. As their horse joined the fray, screaming, rearing, and landing, then rearing again, he felt Frank slip off, and held tightly to the mane, but immediately he, too, was in the air, then pounded into the earth as the hooves of the frenzied horse kicked the ground around him. He thought of Frank, and then he thought no more.

Chapter Eleven

August, 1778

AS PRE-DAWN SHADOWY fingers of light edged through the slits between the curtains, Lucy willed her eyes to show her the whole room. Still and silent, she strained to hear what had wakened her. Was it only a dream? No, she was sure she had heard something in the room. Her eyes were adjusting now.

Where was the gun? Not on the bed. Slowly she moved her hands for the gun beside her. No gun. The chair in the corner. She had left the gun there. She tried to see it. Instead, a human form became visible. She gasped.

A man was slouched in the chair. She couldn't see who, but it was definitely a man. Was he asleep? Maybe she could creep out of the cabin without waking him. She slipped her legs to the side of the bed.

Squeak. Squeak. Rigid, she stood on the floor hoping he hadn't heard. Silence. She edged along the wall to the curtain door, feeling her way in the dim light.

"Where do you think yer going?" The man's voice was rough and mean. She recognized it. She swept the curtain aside and ran for the door but the bar was still across. From behind he grabbed her waist.

"Let me go. Let me go." She fought against the rough hands with all her strength but he was too strong.

"Yer just a terrible wild thing, ain't ya?"

Hairy, hard hands held her arms locked. She couldn't move. "Let me go, you pig. My husband is going to thrash you when he comes back. In fact, he'll probably kill you when I tell him how you broke in here." By now she could see the hole where the window should have been and feel the cold breeze blowing in.

"Now you told me that husband story before, but there's no husband, is there? You was sleepin' all by yerself in that bed. There's no husband so don't tell me there is." He pushed her toward the table and forced her to sit, then took the chair opposite.

Daylight streaming through the open window lit Daeger's face. His cold eyes and sneering face made her gag. Lucy tried to look fierce and strong but she was terrified. And freezing. Her long-sleeved, full-length nightdress was not enough for fall's chills. She sat with her bare feet on the rungs of the chair, her hands holding her sides in an effort to get warm.

"I'm freezing. I need to light the fire." She stood and looked at Daeger, who nodded. She moved to the door hook for her coat, then back to the woodbox by the stove, all the while feeling his leering eyes on her. Grabbing the poker she opened the stove door and teased the faltering fire until a lonely flame started up. Kindling first, a couple of small logs, and a larger one crossways over the top.

While she worked, her brain was racing. What did Daeger want? If he was going to hurt her he didn't have to wait till she woke up. Still, she didn't trust him. Oh. Mr. Maycock was in the barn. Did Daeger know that? Or had he killed him? She closed the stove door and moved to put her shoes on, before turning to face Daeger.

"What do you want here?"

"I want your farm. Your land." He narrowed his eyes as he watched her.

"You what?" She dropped to the chair. "This is our land. You can't have it. I have the papers to prove it's ours." She was shouting now. Her fist banged the table.

"Doesn't matter. I'll be taking it all. You have two choices. Pack up yer personal things and get out today, or," his head tilted to one side as he studied her, "stay with me. Farm it with me. I could use the, ah, help."

Lucy felt her face go red. "I'd never stay with you." She jumped from the table and ran for the window, screaming. "Help. Help. Somebody, help!" She tried to hoist herself up to the open window but Daeger was too fast. This time he grabbed her around the waist and hurled her toward the bedroom door.

"Pack up yer things, you witch."

She fell against the bedroom doorway, pulling the curtain down. She staggered, gasping, into the bedroom. Her left hand went to the baby inside her and she moaned. Then she saw the chair. Her rifle was still there. She glanced back at Daeger as she leaned down to grasp the cold comfort of the metal. Her fingers found the trigger. She spun around toward Daeger in the kitchen. His hooded eyes widened as she jerked the rifle to her shoulder and took aim. Boom! Daeger dropped from her sight.

She lowered the gun, confused, as she had not yet fired. In the kitchen Daeger's hand was at his head. Blood poured through his fingers. He staggered toward the window, faltered and fell. Immediately a figure came through the opening.

"Mrs. Garner. Mrs. Garner. Are you all right?" He dropped his gun on the table as he hurried toward her.

"Oh, Mr. Maycock. Thank God. Yes, I'm fine. I was afraid he'd killed you."

Mr. Maycock turned to Daeger. The man lay sprawled, stomach down, across an upset chair, motionless. Blood dripped onto the floor beneath his head.

"I think he's dead."

"He better hope he is," muttered Mr. Maycock. He edged toward the body, careful lest there might still be danger, and prodded with his gun. The head hung still and lifeless as brown-red blood pooled on the floor. Daeger was dead.

"I'll get him out of here. If you're sure you're all right, ma'am?" Mr. Maycock studied her and she felt his eyes take in the night dress and the heavy coat. She touched her flaming cheek, sure he could see a bruise.

"I'm fine, Mr. Maycock."

"All right, then. I'll get this skunk out of here." He tugged the body to the door, lifted the board from its place, and dragged Daeger out of the cabin. Presently he returned, his hands dripping with water from the pump. Lucy gave him a cloth and he stood by the table watching her as he dried his hands.

"I heard you shouting, ma'am. Looked out and saw a strange horse. Went back for my rifle. Sorry it took me so long." Mr. Maycock touched Lucy's arm. "Are you sure you're not hurt?"

"No, I'm just…a little shaken." Lucy sat in the chair and then quickly stood and moved to the other side of the table, away from the patch of blood on the floor.

"We'll get that cleaned up in just a bit, ma'am. Don't you worry about it. Can I make the coffee?" Mr. Maycock moved to the stove and grabbed the coffee pot.

"Yes. That would be good. Thank you."

The warm sun coming in the window streaked across to Lucy and seemed to wrap its gentle fingers around her shoulders. Her breathing slowed as she sat holding her arms crossed over her belly. Gradually she relaxed. She stroked the baby periodically but her thoughts drifted as she tried to control herself. "I shudder to think what would have happened…" Lucy's voice trailed off.

"Now, don't you even think about it. Daeger is dead. He won't be bothering anyone anymore."

"He said he was taking our land. How could he do that? We have the papers to show it's ours."

"Haven't you heard? No, I guess way out here you wouldn't." Mr. Maycock sipped his coffee. "There are a lot of folks across the colonies who need to find land. Because what's here has all been taken and they don't want to go into Indian territory or further west. They look for people whose farms are easy to take and then go in and steal them. The owners are lucky to get away with their lives. Sounds like this Daeger was one of those thieves."

"Does that mean there might be more?" Lucy stared at Mr. Maycock. "More people coming here to steal our land?"

"Now, don't worry yourself, ma'am. I'm sure he's the only one way out here." He frowned. "Your husband will be back soon. Soon enough to help you with, ah," he lowered his eyes and his voice, "that baby." Mr. Maycock looked away. "Pardon me, ma'am."

"No pardon is necessary, Mr. Maycock. John doesn't even know about the baby. I have a letter to send with you telling him. Would you take it, please?"

"I am just that pleased to take it, ma'am. Though I think I'll stay another night here and help you get things looked after, if that would suit?" He glanced at the blood on the floor.

"I am most appreciative, Mr. Maycock. Let me get us some food now." She started the meal while Mr. Maycock went outside.

The day passed quickly with all the work to do. She fed the animals and gathered the eggs. Mr. Maycock fixed the window in the cabin. He dragged Daeger's body over to the horse and hoisted it up and over the saddle.

Not wanting any reminder of what had happened, Lucy had asked Mr. Maycock to bury Daeger in the woods, although even that was no guarantee against nightmares. She tackled the blood spot on the cabin floor while he was gone. On her hands and knees she scrubbed and scrubbed at the stain. She pushed and pounded and poured her anger into the cleaning. Why did the man have to come here? She was doing well enough. She got the grain in all by herself, and the corn, too. The barn was stocked with enough food for the animals for the winter. And she did it all. Herself.

Her thoughts flashed to John. Where was he through all this? Why wasn't he here? She sat back on her heels and wiped at a tear.

A knock at the door startled her. "Come in, Mr. Maycock." She wrung out her cloth and wiped the spot one more time, sopping up as much water as she could.

"That looks good, ma'am."

"I hope it's gone. I think I can still see it and I don't want to be looking at that all winter." Lucy stomped to the door, threw it open and tossed the dirty water into the yard.

At the well she pumped water to slosh out the pail, and then banged it upside down on the porch to dry. Looking up she saw Mr. Maycock in the doorway. "I guess you think I have a temper."

"I think you are doing what needs to be done. You're a strong woman. You'll be just fine now."

She smiled.

"What does a man have to do to get fed around here?" Mr. Maycock turned and went into the cabin. Lucy followed.

That night Mr. Maycock shared the heat of the fire after dinner. Lucy enjoyed his company, even though they said very little. She rocked slowly back and forth, her knitting needles still and silent in her lap, her eyes glazed over with the whirl of thoughts, possibilities, and, yes, dangers to come, until the one candle burned low.

Mr. Maycock stood up. "Time I headed for the barn, ma'am." He looked right into her eyes. "Now, don't worry yourself, ma'am. The man's dead. He won't bother you again."

"You're right, Mr. Maycock. And you've nailed the window from both inside and outside so no one can just pull the nails and get in. Thank you for that." Lucy stood. "Time I got some sleep, too."

Mr. Maycock opened the door and turned to Lucy. "Mind you lock that door, ma'am."

"Don't worry. You'll hear the bolt as soon as the door closes."

Chapter Twelve

THE ROOSTER'S RAUCOUS CROWING woke Lucy from a sleep so fitful and disturbed she was glad to see the dawn. In her dreams she had screamed at John for leaving her here alone but when she woke he was still gone and she was still alone. She might as well get up. Facing the day's tasks was easier than giving license to her nightmares. She dressed, and poked the fire alive, feeding it with fresh wood.

Mr. Maycock swung the axe in the yard chopping more wood for her, even though he had split a huge pile yesterday. Lifting the curtain, she watched him set a large round on the stump. Then with both hands he swung the axe over his head and down onto the wood. He picked up one of the broken pieces, placed it and swung again. Smaller pieces sprayed the area around the chopping block. He was making kindling. Such a kind man. This would last her at least a month.

Her thoughts flew as she set out their breakfast. Having someone to care for felt good. Soon, she'd have the baby to care for. How could she do everything then? She'd find a way. Winter was coming, with less work outside. She would have to get the place in good shape soon, before it became too hard for her. And maybe John would come home. She fingered the letter for him in her pocket and pictured him reading about the baby coming. Surely Mr. Maycock would soon cross paths with him.

THE LATE MORNING SUN slanted onto the porch where she sat resting in the rocker she had dragged out of the house. She had seen Mr. Maycock off, worked for a while and was now having a sit down. This might be one of the last beautiful days before the cold. She wanted to enjoy it. She had to take more breaks now, but today that suited her. Sipping at the coffee in her cup she leaned back in the rocker.

"Oh! You almost spilled my coffee." Her left hand stroked and soothed the tiny shifts and kicks of the baby. She wondered for the hundredth time if it was a boy or a girl. John would love a boy, she thought, but she would love either one. As long as the baby was healthy. She closed her eyes and breathed a silent prayer. She smiled to herself and slowly drifted into sleep.

A frenzied bawling startled her and she struggled from the chair. She took a few seconds to fix on the sound and then hurried to the barnyard. Moo-oo-oot. Moo-oo-op. Molly had never sounded like this before. Rounding the corner of the barn she saw why. Molly was down.

"What's the matter, girl?" She scanned the area but saw nothing. "Oh, my God. You're hurt." Molly's rear leg was split right open with blood oozing from the break and the lower part just lying twisted in the grass. "You've broken your leg, girl. How did you do that?" She tried to touch the leg but Molly jerked it back, flopping it on the ground. She bawled a loud baleful sound. Lucy stroked her forehead. "I don't know what to do, girl. I can't fix this." Molly's familiar brown eyes were wild with pain. Or fright, maybe.

She sat on the grass and stroked the cow's neck, face, ears, all the while mouthing soothing sounds. But she knew what she had to do. Finally, she lurched to her feet. With a look back at Molly, she turned toward the cabin. She had no choice. She grabbed her rifle, checked that it was loaded, sighted along the barrel and marched back to the barnyard, all the while trying to shut out

Molly's terrible sounds. She must shoot Molly in the head. Staring into the cow's eyes, she knelt and laid the rifle on the ground.

"I have to do this, old girl. I am so sorry," she sobbed. Leaning forward she held Molly's head with both hands and kissed the white streak down her face. "You've been a good friend."

She struggled to her feet. With an angry swipe at her tears she grabbed the rifle and marched a few feet off, then turned. Molly lay silent, as though she knew what was coming. Lucy raised the rifle, aimed for the centre of Molly's forehead, between the eyes and the ears, and pulled the trigger. The gun knocked her back but she regained her footing and looked.

Molly lay in the grass with her head tilted awkwardly. Blood oozed out of the small hole in her forehead. The one eye that Lucy could see was wide open but lifeless. She dropped the gun, stumbled over and knelt to close the eyelid. That look was just too horrid. Then the sobs came.

Long, despairing cries howled forth from Lucy as she lay across Molly's lifeless form. So much had happened since John had left. The Indian scare. The days of talking to no one but Molly. Daeger's threats. Him lying dead on her floor—the stain was still there, soaked into the wood. She couldn't bear it.

She should stop. Get up and carry on. She tried to rise, but a new wave of desolation engulfed her and she wept once more. Over and over this happened until, finally, she did sit up and wipe her nose on her apron. She had no more tears but stray sobs escaped from time to time as she walked to the cabin. Now she had to cut up Molly. And use the meat for the winter.

Having never butchered an animal before, Lucy was at a loss. She had seen John and Frank use the oxen to pull the body of their dead pig up so the blood would drain out. She looked across the yard to the old elm tree at the edge of the forest. Could she get Molly over there with the oxen?

She yoked the pair together and drove them over to the carcass where she tied a rope around the legs, wrenching it underneath as well as she could. It was not enough. Molly was dead weight and she shouldn't lift too much. She had to dig a trench under Molly. She grabbed the shovel and made a channel for the rope to go underneath the rear quarters, then tied several loops around Molly's body. She made it good and tight. Hooking up to the oxen was easy and she soon had them lumbering across to the tree pulling their load behind.

Once there she untied the rope from the oxen, threw it over the stoutest branch she could reach, and then tied it up for the oxen to pull again. Slowly the cow's body rose until it hung from the tree. Lucy knew the next part would be gruesome but she didn't allow herself to think. She tied off the oxen so they wouldn't move and ran to the cabin for her biggest knife.

Molly's head hung just above the ground. Quickly she closed the other eyelid. The knife in both hands, she slit the throat from side to side. Blood came pouring out, spraying her dress with the sticky dark streaks. She fell back on the ground. *I should have had a pail to catch the blood. Too late now.*

She left the cow to hang and went back to change and soak her dress. She grabbed some stew and gobbled it down before heading out, wearing John's old shirt and trousers tied over her stomach with a long cord.

The carcass hung from the limb. All trace of Molly was gone, it seemed, and she was just dealing with meat. That made the job easier. She eased the oxen back to lower the carcass slowly to the ground. She would have liked to hang it longer but the afternoon was passing and cutting up the animal would take hours. She just didn't have time. And she didn't know how to get the skin off properly.

She took the knife and slit along the belly, around the legs from one end to the other and eased the hide back cutting where necessary to free it from the body. She couldn't roll the cow over to fully skin it, so she went ahead and made a huge cut down the length of the animal and took out the guts. It was gruesome work, and more than once she staggered back, away from the stench. Knowing she now had meat for the winter kept her going, though, as she carried the guts in a bucket into the woods. She didn't have time to dig them in. The wild animals could have them.

THE SUN WAS SINKING on the horizon and Lucy had built a fire to see by as she finished off the work. Even in the cold night air she was sweating as she cut and lugged the meat to the barn. She hung it in small pieces from the rafters, safe from the animals until she could salt it down and store it. That would be tomorrow's job. She got the rest of the hide off and hung it in the barn as well. She had no time to remove the hair and make leather. This would be a skin with hair on it. They would use it in the cabin over the cold winters once John came back. If he ever did.

Finally Lucy put the oxen back in the barn, fed them and closed up the doors for the night. She had not been able to use the whole carcass—she was just too tired—and she left the rest on the ground till morning. She doused the fire, picked up the gun, and staggered to the cabin where she barred the door, took a long drink of water from the pail, fixed the fire, and collapsed, fully clothed, on the bed.

There were no dreams that night. Lucy slept until long after the rooster had crowed. The sun streamed through the window and still she lay motionless on the patchwork quilt. She had never even pulled it over her. The room was cold. The cabin was silent. There was no cow lowing in the barn.

A streak of morning sun sneaked through the slit between the curtains and tickled the tip of Lucy's nose. She stirred. Her hand went to the baby. "Oh, you're ready to get up, are you?" Slowly she swung her legs to the floor, rubbing her stiff muscles. "Let's get the fire going."

She coaxed the fire to a crackling flame. "I could eat a horse." She stopped and sagged onto a chair by the table. There would be no milk today. And no Molly to keep her company. Her eyes found the milk pail clean and ready to use, sitting by the door. Hands on her belly she rose and heated the stew one more time.

WHEN LUCY OPENED THE CABIN DOOR, her eyes went first to the carcass. She walked to the spot to see if the wolves had come. She had saved all she could the night before and was glad. Bones picked clean littered the area. The head was completely gone, dragged off into the woods. She would have to bury the remains after her chores. She sighed and started for the barn.

The chickens cackled their welcome as on every other day but Lucy missed Molly's soft brown eyes and low croon. She fed the oxen their hay and led them into the yard for exercise. Back to the barn she went to start the long task ahead of her—salting and drying the meat.

THE NIGHT CAME EARLY ONCE AGAIN. She was exhausted. As well as her regular chores, she had washed and hung her dress, salted pounds and pounds of meat, roasted a huge chunk in their fire pit behind the cabin, collected the last onions from the garden and hung them to dry in the barn. Now all was safely stored away and she glad.

Moving the table to get at the cold cellar under the floor had given Lucy an idea. When she swung the trap door shut again, she moved the table to cover the whitened boards where the blood stain had been. She would rather look at the door in the floor than be reminded of Daeger.

At the table she devoured the roasted meat, accompanied by fall's lovely vegetables. Such a treat. And the fresh meat tasted so wonderful she could almost forget she was eating Molly. *You kept me company all summer long, Molly, and now you're going to feed me for the winter.*

She finished her meal, washed and dried the dishes, and took the candle to the bedroom. In no time she stripped off her dress and lay under the quilt. After a couple of minutes she jumped up again. She had forgotten the rifle.

She felt her way to the other room, grabbed the rifle and moved to the window for light. Yes, it was loaded, ready. Back in bed, rifle beside her, she collapsed under the patchwork quilt.

....

THE NEXT DAY, she took a long walk in the forest. Chores finished, she banked the fire in the cabin and started down the trail. Another sunny day. I don't think I'll go as far as the falls this time. Just a short walk for a couple of hours will do. The baby kicked.

"So you want to go walking, too, do you?" Lucy smiled and caressed her belly. Quietly she ambled down the path thinking of the last trip she and John had made along this trail. She had walked quickly then, unencumbered, but today she carried the rifle, the pack with some food, a knife, and a skin with water. She never went into the woods without her pack. But more than all that she was carrying the best thing of all. Her baby. She smiled as she felt the bulge of her belly. Their baby.

"I wonder when your father will get the news."

She felt good today, if a little tired, and stopped often along the trail to sit and ponder. On one such stop she saw a stag. Very still she studied his full set of antlers, his honey brown colour with that blaze of white on his tail. His eyes held hers. She was close enough to see their dark brightness and their wary wisdom.

"I won't hurt you today." She whispered so as not to startle him.

Eventually the stag seemed to lose interest and, turning his head, ambled out of sight. She basked a moment longer in the memory of their time together. She watched the place where he had been and felt a wave of happiness wash over her. Smiling, she breathed deeply of the forest smells. Her legs were stiff as she stood and turned back for home. A little walking would warm her hands and get the blood flowing again.

"Ready to go, little one?" She laughed. "I see that you are."

As always when approaching the cabin Lucy was wary, just like the deer had been, but the chickens were pecking noisily in the yard and the oxen stood silently munching their hay. All was as she had left it.

DAYS WENT BY and Lucy's life was good. She had plenty to eat, the work had slowed down and her baby gradually grew. All was quiet with no one coming to visit. She would have liked company but also enjoyed the solitude with her baby. She talked to the child all the time now, telling the stories of her own childhood and singing the songs she knew from long ago.

She also talked to John, telling him of the baby's progress and asking him what he would like for names. Nathan was her favorite for a boy or maybe John after his father. For a girl she liked Grace or maybe Caroline after her own mother. Both were good names. Maybe she would give her both of them.

She tried talking to the baby and calling it different names to see which it might answer to but the results were confusing. This was a good game to play but not really a good way to pick a name. She wished she knew John's wishes in the matter. She willed him to come home in time for the birth. Then the problem would be solved. And she was so lonely for him.

Meanwhile the snows came and gradually piled around the yard. She kept the animals in the barn all the time now. She had killed four of the hens so as not to have to feed them for the winter, and had made chicken and dumplings, a wonderful change in her diet. The rooster and the other eight birds she kept in the barn now to protect them from the cold and any marauding animals. She might kill a couple more hens later but for now she fed them dried corn from this year's harvest.

Her biggest problem was mucking out the oxen, a heavy job at the best of times but now her energy waned after just a few shovelfuls. Every other day she would dress in John's old clothes and trudge to the barn to clean out the stalls, pitching the forkfuls out of the open window onto the ground outside. If she kept up to it now, when the baby came she could afford to have a break for a couple of weeks.

Lucy thought a lot about the baby coming and how she could possibly manage alone. With all her prayers she wished for John to return so she wouldn't be by herself when her time came.

She thought about the births she had seen in the past, only three, and for most of the time she had been boiling water in the kitchen. She did, however, remember what the midwife had said about breathing properly and she knew she would have to cut the cord. How hard could it be?

She had killed a cow, hung it, and butchered it. She had raised a crop of corn, some wheat, and some hay, and harvested them all by herself. She had fended off a thief trying to take her land. Well, not alone, but she had been strong. As she sat at the table by the light of one candle, listening to the logs crackle and burn in the stove, her hands crept to her face. She held her head and whispered, "Oh, God."

Chapter Thirteen

November, 1778

THAT SMELL. And a pain in his middle. Something tight. His head was flopping down, full of rushing blood. John cracked open his eyes and tasted dirt on his crusted lips. The horse smell overpowered the stench of his own body. He gagged. He was hanging over the horse as they moved along the trail.

"Ho-o-o-o." He tried to shout but the sounds were small. Who had tied him over the horse? He tried to turn his head to see ahead. The pain stopped him.

In a moment he tried looking again, this time without a sound. The path took a slight turn to the right; John could see the horse ahead. The rider was an Indian brave with all his hair shaved off except for a strip down the middle of his head. A Mohawk warrior. He shuddered and felt again the pain in his head.

The Mohawks were rumored to have cannibalistic tendencies. He hoped the rumours were false. The man ahead was not the man who had led them for days. Where had he gone? Slowly he turned to look behind. There was no rider. Wait.

Every muscle wrenched as he stretched his neck and body farther out. Someone was slung over that horse as well. Frank's dirty blonde hair hung down covering his face. Was he dead? Or just out cold as John had been? He watched as best he could but Frank's head only flopped with every step of the horse. John tried to think but his head hurt and he felt his eyes sinking into the black again.

Rough hands pulled him. He struggled but his own hands were useless blocks. Why wouldn't his fingers move? He hit the ground with a soft thud and forced open his eyes. An Indian held something hard to his lips.

John flinched and twisted his head, then felt liquid on his chin. He licked his lips. Water. He opened his mouth for more.

"Who are you?" he sputtered.

The Indian gave him more water.

"Where am I?"

The Indian shook his head and muttered something unintelligible.

"Do you speak English?"

"English bad." The words were clipped and almost unrecognizable.

John tried to sit up. The Indian reached to support his back. "I guess you're friendly. English?" John pointed around at the camp hoping there was someone there he could talk to, but the man simply pursed his lips and muttered, then pulled the water skin away and stood. He moved a little way off and knelt again.

He gently lifted the head of another and offered water. Frank. But his head lolled to one side and his eyes were shut. Blood caked his hair and face. He looked like a scary being from Hell.

John crawled over. He held out his hand and the man handed him the leather flask. John poured a little into his hands and then rubbed Frank's face, washing away the bits of blood and dirt. Over and over he rubbed his bare hand over Frank's warm skin until he felt his friend stir.

"Frank. Wake up."

"My head." He reached up to touch his head but John stopped him.

"Not so fast, Frank. You've got a nasty gash there. Don't touch it."

"Did we get shot?"

"I don't think so. We fell off the horse and got caught under the hooves. First you, then me. When I woke up I was face down over another horse and we were bumping down the trail. You're lucky you don't remember that trip."

"You don't have blood on you."

"No, but I've got a goose egg the size of a milk pail over my ear." He barely touched his hand to the spot. "These are the Mohawks, Frank, and they don't seem that anxious to kill us. But no one seems to talk. Either they can't speak English or they don't want to."

Frank's eyes shifted away as another Indian came toward them with pieces of dried meat. Frank lifted the meat to his mouth and chewed. "This stuff never gets any tastier." He reached for the water.

Soon the whole band was back on horses. John and Frank each sat on their own, although the horses were still tethered together. With every step of his horse John winced at the pain in his side. He must have got a good kick there, too. When they stopped he would have a look.

He turned to check on Frank. His friend could sit the horse but he was bobbing noticeably and a fresh stream of blood trickled down his forehead. Frank raised his hand weakly; a thin smile creased his face.

"He has a lot of guts. I hope he's going to make it," John muttered. He smiled and nodded to Frank.

By the time the daylight streaks were disappearing in the trees, John was almost unconscious again. He held his reins with curled hands that seemed to be fixed forever into a curved, pointy-knuckled grip. He was long past thinking. From a place far down inside him came the instinct for survival. *Hang on. Hang on. Hang on.* Eyes were slits, throat was parched and pain was all.

He jerked in his saddle. His eyes opened slowly. Stopped. Horse ahead. He tried to shake himself alert but his head barely moved. He was falling off the horse. Hands caught him. Strong hands, under his arms. He was on the ground…

He dreamed he was drinking water, long cool gulps of it. Then his head was high as he rode with Colonel Butler into battle along-side Frank. Maudie snorted and jerked at the bit but he held her fast.

Shouts and screams assailed them as they rode right at the trees and bushes which held the enemy, the murderer. Horse and rider flew as one into the rain of gunfire. John held his musket like a lance. A man stood to take aim but before he could shoot, John bayoneted him. He jerked out the blade. The militia man's blue-green eyes stared unseeing. No, wait.

The eyes were coming right out of their sockets, following John, chasing him. He shouldered the gun to shoot but it wasn't primed. His heels dug into Maudie and she reared up, then landed in a wrenching thud and ran. A horse came on his left and he turned. Frank rode for his life but his arms were gone and his head streamed blood.

"Oooh," he groaned. Suddenly Maudie stopped dead. He pitched over her head, kicking wildly through the air. He tried to steady himself with his wings but he felt a shot from the ground. It was hot in his belly. Cold on his face. He twitched but the cold followed him. *When would he hit the ground?*

Water trickled from his face slowly down his neck. *Oh, that's good.* Something seemed to wipe the care and hurt right out of him. His eyes snapped open and he wrenched himself up. "Where am I?"

A dark-haired Indian woman's eyes met his. "Humh." Her low grunt was barely audible. She wiped his brow again with the cool cloth, and then his hands. The water felt good. She reached for a bowl, dipped into it, and brought the spoon to his lips.

"Onenhsto." She pointed to the soup.

His eyes never leaving her face, he slowly parted his lips and a wonderful taste of corn took his attention. He opened his mouth for more.

Black hair framed the woman's oval face. Her nose was flattish above wide ruddy lips. Her brows were black as well, but not as dark as her eyes, which she kept trained on the spoon, only glancing up periodically. He had never seen such eyes. Black like shining coal they were, and deep. What was behind them?

The woman held a cup to his lips. "Hnekirha'." She urged him to sip. He opened his mouth and drank fully.

"Where am I?" John lay back on the bed and gestured around.

"Kahnyen'kehàka kanonhsehs." She swept her left arm back, around and up. She pointed at herself, held up one finger, and then many more, opening and closing her hands many times as though she were counting. He did not understand her meaning.

He looked beyond her. They were in a very long, roofed structure, made of wooden poles stuck into the ground and then covered with large pieces of bark. There were lots of people cooking and eating. This was a whole village.

Close to him another woman was bent over a fire, stirring a pot. He, himself, lay on a bed covered with furs about a foot or so off the ground. The wall beside him was hung with furs as well and he saw a platform a few feet up which made a ceiling for the sleeping bench. He seemed to be the only one still lying down.

John sat up and moved his legs off the bench, ignoring the throbbing of his head. He turned to the woman. "Where is my friend?"

The woman shook her head.

"What does that mean? Where is he?"

Shaking her head again, she glanced down.

He felt the old fear coming back. "What have you done with him?" He pushed off the bench and shouldered her aside. "Frank. Frank. Where are you?"

Faces all up and down the longhouse turned to the noise. A man close by rose from his seat and glared at John. He held a knife at his side, ready.

John turned back to the woman. "I need to find my friend. Is he here? Or outside? I need to know."

Finally she seemed to understand and led the way past the silent, staring Indians to the door at the end of the longhouse.

After the gloom of the longhouse, John blinked at the bright, white camp. Snow had fallen in the night. His hands shielded his eyes.

There were many longhouses of the sort he had been in, and Indians moving to and fro among them. He hurried to keep up to the woman who led him through the village. They passed Indians building fires and scraping hides, but no one paid the slightest attention. He and the woman might as well not even be there.

Soon enough they approached another longhouse. The woman opened the door and stepped inside. He followed.

In the darkness, he saw nothing. He rubbed his eyes and gradually made out the fire in the middle of the longhouse. Standing about twenty feet from him, down the centre of the structure, the woman motioned to him.

"Come," she said.

He followed her down the central aisle past the fires and women cooking. A heavenly aroma rose around him. He was still hungry. His guide stopped and spoke to another woman and he looked past her.

There, on the sleeping platform, lay Frank, motionless. John forgot his stomach and stepped closer. In the dim light he saw a tattered bandage on Frank's head, a telltale dark patch seeping through the white strips. He held his fingers under Frank's nose and felt a soft flow of air. He was alive.

"Frank." Nothing. "Frank." John pushed at his shoulder. "Come on. Wake up." He looked at the woman. "How bad is he?"

She leaned over and touched the damp forehead softly pushing the hair from his eyes. "Maybe not wake. Maybe wake. I not know."

"I'll stay here with him." He took the cloth and bowl from the other woman's hands and sat on the edge of the sleeping platform beside Frank. Gently he wiped the cloth over Frank's face, talking softly all the while. He tried not to notice the still pallor of Frank's skin and the way it seemed to be stretched over the bones of his face. He longed for Frank's mouth to relax into that ready smile he knew so well.

He continued talking to Frank, wiping his face, and every so often nudging his shoulder but he slept on. John sat back. This longhouse was smaller than the one he had been in, maybe about half the length, but it was made the same way. Frank rested on a raised sleeping platform covered with furs just as his had been. He looked warm and comfortable. The smoke from the fires seemed to know enough to escape from small holes in the roof, making a snug and cozy place, even if they were walking on the bare ground underfoot.

"Where are we?"

He jerked back to Frank. "You're awake."

"Barely. My head." Slowly Frank touched the bandage. "Are we in Heaven or the other place?"

"I see you haven't lost your sense of humor."

Frank smiled, ever so slightly. "What's the stink?" He glanced toward the fire.

John laughed. "I'm afraid that's you. Your clothes are filthy with mud and blood. Never mind. Stink we can fix. We'll take these clothes and wash them." He motioned toward the woman who had brought him.

Chapter Fourteen

JOHN ESCAPED THE WOMEN'S MINISTRATIONS as quickly as he could. Still attracting little attention, he strolled through the village. At the far end of the clearing, on a ridge overlooking the scene, stood a cabin which reminded him of home. Walking toward it he saw several more, set high on the hill looking out over the valley below. His eyes fixed on the drawing of the bear just above the door of the first cabin. He walked on. All of the cabins had the same drawing.

He heard shouts and automatically ducked his head. He had walked into a game of hoops and javelins. The javelin lay in the snow a few feet away. "Beg pardon," he called to the boy running past him for the javelin. "I didn't mean to interrupt your game."

The boy stopped short and smiled. He picked up the javelin and held it out to John. The others circled around. John hefted the javelin into the air and pretended to throw. The Indian boys cheered and stepped closer, gesturing to him to go ahead.

He looked at the eager faces, their dark eyes shining as they urged him on. Three of them were short, about four feet, but the other stood almost as tall as John and had his hair removed except for a narrow band from his forehead to the nape of his neck. The boys were dressed alike in tan deerskin leggings and fur-lined moccasins and overshirts. Even though the air was cold, sweat streaked their faces.

"You've been playing hard."

The boys stared.

"Can you speak English?"

"Little." The tall one nodded.

"What is that bear over your door?" John pointed the javelin toward the nearest cabin.

"Clan bear." He pointed to himself. "I am bear clan." He stood a little taller.

"Do you live in these cabins?" John swept his arms toward the cabins.

Suddenly all of the boys were talking and gesturing, pointing out where they lived. The younger ones pulled on his arms to draw him to their homes. As he was led away, he looked back at the tall boy standing motionless, his eyes partially closed, his arms crossing his chest.

After the tour of the cabins John and his new friends marched about the camp, pointing and gesturing to communicate. The boys laughed as he pretended to pluck out his hair. He pointed toward the horses tethered together eating their hay and the boys led him closer.

In a large fenced area against the wooden stockade wall, John counted thirty-two horses of different colors and sizes. One of the boys slipped through the fence into the enclosure. Grabbing a hank of mane he hoisted himself bareback onto the horse, kicked his heels into the flanks and rode hollering around the pen.

For the first time in a long while, John laughed. His arms resting on the fence, he breathed deeply and relaxed. He smiled at the small rider's antics as he circled the area, scattering the horses with his whooping and hollering.

Suddenly John straightened. That horse over by the palisade wall. It looked like…no, it couldn't be. He whistled his low call. Up came the horse's head and she started toward him. It was Maudie. Over the fence he went to meet her.

"Maudie. Oh, Maudie, it's so good to see you." He stroked the white streak on her head, looking into her eyes. "Where've you been, girl?" He held her head, walked around her to check her hoofs, which needed trimming, her full belly, and her strong legs.

Circling back to her head, he became aware of the quiet. The Indian boy was no longer whooping it up on his horse. He had, in fact, jumped off and gone to stand with his friends. There was no sound of cheering. With somber faces, the boys stood stock still, peering at him. He dropped his hands and took a deep breath.

"Beautiful horse." He turned to point to her and realized she had followed right behind him. "I guess she likes me." He grinned. The sober young Indian rider said something to his friends. They nodded, still staring at John. The rider stepped toward John and took his arm, and pulled him toward the fence. "I guess you want me to climb over, do you?"

No one spoke on the walk back to the longhouse. One of the boys led the way while the other two walked behind, surrounding him. They were more like a prisoner being herded by his captors than the group of friends they had been before, and he thought again of the tales he had heard of the Mohawks. Was he about to become their dinner?

He smelled smoke in the air and glanced off to the left where a huge fire raged in a stone-circled pit. The thick pole rigged above it was large enough to cook a whole animal. John's stomach turned and he looked again at the boy in front. Their little procession drew attention this time. Furred women stopped in their tracks and turned to watch.

Although not a word had been spoken, the watchers seemed to know something had changed. Blanketed men glanced up from their circle, their pipes poised in midair. Little children, looking like balls of fur in their warm clothing, stopped playing in the fresh snow. They fell silent and stood still, blinking their staring eyes in the sun.

"Here!" The sound pounded into the silence.

John was led into the longhouse. He noticed a fish painted beside the door on this one, and then they were inside. Seeing was impossible in the gloom. They stood a moment; hands pushed him forward. Gradually he could see in the dim light. The long-house certainly earned its name, he thought, as they walked a good way past cooking fires, old men nodding off, and women tending children. One was suckling a baby.

Ears of corn tied in bunches hung from the poles overhead. There were baskets on high shelves along the walls, overflowing with squash and other food from the harvest. Furs lay on low sleeping platforms along the walls with sticks and short branches stored underneath. On one bench a child lay snug under some furs, only its contented face showing. On another John saw the bone-stretched skin of an old woman. Her staring eyes peered into his. He looked away.

The boy ahead of him stopped so quickly John almost ran into him. He stepped aside and John met the dark eyes of a chief staring at him. The eyes were set in a broad, determined face with a full nose, thick lips and a dark cleft in the chin. He wore a feathered head-dress, a mark of his rank, but his clothes were not Indian. Rather he wore a tan, collared shirt, and breeches of the white people.

"Who are you?" the chief barked.

"John Garner, sir. I have a farm in New York."

The Indian stared at him.

"What is your name?" John thought he knew.

Still the Indian was silent.

"Are you Joseph Brant?"

"I am Thayendanegea, chief of the Mohawks."

"I am honored, sir." John dipped his head respectfully. "Are you known as Joseph Brant?"

"How do you know the horse in the pen?"

"I beg your pardon?" The topic change had jolted John. He stood tall and swallowed, breathing in the fumes of the fire. "That is my horse. It was stolen from me a few weeks ago a long way from here." He stopped as the Indian stiffened and glared at him.

"Are you a fighter? A militia man?" The chief looked aside and his voice was soft.

John thought quickly. He didn't know what the right answer was but he had to take a chance. "Are you Joseph Brant?"

The Indian chuckled. "I am Thayendanegea to all the Mohawk people but, yes, I am also known as Joseph Brant, friend to the great King George in England." Suddenly his eyes bored right into John and he barked. "Who are you?"

John smiled. "I am John Garner, a cavalry man with Butler's Rangers. I, too, am a friend to the British."

"Sit."

John sat cross-legged by the fire. Its warmth cast a ruddy glow over his face as he stretched his hands to the heat. "Do you know where Butler's Rangers are now?

Brant did know and wasted no time sharing with John, who began to trust him.

"But how did you get my horse?" John finally asked.

Brant's eyes were patient. "We did not steal your horse. One of our hunting parties met a band of the Tuscarora, those that are fighting against the British. Our braves relieved them of the burden of their horses and brought them back here. You may have your animal back." He nodded at John.

"Thank you, sir. My friend, also with the Rangers, is here wounded. His horse was stolen, too. May I have it back as well?"

"Certainly, if it is here. I trust your friend will soon be well." Brant made to stand up and John hurried to do the same.

"Thank you, sir."

Back outside, the camp had changed again. The bright sun had sucked up the snow and the fresh air tingled with warmth. Indians smiled as he and his young guide threaded their way back to Frank's bedside.

"You look a little better." John peered at his friend.

"And you, too, my friend. What did you find out?"

"Joseph Brant is here. This is a Mohawk camp. They're friendly."

"Good. We do seem to know how to land on our feet, don't we?" Frank chuckled. "Well, you're better than I am."

"Glad to hear you joking. Must be on the mend." He looked at the bandage on Frank's head. "Has anyone checked that?"

"I think so. I woke up feeling someone's hands on my head. Then I went right back to sleep. That's what I'm best at, just now."

"Never mind. We'll soon be out of here and back with Butler's Rangers. Oh, I forgot to tell you. They have our horses."

"What? How?" Frank's eyes shone.

Quickly John sketched the story and then went on to what he had learned from Brant about Butler's whereabouts. Apparently the Rangers had made it back to Niagara and were in winter quarters on the west side of the river.

"When you are well, we'll join them."

FOR THE NEXT FEW DAYS he watched Frank mending under the watchful eyes of the Mohawk woman. His eyes lit up whenever John came near and a funny quip was out of his mouth as often as not. Soon he was sitting, then standing, and taking a few steps in the longhouse. Outside the wind blew cold and the sun had no warmth, but both men longed to rejoin Butler in his winter quarters at Niagara or go home.

"Are you ready?" John stood wrapped in his blanket before Frank's bed.

"You mean it? Today?" Frank's eyes glowed.

"Not to leave, just to go outside and face the weather. It's changed quite a lot since you've been in here."

"Of course I'm ready." Frank sat up slowly and began to put on his heavy coat.

"We'll take a turn around the camp, if you can make it."

"You'll have to keep up to me, old friend. I'm just itching to get out of here." Frank followed him along the center of the longhouse toward the door at the end. Every few feet John turned around.

"Keep moving, John. Don't worry. I'm right behind you."

As John opened the door an angry wind pushed inside. Frank gasped but followed his friend outside.

"Are you all right?" He glanced at Frank.

"That wind is like a cold knife against my ribs. But getting out of the longhouse is almost worth it."

John laughed and took Frank's arm. As they walked he pointed out the playing field and the huge fire pit, the other longhouses and, further on, the cabins of the bear clan. Very few Indians were out in the weather and those that were hurried about their chores with barely a glance their way. John steered Frank toward the horse pen, where the animals stood in a tight group facing into the wind with their thick winter coats and their glazed eyes, still as death.

"I don't see Maudie or Jackie. You sure they're here?"

John pointed to a spot up against the palisade wall. "I think it's time to get them home as well, don't you?"

As Frank gave a whistle John called to Maudie. "Come on, girl. Don't you recognize me?" Slowly the horse cantered toward the men, Jackie following. John stroked his animal, talking softly and rubbing her nose, lost in his dream of home.

BACK IN THE LONGHOUSE Frank sat on his bed watching the fire's brightness. John held his hands over the flames.

"Another couple of days and we'll go. You should get a little stonger." He looked at Frank. "What we need to decide is where we'll go. Home, or to Niagara."

Frank's head shot up. "Where are we now? I mean, how far from home?"

"I figure we're closer to home than Niagara. The thing is, it's winter and there will most likely be nothing happening with the Rangers until spring. I don't want to desert, that's for certain, but we're this close and have the opportunity..." He paused and slapped at a wayward spark with his hand. "What are you thinking?"

"Love to be home. Father will be missing me. On the other hand I don't want to be branded a deserter for the rest of my life."

"We don't have to decide now. Two days." He turned and headed out of the longhouse.

Chapter Fifteen

December, 1778

DECEMBER WAS WELL UNDER WAY and the farm had snow to prove it. Lucy had shoveled a path to the barn and another to the privy. The snow had come late one night as she lay in bed, shaking and listening to the wind terrorize her land. She had snuggled deep under the quilts, exhausted, but unable to sleep.

In the morning as she opened the cabin door to a glistening white marvel, the bright sunlight had so blinded her that she didn't realize the little snow pile in front of the door had fallen into the cabin. When her eyes adjusted to the brightness, she could not close the door until scooping out the snow.

That day she had been torn between loving the look and the feel of the snow and hating the extra work it gave her. Since then she had added keeping the paths clear into the rhythm of her daily chores, a rhythm which helped her to focus on one day at a time and on doing what needed to be done.

Christmas was coming but she barely gave it a thought. She was knitting socks for John although she began to wonder if he would ever wear them. John's smile she could conjure only if she pictured an event. Otherwise she needed to look at the little engraving of the two of them on their wedding day. Hard and serious he looked in it and she so innocent; neither was a true likeness then, and now, almost two and a half years later, the picture looked like someone else.

"And what do you think?" She stroked her belly. "Does this look like your daddy?" She watched her skirt rise and fall as the baby shifted. She pulled her jacket apart to see a sharp point actually sticking up. Her hand closed over it. "Hello, my little one. Are you poking at me? Do you want me to notice you?" Soothing the baby with her gentle caresses, she smiled. "I will be so glad to hold you in my arms. When will you come?"

She glanced at the stove where she kept the huge pot filled with water. Her woodpile had grown with all she had brought inside and just off the porch a huge stack lay under a blanket of snow. She blessed Mr. Maycock for having split so much. That was one job she wouldn't have to do for quite some time after the baby came.

Lucy had fed the animals for the day and made sure all was secure. The chickens followed her to the barn door but, as she opened it, the blast of cold air sent them scurrying back. She was not shoveling the dung. It would just have to wait until she was better able, maybe even until spring. It would pile up until the oxen gradually stood high in the pen.

She couldn't help it. She could only do what she could do. Besides, the oxen were content with the fresh straw she added every day. She dug in the snow to the chest where she had stored some of the meat to keep it cold over the winter. She reached beyond her huge belly and pulled the latch to retrieve a large frozen chunk of venison.

Inside again, she barred the door without even thinking. She hung her coat, removed her heavy boots, and placed them near the door.

Pain ripped through her. She clutched at her belly. "That was some kick." She stood still, caught her breath, and the pain was gone.

She put the meat into a stew pot, filled it with water, and set it on the hot stove. Into her dried spice chest she went, finding the flavorings she loved. She added mustard seed and an onion from the root cellar. Carrots and potatoes she prepared now but would put in later. This would keep her going for a few…

"Ohhh." Was the baby coming? "It's too early, little one." The pain eased and she rested her hand on her belly.

She sat in the chair by the fire listening to the water in the stew pot hiss and gasp. When the telltale wisps of steam turned into full scale eruptions she stood and lifted the pot to the other side of the stove. "There. Now you can gently bubble for a few hours."

Again she sat. If the baby was coming, was she ready? She had made a soft blanket from an old nightgown. Over the past months she had knit a tiny cap and booties but she didn't have enough wool left for a sweater coat.

She had planned to unravel that shawl that had been her mother's but hadn't got to it yet. And tiny shirts. She had done her best but the baby would need more. She just didn't have anywhere to get what was necessary. The few nappies she had made would have to do. The fire would dry them quickly here in the cabin.

When it was time, Lucy added the vegetables to the pot. The sharp pains had stopped. She was glad, but a small part of her was sad. She was ready to see and hold her baby. Presently she dipped the large spoon into the broth and drew out a taste. She blew on it. "Mmmm. Good. We need some more of that, don't we, baby?"

LATER LUCY TUCKED INTO BED for a warm night's sleep. Her back had ached all day and she shifted to get comfortable. She turned on her side to rest her large belly on the bed. Better. The wind shrieked outside and whistled down the chimney. She was glad to be out of it.

Something made her open her eyes. Moonlight streamed through the gap in the curtains and streaked across the patchwork quilt, lighting the dark blues, reds and greens of her childhood dresses. She remembered her mother buttoning her pretty dress for her and then turning to do yet another chore. Maybe she was carrying a little girl and would be doing the same. Her eyes closed and she smiled herself to sleep.

Elaine Cougler

Floating on a soft pink cloud, Lucy felt her eyes sink into her head and the feathery brush of a hair across her cheek. No, it was a hand. John's hand and she turned into his arms but couldn't reach him. Something was in the way. He drifted off and she was holding only his shirt. She reached and reached, but he was gone.

She heard his empty boots stalk across the cabin floor; the door opened and a flood of white sunshine pushed in ahead of the cold dark night. Hard hands held hers tightly against the pain. "Let me go. Let me go."

She rolled away but hurt more and, suddenly, she realized she had been dreaming. She opened her eyes in the dark, stroking her belly. The baby was quiet now but she was sure she had felt something. It wasn't just a dream.

She lay on her back wondering what had wakened her. Huge searing jolts flamed through her middle. She clenched the quilts and squeezed, her belly muscles stretching and straining. The baby was coming. Her legs pulled up on their own and then slowly eased down again as the pain ebbed. She had to get up. She needed to heat the water and light some candles.

Sliding from the bed Lucy pulled on her shoes against the cold of the floor. She lit the night candle and wrapped the quilt around her. She was feeding the fire when she felt the start of another pain and just had time to reach the chair before the contraction hit her full force.

Her hands moved from gripping the table to rubbing and massaging the hard knot of her belly. Nothing helped. She could hardly breathe. She panted short tiny breaths and that seemed better. She thought about those breaths, every single painful one of them, but didn't want to think about what was happening to her body. The breathing she could control.

She panted and panted and gradually the attack lessened. Soon she leaned down—oh, so carefully—and picked up the fallen quilt to wrap around her shoulders.

Now her time was near, she was afraid. Her mind was full of horrible birth stories, especially the one about her cousin, whose baby had to be pulled from her body piece by piece. She died soon after and Lucy never knew her.

She prayed her birthing would go well. The water was boiling on the stove. She had piled three quilts on the floor by the fire and lay there waiting for the next pain. Alone she was and would have to do it all herself.

John would be so proud of her when he came back. And she'd have a baby to show him. A real, live…"ohhhhh. You're coming soon, aren't you? Ohhhh." Lucy held her belly. "Breathe. Breathe."

Her eyes squeezed shut with the effort and she gasped short puffs through her mouth. She screamed. Breathe, she tried to tell herself, but the wall of pain and fear was too high. Her hand wiped wet from her forehead. She didn't notice. All of her attention was on fighting the mountain of pain which ripped at her. A moment later she lay back and slept.

"Uhah." Lucy's head flopped to the side and her eyes flickered open. The attack was on again with even more force than before. Like a crazed animal with no thought but survival, she plunged through the next contraction, then the next and the next, till she could not think where she was or what was happening.

THE FIRST SHARDS OF DAYLIGHT were long past and the winter sun lit the farmyard outside. The rooster had long since crowed and the chickens scratched fruitlessly in the dirt of the barn floor. The oxen stood by their empty manger and watched a tiny mouse flit back and forth, all of them following the call within. They were hungry.

Lucy had no thought for them, nor was she hungry. Her work was before her and her body knew its job, rhythmically pushing, relaxing, pushing, pushing, relaxing, and again pushing the baby along its way. She worked when necessary and rested for scant seconds between the contractions.

Soon she had no time to rest and the pain rose and rose and rose and never stopped, taking Lucy with it, up and over the mountain, searing her whole body with need. Need to be done, to birth this baby, to win this war, right here, right now.

The screams became endless grunts and groans. Her eyes felt like they might pop out of her head and her sweat smelled sweet and musty. She fell back, spent. Her eyes closed. Relief. Blood seeped back into her brain. "Baby..." She struggled up on her elbows to look. "My wee child." She saw the still, bluish object between her legs and struggled to reach it.

She hardly knew what she was doing as she stuck her finger in the mouth and pulled out wet slime. She held the baby by its feet and slapped its backside. And waited, terrified, sobbing. "Oh, baby, my baby. Breathe. Breathe." There was nothing. She jerked the baby to her bosom and held on tight, squashing it to her, crying and crying.

And then she wasn't crying alone. She heard the sweet howl at the same time as she felt the baby's chest move against hers. "You're alive. Oh, honey, you're alive." She lay back down and rocked the newborn against her.

What would John say when he knew he had a... son or daughter? She held the baby away from her and laughed. They had a son. She couldn't believe she hadn't even noticed before, or thought to look.

Now pictures flooded her mind, of John and their baby, of John and their little boy, of herself teaching him his letters, of John teaching him to ride, to shoot, to hunt, to do everything. Their whole future was spread out before her in her mind's eye and her smile came unbidden as she lay the wee babe down.

The cord pulsed big and blue out of her child's belly. As the blood flow slowed and stopped she knew she must cut the cord. The knife lay beside her, ready. She had to slice through the line connecting her and her son. Her hand was wet with sweat. She reached for the knife.

And dropped it. She began to cry. The baby wailed with her. She took a deep breath, looped the slimy cord over her hand, and sliced it through. Through her tears she saw that her boy was safe, his colour was good and his lips moved. He was hungry.

She gave him her breast. He seemed to know just what to do with it.

....

Soon he stopped suckling. She studied his closed eyes, tiny upturned nose and his dark lips periodically sucking at nothing. His right fist was tightly clenched next to his mouth, each little finger a wrinkled wonder to Lucy. She wrapped him in a large shawl and placed him in the basket near the fire, glad her ordeal was over.

SHE LAY ON THE BED with the boy beside her and slept. She had cleaned up as well as she could but she hadn't gone to the barn. The animals would have to wait until tomorrow. For now she slept with her boy.

Sometime later Lucy jerked awake. Her baby was crying. She brought him to her breast and fondled his smooth bald head and tiny perfect ears. She touched the soft spot on the top of his head and marveled at the pulse she felt. His miniature mouth didn't look large enough to suck so hard but suck he did, his eyes closed as though he concentrated on that one thing. His reddish cheek was a wonder so soft she felt her finger would push right through the skin if she pressed harder.

His eyes popped open and his mouth stopped for a moment. His deep blue eyes seemed to be looking right at her. "Well, hello there, little one," she whispered, but his eyes closed and his lips fastened onto her once again. Soon he slept once more.

She left the baby on the bed, wrapped tightly in his shawl, and waddled to the stove. She added more wood and stirred the fire. The stew was still on the top and she ladled a plate to eat. Even feeling as tired as she did she knew that keeping her strength up was very important. Besides, her stomach was growling again. This birthing business was hard work.

Yes, she was tired, but underneath it all she was elated. She had birthed her own baby and she felt good. She took stock. There was washing to do and animals to feed tomorrow. She had to tend to her own needs, making sure not to do too much. For now she could not help sneaking a peak at her slumbering son's face as he lay in her bed.

LUCY HAD WRAPPED HER SHAWL around her shoulders and sat in John's chair staring off into space. The sun had not waited for her but had gone down some time ago and she hadn't even been outside except to dump the slop pail over the end of the porch into the snow bank. The day was done.

She was anxious to go to bed but reluctant to leave John's chair, her only connection with him. "Where are you? Why haven't I heard something? Do you know you have a son? And we have to name him. Or rather, I have to name him." Her head nodded against the back of the chair and her eyes closed. She dozed.

She jerked awake, dropped the shawl, rocked to her feet. The knocking came again. She stood, motionless, hands clutching at her skirt. She crept toward the window to peek out between the curtains. And saw only black nothingness.

Chapter Sixteen

Boston, Fall, 1778

"I SHOULD ESCAPE THIS CITY, MARY. But I surely cannot leave you."
William Harper knelt and brushed the wet snow away from the
plain black stone. He took off his knitted muffler and polished
until the stone shone dry and clear in the moonlight. "I just don't
know how long I can hide in the house here, digging carrots and
potatoes from the garden in the dark. Hoping no one sees me. I
should have gone with the others."

He stood, glanced right and left and followed the path to the
back door. From the back lane he heard a commotion. He crept
back to the fence. Smoke. He could smell smoke. Then he saw
flickers of light. Torches. A bunch of unruly ruffians hustled
toward him.

He raced to the house for his gun. Not fast enough. By the time
he reached the porch a second group had circled around from the
front. They grabbed him before he could get inside. He thought
they would pull his arms off with their jerking and rough handling.

"King's man," someone snarled in his face.

"Traitor."

"Turncoat."

The whole crowd shouted and hooted dirty names at William.
He thought he was going to the hanging tree, for sure, but they

had other plans. They started a fire right in the garden near the porch and used his own woodpile to fuel it into a roaring, soaring thing. He was afraid his attackers were going to throw him on it, too, but someone brought out his large kettle and they dumped tar into it. When the pillows from his house appeared, he knew what was coming.

He rammed his boot down on the foot nearest him. Its owner screamed and let go. William tried to run but he couldn't fight all the hands that held him. This time they jerked his arms tighter and tied a rope around his middle, wrapped it around the pole of the porch, and winched it so hard he could hardly breathe. He couldn't move.

When the tar was hot, someone loosened the rope enough to strip off his jacket and shirt. He struggled but they held him tighter. He heard the slice of scissors and realized they were cutting his hair. He could do nothing. He was on the ground when the tar scalded his chest and they dumped feathers over him. They tarred his head and pushed it into the feathers as well.

He lay on his stomach. Heat seared down his back from his head to his waist and even through his britches. He shrieked. Somehow he wrenched his arms from the grip of the madmen. Then he was running and screaming, so crazed from the fire on his skin that no one could grab hold of him. He careened down the lane, his heart banging in his chest. Some followed but soon left off. They had done the thing and were happy.

In moments the heat had gone and William was able to think. He stopped screaming and looked for somewhere to hide. He found a cellar door slanted against a house. He lifted it just enough to crawl in. There on the cold stone steps he spent the night hugging his arms to his body, afraid to go into the root cellar lest he be heard, and afraid to go out in the cold night lest he be seen.

When morning came he realized what a mistake he had made. He couldn't go out in daylight because someone would definitely see him. He huddled in that cramped space the whole day, listening to every sound, afraid someone would open the door, feeling his hunger gnaw at his innards every minute, and picking pain-fully away at the feathers stuck to him.

Finally the shards of light slipping between the boards above him dimmed and disappeared. Darkness had come. He strained his ears but heard nothing. He crept out into the night. He made it back to his house where lights glowed in the windows and shadow figures moved about. He dared not go in. His clothing still lay on the ground where the men had tossed it and he inched his cold shirt on over the tar.

During the day he had planned his escape. Now he struggled to carry it out. The week before he had wrapped his money in a tin along with some dried meat and apples and buried it in the yard. Now he took a charred slab of wood from the fire's ashes and scrabbled in the dirt where he thought the packet lay. He found it quickly and ran off down the back lane, hiding in shadows, avoid-ing people.

Chapter Seventeen

LUCY JUMPED BACK FROM THE WINDOW. In the bedroom the baby cried. The knock came again, louder, and she moved to the door.

"Who's there?" Her fingers clenched the cold trigger of the rifle.

"Open the door. It's freezing out here."

That voice. She knew it, but... it couldn't be. She lifted the bar and set it against the wall. In the dim light she saw the latch lift even as she reached to pull the handle and let in her visitor.

"Lucinda. Oh, Lucinda." The man stood before her covered in heavy coat, scarf and dog-eared hat, the snow clinging to him everywhere, even to his bearded face and bushy eyebrows. She knew him but still she held back.

"Lucinda. At last I see you again." He closed the door and brushed the snow from his arms and face, removing his wet clothing piece by piece.

She took the things from him and hung them to dry. Her mind whirled. She had not seen him for two and a half years and had heard nothing in that time. Now, he was here, in her home. She turned to greet her father.

He stepped toward her and she walked into his open arms.

"Father..." She looked into his eyes. "I am so glad you're here. I've missed you."

"Shhh. I'm here now." He patted her head. "I am so sorry I opposed your marriage. I was wrong and I've lived to regret the things I said."

She stepped back. "It doesn't matter now. You're here. Sit down." She led him to the table. "I'll light another candle."

"What do I hear in the other room?"

Lucy smiled and turned toward the sound. "A baby. My baby. Our baby." And she started to cry again as she went to get the child.

A moment later she was back with the howling baby in her arms. "He's hungry."

Her father peered into the tiny bundle and smiled. "He's awfully small. When was he born?"

"Today, just this morning, just me, no one to help," Lucy wailed.

"Shhh. It's all right now, my dear. I'm here." Her father stood quickly and held her and the baby together. "Seems you did just fine."

Gradually Lucy got hold of herself and smiled a crooked grin. "I am so glad you're here."

He helped her to John's chair and turned to feed the fire while she nursed the child.

He lifted the lid of the pot on the stove and sniffed. "Might I have some of this stew?"

"Of course you may. And there is bread in the larder. You must be famished. How long have you been on the road? Why did you come? Why didn't you write to me?"

"Wait a moment. I can't eat and answer all your questions at the same time."

"I'm sorry. It's just such a relief to have you here." She glanced around the cabin.

"Where's John?" Her father's eyes narrowed and his eyebrows lifted hesitantly.

"He is fighting with Butler's Rangers. At least I think he is. I haven't heard a word in months. He doesn't even know about the baby." Lucy sniffled once but held herself together.

"And you've been here all this time, alone?" Her father's spoon stopped in mid air.

She nodded. For the next while she recounted what had happened in the months since John had left, leaving nothing out. She mentioned the Indians coming, and returning with the wounded man for her to nurse. She touched on the crops and the animals, on feeding and harvesting, on walking in the forest and talking to herself. She told of Molly's accident and having to shoot her cow.

"With the rifle you gave me." She shifted in the chair and put the baby over her shoulder, patting his tiny back as she continued. "A man came here a couple of times and…he terrified me." Finally, she told him of Daeger's attack and her luck that Niles Maycock happened to be in the barn that day. Her eyes went to the place where Daeger's body had lain, but immediately she looked away, at her father's face.

"I am so glad you've come, father." She smiled at him.

"I wish I had been here before. I should have come sooner." He dropped his eyes. "But, as I said, I'm here now."

Lucy laid the babe in the bed and slipped back to her chair. Her father's hair was much greyer than she remembered and the bones above his eye sockets seemed to jut out more, shadowing his eyes as they talked. She noticed the unkempt beard and shaggy hair of someone who hadn't had a good cleanup in weeks. His scrawny hands went often to his face, his hair and then to his lap as he talked.

"Where have you been all this time, father?" She knew Boston was a mass of revolutionaries.

"It's a long, sad story, Lucinda, and I'll tell it to you, but not now. My aching bones just want to lie down and rest awhile in comfort. Tomorrow. I'll tell you tomorrow." He stood to accept the buffalo robe and bear skin and spread them on the floor. Lucy dug another quilt from the chest in the corner.

"Will that be enough? I have more." She peered into his face.

"Much better than I've had for weeks. Don't you worry. I'll be warm and cozy here by the fire." He settled into the bedding, his face to the wall. She banked the fire and moved to her room where the sleeping baby lay on the bed. Carefully she moved the wee thing under the blankets, undressed, and slipped in beside him.

Her deep sleep was broken only by the baby's cries. She fed him and drifted back to sleep, lulled by his periodic gurgling.

Chapter Eighteen

"YOU AND JOHN ARE COMFORTABLE HERE," William called, "but I'm amazed he left you all alone."

She had heard him up early poking the fire. Now he sat in the chair by the table. He looked up as Lucy came from the bedroom carrying the wailing child.

"Good day, daughter. Did you sleep well?"

"Yes, father, even though the baby cried for feeding twice in the night. I hope we didn't wake you?"

"No, you didn't. I slept like a dead man."

"Can you hold your grandson a bit?" Lucy placed the babe in his arms and turned to put the large water pot on the stove. Today she would bathe both herself and the baby before she did anything else. Turning she caught her father's delighted glance at his grandson. "Maybe he, too, will have your deep blue eyes."

William looked up quickly and smiled. "Or yours." He smiled. "I only ever see that colour when I find a looking glass clear enough to see." He cleared his throat.

"What is it?" She saw something was bothering her father.

William walked with the baby to the window. "What was John thinking, leaving you here all alone?" He faced her. "And with a baby."

She turned away. "We are both doing what we must, father."

"I'll be having a word or more with him when next I see him." He handed the babe over and put on his heavy coat. "I'll do some work in the barn."

She settled into John's chair to nurse the baby. Her father's story would just have to wait. She watched her son suckle and gloried in the exquisite pleasure of feeding him. His little lips grew more powerful with each pull. In a few moments he had finished and, reluctantly, she put him to bed. She had to prepare food for her father who had come back inside.

"Your animals were bawling, Lucinda. They're fed now, though."

"I just couldn't get out to them yesterday, father. You know that."

"Yes. And you did right. They'll be fine. One day's hunger won't hurt them at all." He sat at the table and concentrated on his food. "Home cooking is sure a treat after what I've had to eat the last while."

"Tell me about your trip. I'm just that anxious to hear what happened, father." She sat forward on her chair.

William stared at his porridge. His shoulders drooped and his eyes were hidden. He picked up his spoon and stirred the colourless mixture. A long sigh escaped as he began to tell of the terrible political climate in Boston after the tea dumping, the danger he felt all around, the tarring and feathering, and his escape.

Lucy could not believe his suffering. She tried to keep silent and let him finish but could not.

"How did you get the tar and feathers off? It would surely be obvious to everyone who saw you."

William smiled. "Of course, you're right. I had no turpentine so I just picked away at it during the day while I hid and eventually I got most of it off. One night I peeked into a barn where I did find turpentine. I stripped to the waist and rubbed off what was left, a lot of my skin along with it."

"Did it hurt?"

"The pain was terrible but I had to keep quiet. Afterwards I washed with water from the pump in the yard, thinking I'd get caught. But no one came out."

"Then how did you get here?"

....

"I found my way to the harbor and managed to stow away on a rebel ship going south. Luckily I made it to New York." William paused.

"But New York is British. Your ship couldn't land there."

"No. I heard the boatmen talking and knew we were close to New York. That night I lowered a small rowboat. No one heard its splash. I climbed down and rowed toward the glow of lights in the distance. Hours later I made it to shore and found a riverboat going up the river.

"I thought of coming to you. I met a man who knew exactly where you were. He gave me directions and here I am. And not a moment too soon." William smiled.

"Who was the man?" Lucy peered at her father.

"He said he knew you. That he had been here."

Lucy laughed. "Who was it?"

"Ah, you'll have to guess." At that he stood, grabbed his coat and was gone before Lucy could ask if the man was Niles Maycroft.

Chapter Nineteen

December, 1778

FRANK RAISED ONE FOOT to the mounting block and turned to look at John. "Which way are we going? Winter barracks and boredom or home sweet home?" Of course they both knew that second choice might in the end mean a court martial and a firing squad. Frank grabbed Jackie's mane and pulled himself up onto her back, already loaded with bundles of food and furs.

"We have to decide," said John.

Together they rode one last time through the awakening Mohawk village. "Brant is pretty close to Butler. Butler will know where we are before long. I'd like to go home but I just don't think we can risk it." He looked over at Frank but got no hint of what he was thinking.

After a few seconds Frank spoke. "They are in opposite directions, aren't they?"

John pulled up at the edge of the village. "No. If we go west, we're going to Niagara. Southwest, home."

"A fine pickle we're in." He glanced over. "But I'll do whatever you say, John. You're the one with the pretty wife at home."

John closed his eyes and his head tipped forward. He so wanted to see Lucy, to check that she was all right. His hands tightened on the reins. Suddenly he pulled back with his left hand and kicked Maudie. She lurched through the trees on the more southerly trail.

"Yes, sir. We're going home." Frank hollered, "Wait for me."

The day was cold. Wind tugged at their packs and tore at their coats. John wrapped his woolen muffler around his hat and his whole head but the cold still spiked into him as he followed the barely recognizable trail. Glancing behind, he saw Frank's eyes were mere slits and he was struggling to keep up. He was not as well as John had thought. They would have to stop often to rest.

At least they didn't have any worry about armies attacking in this weather. All sane people were nodding off in front of their own hearths. He thought of home and the huge stove that Lucy had insisted they bring from Boston. Quite a trip that had been, hauling it by wagon and boat, paying off everyone to even accept it. But it had been well worth the trouble.

He pictured Lucy warm and happy in his chair near the stove, and thought of her surprise when he opened the door, a huge snow-covered hulk, hardly recognizable in his furs and muffler. But she would know him and they would hold each other forever. He squeezed his eyes shut and blinked back a sudden wetness.

Frank was bobbing on his horse and looking unsteady. John looked for a clearing and pulled Maudie up short. "Come on, Frank. Let's have a break."

BY NIGHTFALL THEY HAD COVERED a lot of territory but still had quite a distance to go. They were following the Mohawk River now. John judged they had five or six days before they reached home. As long as the weather held and they had no problems.

They brushed the snow back, pitched their tent before the roaring fire and stood holding their icy hands over its warmth. The blanketed horses were tethered close by the heat. From their packs the men took dried meat and apples and wolfed them down, then crawled into the tent and dropped off to sleep. Used to the warmth of the Indian longhouses, they slept fitfully on the cold, hard ground.

....

IN THE MORNING they covered the fire's ashes with snow, saddled up, and headed east. The puny sun this day warmed their spirits, but not their bodies. They rode slowly and didn't see a soul, either on the trail or the frozen river whenever they came near it. That night they pitched camp early and Frank dropped a line into a hole in the icy river to catch a fish but nothing bit the bare hook. He gave up and tucked into his provisions.

The days went by with little to think about except eating, sleeping, and riding along the river, and the many rest breaks along the way. Frank seemed to have hardened into the trip, for which John was thankful. He really didn't want to spend any more time on this trail than absolutely necessary.

They saw very little movement in the forest as the bears were hibernating and the squirrels and raccoons knew better than to be out in this frozen landscape for anything but grabbing a quick meal. Still, from time to time, red cardinals and scrawny jackrabbits broke the monotony. At night owls hooted and sometimes the men would hear a far off wolf howling its fury at the moon. But they collapsed into their blankets to try to keep warm.

They had been traveling a full week when the trail started to look familiar. The bend in the river suggested that been-here-before feeling and the two friends pulled their horses to a stop.

"Not much farther now, Frank. Can you make it?"

"I could ride to Hell and back today." A lop-sided grin lit up his white face.

"We'll be at the turn off soon. Do you want to come with me and rest up a day or so?"

"I'm thinking Lucinda would not thank me for that. She'll be wanting you all to herself." He laughed.

John smiled and clicked his horse ahead. He could almost smell the cabin's fire. Soon he pulled his horse up short. "Sure you'll be all right?" He leaned over and grasped Frank's arm.

"I'll be home in no time, toasting my feet by the fire. I'll tell my father lots of tall tales about the last few months. You go ahead."

He waved and turned away. He dug in his heels and shook the reins. Horse and man drifted off into the wintry white.

John turned homeward, longing for Lucy. As the afternoon wore on he kept a close eye on the lengthening shadows of the trees, gauging how much daylight he had left. He was sure he could get there before dark but the snowed-over path seemed endless with trees, trees and more trees.

All lay still in the forest. Even the waterfall where once he and Lucy had lain pressed together in the long summer grass was frozen to a trickle. He would have liked to stop but wanted to get home much more.

Maudie pushed herself on through the deep punishing snow, faster and faster. He felt her excitement and leaned forward to pat her neck. "Not long now, girl. Don't rush too much in this snow. Calm down. We need to get there safely."

His thoughts rambled with the rhythm of Maudie's muscles rocking him homeward. He pictured the small clearing, the sturdy barn, the small, fenced fields, and the cabin nestled in the middle of the snowy landscape with smoke curling from its chimney.

He blinked at the wetness in his eyes and forced himself to smile the tears away. No reason for tears. She was less than an hour now. Far in the distance he saw the break in the trees at trail's end. Maudie trotted faster.

The sinking sun was an orange-red curve through the black trees poking out of the snow. It bathed the scene in pinkish mist. Just as he had imagined, smoke curled from the chimney and all looked serene.

But wait. Someone stepped onto the porch. A man. John yanked Maudie to a stop. The man kicked the snow off his boots, opened the door and walked in without knocking. He clicked Maudie on toward the barn, stepped down and tied her just outside. He pulled his musket from the pack, checked it and crept toward the cabin.

His boots crunched softly on the snow-crusted porch. He stood beside the window, leaned to look. Through the small slit between the curtains, he saw a grey-haired man sitting in his chair, his back to the window. Lucy was nowhere to be seen. He pulled back. Cooking sounds and the smell of a good stew seeped out to where he stood.

He tiptoed to the door and tried the latch. Locked. He would have to knock and be ready. Knock, knock. The loud sound shocked even him, but he stepped back and raised his musket.

As the door edged open, firelight and the smell of delicious home cooking washed over him. He gripped the gun, ready to shoot. He couldn't miss at this distance. A small man with blazing blue eyes stared at him. "Who are you?" John growled.

And then, behind, he saw a whirl of red hair flying toward him, pushing the man aside. His musket went up and he fell backwards, down the steps, and into the snow.

She was hollering, and laughing, and holding him. He felt the cold snow on his neck and the warm kiss on his lips. His arms came around and he held her tight. "Lucy. Aw, Lucy." Tears tried to come but he forced them back and held his wife in the snow.

"Seems like the wandering soldier has returned." The man stood in the doorway. "Lucinda, you might let him up and into the cabin. It's cold in the snow." He turned and closed the door part way, keeping the fire's heat inside, and leaving the young couple the privacy of their own warm reunion.

John came to his senses and tried to get up. "You'll have to let me up." He laughed as she squeezed his neck more tightly. "Come on, Lucy. Let's go inside."

His back against the closed door, John glanced at William.

"You don't know me, do you, John?"

"It's my father, John. My father." Still holding his arm, she stared into his eyes. He glanced from one to the other. Those eyes that he loved in Lucy smiled at him from across the room.

"Of course. Welcome, sir."

A wail from the bedroom cut into the happy scene. John pushed Lucy behind him and grabbed his musket. He fixed his eyes on the curtain to the bedroom as the wail split the air once more. Lucy's hand grabbed his arm pulling his aim off. He looked at William whose grin shocked him. Why weren't they frightened?

"Wah, wah."

John turned to Lucy and lowered his gun to the floor. "A... baby? You have a baby?"

"No, WE have a baby. A baby boy, just a week old." Her smile faded and her forehead creased. "You didn't get my letter, then."

"No. I haven't been with the Rangers for some time. Frank and I got left behind. It's a long story." His eyes went toward the bedroom. "Can I see him?"

"Of course." Lucy tugged at him but he held back.

"My horse. I have to look after Maudie. She's outside in the snow." William pulled on his warm coat. "Don't worry about that, John. I'm needing some fresh air myself." The cabin door closed on his last words and John followed Lucy to the bedroom.

CHRISTMAS WAS ONLY A DAY AWAY and the little cabin had been full of rejoicing for a week. Lucy was glad now that she had finished the socks she had been knitting for John but she had nothing for her father. Of course, the baby was too young to care. Maybe they could finally give him a name.

She chuckled. Now she was glad she hadn't picked it. So much better to have John here. What she could do was bake a cake and kill a chicken. They would have wonderful food. She had squash and potatoes to cook. The dried berries would make a delicious pie. While the men talked at the table she hung two washed nappies over the stove. Then she started with a fresh loaf of sourdough bread and the pie—better make two, one berry and one apple.

The baby cried and John jumped to get him. He had learned to change and swaddle his son the morning after his return, holding the tiny baby almost in one hand, ever so gently, as though he might break the wee thing in two. She nursed him and when he fell away, asleep, she passed him over to his father to burp and went back to her happy preparations.

John came from the bedroom smiling. "He is so tiny. Like a baby raccoon."

She grinned. "You should have seen him a fortnight ago. Just a little bit of a thing."

John threw on his coat. William joined him. They had chores to do in the barn and wood to bring in.

"Could one of you empty some of the ash from the stove, please? I need a good fire for all this cooking today."

"I'll do that, Lucy." John grabbed the metal pail and opened the door of the stove, while William headed out the door.

THE SKY GLOWED WHITE with frosty clouds blanking out the sun that day as William grabbed the shovel and started to clean out the path to the barn. The sides were high now, about two feet, and the snow drifted in with any bit of wind. The winter was full upon them. John worked alongside his father-in-law.

"You're a grandfather now, William."

"I guess I am. Hadn't thought much about it." William stood still a moment.

"Are you Papa or Granda? What will the baby call you?"

William grunted under the weight of the snow. "Really doesn't matter much. We'll work it out tomorrow. I'm more interested in naming that boy."

They finished the trail to the barn. Side by side, they mucked out the oxen pen, tossing the manure through the open window to the growing pile outside. John was glad of the bracing breeze coming in to freshen the stale air. There would be baths tonight for all of them before the celebrations tomorrow.

CHRISTMAS DAY HADN'T YET DAWNED when Lucy heard the familiar cries of her son. She changed his soaking clothing and sat in the chair to nurse him.

In the cool room she was glad of the heavy quilt which she pulled around her shoulders. She wrapped it tightly around the baby, cocooning them together. He suckled hungrily and she drifted into her thoughts of John, baby, Christmas, her father, the chicken they would kill this morning, the pies. Dozens of details crowded her mind. As the baby tugged insistently, she stroked his tiny head, soothing him and herself. Soon he lay sated and dozing. She patted him and put him back to sleep, then crawled in beside John's warm body and drifted off herself.

Chapter Twenty

FRANK AND JACKIE CARRIED ON through the snow but the trail was tough going and neither he nor his horse had the strength to push hard. Eventually, though, he started to see things he knew and hurried on. He was anxious to get home.

Jackie whinnied. He figured she smelled home but she slowed to a walk and then stopped.

"What's wrong, girl?" Nothing seemed out of the ordinary but he dismounted and went to the horse's head.

Her eyes were wild and white. She jerked her head up and away. He could barely hold her. He looked all around. They were alone on the trail but the forest was silent as death.

Off in the drooping trees there arose a fluttering of birds. Something was on the ground. Something dark. He tied Jackie to a tree, grabbed his gun and set off to investigate.

It was a body. And animals had been at it. He moved closer and saw the green coat. He ran. Even with the face gone, Frank knew the blood-smeared coat was his father's. The hands were bloody bones, and a huge gory chest wound gaped open, shards of ice blood frozen red-black all around the hole from which his da's very life had drained away.

"Da. Oh, Da." Frank ran his hands over his father's frozen legs, the only part not bloodied. "Who did this? What happened?" he moaned. But there was no answer. He looked away, unable to think or even to feel.

When the bitter cold had pervaded his thoughts so completely that he finally noticed his icy breath and stiffened fingers, he loaded his father onto Jackie and headed for home, wondering what he would find. Someone obviously shot his da. Maybe they were at the farm? Maybe they dumped him in the woods rather than try to bury him in the frozen ground, figuring the animals— his breath caught—would look after the body.

Soon he saw the clearing ahead. He tied his horse to a tree and crept on, his musket primed and ready. All was quiet. He thought the place was deserted until he caught a whiff of wood smoke.

He peeked around the wall of the old shack. The tall tree shadows reached right across the clearing. They were pointing at the cabin. His neck hairs stiffened. There was smoke from the chimney.

He drew back out of sight and felt the heat of his blood gushing through his body. He took a deep breath and edged from his hiding place. He crept across the long white expanse of the yard all the way to the cabin window and peered inside.

Three men were sitting at his table, eating his da's food, and having a fine old time of it. They had found the hard cider, too, and were well into it. He knew he should leave but couldn't. They had killed his da and taken the farm.

He would only get one shot with his musket but he had his knife and surprise was on his side. He could get them all before they could grab their weapons. He was crazy with anger and not thinking too well. He forgot how sick he had been.

He tried the door. It was unlocked. He raged in and shot the first man dead. He plunged his knife into the second one before he could react. As that man dropped to the floor clutching his chest, Frank felt hands on his neck. He drove his elbow backwards and caught him in the gut. He released his hold just long enough for Frank to turn. As he raised his knife to strike again, arms tightened around his belly.

There were four of them! And the fourth had his arms locked around Frank. He kicked and slashed his knife down and back; the man loosened his hold. The other one was at Frank's face and he jabbed up at him but missed and lost his balance.

He tried to run for the open door but the two of them pulled him back in and he slashed wildly. Kill them. Kill them. His knife flew from his hand and he fell to the floor, rolling over. Hands choked him so hard he thought his wind pipe would break. He kicked again and his boot found a foot and mashed it into the floor. The man fell howling, the table leg broke and the table crashed on top of them as they hit the floor.

Somehow he got to his feet and drove the bigger man into the stove. The pipes fell and black soot flew everywhere. From behind the other one tugged at his clothes, his hair and his neck. He ducked down and snatched up his knife from the floor. The man lost his balance and flew right over Frank against the stove, knocking it over onto the floor.

Smoke stung his eyes. He had to get out of there. He made it to the door but he was attacked again. This time he slashed to the right and hit flesh. The man fell away from him. Frank tripped over his gun, grabbed it up, and ran like a wild man from the fiery smoke. Over his shoulder he saw two figures stagger out into the night, one hollering like the devil himself, the other weaving away from the smoking cabin and waving a gun.

He ran for the woods and Jackie.

Chapter Twenty-One

SOFT RAYS OF COLD SUNLIGHT washed over the patchwork quilt as John and Lucy woke to Christmas Day. The baby still slept but they could hear William stirring the fire. Quietly they checked the blankets over the babe in his new crib and stole from the bedroom.

A few moments later Lucy placed a cup of steaming coffee on the table before William. "Happy Christmas, Father."

He smiled and squeezed her hand. "Happy Christmas, Lucinda. And to you, too, John. This morning, I am happy." His voice rose emphatically.

"No one is more pleased than I, to be home, to sleep in my bed, to be a father—all good things." His arm slipped around Lucy's waist as she placed a mug before him. "Although sleeping in a bed is not easy after months on the hard ground."

"You'd rather be on the ground? We can arrange that." Lucy smiled up at him.

Laughing together, they prepared for the day. William did the barn chores. John found a plump hen and wrung its neck before plucking and cleaning it, ready for roasting.

Lucy had vegetables to prepare, baby to tend, well-water to draw and a million other things before their celebration dinner was ready. For all of them the work was a joy this day when the best gift of all was just being safe together.

By mid afternoon the meal was ready, and a good thing it was as no one had eaten since their quick cup of morning coffee and slice of bread and jam. Lucy nursed and settled the baby. She came from the bedroom and clapped her hands.

"We're ready. Let us eat this wonderful food." Steaming potatoes, sliced chicken, baked squash, pickles, bread, applesauce, and much more waited on the table. They served themselves and passed the bowls to the sideboard which Lucy had cleared for the purpose. Finally they were ready and, smiling, joined hands.

John said the blessing. "Grant, O God, thy blessing upon us and upon this food before us. Pardon our sins and bless these mercies to our use, for Jesus' sake. Amen." He squeezed Lucy's hand. "Everything smells wonderful. You just don't know how I've dreamed of this."

She squeezed back. "Then let's get started."

When they had finally eaten their fill and pushed back from the table, John turned to Lucy. "I have no gift for you. I'm sorry."

"You've brought me the best gift of all. You. Can you think I need anything else?" She stood and slipped to the chest in the corner. "I only have these for you." She passed him the newly knitted grey socks. "Of course the baby is the real gift, wouldn't you say? To both of us?" She stood behind John's chair and wrapped her arms around his neck.

He patted her hand. "The best surprise I've ever had."

"Well, I have a gift for each of you." William went to his pack in the corner, quickly drawing out three things. "For you, John, this hunting knife. I don't need it anymore." Turning to Lucy he held out something shiny. "Here's something I kept to give to you but I think I'll just give it right to the baby. You ate from it when you were a child."

"A silver spoon. My spoon. Oh, how perfect. Thank you, Father." She moved to give him a hug.

"I'm not finished. I found these in one of your mother's chests. Lucky I had them in my secret box in my yard. Thought you might like them." He held his closed fist out and instinctively Lucy put her hand underneath. Something dropped into it.

"Buttons. Beautiful buttons. I need these." She dropped the handful on the table by the candle. "And I remember Mother's dress with these shiny silvery ones." Lucy fingered through the tiny pile. "Thank you, Father," she whispered, staring into his eyes.

"I have one more thing. A gift from the man who told me where to find you." William pulled out a bushy striped tail, and turned to John. "I believe this is from your wife."

"What?" John looked from one to the other.

"Oh. Niles Maycroft. He gave you that, didn't he, father?
William smiled and nodded.

Lucy laughed as she grabbed the tail and held it against her cheek. "John, don't you recognize the raccoon you skinned before you left?"

"Yes. Thank you, William. For the gifts and for all you've done." John reached across the table and shook his father-in-law's hand. Lucy hung the tail on the hook by the door.

Suddenly the door crashed back. In stepped a snowy, bundled giant of a man. John grabbed the knife on the table and jumped to his feet waving it before him. William held a chair in front of him, ready to charge the man. From behind the door, Lucy ran to the stranger and threw her arms around his neck, choking him from behind.

"Whoa. Wait." The man's arms flew up to loosen Lucy's hold. He backed away a step. "Don't you recognize me?" He peered at John. With one arm he held off Lucy's kicks. With the other he took the snowy muffler from his face.

"Frank. I should have known." John dropped the knife and bearhugged his friend.

"Let's get this door closed." William moved to keep out the cold. "And this time we'll bolt it."

"Oh, Frank. I didn't recognize you." Lucy bustled to help him with his wet things. "Happy Christmas."

Frank handed his coat to her and smiled. "Is that how you welcome visitors?"

HE HAD EATEN HIS FILL of the remnants of the Christmas feast. He pushed his chair back from the table and glanced from one to the other of his hosts, his sad eyes resting last on John.

"What is it, Frank? Why are you here?" He knew nothing would keep Frank from spending time with his father.

"I had to come." His voice was low and hard. He sat silent, staring at the candle as the wax slipped slowly down its side and puddled forlornly in the saucer below. The others waited.

Frank's shoulders sagged. He seemed to slip down in the chair. His head flopped forward and stayed there a moment. Then he took a deep breath. His shoulders lifted up and back and gradually his head came up. He opened his eyes and stared at John.

"My da's dead." He choked out the last word.

Everyone spoke at once, a sudden cacophony of exclamations and condolences, which died down almost as quickly as it had started.

"What happened, Frank?" John asked.

As the three listened, Frank told of finding his father's body and of the thieves and murderers who had their farm. Of the cabin which was no more. His eyes glazed over as he described the fire and his escape.

"I found my horse, pushed da's body forward and jumped up behind him. As fast as I could, I rode away from my home burning behind me. By then the snow was coming hard. My trail would soon be covered. In the dark we rode on, Jackie and I, for what seemed like forever, carrying my da.

"When I was certain no one was following, I took Jackie into the trees and made a camp for the night under a big fir tree. I was just plain worn out. And I needed time to think."

"But where have you been since then?" John stood to add wood to the stove. "That was seven days ago."

"I'll tell you." Frank wiped his hand across his face, pushing his hair out of his eyes. "Jackie nickered and woke me. It was still dark. I was stiff and frozen up like a block of ice from the river. My toes would hardly move. I was afraid I'd have to say good-bye to a couple of them. I had no choice. I had to risk a fire or freeze to death.

"I managed to find some dry pine cones and low branches with little snow on them. Luckily a dead tree sagged to the ground near me and I pulled at it in the dark to break off as much as I could to get the fire going. Its tiny light helped me see and I gradually added more dead wood until I had a roaring blaze.

"The idea came to me as I stood bathed in the fire's heat. I couldn't bury my father in the frozen ground and I sure couldn't take him with me. There was nothing else to do. I would burn his body." Frank stopped a moment, swept his hand over his broken face, and carried on. "His clothes weren't worth saving but I stripped the buttons off his jacket and slipped them into my pouch. I would have kept that jacket, if I could. He had worn it forever. I…liked it."

Frank sat at the table and caressed his coffee mug as he stared at something far away from the cozy cabin. "You don't know how long I stood there. I knew what to do but could not do it. The fire started to burn lower, though. I had to throw him on.

"Finally I just grabbed his shoulders and dragged him over. He was no weight to lift, like he was just a wraith already. His body hit the coals with a sickening crack and I didn't know if the breaking sound was his back or the wood underneath. A spray of sparks shot up in the dark night. The flames grabbed at him, swallowed him up."

Frank paused and stared at his hands on the table. In a monotone, he continued. "I flung more and more wood on the fire. I was crazed. It was worse than anything I ever had to do in battle. To burn my own father." He dropped his head to the table and his shoulders shook with sobs.

Lucy went to his side and touched his head. "Frank, it took courage. You had to do it."

"Yes, you did what you had to, Frank. And I think your father would have approved." John stood by the table, his eyes on his friend, and rubbing his hands together. He moved to the stove. "Here, have some more coffee."

Frank sat up, swiped at his eyes, and slowly reached for his coffee. His long fingers curled so tightly around the brown mug they went white except for the rising red in his fingernails. Gradually, though, his fingers relaxed and he faced Lucy. "I'm sorry. I can go on now."

"How long did you stay there?" Lucy sat again.

"I….for hours. I added wood and more wood. Kept the flames high in the air as the daylight crept up on me. Once I started I had to keep going. Until he was gone. Father, I mean. You just don't know how long it takes to burn a body. Or how the smell clogs your brain."

He shuddered. "I stayed and I watched and I did nothing but feed the fire and think about those men who killed my father and stole our property. The more the fire raged, the angrier I got. I kept that fire going strong for the rest of that day and most of the next before I let it die down. By the embers that night, I made my plans.

"The next morning I pulled what bones I could still find from the ashes and wrapped them in my pack. I'll bury them properly in the spring. It's the least I can do for him." He glanced at the three nodding faces.

"I hadn't eaten for most of two days and my stomach growled. My dried meat was gone. I needed to get back to our cabin and the winter stores in the cold cellar. I wasn't going to let those murderers have the farm without a fight. Father would have wanted me to fight for what was ours. In the silent snow Jackie and I picked our way back down the trail to get our…my property back.

"On the edge of the clearing, I slipped off and tied my horse, just as I had done three days before, but this time I knew what lay ahead. There was a burnt smell in the frosty air and it wasn't fresh. I looked for footprints and found nothing. No signs of life.

"I sneaked to the shack and peered around the corner. Across the yard, wisps of black smoke still spiraled up from the charred remains of our cabin. Our home was gone, my father was dead and all our work was destroyed. I dropped my head and noticed the scuffled snow right in front of the door. They were inside the shack. Those murdering thieves relaxed just a few feet away from where I stood. All I could think of was my da's body, broken and bloody, and…" Frank looked at John… "I lost my temper again."

"I rammed against the small door and slammed it open. For a moment the darkness blinded me and I stood dazed looking at the embers of a fire in the pit. A shape loomed beside me and my head broke apart. At least it seemed so. I went down without a whimper. Didn't even get to fire my gun."

"But how did you get away?" Lucy croaked, sliding forward on her chair.

"When I woke I was tied hand and foot and my head throbbed as though I'd been trampled by ten oxen. I was still in the shack but not alone. Across the fire pit, two pair of eyes cut into me. Mean eyes squeezed almost shut. In filthy faces, with matted hair straggling over them. Hate. Murderous hate. That's what I saw in those eyes."

"Oh." Lucy's hand went to her mouth. "Sorry. Do go on, Frank."

"Well, there's not much more to tell. Those murderers had me and I couldn't do a thing. They left me tied up for most of the time. Although they did give me food to eat."

He snorted. "Had to chew from a plate, with no hands. Anyhow I asked a lot of questions but they weren't talking. Even when they let me outside to, ah, do my, ah, business, they kept a rope around my neck. At least I could stretch my legs. They untied my hands but kept that rope tight while I stood in the frosty air, trying not to think of my audience."

He chuckled, the old Frank coming back, but sobered immediately. "The next day I managed to get them to untie me for my meals but they still weren't talking. I thought maybe they were waiting for something, or someone.

"We spent another night together and I fumed for most of it. Were we going to go on like that till spring? In the morning the taller fellow bundled into his coat and muffler and left. Didn't come back for hours.

"When his partner, the one with burns on both his hands, came to untie me to eat, I smashed the plate in his face and tackled him. He was on the floor in a second and screaming at the pain in his hands as he tried to defend himself."

Frank stopped and looked straight at John. "I broke his neck and didn't even think about it. He was dead on the dirt floor."

"You did what you had to do, Frank." William spoke in a low voice and the others joined in.

"Yes. And I'd do it again. When the big fellow came back a little later he met a similar end. I dragged them both out and left them for the wolves. Even that was too good for them.

"I checked the barn and found their two horses, my cow and my own Jackie. They must have found where I tied him. My bull was gone, though. Maybe my da had to butcher him, I don't know. Anyhow, I stayed in the barn that night, last night, before coming here. Couldn't bear to be in the shack where that trash had been."

He jerked his head up. "I've got to go back. You know, to feed the stock, and to protect the farm. There will probably be more of those types coming this way. That's why I came here, John. To tell you, warn you, so you could be ready."

John jerked his head to Lucy but she ignored him.

Frank picked up his mug. "I've outstayed my welcome. My cup's empty."

Lucy went to the stove. "And the pot is, too. I'll make more."

"No, don't you bother yourself, Lucinda. I've had enough and it's time I was away home." Frank strode to the door, bundled on his greatcoat and his heavy woolen muffler, and set the bar aside.

"Here, take this package of food." Lucy passed the sack to him. "You'll be glad of something later."

"Thank you, Lucinda. And thank you to all of you. I needed some place to collect myself. I do appreciate your kind hospitality." He smiled and strode out the door, John close behind him.

"I should come with you. You don't know what you're going to find or if someone else is coming." John followed Frank through the snow to the barn.

"Your place is here with Lucy. I'll be watching now. I can take care of myself."

"Are you sure?"

"Give me a week, John, and then ride over if the weather's good. If not, as soon as you can. I'll be glad of the company. Bring William. Maybe we can start cutting logs for the new cabin. I wish I had room for all of you to come but that old shack is just not a place for Lucy and the baby."

He swung up into the saddle and reached his hand to John. "Thank you, friend."

"Happy to help, Frank. You know that." He stepped aside to let horse and rider go. "A week, Frank. We'll be there," he shouted. Frank turned and waved, then rode into the trees, a black speck in the wintry white.

OVER THE NEXT FEW DAYS they settled into a comfortable pattern of chores and talk and plans for their future. They had all thought the war would be over in no time; that the British would check the colonists' revolutionary tendencies and life would get back to its normal peaceful rhythm, but such was not the case.

William had brought news with him that the colonists and their militia, along with Washington's continental army, were putting up quite a fight. France had even declared in favor of the revolutionaries and a man named LaFayette was making a considerable difference in the training and outfitting of the Americans. Americans. For Loyalists like John and Lucy and her father, the name was anathema.

"WE HAVE TO FACE THE FACTS, LUCY. We might not be able to stay here even after the war." John's earnest tones voiced Lucy's fears as she fidgeted at the table beside her men.

"I can stay and help. Nowhere else to go." In the flickering candle-light William's blue eyes clouded over for just a moment. He glanced at Lucy. "Besides, the future is here, with little Harper John."

"If father stays with me, we'll be fine come spring when you have to rejoin Colonel Butler again. Don't you think so, John?"

"I think you should take the baby and head for Niagara with me in the spring. When I have to rejoin the Rangers. You'll be safe there." He put his hand over hers and squeezed.

Lucy pulled her hand back. They had been going in circles like this for days and she still was not convinced they should abandon their farm. She had lasted over nine months, done all the farm work, birthed a baby, even shot and disposed of their cow, all without John. Alone. And now with her father here she knew they could hold on.

She leaned back and crossed her arms. "No, John. I can't do it. I won't have you give up everything we've worked for because you're worried about us. I won't have it." She glared across the table at John's frustrated face.

"Perhaps we could set this aside for now and decide later what to do." William looked from one to the other. "In the morning we have to help Frank. And I need sleep."

"You're right, William. Morning will come early. We can decide later."

Lucy stood and banged the chair in against the table. "As you wish, gentlemen." She glared at them both. "But I'm not giving in." She stormed off to the bedroom.

BEFORE DAYLIGHT John heard William rustling in the next room and stole from Lucy's warmth. He dressed quickly and tiptoed out, hoping to let her sleep longer. They had packed the day before, putting in extras they thought Frank might need to replace his possessions. The horses would be loaded down but they would still make the ten miles by noon.

He fed the fire and put the coffee pot on to heat. They wouldn't eat again until Frank's.

William had poured coffee and John was slicing some ham when he heard his son's cry. The bed creaked and Lucy whispered to the baby. *Good. She's awake.* He wanted to say goodbye.

Moments later Lucy swept the curtain aside and emerged holding the wailing Harper John against her. "He's impatient this morning." She sat in the rocker and settled the babe at her breast.

John smiled as the firelight from the open door of the stove lit up her hair. William was already outside getting the horses. He must hurry. He put his mug in the dry sink and turned back to his family. "I've got to go."

He loaded another log into the stove and closed the door. Struggling into his clothing, he kept his eyes on her. She tried to stand, with the baby at her breast, and he moved closer. "Don't get up. I can kiss the both of you."

He knelt before her and touched the blond fuzz of his son's head straining to remember everything about the scene—Lucy's beautiful auburn hair sparkling in the candlelight, her brilliant blue eyes burning into him, and Harper John's powdery baby smell filling his senses. He laid his head over the baby and against her chest and wrapped his long arms around them. He held them and held them as if he would never let go. His voice came in a whisper. "I...I...don't want to leave you both alone."

"I know, John," she whispered, and breathed deeply. "We'll be snug and cozy here in the cabin. I'll keep the door barred when I'm inside and my rifle handy when I go out." She squeezed her eyes shut and took a deep breath. "You know we love you." Her soft voice broke. "Come back safe."

"Two days. Three at the most." He pulled away from her and crossed quickly to open the door and step into the darkness. A cold blast came past him into the cabin before he yanked the door shut. "Put the bar across, Lucy," he yelled.

"I will, John," she called back but in answer heard only the wailing wind.

Chapter Twenty-Two

January, 1779

A LIGHT SNOW FILTERED through the trees as John and William took the path to Frank's farm. In spite of the snow, the horses had firm footing and the pair made good time, arriving at the farm as the sun stood overhead. As they rode past the shack with its wisping smoke, Frank's voice cut the air.

"Hello. Welcome."

"Good day." John smiled into his friend's ruddy face.

William struggled off his horse and reached out his hand in greeting. "Hello, Frank."

"Looks like you've been busy." John nodded at the neatly stacked piles of charred wood and the exposed black earth of the cabin floor. "How did your cellar fare? Did the fire destroy anything?"

"Luckily, no. Fire went up, not down through the rug-covered slab and the iron grate." He led them to the newly blanketed spot. "Used my pack blanket over the grate, and criss-crossed branches. Have to keep the varmints and the snow out."

"Where do you want to start?" William picked up a board and tossed it from the site.

"Slow down, William. Let's eat." Frank led the way to the shack.

AFTER SALT PORK AND JOHNNY CAKES, the men started cutting and trimming trees. They were too green and wet to use just yet but in the spring they would be ready for building the cabin again. This time there wouldn't be a dirt floor. Frank planned a proper raised floor with steps up to the front porch. The cabin would still be small but better than Frank and his father had had before.

John questioned whether this was the time to build when the war was going badly for the British but Frank was adamant. He would be coming back to his father's farm and that was that. By nightfall the three were ready for food and sleep.

The next day they hitched up the oxen and pulled some of the smaller logs to the cabin site. Using the crosscut saw, John and Frank sliced the logs and laid them near the cellar opening. The pile of useless charred wood, they burned.

Frank became quiet as he fed the flames. John thought he missed his father or maybe he was wondering about the wisdom of rebuilding the cabin. He, himself, thought of Lucy, alone with the baby, half a day's ride away. Both he and Frank had to rejoin the Rangers. No one would be here to protect either farm. He shuddered.

THAT NIGHT, sitting around the tiny fire in the shack, the men made a plan for the morrow. They would spend the morning burning the rest of the charred bits, cutting trees and dragging them to the site, and tidying up the space as best they could. Then John and William would strike out for home, hoping to get there before dark. No one questioned cutting trees for a new cabin.

The morning came and went and John and William were saddled up, ready to leave, about three hours after midday. They stood before the shack, holding their reins and surveying the property.

"You'll be fine here then, Frank?"

"Certainly. I'll be finer than a beaver building a dam beside a grove of birch trees." He laughed and then sobered. "I need some time alone. With my father."

"Of course. When will we see you? You know you can come any time. And that offer still stands to bring your animals and stay with us."

"Thank you for that. I'll think on it. Meanwhile that sun is moving and the day is wasting. Goodbye."

John and William mounted and made for the trail.

"Tell Lucinda thank you," Frank shouted.

The trip home was cold and monotonous. They saw no one, and nothing moved. The snowy woods were still and quiet. They trotted on bare stretches but walked the horses in the deeper snow. Daylight seeped away as they gradually made their way toward home and Lucy. Once they made a quick fire to warm themselves and rest the horses. Lukewarm coffee from their pouches revived them a little.

"I've been thinking about spring again, William. I just don't want to leave you and Lucy on that farm alone."

"I understand, John, but Lucinda is a very strong-willed young lady. You'll have a time convincing her to leave everything behind. Why not do it her way? I promise I'll get her away at the first sign of trouble. I had enough of that in Boston."

"It would give Harper John a couple more months to grow and get stronger for the journey. And I know there'll be a journey, William."

"What do you mean?"

"I didn't tell Lucy just how badly the war is going for the British. Loyalists are losing everything for their beliefs and are dying every day. I fear for our future here."

"You're right, John. Leave it to me." He struggled to his feet and untied his horse. John followed.

Chapter Twenty-Three

January, 1779

LUCY STIFFENED. Someone was at the door. Wrapping her shawl around her in the dim light she inched to the door. "John? Is that you?"

"Lucinda. Open the door. We're back."

She hoisted the heavy bar up and pulled open the door to a snow-covered man, whose bright blue eyes shone from under his frosted white eyebrows. "Father." She stepped back to let him in. "Where's John?" She glanced around him but he pulled the door closed.

"Just putting the horses in the barn. He'll be right along. Are you well?"

"Everything is perfect, now that you're both here." She relit the candle and turned. "Are you hungry?"

Before he could answer the door opened again and John came in with a blast of cold air. Lucy saw his eyes light up as he looked at her. "You must be exhausted. Did you eat?"

"Yes, but we had a time getting back with all the snow and breaking trail most of the way. There isn't a soul stirring in that cold woods. And the wind came up, blowing the snow in our faces. We couldn't see a thing. Right now I just want to sleep. You too, William?"

"Yes, that's it. My bones are aching."

WHEN LUCY ROSE to Harper John's first whimper, no one else stirred. She changed, then carried the babe to the rocker and sat to satisfy him. From the corner she heard the soft rumble of her father's snores and John's fainter breaths in the bedroom. Her men were all with her. She smiled. Resting her head against the rocker, she stroked little Harper John's cheek once more.

IN THE SEVERE WINTER that year the snow piled up so high around the cabin that the trail to the barn snaked between shoulder high snow banks. It needed constant shoveling in order to reach the animals in the barn; they had almost given up using the privy behind the cabin, because getting there was so hard.

Lucy cooked, washed and cleaned, as well as cared for the newest member of the family. John and William did chores and even went hunting for fresh meat, bringing home a stag and multiple rabbits.

With the stores in the cellar the family ate well and the hunting relieved the monotony of the same food day in and day out. But the cold was ferocious. On more than one freezing night Lucy and John snuggled their son in bed with them to keep him warm against the howling wind screaming its way into the cabin.

After such nights Lucy mopped up little piles of snow which had sifted in through gaps between the logs where the chinking had blown out and John or William would patch the holes once again.

She tried not to think of spring because John would be leaving her again. Worse, he might force the issue of her going with him to Niagara. And sometimes she wondered if she should leave. She had Harper John to think of now and couldn't picture herself escaping to the woods with him to tend. What to do? She was not at all sure.

After one particular patch of freezing cold the family looked out to blue skies and a yellow sun which had warmed the roof snow so much that little dripping icicles formed over the door. Returning from the privy Lucy stopped on her porch and turned to feel the sun's warmth on her face. She smelled that wet clean air of spring and smiled. When she stepped into the cabin, however, her face clouded over. John was packing.

"Are you leaving?" She tried to keep her voice calm.

"Aw, Lucy. I have to go. Brant will have reported where I was to the Rangers. Besides, Butler needs all of us if we're to win this war. This break in the weather is a perfect time to go." He took her hands in his. "Are you sure you don't want to come with me to Niagara? We could start again there. And, when it's safe, we could come back here."

She stared into his earnest eyes, memorizing their greenish blue shade. She wanted to keep his face in her mind. Not lose it as she had last fall.

"Say something." He squeezed her hands.

"I don't know what to say, John. I'm not sure what is best but I know travelling that long distance with a baby would be very hard. Harper John is safer here, I think. Don't you?"

"I really don't know, Lucy." He pulled her close and wrapped his arms around her. "I don't want to leave you, or him."

She heard his voice catch and pulled back to study his face again. His eyes were glistening now and she realized how hard this was for him. "I'll be fine here. We'll be safe together. Father, Harper John and I. And we'll look after the farm until you come back." She kissed his cheek and turned to the stove. "Let's get some food ready for you to take."

THEY KILLED A HEN THAT DAY to make a fragrant feast of chicken and dumplings. He left the next morning with large pieces of it wrapped in corn bread in his pouch, along with dried venison and withered apples.

Lucy was alone, as William had accompanied John in order to bring back Frank's animals to their farm where she and her father could tend them. The men would stop only long enough for Frank to get ready and then turn back along the track together driving the animals until they reached the turnoff. William would turn south toward her and the farm. John and Frank would head west searching for Butler's Rangers and the war.

Lucy knew that driving the oxen and cow from Frank's place would slow them considerably. Several days passed before she heard her father's call as he herded the animals into the yard. Together they secured the barn, full to overflowing with the extra stock.

"We'll have to get them out on the grass as soon as possible." Lucy had checked the loft. "The hay and corn just won't last with twice as many animals, even with what you brought in Frank's wagon."

"We'll be fine, I think, but if we have to, we can butcher something. One less animal to feed and more food for us." William turned toward the cabin.

"Are you hungry, father?"

"Yes, and I need to clean up. I'm looking forward to a warm night's sleep, too."

As they reached the cabin a plaintive wail came through the door. William chuckled. "Sounds like someone else is hungry, Lucinda." Lucy hurried to the bedroom.

THE DAYS LENGTHENED and the nights grew shorter as gradually the winter loosed its hold over the small farm. Slowly the snow banks shrank and the lively sound of running water dripping off the roof and trickling by the porch steps filled the days. But as darkness fell the cold grabbed hold again stifling the sounds of spring.

Looking after extra animals took time each day but the promise of spring brought a new hope to Lucy and William. Perhaps the war would end this year and John would be home. She counted on it, although to her father she never mentioned the possibility.

One evening, as she and William sat at their supper table drinking the last of the coffee, they spoke of John.

"I expect he and Frank are in Niagara now, with Butler's Rangers again."

She looked at her father. "Do you think Butler will punish them for being gone so long?"

"Oh, that's possible, but more than likely he'll be glad he didn't have to feed them all winter."

"I hope you're right."

William jerked his head to the left. "What was that?" he whispered and put his finger to his lips.

"On the porch. Someone's on the porch." Lucy jumped up, her heart thumping, as she checked the bar blocking the door.

"Calm down, Lucinda. We don't know who it is. Could be nothing." William stood quietly and reached for his gun. Lucy did the same.

"Who's there?" she called.

No answer. Then shuffling.

"Who's out there?" William barked.

Still no one answered.

William moved to the window and pulled the curtain back slightly. He let go like it was a hot coal and turned to Lucy's staring blue eyes. "Indians! A whole pack of them!"

Lucy shot a glance toward the bedroom, then looked at William. "They might be friendly. I had some here twice before who were. Let's open the door." She stepped forward and nodded at her father. He lifted the bar.

"I hope you know what you're doing." The bar fell to the floor.

Clutching her rifle, she flung open the door. The sudden gust of frigid air made her stumble backwards and she fell to the floor, her rifle clattering down beside her.

Chapter Twenty-Four

April, 1779

"HALT! WHO GOES THERE?"

John pulled Maudie up short and glanced at Frank, then back at the wall before them. They had ridden most of the day without stopping, knowing they were close to Niagara and Colonel Butler.

What they didn't know was which side now controlled the fort before them, but they had decided to take a chance. The British had held it since the French and Indian wars so most likely still did.

"John Garner, a farmer. We need shelter for the night."

"And your companion, sir?" The voice boomed down.

"Frank Smyth. A farmer also."

The horses shifted and whinnied in the silence. "Steady, girl." John stroked Maudie's neck, his eyes scanning the walls before him.

Both men had primed their weapons and held them ready across their saddles. Frank spoke softly. "We're as welcome as foxes in a henhouse." He shifted his musket.

"Hold on. We don't want to take on the whole garrison." John studied the structure. Sturdy young trees had been cut and fastened securely together. Little could be seen through the tiny gaps. The height was that of about two or three grown men and the tree tops had been angle cut to make scaling them treacherous. Huge gates reached almost as high as the walls themselves.

He could just see the heavy bar locking the gates shut. Some-one was there. The bar was rising. The gates opened and a soldier beckoned them forward.

He and Frank exchanged glances, then chucked their horses onward into the fort. They met a line of three men pointing weapons at them.

"Get down." The middle one barked the words. The others narrowed their eyes, taking aim.

His movement was slow and deliberate as he stepped to the snow-packed ground and turned to face the uniforms. British blue and red they seemed to be but he was not at all sure. Frank's horse whinnied and John sensed rather than saw his friend quiet the ani-mal in the stillness.

"Do you have a place for us to bunk for the night?"

"Who are you? And why are you out in this freezing cold?"

"I am John Garner and this is Frank Smyth, as we said. You're not flying any colours. Is this a British fort?"

The man stared right through him, then turned to Frank. "What's your story?"

"I don't have a story. I'm cold and hungry and my bones need a warm place for the night but if you can't give us that we'll be on our way." He turned to John. "Let's go."

Just then a commotion off to the right took everyone's atten-tion. "Garner. Is that you?" A man strode toward them. John smiled and passed the reins to Frank. "Indeed it is." He stepped forward to shake the hand of Joseph Brant. "Very good to see you, sir."

"What are you doing here? I thought you would be across the river with Colonel Butler." Brant led the two toward the first build-ing inside the fort. "But I am sure you need to eat before we talk."

AS DARKNESS FELL the men tended their horses and found space to sleep in the crowded guard room on the second floor of the so-called French Castle, named because it had been built by the French when they controlled Fort Niagara. There they dropped their packs and went to join Brant.

"We're not officers. I'm not sure we should be in the officers' mess." Frank spoke softly as the two stood before the open door.

"This is where we were told to meet him so this is where we go." He stepped into the room and scanned the small crowd of laughing men eating at tables. He saw no one he recognized.

"Ah, you are in good time, my friend."

He turned around to meet Brant's smile. "Yes, thank you, sir. We are not officers, only cavalry. Are you sure we should be here?"

"The food certainly looks good. I think we can stomach it." Frank's eyes widened at the mutton pie being carried on platters to the long tables.

Brant smiled. "Do not worry. You are my guests this night." He turned to Frank. "You are sounding much better than when last we met, Mr. Smyth."

"To be sure I am, although I probably would have died if your people had not cared for me. Again, I thank you."

The men sat at one of the tables and ate everything put before them: a pomate of parsnips on three grain bread, seed cake, apple dumplings and, finally, a steaming cup of chocolate. The space was warm, the food was hot. The sense of safety was welcome after so many days and nights traveling the wintry trails and sleeping under canvas trying to keep warm. And never knowing when they would be discovered by enemies and have to fight for their very survival. Yes, this was good.

But it couldn't last.

IN THE PREDAWN LIGHT the bugle blared waking John and Frank and the soldiers whose billet they shared. In a muttering, stumbling confusion, they rose and very soon stood at the river's edge, looking for the boat Brant had said last night would take them across the river.

There still remained much ice along the banks and out into the water. The crossing would not be easy. In fact, ferrymen often refused to go out in such treacherous waters. Nevertheless John's offer of coins persuaded the fur-clad, French boatman to load the two men and their horses and strike for the other side.

The craft had not been long in the water when one of the oars hit a block of ice. The crack of splintering wood cut the frigid air. All eyes were on the oar as the boatman lifted it out of the water. Useless. The end of the thing had split right off leaving only a jagged splinter.

"Looks like we'll have to swim," Frank muttered.

"Non. N'inquietez-vous pas. Paddle. J'ai un paddle." Reaching down under the gunwale the boatman brought up a stumpy hand-hewn paddle. "Need help." He thrust it at Frank.

"Give it to me." Frank took the thing in his hands. "Anybody know how to use one of these?"

"Awwh, this is no time for jokes, Frank." The horses were jittery and John stood between them trying to calm them. When he looked around, Frank had dipped the paddle and was matching strokes with the boatman's oar, not an easy task. The boat jerked to the right and to the left but eventually the two got their rhythm and made progress toward the opposite shore.

"I should get my money back on this trip, don't you think, boatman?" Frank asked.

"Just get us there safely," John sputtered. He stood before the two horses whose eyes he had covered for the trip and held them tight. He whispered all the while, soothing the horses but also himself.

"Can you not keep this boat from lurching, fellows? These horses are skittish. If they take a notion to both head for one side, they'll tip us for sure."

His arms ached with the constant tug of the horses. He kept his eyes on them for the most part, with quick checks on the far shore to gauge the boat's progress. Safety was much closer now.

Through a sudden gap between the two animals John noticed Frank's red face. In the cold morning air, his breath wisped from his open mouth. He struggled to keep his paddle in sync with the long oar of the boatman whose face was a tangle of scraggly black whiskers. A broad-brimmed hat was pulled low over the man's eyes. At least he didn't seem to be too worried. The horses sidled together again.

"Everyone all right back there? Frank? You all right?"

"Fine. Much further?" He spat the words.

"Not far. Soon land. C'est si bon." The man nodded his head in the rhythm of his oar-pulling.

Now chunks of ice were striking the boat and the horses shied again at the noise but John could see the water was open right to the dock. *Just a little longer. Hold on just a little longer.* Soon they pulled alongside the wooden dock, close to the shore.

The boatman jumped out and tied off the lines. On the treacherous ice of the rocky beach he let down the ramp and placed heavy planks side by side in the boat for the horses to climb out one at a time.

Maudie went first, the boatman leading her up the planks onto the ramp and down onto the icy shore. John took her reins and held her. Frank repeated the process with Jackie. Soon they were stepping carefully up the rocky slope to the trail, where they mounted and rode on.

"Next time we'll take a bigger boat. Or maybe just fly over like birds." Frank rasped.

"Are you all right?" John pulled up and stopped to take a good look at his friend. Frank's face was white and wet with sweat. "What is it?"

"I don't know. I think I'll be fine once we get settled in the barracks. Let's go." He motioned down the trail.

"Go ahead. I'll follow you."

The sun felt soft and warm on John's face as he followed Frank along the wooded path. He glanced up and saw a perfect blue sky dotted with white clouds, the friendly kind he and Lucy had watched as they lay in the grass one summer afternoon at the farm, a lifetime ago.

He loosened his shirt. What would their reception be at the barracks? To be thrown in the brig for the summer would make this trip useless. Hopefully their friendship with Joseph Brant would count for something. They would soon know.

Chapter Twenty-Five

THE GROUND SHOOK with the deafening roar of cannon fire. The next moment the two vaulted off their recoiling horses, and yanked them off the trail into the bushes. Heads low, John and Frank lay flat on their bellies, their darting eyes searching through the trees, until the thunderous roar died away into eerie silence.

"What do you think, Frank?"

"Can't be battle. Too quiet."

"Let's walk on."

"Better on horseback, don't you think?" He looked at John.

"You may be right. Let's go." This time John led, his musket primed and lying across his lap as he watched the trail widen into a road. A large building appeared through the trees and, in the distance, people. Soldiers. Marching across a bare expanse. Stopping on command.

Across the space shouts echoed. "Prime and load. Handle Cartridge. Prime. About."

"Halt." From the left the command came. "Name yourself." John pulled up and turned to see a pair of muskets aimed right at them held by two soldiers dug solidly into the snowy ditch five paces away.

"We're Rangers. Butler's Rangers," he answered. The guns still pointed right at them.

"This is John Garner and I'm Frank Smyth," Frank said. "We got separated from the rest of the Rangers a few months ago."

The rifles inched downwards ever so slightly. "Where?" The voice cracked out the question.

"On the march north along the Susquehanna River." Frank and John sat motionless, waiting for the guard to process this.

"Get off your horses. Head for the barracks. We'll be right behind you all the way."

Moments later they tied their horses, packed their muskets, and marched into a familiar tent where the colonel himself sat at a large plank desk, engrossed in his writing. Above him a tattered British flag stretched between two tent poles; the red was faded to a putrid pink and the blue was rotted right through while the white that was existed only in the minds of those who followed the way of the King. Colonel Butler dipped his quill into the ink-well on the table, held it mid-air, and lifted his tired eyes to the group before him.

"I wondered if we'd ever see you two again. You know desertion is a hanging offence. What have you to say for yourselves?" He sat back in his chair and stared from one to the other.

John spoke first. "We didn't desert, sir. We got left behind by accident and then we took the wrong trail."

"Indians ambushed us and stole our horses, and then more Indians attacked them and rescued us, sir." Frank's words tumbled out. "By that time we were both wounded and they took us back to their village."

"That's right, sir. Frank was pretty badly off. Didn't know if he'd make it or not."

"Who were these Indians?" Butler cut in.

"We didn't know for the longest time but it turns out they were Mohawks, sir. I met Joseph Brant there. He's across the river at Fort Niagara just now."

"We talked to him last night, sir," Frank put in.

"Sounds like you had quite an adventure and I'd like to believe you. But you haven't told me where you've been since, since…you recovered. Out with it."

"We're sorry, sir, but it was winter…and no chance of fighting." John spoke slowly.

"And we were so close to home." Frank's hands flew up as he spoke.

John glanced at Frank, then looked back into Butler's eyes. "We wanted to check on our farms. I know we should have come here, sir. Sorry, sir." His voice fell as he dropped his gaze to the floor.

He waited. The colonel was so short his body was almost hidden by the makeshift table. His hair was long and almost completely white. Black eyebrows bushed over the dark eyes trained on the pair. His large nose was red with cold or illness, John couldn't tell which, and the man seemed content to keep them standing forever. Finally his pursed lips softened and a ghost of a smile flickered.

"As it happens, Garner, and you, too, Smyth, we have had too many to feed here this past winter. You both look healthy enough, healthy enough. Most likely you did the right thing. And your, your horses?"

"Yes, sir. The Mohawks had them and gave them back to us. They are in fine shape."

"Good enough, men. Welcome. Welcome back. You can go." He dipped his quill in the ink and focused on his writing.

Dismissed, the two headed for the door but before they were out, Butler spoke again.

"I hope you found all well at home?"

John turned back. "Yes, sir. I did. I have a son."

The colonel smiled at John and nodded, then turned to Frank. "What about you, Smyth?"

"My farm was taken over by riffraff and my cabin burned." He paused. "They murdered my father, sir."

"I am sorry to hear that, sorry to hear, Smyth." He rose and strode to them by the door. Putting his hand on Frank's arm, he spoke. "We all have our sad stories in this war, son. But it will get better with good men like you fighting."

"Thank you, sir."

The colonel stood for a moment, nodding, then walked to the table again. "Dismissed."

JOHN AND FRANK soon settled into life with the Rangers, renewing acquaintances and taking stock of Loyalist recruits who had joined over the last few months. Food was scarce and more than once he thought he should have stayed longer with Lucy where there was plenty.

They spent their days drilling, mending their uniforms, eating what food there was, and speculating on the campaign to come. It was 1779 and the war had been raging for three years. The men were tired and ready to move on with their lives. Many had no home to return to, but others, like he and Frank, longed to finish the fighting and go back to their farms in New York. They were beginning to wonder, though, if that would ever happen.

John would have been much happier if Lucy, her father and the baby had come with them to Niagara. She could be a stubborn woman.

The days grew longer but the food supply grew shorter. As the winter stores of corn were long gone, the men had to survive almost entirely on meat. Hunting details set off into the forests daily to find game to feed the community of Rangers at Butler's Barracks.

Sickness assailed many, the bloody flux being most prevalent. John and Frank were lucky to have eaten well for most of the winter and thus avoided illness. Everyone wondered when new supplies would come to the beleaguered settlement until, one sunny day, sails appeared to the east on the lake's blue horizon.

The barracks was alive with activity. Details formed to unload the barrels and tubs from the hold of the ship. Soon the cooks were preparing salt pork and dried apples with johnnycakes and the season's first maple syrup.

....

As the men sat eating this spring bounty, talk died into a split second of sudden silence before they staggered to attention. Outlined against the sunlight in the open door of the barracks stood the stocky form of Colonel Butler.

"Easy, men." The short man stepped to the centre of the long room. "As you were. I am pleased to see you eating well again." He looked from one to another, his eyes pausing on each pallid face staring at him. "We'll take some time, some time, to get you all healthy again and then head out to settle this war. I expect there are many of you who are tired and just want it to be over."

Heads nodded as the men started a low buzz of agreement. Butler shifted on his feet and absently lifted his hand to his hair. "We'll take some time to get you healthy. Yes. We'll take some time to get you healthy." The words tumbled out. "Then we'll be ready for battle." Butler turned and strode to the stairs, followed by his aide. They pounded up to the little used storage room which had been built for the Colonel, although he preferred his tent in the open air.

"He seemed surprised to see the sickness, didn't he, John?" Frank turned to his friend who had sat once again.

"I saw that. He was ready to announce plans but the state of the men shocked him. Maybe he's been spending too much time in that tent with his papers and not enough with the troops."

"Maybe."

"I wonder where we're going."

"We'll hear soon enough. I just want this whole thing to be over. I don't want to spend another winter as a Ranger."

"And we got to spend most of this one at home." John shook his head as he finished off his plate of food. "Look at the rest of these poor fellows."

ONE FINE DAY IN APRIL the orders came. The Rangers were on the move again. The spring sun shone on the lines of men snaking down to the river for transport to the Fort Niagara side. The boat was much larger than the one in which John and Frank had crossed before and the horses easily stepped up the gangplank for the quick crossing.

Along the track toward the eastern settlements the men marched, although no one in the ranks knew exactly where they were headed. They slipped into the old drill of marching, stopping, marching, stopping for the night, sleeping, marching again, eating—it all became rote.

No one bothered them. The Americans were somewhere else, it seemed, leaving the Rangers to penetrate the land looking for the enemy.

The spring rains started and the trail became a slithery sea of mud. The men slipped to their knees and even fell right down in the goo. Over and over they fell and staggered to their feet again lifting their faces so the rain might wash them.

Warm weather had accompanied the rain so that cold was not a problem till the night. When the halt was called, if they were lucky, the soldiers were able to build huge fires to dry themselves. If the rains were too intense, though, the men had to settle for cold food and a cold tent with no way to dry off. The shivers would come in the night as the temperatures dipped to near freezing again.

From time to time a messenger brought news of faraway events, such as the Loyalist raid on coastal towns in Connecticut, or the success of militia men picking off Rangers scouting ahead, but it all seemed not to matter in the watery minds of Butler's Rangers. They concentrated on surviving, hoping that there would come a time when they would be dry again.

And come it did. The Rangers trudged one behind the other through the forest as the sun broke through the dripping canopy of trees. The track was narrow here, ideal for ambush, but no one thought of the danger, so happy were they to see the blue sky and feel the warming rays of the sun.

The command came to make camp early that day and the men set about making a semi-permanent camp on a large flat hilltop from which they could see the valley to the east and west. That night the fire lit the faces of men finally dry and full of a good supper. They talked and laughed and made wry faces as they boasted about surviving this punishing march.

"YOU FELLOWS ON HORSEBACK HAVE IT EASY."

The words flew at John as he walked back with his plate of food to his and Frank's tent. He glanced toward the sound but kept moving. "I guess you're right, although finding food for the horses isn't always easy." He kept his voice low.

"Ah, you weren't even here all winter. You don't know what it feels like to be starving and freezing all at the same time. Pair of pussies, you two are." The man's voice rose as he stood and tottered toward John. He stopped and turned.

"If we'd been here for the winter that would have meant even less food for the rest of you. The colonel is glad he didn't have to care for us and our horses. And that's the end of it." He glanced at the drunken soldier—someone he didn't know—and moved off. His food was getting cold.

"Mighty fine to see you, John, tho' I'm not sure what you'd be doin' with the likes of that trash back there." By the light of the fire Nat's eyes twinkled.

"Good evening, Nat. Can you sit a while?" John pointed to a nearby log. "Can't promise how dry it'll be, though."

"I'll jist stand a moment. Wouldn't want to get folks all in a flutter. Jist wanted to welcome y'all back."

"That's kind of you. Thank you, Nat."

"Come to teach us some more of that voodoo magic of yours, Nat?" Frank hadn't forgotten the smallpox scare.

"No, sir. Jist come to pass the time with ya both. Good to see ya made it through the winter so well. Much better'n we did."

"Perhaps this will all be a memory by the time next winter comes. What do you think?" John stood to pack away his plate and spoon.

Nat glanced around and then spoke softly. "I's afraid we might not win this'n, John. I'm thinkin' that land around the barracks on the other side of the river might end up home to us all." His hands flew up. "But what does a old black man know?"

Frank stared at Nat. "Where's your home, Nat?"

"Ain't got no home now. It's long since burned and my folks buried, all 'cause of this cursed war. I'll be startin' new when it's over."

"Sorry to hear that, Nat, but you won't be alone. If the British lose this we'll all be hightailin' it to Canada somewhere, anywhere, to escape the Americans." His voice trailed off as he thought of Lucy and Harper John, and Lucy's father. He grabbed a branch and poked furiously at the fire, every spot he touched leaping high with angry flames. "I just want it over," he whispered.

THE NEXT DAY THE RANGERS dug in to their new camp, building trenches and cutting trees for protective pikes pointing outward toward any attackers. The fortifications would give a measure of security for a few days or however long Butler kept them here on this hilltop.

The weather had improved and the sunny days dried up the camp and lifted the men's spirits. They thought of maybe winning the war and getting their properties back again. The food was plentiful for the moment what with army stores and the abundance of wildlife in the area.

As the season progressed the men were on the lookout for new shoots of edible plants to supplement their fare. Soon wee bits of dandelion and lamb's quarters provided greens for their meals and tiny white strawberries pushed forth promising a treat when they ripened.

The scouts went in and out of the encampment bringing their messages to Butler but, for the most part, not much was happening and the Rangers were kept busy just drilling and training on the ridge. Occasionally news would filter in of the exploits of other Ranger companies. The men would become anxious to get moving and accomplish something. The war would never be over if they just camped on a hill all summer.

On a cool day toward the end of July, Niles Maycock came pounding into camp, jumped off his horse and, handing her off to a Ranger, ran to the colonel's tent. He was admitted immediately.

"Wonder what that's all about?" Frank and John were brushing their horses.

"Haven't seen Maycock for a long while. Maybe he came past the farm." John's hand stopped as he stared across Maudie's back at the colonel's closed tent.

"I expect we'll know soon enough," Frank replied, and even as he spoke the tent flap opened and Maycock emerged.

"He's moving slower now. Maybe we can catch him before he rides out again." John threw the words over his shoulder as he walked toward Maycock.

"Mr. Maycock. Mr. Maycock."

His remounting interrupted, the dusty man turned to the noise. "Garner. How are you?" He reached to shake John's hand.

Maycock's clothes were ragged, his hat a scrunched and well-used piece of felt, and his once-sparkling eyes, although still kind, had lost their luster. The war was taking its toll. "How are you, sir?"

"Well, thank ye. Well. Although I'd be a lot better if this war were over. I've got saddle sores in places I didn't know I had." Peering closely at John, he added, "How's that wife of yours?"

"I was just going to ask if you had come that way, but I guess you didn't, did you?"

"Actually I did come by your farm again. Is that where you left her?"

"Yes." John moved closer. "Didn't you see her?"

"I didn't see her, and what's more the place was deserted. I didn't see a living thing."

Chapter Twenty-Six

April, 1779

STEPPING OVER LUCINDA'S STILL FORM, William filled the doorway. He raised his rifle, ready to shoot into the mass of Indians crowding onto the porch in the dimming evening light. Black hair and feathers, war paint and naked bodies all threatened to overwhelm him as he breathed in the stench of tar and sweat.

No one moved, neither the Indians, nor William. He trained his gun on the muscular bare chest of a black-eyed brave inches from the end of his rifle.

"What do you want?" He spat the words into the open air.

Silence. As in a motionless parlor tableau everyone stood still like time had stopped. Over the pounding of his heart, William heard a faint cry from the bedroom. He clenched his trigger finger a little tighter as the Indians looked at each other. Lucy shifted behind him. She was coming out of her swoon. He spoke again.

"Who are you? What do you want?"

The brave before him glanced to the side before speaking. "Oneida. Oneida tribe. Hungry."

"Is that all? You're far from home, aren't you?"

"We go home but need food." His eyes took on a pitiful look to match his pleading tone. He looked from side to side and the others nodded.

Harper John wailed again but this time he didn't stop. Lucy sat up and glanced toward the door. She got to her feet, grabbing the door to keep from keeling over again. "Father? Is everything all right?" She glanced at the bedroom curtain.

"They want food, Lucy."

She looked at her father's face, his pointed gun and then at the band on the porch. "We can give them food." Turning, she motioned the Oneidas back. She stood fast and stared at the band. Slowly they moved off the porch.

"Wait here. I'll bring food." She stepped back into the cabin, William backing up beside her, his gun now at waist level.

She whipped the door shut and leaned against it for a moment while William moved to the window. Ignoring Harper John's wailing she set about gathering bread, the last of the corn, and a large chunk of boiled meat. It would have to do. She needed to keep enough for their own use until the crops came on.

"Do you think that will be enough to satisfy them?" William watched his daughter's movements. When she had tied the food into a large bundle she nodded to her father. Stepping to the door she opened it with one hand and passed the bundle to the nearest brave. William held his gun at the ready.

"This is all we can spare. I hope it is enough to get you home." Lucy passed the bundle over and stepped back.

"Good. Very good. Thank you." The man nodded and turned to his comrades. In the light of the doorway they tore open the bundle and latched onto the food. The bread fell to the black ground but was soon snatched up and torn into bits for sharing by the hungry men. She edged back into the house and closed the door. William dropped the bar in place and took up his watch at the window.

"I'm coming, Harper John, I'm coming." She took a deep breath and headed for the screeching baby.

HOURS LATER SHE LAY IN BED unable to sleep, still thinking about the Indians. For all her fear of them they had not been nearly as dangerous as some of the non-Indians she had met of late. She shud-dered at the thought of Jacob Daeger and the blood on the floor washed clear away but still darkly red in her mind's eye.

And those poachers who had killed Frank's father and threat-ened to kill him. Her arms tightened across her chest as she saw again Frank's shaking form at the table as he relived his father's funeral pyre.

She had been luckier than some. That was for sure. Her father was sleeping in the next room. What would have happened if he had not been here when she fainted? She didn't want to think about it. She forced herself to listen only to Harper John's sweet snuffling sounds as he slept and soon she drifted away as well.

All was dark but safe in the cabin with the fire banked and the door barred, the window covered and locked and the water pail waiting for morning. Nothing moved but the steady march of the moonbeams slitting through the shutters, keeping watch, keeping watch.

THE RAUCOUS CROWING OF THE ROOSTER lifted Lucy from her sleep and her pillow until she realized what it was and sank back. She lay quiet hoping Harper John would sleep longer but he seemed to be on the same schedule as the rooster.

Her father rattled about in the next room and the faint smell of cof-fee drifted to her nostrils. She leaned over the crib and smiled at her baby's bright eyes on her, little fists waving his joy at the new day.

"Good morning, my little boy. Good morning." She snatched him up and felt his sopping clothing. "We'll have to get you changed, won't we?" She slipped off the wet clothing, swabbed his tiny bottom and tied him into dry things. "That's better, isn't it?"

She pressed him against her and nuzzled his rosy cheeks, then held him with one arm while she swished back the curtain with the other.

"Good morning, father. How did you sleep?"

William sat at the table working with his gun. His wan face was pinched and drawn. Lucy hesitated. "What is it?"

"Look outside."

She moved to the window and cracked open the shutters. "My God." She snapped back and faced her father. "What happened?"

William had finished with his gun and stood to join her looking out at the yard. In the dim light of dawn, bodies were strewn in the grass. Indians. They hadn't left.

"Are they dead?" Lucy whispered.

"I don't know. I don't think so." Even as they spoke first one, then another of the Indians stirred.

"Why didn't they leave?" Harper John's cries forced Lucy to the chair where she gave him her breast. "I thought they were gone last night."

"I don't know, but I suspect they want more from us. Is your rifle ready?" William turned to Lucy.

"Yes. Do you think we'll need to fight?" She held the baby tighter and felt tears start as she stared at her father.

"Perhaps they'll just wake and go, Lucinda. Don't worry."

They lapsed into silence. The only sound was the baby suckling and gurgling, unaware of the danger. William kept watch at the window while Lucy's eyes stared off into the unknown.

Her vivid imagination was a hindrance just now as visions of tomahawks and knives, bloody scalps and fire-wielding savages circling the cabin flooded her thoughts. Absently she stroked Harper John's head. She had to protect him. She just had to.

Tears, first one then a stream of them, silently dripped down Lucy's cheeks. With the corner of Harper John's blanket she dabbed at her face. She touched his cheeks and smiled at his blue-green eyes staring at her. "We'll keep you safe, little one. We'll keep you safe."

At the sound William turned toward her. "They're leaving, I think. Lucky thing, too. We can't fight nine Indians." He turned back to his watching.

"They're going in the barn. What are they doing?" William pulled open the shutters to better see. "They're taking the cow. Frank's cow. I've got to stop them." He moved to lift the bar on the door.

Lucy blocked the door. "Father. You can't go alone. Let them have the cow."

"No. I have to try."

"And leave us here undefended if they murder you?" Lucy was on her feet now and Harper John, eyes wide, lay in her arms, motionless.

William stopped dead and dropped his hands to his sides. His head fell. "You're right." Slowly he replaced the bar and moved again to the window. "They're leaving with the cow, but that's all. I suppose we should feel glad of that."

"One less animal to feed." Lucy spit out the words and sat down again with the baby. "Are they really gone?"

"I think so. I'll go out in a bit and check on everything. You keep the door locked while I'm gone. Make sure."

"You don't have to worry about that, Father. I've spent the last year making very sure that bar is across." Her voice rose. "And I'm getting tired of it. When is this war ever going to be over? I don't want to spend my days afraid for my very life. And for John's life. And Harper John's. For yours, for everyone's. I just want the world to go back to what it was," Lucy cried, and Harper John began to wail, a simmering, smoldering sound which rose to a wrenching, piercing scream.

William moved quickly to them and knelt by the chair. His hand barely grazed her cheek, then her child's red face. This tenderness was new and she immediately began to feel calmer. "I'm sorry, Father."

"There, there. Nothing to be sorry about."

Presently William gave Harper John one last pat and slowly got to his feet. "We'll all be fine, Lucinda. You'll see." He took up his position at the window again and stood gazing out for a very long time.

Lucy sat on with Harper John long after he had nursed, burped and fallen into a contented sleep. She held his tiny body next to hers comforted by the calm rhythm of his breathing. Did he know where he was or that his dada wasn't there? Did he miss John as she did? Hopefully not.

Rocking the chair forward she tipped to her feet and carried the babe to his crib. Time to start the day. As she came back into the room, she glanced at William. Still and silent he now sat, his grayed head bent, staring at the table before him. She touched his shoulder.

"Oh. I'll be going out for the chores now," he said. He grabbed his coat.

"Be careful, Father." She reached up and kissed his cheek, then pulled open the door.

Chapter Twenty-Seven

April, 1779

THE SUN WAS FULL UP and shining across the yard with a blistering heat unusual for late April. William stood on the porch and listened to the bar slide into place while he stared around the yard. All was as it should be. He moved along the path to the barn every nerve ready to pop at the least little noise.

The hens were cackling in the chicken coop anxious to be fed, and the neighing of his horse called him to the barn. He paused at the door. The Indians had closed it to keep the other animals inside. Amazing. Why didn't they steal all the animals? And what made them close the barn door?

His gun at the ready William stepped into the gloom and waited a moment for his eyes to adjust. He let the oxen out to the yard and carried hay to the manger for them. Now he breathed easier and concentrated on the rest of the chores, happy even to muck out the pens as he considered what this day might have been.

IN AN ATTEMPT TO LIGHTEN HER MOOD and ease her mind, Lucy hummed as she prepared their first meal of the day. Harper John slept soundly. She felt the familiar relief that his needs were looked after but more the utter joy that the Indians hadn't been savage and they were all safe.

The Oneidas had not sided with the rest of the Iroquois Confederacy. They were fighting on the side of the Americans. That made them enemies of the British and the Loyalists. She felt lucky they had only stolen Frank's cow. Surely he would understand.

Setting yet another bowl of stew on the table for their breakfast, she slipped to the unshuttered window to check on her father. He was coming along the path. She lifted the bar and let him in, breathing in the sweet heat of the day and his sweaty work smell.

"You're just in time for food, father." She slid into the chair opposite.

"I've been thinking, Lucinda. Maybe we should have gone with John to Fort Niagara."

Lucy studied her father's furrowed brow over his troubled eyes. "I know. I've been wondering myself."

"The trouble is that when we're locked inside the cabin all anyone has to do is set a fire and we're done for. Maybe we should leave this country like so many of the Loyalists have already done." He paused with his spoon in mid air. "We could go to Fort Niagara. A lot of British supporters have already gone there."

"It's such a long way, father. How would Harper John make the trip?" Lucy dropped her spoon and leaned back.

"We could take the oxen, one pair to sell and the other pair to pull the wagon with all we could put on top. We could do it, Lucinda."

"Maybe we could, but how would John find us?" Lucy's voice caught.

"We'd leave a note here for him. Somewhere only he would look. And we would probably be there before he even knew we had left the farm. I think we could do it, Lucinda."

"But should we? If we go, John will lose everything." Lucy had jumped up and now stood looking out the window. Her voice was a whisper. "I love this little farm, father, and John does, too."

"I know, Lucinda, but we are in danger here. If we don't go, John could lose the farm and you and his son as well. He would want me to protect you. This is the best way I can think of to do that, daughter."

"Just let me think about it. I need to be sure." Lucy sat again. "I need to be sure." Slowly she lifted her spoon and ate.

FOR THE REST OF THE DAY William left Lucy alone as he took stock of their possessions and decided what they could safely take. He tightened the wagon wheels and applied a coat of bear grease to the axles.

He planned to follow John's path along the river toward Niagara. Maybe they'd even find John and the Rangers along the way. He had no clear idea how much they could take but would pack the wagon as full as possible. Driving an extra pair of oxen would be cumbersome but they could be useful if the wagon got stuck in the mud. Hopefully, before they got too far, he would find a buyer for them.

When supper time came William found his daughter strangely quiet. She set the food in front of him with not a word of conversation. He let her be and calmly studied his plate of food.

He was getting tired of stew but knew that food on their trip would be much less inviting. Dried meat, salted pork, the odd rabbit he might kill would be the staples, along with fresh greens they might find along the way. His mind raced with the enormity of the journey.

"A ha'penny for your thoughts, father."

William jerked up to Lucinda's staring eyes. Her eyebrows were up. How long he had been day dreaming. "Oh, sorry, my dear. I was just mulling and musing."

"I've decided we should go. And the sooner the better, I think."

"Very good, Lucinda." He relaxed and reached for both her hands. "I am glad you agree."

"When, father?"

"As soon as we can. The day after tomorrow? Can you be ready by then?"

"I think so. We'll have to decide what to take and what to leave behind." Her voice broke and he knew she was thinking of her dear possessions, her stove, her mother's things.

"How will we ever decide what to take?"

"We'll do the best we can. We can start first thing in the morning, or tonight, if you wish." William patted Lucy's hand. "It's all for the best, Lucinda. All for the best."

THEY SPENT THE NEXT DAY deciding what to take and what to leave behind or try to sell on the way. The stove was just too big with all their other things but they opted to take her chest filled with a few mementos such as the silver spoon and her mother's buttons along with the baby's clothing. John's chair would go on top of the load with the table and two of the side chairs. The bed, the buffalo robes and the blankets were necessities as were their few pots, pans and dishes. After all, they had to have something to start a new life in Niagara. As the candle began to sputter she fell into the rocking chair, exhausted but strangely exhilarated.

"Time to rest, father."

He finished tying the knot around the pack of blankets. "You're right, Lucinda. Tomorrow will be a long day." He moved toward the door, lifted the bar and turned to his daughter. "Do you want to use the outhouse first?"

"Thank you, father, I do. Can you check it?" Her meaning was clear. She still expected the Indians to return.

William nodded, reached for his loaded rifle and cracked open the door. Listening for a moment, he peered into the black night. "All's well, Lucinda. All's well." He motioned for her to bring the lantern she had lit and walked her to the privy, then stood waiting a few paces away.

He peered into the clear sky and tried to name the stars he knew. The big dipper stood out against the inky night. A few others seemed brighter than their partners as they twinkled across the sky. There was so much beauty and order up above. Why not here below, he wondered?

Lucy joined him, handed over the light and waited as he walked to the privy. When he came back, she, too, studied the sky. He stood beside her and put his arm around her shoulders. "It's a beautiful sight, is it not?"

"Oh, father. I am so sorry to leave. And it's the only home John ever had." She trembled against him. Her voice shook. "I want to remember it all. The sky, the stars, the moonlight over the barn roof. And the smell of spring on the evening air."

She looked toward the cabin. "The tiny glow at the window looks so peaceful and safe I still wonder if we're right to leave." She sniffed and laid her head against him. "But we will make a new home, won't we? And John will find us and we'll all be together." She moved toward the cabin. "Surely at Niagara we'll be safe."

William followed. "Yes. We will," he said, and wondered how he could ever promise that. There was a very long journey between this little cabin and safety. He caught his breath and held it, against the tight pain in his chest.

Chapter Twenty-Eight

MORNING CAME EARLY AND CLEAR, bringing a hint of excitement to the little cabin. Even the rooster's crowing took on an urgency it hadn't had before. Lucy felt it herself. She nursed Harper John and urged him to finish quickly. She had so much to do.

William had already gone to the barn to feed and prepare the animals. He had made slatted boxes for the rooster and hens. Some would not make the whole trip. They would be food along the way. When the family reached journey's end they would still have a pair left to start a new flock.

While the chickens pecked and the oxen munched, William and Lucy loaded their possessions on the wagon which sat forlornly in the middle of the yard waiting to be hitched up and pointed toward the road ahead. She ran back and forth adding a pillow here, a pot there.

William loaded on the single furrow plough. The handles stuck out the back of the wagon at an odd angle resembling a rough-hewn clothes rack. She tied a cloth near the top like a kerchief and they laughed at the effect. They hitched up one pair of oxen to pull and tied the other behind the wagon. Finally, she plucked Harper John from his cradle and William tied it to the load.

He studied the hot sun and turned to her. "We had best get started before the sun gets any higher, daughter."

She handed Harper John over and strode back into the cabin for a last look. In minutes she appeared at the doorway holding something. "We almost forgot this," she called and strode to the wagon to pass her treasure to him. It was the patchwork quilt.

She turned to the cabin. Her back was straight and her head high but her heart was a pumping lump in her chest. How could she leave? Would she and John ever find their way back to their fresh new life as it had been here? She stood a moment, took a hard breath, and swiped at her eyes. Then she stepped back, straightened up and turned toward her father and the wagon.

He kept his eyes on the oxen as she climbed up beside him and took the baby into her arms.

"I'm ready, father. Let's go make a new future."

ALONG THE TRAIL she had walked so many times, the oxen pulled their wagon load of possessions. William's horse and Frank's oxen brought up the rear. Slowly they made their way from tree to tree, from gorse bush to thorn thicket and across open spots of warm sunshine. The wagon bumped through huge holes and over fallen branches, stopping at times when William had to clear them out of the way.

Lucy held Harper John in her arms to soften the bumps but, jolted awake, he whimpered often and couldn't settle. They stopped for her to nurse him and all were glad of the respite even though it slowed their progress.

They stopped in a small clearing and prepared for their first night on the trail. William spread the buffalo robe under the wagon and rigged blankets hanging from the sides to provide shelter underneath for them to sleep. While he tended the animals, Lucy warmed stew over the fire.

Before long they had eaten their supper, banked the fire, and crawled under the wagon, where Lucy snuggled Harper John to her breast. As she closed her eyes she felt again the bumpy ride that day. She was still in the wagon and her body just kept lurching as she held on to the baby. The feeling came in waves, broken only by the sounds of the night outside their small refuge.

Whoo-oo-oo. Her eyes sprang open and she gripped the blanket. Just an owl. Her father's steady breathing came from the other end of the wagon. It soothed her and she relaxed into sleep once more. This time she heard nothing until morning when the rooster roused them all to another day of travel.

SLOWLY BUT STEADILY William and Lucy made their way west by northwest toward Niagara where they hoped to find sanctuary with other Loyalists like themselves. The rhythm of their days became second nature, the only variation coming with rain or meeting someone else on the trail.

She became used to the shifting of the wagon and her body easily responded to the jolts. She could even hold Harper John and nurse him as he, too, adjusted to their changing circumstances.

The little wagon wound along the river trail, snaking its way between tree-covered mountains that seemed to reach into the sky. Lucy was mesmerized by the beauty of the sun streaming through white clouds in a brilliant blue sky above the hills on the horizon. Sometimes, as far as they could see, they were surrounded by green topped off with a roof of blue sky.

Of course the sun shone hotter as the days went by, causing William to roll up his sleeves and Lucy, from time to time, to lift her skirts and let the breeze cool her legs.

Harper John fidgeted in her arms so much that she found a way to rig his cradle with the patchwork quilt as a fluffy bottom that softened the bumps. He seemed happier sleeping there just behind their seat with a net of cheese cloth over him to keep off the pesky flies and the sun.

On one such day about a fortnight into the journey, the little wagon had left the mountains behind and trundled along a great flat plain. In the distance as Lucy watched, the afternoon sun seemed to be boiling up the horizon.

"Look at that, Father." She pointed ahead. "Clouds are rising from the earth, up into the sky."

"I can't see that far away, Lucinda. Describe it for me."

"Well, it's just that, except the clouds are getting bigger all the time. I think it's someone coming."

"Are you sure?" William squinted into the distance. "Get the guns ready."

Lucy reached under the seat and pulled up their rifles. First one, then the other, she checked then sighted into the distance. By now she could make out four riders coming quickly and her heart pounded in her chest as she watched. She took a quick glance at Harper John. Asleep.

The horsemen came on.

"They're not soldiers, father. No uniforms."

"They could be militia or soldiers without uniforms. Let's hope they're not more of those ruffians who murdered Frank's father."

His tone was soft but something about it made Lucy glance at him. His eyes were almost shut against the sun and his 'worry' vein pulsed rapidly. Trying to see ahead he held his mouth in a type of tight grin with nary an ounce of humor in it. The angry red welt on his cheek, scarred over from the hot tar of Boston, burned bright. She turned away.

Now she could see the riders clearly. Black. Or dusty grey clothes. Even their blurry faces were dirty smears. Their horses frothed at the mouth, straining under the heat and the weight at such a speed. The first rider raised his arm and they all slowed.

William pulled the oxen to a stop and took his rifle into his lap, his finger on the trigger.

"Good afternoon, gentlemen." His voice was low but firm.

The four riders stopped at the leader's signal. He walked his horse towards the wagon, alongside the oxen, and jerked to a stop scant inches from her. As a cloud of dust washed over her, Lucy covered her nose and drew back. He had not washed in a long time.

"Good day, sir. Ma'am." He looked from William to Lucy, his eyes holding hers just a moment too long. "Where are you off to?" He looked back at William.

"We're travelling. And you? Why are you hurrying so quickly?"

"We're just out for a little pleasure ride, aren't we gentlemen?" They laughed and nodded. The leader moved his horse a few steps closer. "Where would you be going with a wagon load of all your possessions? You can tell us."

"We're settlers, heading further west."

"I see you have a cradle. Is there a baby in it?" He leered at Lucy.

"Yes, he's sleeping just now." She spoke firmly as she stared back at the man.

"We'd best be on our way. We have a long way to go before nightfall. I wish you good day." One hand holding the rifle William picked up the reins with the other and chucked the oxen onward. The riders moved aside.

"Pleasant journey, ma'am." The leader sang out the words, making her skin crawl.

William cracked the reins hurrying the oxen. "Good day, gentlemen."

As they pulled away Lucy sat sideways and watched the riders regroup. They seemed reluctant to move on but finally the leader slowly raised his hat in a mock salute and turned east once more.

"They're going."

William let out a breath. "Thank the Lord. Let's see how much distance we can put between us, shall we, daughter?" He smiled at Lucy and released his grip on the rifle but he kept it across his lap. She did the same and they rode on in silence. She turned often to look back and not just at Harper John.

Chapter Twenty-Nine

July, 1779

"WHAT DO YOU MEAN? I left her and the baby and her father safe on the farm." John grabbed the bridle of Maycock's horse. "Tell me what you saw there."

Niles Maycock sighed and swung down off his horse. "Could we just sit a moment, Garner?"

John felt his face flush. He spoke again, more softly. "I beg your pardon. Come this way." He hurried Maycock toward his tent, Frank following.

"Let me hold your horse, Maycock." Frank reached for the reins while John pointed to stumps before the fire pit. They sat.

"What did you see?" he croaked.

"Well now, Garner, I didn't see much at all. When I saw your wife the last time, she gave me a letter for you but I'm afraid it is long gone."

John grabbed Maycock's arm. "What do you mean, the last time?"

"I was there late last year and she gave me a letter for you. But I've lost it." He stared at John. "I'm sorry. This last time the place was deserted. No animals in the barn. The cabin was cleared right out. Only that great stove left inside looking lonely and cold."

"Was there, ah, was there any, ah, sign of fighting or the like?"

"No. Definitely not. The farm was abandoned. As if they had plenty of time to pack up and move out. I'm surprised some of those farm-stealin' ruffians hadn't moved in, but there was no sign of anyone."

"Maybe they decided to follow you, John. Because of the war," Frank said.

"Or maybe they started for Niagara but never made it. When were you there, Maycock?" John peered at the bedraggled man.

"Must be about three fortnights ago, along about the first week in June."

"And crops? Was there any planting done?"

"No. The land had not seen a plough."

"That means they left early on, maybe soon after you did, John." Frank looked away. "Maybe Lucy's father took her somewhere else, or…" He stopped.

"Or maybe they're in trouble," John said.

"I'm that sorry to bring you this bad news, Garner, but I have to be going. I will keep a sharp lookout for them."

"Yes. Thank you for the information, Mr. Maycock. I do appreciate it."

Taking the reins from Frank, Niles Maycock gentled his horse and put his boot into the stirrup, paused a second, then made the effort to mount. Once up, he looked at John. "I wish you well, Garner."

He pulled to the right and the horse lumbered off. Maycock's shoulders were hunched and his head drooped low but he dug his heels into the horse and galloped out of the camp.

"There's a man with a lot on his mind, John. He has really changed in the last year and a half." Frank turned. "You're awfully quiet. What do you want to do?"

"What can I do, Frank? I have no idea where she's gone. The colonel wouldn't let me go after her anyhow." He turned away and stomped off.

THAT NIGHT HE LAY, SLEEPLESS, on his straw mattress and pictured Lucy as he had left her. Sitting in the rocker with Harper John. He thought of their time on the farm before he joined the Rangers, of their walks in the woods and that last one. His body remembered, too, and the thought of Lucy beneath him near the waterfall stole into his mind.

He swiped at his eyes and rolled over, away from Frank's rough breathing. He had to find her. And Harper John. He would speak to the colonel in the morning.

"I NEED YOU HERE, GARNER. Do you not think every man here has a story about his family? Most of them know their wives and children have been captured, killed or worse and, still, they fight, they fight on to save this country from those patriots. Patriots." He spat in the spittoon. They're ruffians. Just lowborn ruffians. And that Washington doesn't know, doesn't know what he's doing, leading his gang against the British. Against the British. The best army in the world." He sat at the small desk and stared into space.

The silence grew. John watched the colonel's lined face and hunched shoulders atop that corpulent body. He sat short behind the desk. He would not be intimidating at all were it not for his flashing eyes. Butler's brow was creased and his set jaw clenched his remaining teeth. The man's face softened as, once more, he focused on John.

"Sorry, Garner. I understand your worry." His eyes stared into John's own. "I can't let you go. We have orders, and so many are sick. I need every healthy man." The Colonel stood up. The interview was over.

Outside he fixed his eyes on the orderly camp, the Rangers going to and fro, horses being groomed, straw mattresses being shaken, the clank of the pots as the cook prepared another monotonous meal. But he saw none of it. His feet took him to their tent where he perched on a stump. Stowing away on the ship and sailing to New York with hardly a thing to eat had been frightful but this was worse. He could do nothing to help Lucy. She might be lost or captured or dead. And he could do nothing. Head in his hands, he barely held back the frustration.

Elaine Cougler

"She's strong, John. She'll be all right." Frank spoke softly right next to him.

"With a baby?" He stared at Frank. "I'm afraid for them."

"What do you want to do?"

"Butler says he has orders. We may be marching. If we're wounded or worse, who will look for them? Who?"

THAT AFTERNOON, AS THEY DID EVERY DAY, the Rangers drilled in the clear space behind the tents. Though they were cavalry, John and Frank stomped and sweated with the others but John's mind strayed far from the parade ground.

He thought of Lucy, imagining where she might be, even attempting to talk to her in his mind. Maybe her whereabouts would come to him. Maybe she was calling to him even as he thought of her.

"Garner. Attention. Where are you, man?" The sergeant's bark cut into John's thoughts and he struggled to keep with the others. Beside him he felt rather than heard Frank's comforting presence.

Would Frank desert with him? Should he ask him? More than likely he wouldn't be able to keep Frank from coming. Well, that was all right. They were a team. He wondered when to leave, and where to start looking. How could he pick up Lucy's trail? Maybe he should just stay here till he heard from her.

Eventually the day's drill was over. John and Frank took their horses and rode out with the other cavalry to exercise the animals and to provide an escort for the cook's detail filling the water barrels at the river. Frank came up alongside John. They rode in silence. Where the trail narrowed, the horses were almost touching and Frank turned to him.

"What are you thinking?" His voice was low.

"I cannot decide what to do. If I go looking for them, I don't know which way to go. They could be anywhere." Desperate, John looked at Frank. "What do you think?"

"Let's talk tonight. Alone." He cracked his reins and moved ahead.

HE WAS ALMOST FINISHED his evening meal by the time Frank finally made it back to the fire and sat with him to eat.

"This salty stuff is a touch nasty, tonight. My lips are about to shrivel up and die. If I never eat salt pork again, I'll be happy." Frank grimaced as he took another mouthful.

"I didn't really notice," John said. He turned and stared at Frank. "What can I do?"

"I was talking to the sergeant. It seems that two Rangers, while searching out the American defenses along the north river, were recognized and murdered. Hare and Sergeant Newberry. You remember them?" He lowered his plate and turned to John, who nodded. "They hanged Hare on a gallows erected in front of his own house."

"My god, man. Is there no limit to the cruelty in this war? And what about his wife and family? Did they have to witness that?"

"I have no word on that. Perhaps they were already away to Nova Scotia with some of the other Loyalists."

"Nova Scotia. Frank. You don't think Lucy and William went there, do you?"

"I suppose it's possible, but why would they do that when they know you are with Butler?" Frank poked at the fire. "More likely something has delayed them coming this way."

"Or they could have gone right past us on a different trail and be at Fort Niagara by now." He spoke quickly and his eyes opened wide in the firelight. "It could be that they are safe there, couldn't it, Frank?"

"Yes. Let's hope that is the case." The two friends stared at the flames leaping higher as Frank prodded the logs. Showers of sparks flamed up and vanished into the soft night air. "I'm ready to get away from this fire. What about you?" Frank asked.

"Getting a little too hot. Time to turn in." He stretched. "Good night, Frank."

THE WRETCHED AND SCANT MORNING FOOD had the whole camp complaining. "When are we going to get something better to eat?" Frank asked the cook, but the man just shrugged and doled the nasty salt meat out to the next in line.

Unlike the summer before, the Rangers couldn't forage food from farms along the way as no crops had been planted. What animals there were had been confiscated by the Americans. Men dragged their feet in the midsummer heat, too tired and hungry to do more.

The small sick tent could not hold all those with dysentery and fever and the colonel could do little to alleviate the situation. He depended on supplies from Niagara. Those few shipments that did come were scant and didn't last long. Butler would have to do something soon or he wouldn't have anyone left fit to fight.

In a desperate attempt to feed his Rangers, Butler decided to move them two days' journey to Genesee Falls on the lake. That would allow the men to eat fish and enable boats from Niagara to provision them. They would be able to move by boat up and down the lake wherever they were needed. The news came to the men with the morning roll call and was well met by those who were healthy enough to attend. John studied the soldiers around him. How would it all turn out?

After the meeting he and Frank prepared to leave. "How are we going to get all these sick people there?" He shook his head as he brushed Maudie's mane.

Frank turned. "What do we always do? We'll walk, we'll ride, we'll make litters to pull behind the horses. And we won't think, will we, John? We'll just do it." His shoulders sagged as he drifted away to prepare for the next day.

HEAT SEEMED TO SIZZLE IN THE TREES OVERHEAD, frying up any little bits of moisture long before they could reach the struggling line of bedraggled Rangers who sweated under their packs in an endless line of despair. At least the trail had leveled out and the hills were small here.

John and Frank shared their horses with some of those who most needed the rest. Unaccustomed to marching, their feet swelled and blistered in the monotonous stamp, stamp of the march. This was the second day of their trip to the lake. Ahead of John, a man staggered and fell. He almost tripped over him. He stopped to help and realized he was holding Nat, who had saved them from small pox.

"Nat. Nat." John wiped Nat's brow and gently slapped his face.

"He needs water and a rest." Frank had knelt on Nat's other side.

"Don't we all?" Standing up, Frank motioned to those on horseback. "You'll have to let Nat have a turn, boys."

"And someone else," John added.

"Here, Nat, drink something."

"Don't use all your water, Frank. We don't know when we'll get any more."

"Just now Nat needs it more than I do."

Once the men made the changes and Nat was safely on John's horse, alert enough to ride for a bit, Frank moved alongside John. Both men were leading their horses.

"I've been thinking about Lucy, John."

"What?" John swung to look at his friend.

Looking around, Frank moved closer to John. "I think we should look for her. She might need help."

"What do you propose?" John whispered.

"We make the lake and get some good food into us, rest up a day or so, and strike out."

"I can't ask you to desert, Frank. And the colonel will know where we've gone." He paused. "I do appreciate ..."

"Think about it." Frank led his horse ahead, with its burden swaying and jolting at every step.

THAT NIGHT THEY REACHED THEIR JOURNEY'S END, and none too soon. The cool lake breezes brought some relief and the men who were able picked their way down to the water to dip their feet. Several stripped to their skivvies and, like children, swam out into the current. Frank and John had never learned to swim and contented themselves with sloshing water on their faces and bared arms. Nat watched from the bank.

"Come on in, Nat." John called.

"No, sir, John. I'm not going to be putting these parts in that water. Too cold. And too many things swimmin' around in the dark."

"Suit yourself. It does feel good." John laughed and turned when Frank splashed him. "Hey. Stop that. I don't want my clothes all wet."

"They could stand a good washing, don't you think?" Frank sliced his cupped hand through the water again and John was doused. Laughing, he reciprocated and soon both were leaping, fully clothed, in the shallow waters.

IN THE MORNING the antics of the night before seemed less amusing as their clothes were still damp. John pulled on his homespun shirt, his woolen stockings and his soggy breeches. At least the stockings were dry, although not that clean. He would wash them later and dry them in the sun.

The smell of wet wool pinched his nostrils and he moved quickly to get out of the tent. Frank did the same. Their combined efforts had made the small tent hot and humid, even that early in the morning. The day was going to be another scorcher.

Their meal was fresh fish. Even those who didn't quite relish fish found it to their liking after such a long diet of salt pork. Men ate in small groups, talking between mouthfuls. There were even fresh boiled potatoes, small but tasty, and johnny cake, which was manna after the brick-solid hardtack they had been eating. Men smiled in the sun and joked with their fellow Rangers.

"Surprising what a little good food can do." John nodded toward the soldiers.

"Everything looks better on a full stomach."

"Almost everything." John studied his plate.

"We'll find her, John."

Chapter Thirty

AT ROLL CALL THAT MORNING, the men had full stomachs for the first time in weeks. They breathed easier and answered louder, even though the hot sun beat down on their covered heads and sweat trickled under their homespun shirts.

Colonel Butler had news. A small squad would be sent out to reconnoiter to the east along the lake and down into New York State toward the Mohawk River. He warned them all that the war was still very much alive and they had better look to their weapons, their fitness and their horses, those that had them.

John was lost in thoughts about Lucy when he heard his name.

"...Garner, James, Smyth and Sergeant Mabee. You men report to me immediately upon dismissal." The colonel narrowed his eyes as he studied the rows before him. "We're all needed here, men, even though most of us would like to be somewhere else. Remember that you're fighting, you're fighting for your homes, your families, your land and your king. Your king." He turned and marched away, his aides following.

Dismissed, Frank and John walked toward the colonel's tent. John looked at his friend. "This could help us find Lucy."

"I expect you're right." Frank nodded toward the colonel just disappearing into the command tent. "Do you think he'll want you looking for your wife?"

"Maybe he put me on the detail so I could look for her. I just don't know. Who else is going with us?"

"He named six men and said there would be some Mohawks with us as well."

"That's interesting. How many?"

"Two."

Stopping before the tent, John studied the others whose names had been called. Six altogether. Sergeant Mabee stood to one side, his squinty eyes taking the measure of his force. He stared at each man with a horse trader's slow calculating eye.

John nodded at Nat James, glad of his wisdom and his friendly face among the group. William Ford sidled up to Henry Marcellus and nudged him, glancing pointedly at Nat. There might be trouble there.

Even though the Negro soldiers had fought bravely and well, there were still those who resented them and, despite specific orders from Colonel Butler, also harassed the black men. In this company John was glad to have Frank by his side yet again. This would be the party, along with the two as yet unnamed Indians.

The tent flaps parted and Butler's aide appeared. "He'll see you all now," he said, and stood aside to let the group crowd into the tent.

"At ease, gentlemen. You know generally what is expected of you but you do not know everything, know everything." The colonel sat on his camp chair behind a small table, studying each of them in turn. When those questioning eyes settled on him, John struggled not to blink or look away.

The general moved on. "I have picked you for your skills, gentlemen, and for your loyalty. I am not going to tell you the whole mission yet, only that you are going east, going east. The sergeant will enlighten you as needed. Let me just say that the Americans—that's what they call themselves now—the Americans are getting stronger and stronger. The war is going badly, badly for us. Your successful mission will help. To turn the tide."

The colonel paused and stood up. "We need you to come back, men. Look to your own safety." He turned toward the corner of the tent and stood silently for a moment, then quickly turned back to face the men. "Dismissed."

Outside the tent the sergeant spoke. "We leave at daybreak. On horseback. Do not take anything more than necessary. Dismissed." He strode off.

John and Frank headed for their tent. "What do you make of that?" John spoke softly.

"I'm sure we'll learn what it's all about soon enough. And then we'll wish we didn't know. Sometimes ignorance is bliss."

THE NEXT DAY found the eight men outfitted in their Ranger uniforms as they picked their way through the woods away from the trail. Huge thorny bushes loomed beside them and they took care to avoid brushing them and the low branches of wild apple trees. The ground was barely visible covered as it was with brambles and purple thistles, goldenrod and lacy white flowers which stood half way up the horses' legs.

Thwack. John recoiled from the branch flung in his face as it was released by Frank ahead. "Watch it, Frank." he called out.

"Silence." The sergeant hissed back at them.

Frank shrugged at John who shook his head and rolled his eyes. *Crazy. We're all just crazy to be out here not even taking the trail. If I knew what we were about maybe I'd understand it. I'll think about Lucy, and how I can find her.*

She lay sleeping under the quilt, Harper John in the cradle beside her. Her face was calm, eyes closed, and light brown eyelashes fluttered gently over her eyelids as the sun streaked in the window. A golden haze formed in strands of light and tiny dust motes danced above Lucy's still form.

He could almost reach out and...but he didn't want to wake her. She turned on her side and smiled, reaching for the pillow beside hers. Her hand stopped and her smile slid away. Her eyes opened, taking in the empty pillow, and then squeezed shut again.

His own eyes blinked repeatedly. His shoulders drooped as his head fell forward onto his chest and his horse lurched over yet another fallen log.

He had been daydreaming. Lucy was not in their bed. Not even in the cabin. Lucy was lost, he knew not where she was, and he was helpless to do anything about it.

He shook his head and tried to watch Frank's bobbing form ahead. He sensed rather than saw a movement to Frank's left. He looked and listened, every nerve taut, but only heard the horses picking their way through the underbrush and the branches swishing back into place.

But there were no birds, no crickets, no cicadas starting their fall chorus. He whistled a low-pitched call at Frank who turned in his saddle and stopped. He waited for John to come alongside.

"What is it?"

"Don't look now but we're being watched."

Frank's hand went immediately to his musket, primed and ready, across his lap. He raised his eyebrows in question to John.

"Off to the left."

"How many?"

"Only one that I could see so far. And it could be nothing. Pass the word up to Sergeant Mabee."

Frank sprang ahead to catch up as John dropped back to tell Nat. Quietly the word spread to the group of eight. Moving steadily ahead they doubled their attention to the woods surrounding them.

Strain his eyes though he might, he saw nothing else and began to think he had imagined it all. Frank glanced back, his brows raised in question. John nodded, sure there was something wrong, although he had no idea exactly what.

When the group reached a tiny clearing they circled around Sergeant Mabee whose eyes continuously raked the trees in every direction.

"What did you see, Garner?" he hissed.

"Movement. About thirty feet to the left."

"And the quiet," Frank added softly.

Mabee nodded. "You sure?" His eyes bored into John's face.

"Yes." John nodded and stared back.

"All right, then. Everyone keep your eyes sharp. Give a whistle if you see anything." He led off into the trees.

"Whee-ooop! Whee-ooop! Whee-ooop!" The calls came from every direction throwing horses and riders into chaos.

"Form a circle. Form a circle, men." The sergeant shouted. The eight regrouped and faced the sounds coming from the woods.

Shouting, screaming Indians came running at them from two sides. War paint and feathers were mixed with random bits of white man's clothing. They were on foot and they were many. He raised his musket and shot into the mass.

He heard Frank's gun beside him as he rammed his own shot home and prepared to take aim again. He brought the gun to his shoulder. He only had time for this one shot, the Indians were so close. A tall Indian in a blue soldier's jacket raised his tomahawk.

The man's bloody eyes bored into him. John pulled the trigger, praying that the shot would find its mark at such close range. The Indian fell. John tried to reload. Another one grabbed his horse's bridle and pulled. He sliced his bayonet straight into the enemy's chest. The Indian's eyes grew wide and his tomahawk slipped out of his raised hand. It landed, flat-sided, on his own head, then glanced off and down into the melee below. The man sank to the ground.

To his left Frank screamed and slashed wildly with his bayonet. John edged Maudie in closer and together the men stabbed and sliced, pulled back and pitched forward again, wild with the threat of death and the hope of victory.

John could feel no more; he thought only of knifing, slicing, of striking out, of killing everything in this cursed war that had ruined his life.

He dug his feet into Maudie's side and she leapt forward with flashing, frightened eyes, her head thrashing from side to side. She wanted to escape but didn't know which way to go amidst the fury. And then the push subsided and he stood still, struggling for breath. He glanced to his left but couldn't see Frank. He jerked every which way. An Indian stood over someone on the ground, fumbling for his knife.

He rode at the Indian and, just as he grabbed the hair of the man on the ground, bayoneted him. The Indian fell across the Ranger. John jumped down and pulled him off. The still form was Frank. His open chest oozed blood.

"Frank." He reached for his friend's head, but sensed movement to his left and threw himself back and away. He scrambled to his feet and grabbed the knife-wielding Indian around his middle, upsetting his balance. The two of them fell across Frank's legs, scrambling to get control.

He had the Indian in a bear hug of a grip, squeezing the very life out of him. The knife had fallen but the Indian kicked and screamed, a blood-hungry scream, maddening John even more. His arms were stretched to breaking, but he was oblivious. Kill, kill, his brain roared.

John obeyed. He heard bones cracking and hoped they weren't his. The man's body sagged. Not taking a chance that his prisoner was feinting, John grabbed the Indian's arm and smartly twisted it behind and up.

The Indian screamed as his whole body rose against the searing, bone-breaking force. Pop. The arm went limp. He wrenched the useless limb up over the Indian's head. He let loose a high-pitched scream and John yanked him around, jammed the knife up under the ribs, grinding and pushing until all was still.

Standing motionless with the man's weight against him, he felt the warm slime on his knife hand. He pushed the man away and pulled out the knife. The body slipped to a formless heap on the ground. He straightened up, took a step back, and registered the silence of the woods.

Chapter Thirty-One

July, 1779

"DO YOU THINK WE COULD DO WITHOUT A FIRE TONIGHT, father?" Lucy was changing Harper John on a blanket spread on the ground. She looked up at William leaning against the wagon. They were stopped a small distance off the track, on the only dry ground in the middle of a reed-filled swamp.

"Finding wood might prove impossible. And," he added, "we don't want to risk letting anyone know we're here."

She paused a moment letting the baby's legs swing free in the air while she studied her father. His shoulders seemed more rounded every day and his dust-caked face, worn thin and deeply lined, was old. Those brilliant blue eyes had lost their luster, partly shaded as they were by his wrinkled eyelids which threatened to close his eyes completely. This journey was taking its toll.

"Don't worry, father. We've been safe so far, haven't we? Let us just have some food and sleep. The new day will make you feel better." She finished bundling Harper John.

"I'll keep watch for a while tonight, just on the chance those men come back." He turned back to unpacking the buffalo robe and hanging the blanket curtains.

"Wake me and I'll take the second watch." Lucy voice was soft and calm but she squeezed Harper John a little closer to her breast.

In the night Lucy's dreams were interrupted by the soft whimpering of her son and she struggled to wake. He was sopping. Automatically she reached behind for dry clothing and quickly changed him before lying with him at her breast, her eyes closed.

Harper John's strong suckling satisfied both their needs and lulled her to think of nothing. She slept. A sharp nip, though, and she was fully awake once more. She heard his burp and shifted him to the other breast.

This time she noticed the silence under the wagon; her father's heavy breathing was missing. She remembered he was keeping watch and wondered why he hadn't wakened her. As soon as she finished with Harper John she would go out. Meanwhile she rested.

THE ROOSTER'S CROWING JOLTED HER AWAKE. She shook her head and opened her eyes, sat up and looked for her father in the dim daylight at the other end of the wagon. The space was empty. She edged away from the still-sleeping baby and crawled out into the grey dawn.

"Father," she whispered as she scanned the area. She walked toward the oxen, all four of them hobbled with the horse, and noticed something on the ground.

"Father," she shouted, and ran toward the face-down figure. His legs. One of them was bent at the knee and below it. She knelt at his side and eased him face up.

"Ahh." William moaned and his eyes opened. "Lucinda." He blinked at her and closed his eyes once more.

"Father." She shook him gently and he looked up again. "Your leg. What happened?"

William sighed and blinked his eyes repeatedly. "Caught in a woodchuck hole, I guess. It just grabbed my leg and the rest of me pitched forward. Leg snapped. Pain. That's all I remember." He flinched.

She felt tenderly along each of his legs. The left one was fine but the right was badly twisted. The broken bone felt jagged, like a split turkey wishbone. Her father cried out. "I'm sorry, father. Your leg is broken clear through. I'll have to set it and splint it."

....

220

She moved to the wagon for her medicines, glad of the laudanum to dull the pain. Luckily the bleeding had not been severe or he might be dead. Bandages and bottles in hand, she returned to where her father lay.

She told him to drink as much laudanum as he could while she searched the area for splint material, but this swampy area had nothing suitable. She pulled a chair off the wagon and grabbed the axe. The spindles separated easily from the back.

Her father's eyes were closed. Could she set his leg? And would her exhausted father survive? She knelt beside him and pushed her hair back and began cutting away the cloth exposing an angry purpled wound. In its centre a jagged end of bone broke the skin. Crusted blood surrounded the opening. Lucy stifled a gasp and sat back a moment.

"Bad, is it then?"

She jumped. "Yes, it is, father. But not so bad we can't fix it." She looked into his eyes. "Do you have any spirits?"

"No, daughter. You know your mother would never allow that." He tried to smile.

"Here. Drink more of this." She passed him the stoppered laudanum bottle.

As the sun crept from its sleeping place beneath the horizon, Lucy washed the wound and waited for William's laudanum to take effect. She knew it would not be nearly enough but it was all she had. She laid out her bandages and glanced toward her father's closed eyes.

This is it, she thought. She put her hands on the leg, feeling the position of the bone, pushing gently, adding more pressure to move the bone back into position. She had seen a doctor do this for their servant but that was years ago when she was young. Most of the time she had just looked away as Matthew's screams got louder. She pressed harder and harder until she felt the bone squish backwards. Her father screamed and she screamed with him.

"I'm almost done. Father. Hold still." Frantic, she pushed and squeezed, willing the bone to move until her father's screams were matched by Harper John's under the wagon. The baby would have to wait. She gave the leg one more mighty push and felt the bone slip into place.

She held it there a moment, afraid to let go in case it might slip out again, and then carefully, with one hand, wrapped the leg while desperately holding it still with the other. She grabbed the chair spindles and tied them into the wrapping to hold the leg motionless. She moved to William's still face and stroked his cheek. He had passed out.

"It's done, father. It's done. I am so sorry I had to hurt you." Oblivious, William slept on but his features had relaxed. Maybe he couldn't feel the pain.

She had no time to ponder. Harper John's screams were now great gulping sobs. She dashed to soothe him.

"Shhh. Don't cry, little one. All is well now. Grandfather's leg is fixed. Shhh." She tried to put him to her breast but he was too upset so she changed him calmly, stroking his bare skin and whispering all the while.

Gradually Harper John fixed his eyes on her, and his cries stopped. When she held him to her breast again he latched on immediately, only pausing his sucking every couple of minutes to let the final, shuddering sobs escape. Presently she stood up and cradled him in her arms as she walked to her father's still form and sat. Now she had two of them to care for. She rocked back and forth as the baby nursed and, beside her, her father's chest lifted ever so slightly up and down, up and down. How would she ever do it?

They had made camp here the night before hoping that the very unsuitable nature of the swampy spot would deter others from coming here and finding them, but now that decision weighed heavily on Lucy's mind. Already insects were hovering over the sludge ponds a few feet away and she worked hard to keep the mosquitoes off the baby, her father and herself. She would have to do something.

Once Harper John was napping again, she struggled to her feet and put him into his cradle, covering it with homespun to keep the insects away. She turned to her father and created a makeshift tent over his upper body. When he awoke she would move him.

How could they continue? Were they stuck here until his leg mended? Would the wound heal properly? She straightened up and noticed the pink streaks of sun-seared clouds as the day grew, and smiled. She couldn't think of all that might happen. Everything was going to work out. Just now she needed to find some fresh water.

Amazingly, after a few minutes' walking, she did find a clean bubbling pool where she filled her jugs before carrying them back to the wagon. Harper John slept on but her father's moaning sounds told her he was waking. She pulled the tent back and sat beside him with her basin of water. She dipped the cloth and brought it to his forehead. She pushed his hair aside with one hand and, with the cloth in the other, dabbed carefully at his features. He stirred, groaned, and moved his head away.

"Father."

His eyes moved but the lids stayed shut.

"Father. It's Lucinda. Can you hear me?" She shook his shoulder. William tried to open his eyes but immediately squinted against the sun. Lucy shifted to shade him. "Is that better?"

"Lucinda." He croaked out her name.

"You are going to be fine, father. Fine." She ran her hand down his cheek. "You've had quite a fall, I think." She had noticed the gopher hole. "Did you trip in the hole here?"

"I think so. I was walking and then I wasn't. I remember a rush of heat and… terrible pain. And falling. Over a cliff into blackness, it seemed." He looked around and chuckled. "No cliffs here, though."

"No. I found you here early this morning and tended to your leg." She glanced at the splint. "It's broken, father."

"How bad? Can I walk?" His eyes fixed on Lucy.

"I've set the bone. I hope you don't remember. And I've splinted it. But you'll have to rest and keep the swelling down." She took a deep breath. "We can't go on until it mends. But we will find a better place to camp." She waved her hand at their surroundings. "This place is just too unhealthy."

AFTER FEEDING HER FATHER and Harper John once again, Lucy saddled the horse and set off on a mission to see how big the swampy area was and to find a place to make a more permanent camp. She headed west along the trail until trees appeared on the horizon. Slowing her horse she pondered the distance trying to decide whether to go today or in the morning, but the sun was high in the sky and heading fast to the west. She turned back.

When she returned both the baby and the invalid were fast asleep. Quietly she set about planning the journey and then prepared their evening meal. By morning they would be ready. She glanced at her father and felt a pang. She moved to his side, pulled the covering back and bent to wash his face once more. It felt hot and beads of moisture stood on his forehead. "Please don't get the fever," she murmured and jerked back when he looked straight at her.

"It's just so hot in here, Lucinda."

"Do you think you can get up? If I get the chair from the wagon for support?"

"I'll try, my dear." William lifted the makeshift tent off to the side and pushed himself up on his elbows, then slowly to a sitting position. She tried to lift him.

"Just let me sit a moment." He waved her off, smoothing his shirt and raising his shoulders up and down. "I need to get the blood moving again." He shifted his good leg, then braced to lift the other. "Awh, not good." Relaxing the muscles and looking up to where Lucy was blocking the setting sun, he muttered, "Damn the luck. Why did this have to happen?"

"Don't blame yourself." She stooped to touch his shoulder and look into his strained eyes. "We'll make it. You just need to rest a moment and then we'll try again."

Much later, as she lay exhausted under the wagon, her father near her, sleeping at last, the tears ran slowly down her cheeks. She squeezed tight, to make them stop and forced herself to think of tomorrow when they would move the camp and set it up so that her father could get about. She lay listening to the night sounds—her father's even breaths punctuated by occasional sniffs and snorts, and

....

Harper John's soft, yet quick rhythm, as well as the loud hum of the cicadas outside their sanctuary. Tomorrow would be a better day.

LUCY WOULD HAVE TO LEAVE part of the load behind so that her father could lie down. He was not well enough to sit for the journey; in fact, he could barely pull himself from under the wagon. Holding his arm around her neck, and with the broken chair on the other side for her father to lift himself, she strained to get him upright so that he could slide onto the wagon. She ignored his groans and her own body's hurts until, finally, it was done.

She had already secured Harper John's cradle. Once the oxen were hitched, she climbed up onto the wagon seat, took the reins and made her way back onto the trail west toward those trees she had seen.

Their pace was painfully slow and with every lurch of the wagon her father groaned, each sound a stab to her breaking heart. She stopped often to give him some respite and once to feed Harper John. As the sun rose in the sky, she recognized the need to push on to their destination and make camp before nightfall.

The distance, which on horseback had looked so short, now seemed endless. She scanned the horizon again and again, hoping to see what she had seen yesterday. She had fed the baby again and was back on the driver's seat before her trees appeared on the horizon, a faint smudge at first. Gradually the dark spot grew and grew and she knew. It was the trees.

"Father." Her soft call blew over his still quiet form and his eyes remained closed against the full sun overhead. She wondered if he was sleeping. "Father. Can you hear me?"

Only the sound of the creaking wagon wheels trundling along the dusty track and the sniffing of the oxen interspersed with the horse's heavy breathing broke the silence of the vast plain. She hoped he was asleep. She glanced back again and noticed he had put his hat over his face. Good. Fixing her sights in the west, she held tight to the bouncing lines flipping above the oxen's backs, her thoughts wild and tumbling with every bone-wrenching bump.

What would John do if he were here? Would he camp for a while until William recovered or would he push on to Niagara and get help? She didn't know. In fact there was a lot she didn't know. She thought of the dangers of the road and the fearsome men they had met. If they came back and threatened them would she be able to shoot them if need be?

"I hope it doesn't come to that." Her tongue slipped over her dry lips and she spat out the grit. In the hot sun the oxen had slowed almost to a standstill. She pulled up to give them water, then wiped both the baby's and her father's brow, before gulping a cooling drink herself and climbing back up on the wagon to push on toward the trees.

The sun moved westward and dipped below her bonnet brim to shine directly in her eyes, blocking out both trail and trees. Lucy trusted that the oxen would stay on the trail on their own. Finally the little procession was close enough to the woods that the sun became just a blinking beacon slipping between the trees to light their way. She was so tired she wanted to just stop anywhere but knew they had to find a permanent camp. Into the woods she drove until she heard a rushing stream.

"Whoa. Whoa." She pulled the oxen to a stop. "We're here, father. We're here." She climbed over the wheel onto the step and down to the ground. She rubbed her worn hands and tried to work out the knots in every one of her muscles.

"Father. Wake up. We're here."

While the daylight held, she worked to set up the camp, see to Harper John, prepare their supper, feed and hobble the animals, and, for a few moments at least, uncrate the two chickens she had saved to keep the rooster company. She got her father settled under the wagon. His eyes closed as soon as she draped the blanket over him. Harper John snuffled softly in his cradle at her head. She lay on the buffalo robe and, forced herself to count her blessings: Harper John, John, her father…the animals…

Chapter Thirty-Two

THE ROOSTER CROWED. Lucy rolled away from the sound, her arm over her ear as she tried to slip back into her dream. John had been there. Somehow he found them and wanted to help. She tried to get him back, tried to recapture the story, the story which felt so good, but the cradle shook with Harper John's first thrashings of the day.

She touched the wood and rocked ever so gently, hoping he would go back to sleep but his gurgles turned to squeaky cries which threatened to erupt into full blown wails.

"Shh. Shh. I'm coming, Harper John. You don't want to wake your grandfather, do you?" She eased the tender burden out of the cradle and laid him beside her on the patchwork quilt. "You're very wet." Nearby, her father shifted and grunted.

In the predawn darkness she groped for dry linens and, with practiced fingers, changed her son. She nestled him into the crook of her arm to nurse, while she drifted off to find John again. He wasn't there. She looked in all the soldiers' tents but couldn't find him. His voice, however, came to her over and over.

"Lucy, Lucy. Where are you, Lucy?"

The plaintive sound drove her to look harder, to run, frantic and fearful, to throw open the cabin door and fall into the barn. She heard gunfire and pulled her food packet from its hiding place, opened it and pulled the rifle out. Harper John was on her shoulders digging into her skin with his long fingernails. She felt the blood run down her back, then looked down to see it pouring out of her stomach. John. John. Where are you? Her voice wailed into the darkness.

"Lucy, I need you. Where are you?"

She searched but now, in the darkness, a warm breeze blew her curls into her eyes. Warmth trickled into them and she blinked as she felt her mother's hand slide across her brow, calming and cooling. Tears coursed down her face. She reached to touch the hand. It melted away.

Harper John was in her arms, sucking noisily. "You bit me. And with only the one tooth." She could see his face in the lightening gloom and stroked his rounded cheeks.

"WHEN ARE YOU GOING TO GET the rest of our things, Lucinda?" William sat on the edge of the wagon, his bowl in his hands. He seemed to be enjoying food for the first time since the accident.

"I don't know. What do you think?"

"You need a day or two to rest." He lifted the spoon once again to his lips and paused. "How will you do it?"

"I've been pondering that. I could take the horse, leave Harper John here with you, and rig something to pull the bundle of things back tied behind the horse. The trip there would be fast but I could take my time coming back."

Lucy held her son and watched her father. "Could you look after Harper John for a day?" She leaned against the wagon beside him.

"I expect I could but, daughter, how would I feed him?" He spread his arms wide and stared at her.

"Maybe you could give him water from the cup and some of the soup thinned out with more water. I would only be gone a few hours this time, father. The horse is much faster than the oxen, you know."

"Of course. And no other idea comes to mind." He turned back to his spoon.

"Would you be able to look after Harper John if I went tomorrow? Are you well enough, I mean?"

William smiled at his daughter. "Of course. We'll just stay here together out of the sun, Harper John and I, won't we?" He chucked his grandson under his chubby chin.

SHE LEFT THE NEXT MORNING, having cut and trimmed thick branches for her makeshift cart, which she then tied into a bundle, securing them to the saddle behind her along with the buffalo robe and some dried meat to sustain her. Back along the trail she galloped, raising a thick cloud of dust behind her, as the steamy sun rose overhead.

She squinted against the brightness and tried to make out where they had been camped. She found the spot and began to tie together her contraption to tow behind the horse. She laced the branches together with the few leather thongs she had, spread the buffalo robe over the top and loaded the table, her mother's chest and John's chair. She stood to survey her handiwork.

"It'll have to do."

She took a pull at the water jug and bit into the beef. Even dead, Molly was still helping. She smiled at the thought and then turned to the west. She had a long way to go. At first she walked beside the horse to test how secure the load was. Satisfied, she swished aside her skirts, swung up into the saddle, and nudged the horse ahead.

The trip, which had taken a couple of hours at a good trot, now looked so far she would need a day or more. Her back crunched and her neck wrenched with the horse's every step. Walking the horse was much harder than galloping as their bodies did not seem to move together.

Finally, for relief she got down again and led the animal part of the way, until the heat of the sun burned into her forearms and her steps slowed almost to a crawl. Her bonnet kept some of the sun's heat off her face but underneath the sweat ran in tiny torrents through her hair and down her back. She felt filthy with dust and dirt.

The water and tiny ration of meat were gone. The horse gasped huge heaving breaths but trudged ahead nevertheless. She blinked at the steady stream of sweat running down her cheeks. She stopped a moment to lift her skirt up and dry her face. She pulled the reins back over the horse's head, put her foot into the stirrup and dragged herself up again.

In the distance the trees were getting larger. She would make it if she just kept going. Her eyes were streaming sweat again as, in vain, she tried to see their camp or smoke from the fire.

She had left her father plenty of wood if he cared to—or could—use it but no sign showed. Looking down she noticed the wet circles of her leaking breasts and tried not to think of Harper John. He had to gnaw at scraps of meat for the whole day.

Just a few more steps, a few more steps, a few more—her head dropped and bobbed as the horse kept his steady pace, rocking and rolling, stepping to one side to miss a rock, pulling his load along behind him. Slower and slower he went until he all but stopped and felt no pull nor heard no call.

"Lucinda. Lucinda."

The horse jerked underneath her and she blinked awake.

"Lucinda. You're almost here, daughter. Wake up."

Her eyes opened to the daylight as she focused on the sound. "I'm coming, father." She shook her head and flicked the reins, urging the tired horse the last little distance.

And then they were there. She struggled from the stirrups and swung, shaking, to the ground.

"You made it, daughter. Amazing." William stood leaning on the wagon. Harper John was in his arms and wearing the most welcome smile she had ever seen. She blinked away tears and reached out. She was safe. They were safe. She took her son into her arms.

Later Lucy sat in the dark, Harper John satisfied at last. He had been red and howling with hunger when she finally took him to her breast to relieve their mutual need and his eyes closed while the distant firelight danced over his features.

She had done it. She had made the trek and retrieved their goods. It had been much harder than she thought, but she had done it. Her head tilted back in the chair—John's chair—and she closed her eyes.

"You'll sleep well tonight, Lucinda." Her father's voice called.

"Yes. First I need to get clean." She leaned forward, rocked herself upright, and walked Harper John to his cradle. "How far away is that stream? A few hundred paces?"

"You know I haven't been there, daughter. Besides a few hundred paces in the dark and into a dark stream—not a good idea. Wait till the morning."

"You're right. But first thing. And I'll wash some clothes, too."

Chapter Thirty-Three

July, 1779

HIS EYES DARTED TO THE LEFT AND RIGHT. He jerked around, watching. Finally, he knelt beside the gore seeping from his friend's body.

"Frank." He looked away from the terrible stomach wound, to Frank's face. He found his water pouch, and pried open his mouth. The water ran down his chin, although his chest still lifted ever so slightly with the effort of breathing.

"You're alive, Frank. Wake up." He pulled a cloth from his sack, poured a little water into it and wiped the blood away. He pulled Frank's jacket over the gaping stomach wound. He could do nothing. His friend was dying. He drooped forward with the realization and his shoulders fell. For a moment he was silent. Small sobs escaped. They grew in intensity until his voice rose in a great howl of pain, and shattered the shaky silence of the little clearing.

"John."

The whispered word brought him back to Frank. "I am here, friend." He swallowed, and touched the pale brow. "Does it hurt?"

Frank's eyes were on him, gradually closing, then slowly opening to focus once more. "John." Only the lips mouthed the word.

"I'm here. I'll stay with you." He grasped the hand and held it in his own, watching. "Frank." He willed his friend to live but with every labored breath Frank's hold on life lessened. Finally, his eyelids fluttered shut and stayed shut. His chest lifted with one last heave.

"Frank. Frank." John leaned over listening, but no breath came. He sat silent and stared at the familiar stiff blonde hair and at his eyelids, closed over the twinkling blue forever. He held Frank's limp hand. At last, he let out a long, shuddering sob and let the cold hand lie beside the lifeless body. He stood.

There was no sound but the birds and the branches, no horses nickering, no soldiers' noises at all. He was surrounded by silent forms strewn across the grassy meadow. He wiped his knife clean on the loin cloth of the dead Indian, and belted it once more.

His musket was nearby, a good thing. He primed and powdered it ready for use once more. Stepping across bodies and puddled blood he made a count of the dead: four Rangers, including Frank and the sergeant, and six Indians, two of their party and the rest, attackers. One of the Rangers was missing. Nat. Perhaps he wandered off or maybe one of the Indians had him. He would look for him when the horses came back.

He sat astride a fallen log and tried to recall how many enemy Indians there had been; if any had escaped they might be a danger to him. He had been too busy fighting for his life to see what happened to the others. From the body count the battle had been vicious.

Why had his life had been spared? He sat a long while trying to figure out what had happened, so long, in fact, that the shadows began to lengthen and the songs of the woods to play again in splendid safety. A soft whinny at his side brought him to his feet, knife in his hand, but it was only Maudie come to find him. He stroked her head, worked his hands over her neck and haunches, under the edges of the saddle. He had to move on. This was his chance to search for Lucy.

He found a small shovel on one of the other returned horses and began to dig. He stopped. He did not have the energy to bury all of the dead, but he couldn't leave them here unburied. They would be mutilated. The men deserved more, especially Frank. His stomach knotted.

....

He dragged the dead Rangers' bodies to the middle of the clearing, pulled the enemy to the edge of the forest, and tethered the six returned horses nearby. Even though the day was sweltering, he gathered wood for a huge fire.

THE NIGHT CAME ON SUDDENLY. His hands shook as he struck the flint over and over until the flame flickered and grew strong in the dried twigs. His chest eased and he sat back to watch the flames, his eyes avoiding the dark gloom rapidly closing around him. He would keep the fire going all night to keep the wolves at bay—and anything else that might be out there. He pitched the small tent but hesitated to go inside. In the damp grass, he tried to eat, not from hunger but from need. This would be a long night.

Though he had planned to sit and watch the bodies burn, the day's events had taken their toll. His eyes closed for a few seconds. He jerked them open again, his hands on his musket. But there was no one near. He was alone with the dead. He stood to stretch, then crawled into the tent. Perhaps he would sleep after all.

IN THE EARLY LIGHT OF MORNING, something moved outside the tent. Blinking the sleep from his eyes he felt for the gun beside him and the knife still at his waist. A shadow? The snap of a twig.

Ever so softly he rolled over and crouched by the tied tent opening, listened, heard nothing, and pulled gently on the ties. He picked up the musket, checked that the bayonet was secure and spread the canvas to peer out at the empty dawn campsite. Suddenly he felt a glancing blow down his back. He fell out into the open, got to his feet and lunged for the shape by the collapsed tent.

In the grey light John smelled rather than saw his attacker, an acrid odor of stale sweat. It dulled his senses as he held, then lost the man, who wrenched away to turn and attack again. He saw the raised arm, ducked, pulled his knife and stabbed it at the man's chest.

But his attacker was too fast. John slid off balance and the knife missed its target. He fell. As the knife came down, his hand shot out to grab the arm and hold it—and the wicked blade, a long, shining thing—inches from his face.

Together the two men wrestled in silence, locked together, their muscles stiff and screaming. He held the man's eyes and knew he would die right then, right there. But an instinct, hard and ferocious, rose from deep down in his gut and he howled and held the knife at bay while his right knee came up and crashed into the man's groin. He screamed and his arm went slack. He dropped the knife, and John easily threw him to the ground, pinning him there, where he writhed and groaned under John's punishing foot.

The dawn light was full upon them now. His attacker was an Indian, a Mohawk. As the moments slipped by, the two men glared at each other, eyes hard and chests heaving, the one wondering how long he had to live, and the other anxious to end the struggle. He needed to protect himself, in his vengeance to lash out at anything and anyone. But something held him back. He snatched up his gun and pointed it at the Indian.

"Who are you?" He hissed the words but the Indian stared back at him.

"You're Mohawk." John poked harder with his foot. "Why are you attacking a Ranger?"

The man's eyes widened. "Ranger?"

"Yes, Ranger. I'm a Ranger." John pointed at his own chest. "Do you not see my coat?" he started, but then realized it was in the tent. He had nothing to identify himself. Again he tapped his chest and said, "Ranger," and watched the Mohawk's eyes widen. The man's body slumped as he dropped his head to stare at the sky. His eyes closed and he shook his head, then immediately looked right at John.

"I did not know. I am a friend to Rangers."

John's foot came off the Indian and he stepped back allowing the man to sit but still keeping the musket trained on him. "Who are you?"

"I am a Mohawk, of Thayendanegea's clan." He studied John's face.

"I know that name. Joseph Brant, isn't it?"

"Yes." The Mohawk nodded.

"I am glad to know you. I have met Brant several times and count him as a good friend." John lowered his musket, motioning for the Mohawk to rise. "What are you doing out here by yourself?"

"Scouting for enemies. I saw a great fire and came to look. In the dark I tripped over a body. A large black man. Scalped." He stared at John but went on. "When I reached your camp I saw a battle had taken place. I did not think anyone was still living. I saw the tent but thought it was empty. Until you moved inside." He stared at John. "I thought you were enemy. I am sorry." He turned his head toward the smoldering remains.

"My best friend." John pointed at the ashes and turned away. "I couldn't leave him here for the wolves so I lit the fire and burned the bodies." He paused. "I'll just dig them in." He started toward the pile of ashes.

"Let me help you." The Mohawk stood quickly and together they began to dig.

LATER THAT DAY the two led a string of riderless horses along the trail toward the Mohawk's village. He had decided to accompany James Roberts (the Mohawk's English name), hoping to hear of Lucy and William. Perhaps the Mohawks would know something.

They made good time, stopping only briefly to relieve them-selves and see to the horses. As they rode they nibbled on dried meat and hard tack, trying to make as much time as possible before nightfall, and, before the sun had completely fallen through the trees behind them, the two reached the camp and safety.

After eating and drinking in the familiar longhouse, he ques-tioned his hosts but no one knew anything about Lucy. His search would begin in the morning when he would return to their farm to pick up the trail. For the moment he wanted sleep.

THE DAY DAWNED EARLY and the thirsty sun quickly swallowed up the dew; John knew he was in for a hot ride. Tying his pack behind his saddle he made sure he had lots of water and swung up for the long journey ahead. He turned to James, raised his arm in a silent farewell, and pointed Maudie toward home. He had miles to ride, along a treacherous trail, full of enemies and dangers. But he thought only of his family and kicked his heels into Maudie's sides urging her on ever faster, ever closer to the cabin.

He rode in a blur of galloping, hiding from soldiers and Indians, stopping for short naps, gulping water at the river's edge, and gnawing on his scant food supplies whenever his hunger surfaced. He thought only of finding Lucy. He felt sure she would have left him some sign or message.

Days later he started to recognize the trail. "Come on, Maudie. Not much longer now, girl." He patted her glistening neck and she seemed to come alive at his touch. She, too, recognized where she was. A burst of energy carried them toward the cabin.

He thought of the walks Lucy took, saw her favorite giant pine rush by, and felt his blood rise at the memory of their last walk together before he left for the Rangers. He slowed Maudie to a walk, strained to see, to hear, to know what lay ahead.

The trees opened in the distance and his barn came into view. As he rode into the clearing, he saw no one, heard nothing. No animals, no people, nothing. Near the barn he slipped off Maudie and stepped to the neatly fastened door. He lifted the latch.

Empty.

He turned toward the cabin, leading Maudie along the familiar path now grown over. Grass covered the trail to the outhouse. No one had used it in a long time.

The cabin door stood ajar. A tin cup lay beside the well pump. She should have taken that. He looped Maudie's reins over the rail and approached the porch. As he pushed the door wider and peered into the semi darkness, a sudden crashing stopped him. He jumped to the side. The hind end of a stripe-tailed raccoon dashed by him and wriggled away into the long grass.

"So, someone is home." He spoke aloud in the silent room.

The raccoon had strewn corn cobs, husks, leaves and debris across the bare floor. The huge stove stood cold and dark, useless.

The table and chairs were gone, Lucy's mother's chest, too, and his own chair. He saw the marks on the floor from its rockers and pictured Lucy sitting with Harper John at her breast.

He blinked back tears and entered the bedroom. The room was empty. Dust motes danced in the sunlight streaming through the dirty window, the only life in the whole cabin.

"Ah, Lucy. Where are you?"

He studied the vacant room. His fingers touched the walls, sliding over the familiar places, looking for something, anything to suggest what had happened. He lifted a loose floorboard and peered into the gloom, then reached in and felt around the whole space. Nothing.

He backed out the doorway and began the same process in the main room. The shelves by the stove were bare, the dry sink full of raccoon debris but nothing else. He felt along the top edge of the rafters, searching for a note, for anything from Lucy.

As the shadows lengthened across the floor he continued looking; he even lifted up the cellar boards and inched down into that dark, dank space. But he found nothing.

FROM THE PORCH he watched the sun sink behind the familiar trees—his trees—and his chest tightened. He could not think what to do now, or where to go next. Maudie still stood at the rail munching the long grass of the untended yard, nickering softly every so often, as though to comfort him. But he barely heard her. His brain ached with the effort of thinking. He had searched the cabin, the barn, everywhere. And had found nothing. Maudie nipped at his knee.

He jumped to his feet and ran for the barn. "The hole by the wall. I forgot about the hole." Alongside the barn he searched for the secret place where Lucy kept her emergency box.

With his bare hands he tugged and tore at the long grass but the roots were dense and completely matted over. He knew this was the place. Right beside that big knot hole. He remembered Lucy laughing as she pointed it out. A little more, just a little more. He had the grass ripped away now and could feel something hard.

He tore at the clods of earth covering the box. He kicked with his boot to loosen the box from the earth. It moved. He tugged the dark thing out of the hole and brushed the dirt from the rough wood. He stopped a moment. Maybe she hadn't left him a message.

Slowly his worn fingers inched the clasp open. He blew the dirt off and lifted the lid. His eyes strained. His blood thumped through his chest. He unwrapped a smelly oilcloth pouch and dropped it immediately. The meat had turned rancid.

A sack of potatoes and carrots had sprouted long white tentacles twisted together. He threw them aside and saw the leather case. "Ah. What is this?" He pulled back the flap. Moments later he was reading Lucy's note:

> *Dearest John*
>
> *I am hoping that you will find this if you come back looking for us. That will mean we have not made it to Niagara and Colonel Butler's camp or have missed you in some other way. Father and I made the difficult decision to leave after more trouble with a large group of Indians and the threat of ruffians doing to us what they did to Frank's father. We are leaving tomorrow and hope to make Niagara before summer sets in. We are taking both pair of oxen, the horse, and as much of our furniture as we can fit on the wagon. Regretfully I have decided we cannot take our stove but pray that someday we'll be back to reclaim our farm and it will be here waiting for us.*
>
> *We all miss you terribly but at this writing are in good health and have great hopes of seeing you very soon.*
>
> *Your loving wife, Lucy.*

"Niagara. They went to Niagara. But I never saw them. They never arrived."

He sat in the grass by the barn, clutching Lucy's letter in his left hand, his eyes staring but seeing nothing. He had to retrace his steps and take the trail to Niagara, checking every stopping spot along the way and asking everyone he saw for information. That would be dangerous, but he had no choice.

The sun had disappeared and long shadows covered the yard. The first star blinked in the darkening blue of the sky. Night was falling fast. He struggled to his feet and led Maudie to the barn where she shuffled and almost purred under his quick curry combing.

With his pack he tramped through the long grass toward the cabin and wished for Lucy's light to call him home, but only the cabin's blackened shape stood against the sky. Though the night was warm he made a fire in Lucy's stove and sat on the floor against the wall in the soft light to eat his dried supper. He would have to hunt tomorrow and get some fresh meat. Maybe he'd even see some berries. He'd follow Lucy's path on his way and gather some fresh things. He spread his blanket over the pale spot on the hard floor and lay down to sleep.

Chapter Thirty-Four

DAWN CAME EARLY. He stretched his stiffened legs before rising and stuffing his meager possessions in the pack. He would eat later. For now he made sure the fire in the stove was completely out, checked the windows and latched the door behind him.

He saddled Maudie as she ate bits of hay on the barn floor, tied his pack on her rump and led her outside where she dropped her head to the fresh grass. John turned to close up the barn. He hoped someday to come back and find everything safe and secure. He could not guess when.

As he started along the trail through the trees he was happy. He hustled Maudie as fast as he could while still watching and listening for anything that would lead him to Lucy. He did not know how he would find his family but at least now he was looking for them. He was doing something.

His bag was full of berries and lamb's quarters, hard to find tender enough this late in the season but he was glad he had taken the time to search. Besides, he had thought about Lucy and the times, together, they had done the self same thing. He imagined her hair in the sunlight at their favorite place that last time. He longed to touch its rusty shine again. He dug his boots into Maudie.

"Come on, girl. We have a lot of ground to cover before dark."

The day was hot, even under the trees, and the occasional bare patches of unbroken sun made both John and Maudie pant. They slowed to a walk. Finally, he pulled her up by the river and dipped his feet in the cool water. He didn't have to encourage Maudie—she stood right beside him, up to her hocks in the cool water, slurping long gulps.

"Not too much, Maudie. Not too much." He pulled at the lead, ready to move on.

"A hot day it is, sir."

He jerked his head around and stared at the little bow-legged man leaning against a maple about fifteen feet away. He was rough and ragged but something about him looked familiar. "Yes. The water feels good." He stared at the little man. "Hilton Cross." He motioned with his arm. "Come and get something to drink, sir. Cool yourself."

He stepped aside and Hilton joined him by the water. "Come on, Hilton, take off your boots and dip your toes."

Shaking his head, Hilton Cross remained on the bank but leaned over to splash water on his face, then cupped his hands and drank. He took off his hat—the same bedraggled one he had worn when John first met him. He dipped it into the water and up over his shaggy light hair and worn homespun shirt. He repeated the motion until his whole small form dripped. He wiped his face with his sleeve and smiled.

"I thought it was you, Garner."

The two exchanged stories and traded war news. John, of course, asked about Lucy but Hilton had no news. He was on his way northwest to Niagara to leave New York for good.

"There is nothing left for me here anymore. My family is gone, my wife and daughter murdered in their beds, by American soldiers. My land has been stolen and I have no way to get it back." He paused and took a deep breath. "I have no fight left in me, Garner."

John looked at the little man struggling to keep his composure and spoke. "Hilton, why don't you come with me? I am going to Niagara eventually. As soon as I find out what happened to Lucy and our son. I am sure by now she is there. But I intend to look for her all along the way just to be certain."

"The company would be good." Hilton Cross nodded his head.

"Let us get started, then. We have many miles to cover." John filled his water container.

At every possible stopover place along the way the two men dismounted and studied the ground, the trees, the fire patches, the whole area, looking for some sign. By nightfall they had covered a lot of the trail but had found nothing. John was still confident he was on the right course. Tomorrow they would carry on, and the next day, and the day after that and one day they would find his family.

The heat had carried into the still night. He slept fitfully, pulling his blanket over his head to keep the mosquitoes away and then throwing it off to escape the heat and breathe fresh air again. When the pale threads of dawn streaked the sky the men were up and riding once more, eager to search but anxious about what they might find.

The trail wound along the riverbed, a snaking line twisting and turning beside the water's edge. Back and forth they meandered, searching and stopping, looking and wondering, trying to determine what had happened to Lucy. At night their routine was simple—wash, drink, eat, sleep—and wake with the sun to do it all again.

A few days across the broad expanse of New York, John's hopes evaporated. They had found no sign of Lucy or William or Harper John. His mind ran wild with possibilities as runnels of sweat coursed down his face and neck and inside his shirt. He longed for cooler weather and for some word, anything, about Lucy.

Today they had stopped once for food and were riding west again. The trees and the hills dropped away, leaving a broad expanse of plain full of diving birds and scurrying rodents off to the side of the rutted trail. There had been wagons over this path, a lot of them, and he watched to see where one might have left the track and camped. He had little hope of seeing anything but knew nothing else to do. He would keep going all the way to Niagara this way. He swatted again at the sweat tickling down his cheeks.

Hilton shouted from behind. He was pointing south. "I can see something in that boggy area."

John squinted against the glare and thought he caught something fluttering in the breeze. "Let's go."

"A wagon has been over the track, and animals, too." Hilton watched the ground as he walked his horse along.

"Maybe the extra oxen she said she took. Or the horse. Look, I can see a horse's hoof print just over that wagon rut."

The two men saw where a campfire had been and tried to read the story in the smudged tracks left behind.

"Look here, Hilton." He pointed to blood on the ground beside a hole. "What do you make of that?"

"For sure it's blood."

"They must have camped here. Something happened. Someone got hurt." John swung onto Maudie. "We need to keep going."

Heading back to the trail the men made out two ruts evenly spaced with smudged and brushed marks between them. The horse hooves were close together.

"They were walking here, pulling something."

Hilton looked up. "Someone was hurt, John."

Riding faster they followed the odd markings until suddenly there were no more. Slowly they backtracked and found where the trail veered off into the brush. John looked up at the trees in the distance. He felt his breath catch. "Lucy," he whispered and rode for the trees, Hilton keeping pace just behind.

"There's the wagon." He kicked at Maudie and raced toward the site. From a distance he could not make out anyone but squinted against the afternoon sun for a glimpse of Lucy.

He saw the upended wagon with one wheel lying in the dust, the contents spilling to the ground. The buffalo robe was half under the wagon, a crumpled mess. A corn sack lay ripped and empty in the grass, a couple of hard kernels lost in the dirt. His eyes strayed to the cold fire pit and Lucy's best pot charred and broken in the ashes. The still desolation of the place gradually overtook his senses as he stumbled about. "My God. What happened here?"

"Now, John, we don't know she was here, do we? This could be someone else's wagon, could it not?"

"Oh, it's mine. These things are ours." John jumped from the horse and strode toward the wagon. "And this is the cradle we made for Harper John." He grabbed at it and set it upright on the ground. When his hand came away he felt the stickiness. Blood. On the side of the cradle. John sank to his knees, dropping his head in his hands.

"I should have been with them. I should have protected them. Instead I was off fighting a useless war."

Hilton gripped John's shoulder. "We have to find them. We'll just not know until we do, John."

As the sun slid lower in the trees the two men combed the whole area but found little to help them. They walked further into the trees looking for bodies, or signs, or something, anything. But they found nothing.

John sat on a fallen log beside the cold fire pit and jabbed at the ground with a twig. Hilton was quiet beside him. In the west the sun sank.

Chapter Thirty-Five

July, 1779

THE WATER SIDLED UP HER LEGS and she paused as the cold prickled her thighs. She was reluctant to take the plunge into the running stream, yet wanted to wash herself free of the grime of the last couple of days. Something moved against her legs.

She jumped away and ducked under, the water icy for a second but then a soothing flow against her skin. Lucy splashed and dipped, loving the release of being naked in the cleansing water. She soaped her whole body including her hair and then ducked to rinse clean.

Too soon she made her way back to the grassy bank and stepped carefully over the stones to her pile of clothes. She grabbed them, along with some of the baby's and William's things and knuckled them clean with soap in the river water, tossing each item up on the bank before going on with the next.

She had never done her washing naked before. She laughed aloud and scrubbed a little harder. The laugh felt good. Finishing the last swaddling cloth she turned and took a few steps back into the cool depths behind her for a quick dip and a couple of strokes before heading for shore to start her day.

Back at the campsite William sat against the wheel of the wagon with Harper John crawling in the grass beside him, the pair laughing and giggling so much that Lucy could not tell who was happier. Maybe this would all work out well after all. She spread the washing to dry on the bushes nearby and turned to her men.

"Who wants something to eat?"

"I think you'd best look after the young one, daughter. I can only keep him happy for so long."

She took Harper John and settled in John's chair near the wagon, quickly helping the hungry baby find the breast before looking at her father once more. "That stream was wonderful. I actually enjoyed washing the clothing after my swim."

"I expect the water is not too cold?"

"Oh, it's cold, but refreshing. I wonder how we could get you into the water? Or if we should?"

"Probably not until this leg heals. I'll just have to content myself with pouring water over my head." He chuckled. "Or maybe you would like to do that, Lucinda?"

"Oh, Father. You know I'd never do that." She turned back to Harper John. Soon she handed him back to her father. She pulled some dried deer meat from their stores and mixed it with fresh water in the pot over the fire pit. "How did you get over here to get this started?" She turned and saw William lean toward Harper John to pull him back by one leg.

"Oh, I'm smarter than you might think, daughter. And I certainly cannot be letting you do all the work around here, now can I?" He was happy tending his grandson. She smiled and turned back to the stew.

The days passed with little happening. They saw troops go by—Americans, they were, on the trail in the distance—but kept the fire out and no one came near. Lucy took the rifle and shot a rabbit one day and a beaver another, bringing both back to the camp and to her father, who skinned and cleaned them for cooking. She hung their skins to dry in the trees nearby.

They were self-sufficient and Lucy felt they could go on this way for a good long time. But winter was coming. They would have to get to shelter. Also they had no harvest to store for that winter.

....

She did find leeks and wild onions on her walks through the woods, as well as many varieties of berries, which she would taste and toss if bad but, if good, carry back triumphantly to the camp. As often as she could she dried what they didn't eat, adding gradually to her little store of food, but it was all too pitiful, far less than they would need.

One day, after they had been there for about two fortnights, Lucy came back to the camp to find William hobbling after Harper John. The little boy's chubby legs crawled along the ground toward the wagon, where he collapsed in the grass just as his grandfather caught him.

"Father. You should not be on that leg." Lucy rushed to his side and pushed under his shoulder. "Here, let me help you."

"Thank you." He slipped into the rocking chair. "That little rascal is becoming quite the crawler. I'm going to have to tie him up or he'll be in the fire before I can get to him."

"Or he'll have to come with me as much as possible. We cannot have you on that leg." She gathered Harper John up and held him to her, his little legs wriggling against her until she released him to the ground again. "He's only eight months old. I thought we would have longer before he'd be mobile."

William shrugged. "Sometimes they wait two years before they walk but not this one. He'll be walking next week. And we'll have to watch him every minute."

They rigged a line to Harper John so that he could not crawl into danger, a help to William when she was off in the forest or washing clothes or tending the oxen or doing any one of the many other chores filling her day.

William helped as he was able and day by day she saw his strength returning. The time was coming when they would strike out in the wagon again but she didn't know whether to be happy at moving on or worried about other dangers they might find on the trail.

Her father's pain made him seem old now as he never had before. She heard his sharp breath intakes and saw his grimaces when he thought she wasn't looking. His leg was definitely a concern but she wondered if he had other problems.

At night, dead tired and longing for sleep, she lay listening to her father's groans as he tried to shift his injured leg. His breathing was often fast and then, sometimes, she couldn't hear him breathing at all. Once she had crawled over to him to hold her fingers under his nose just to make sure. Relieved she lay down again and prayed that she would be able to get them to Niagara soon.

In the daylight she worked hard and longed for the good times ahead when John would be with them and they would be a family once more. Sometimes he just stole into her thoughts, taking her unawares, and she visited with him for a wee bit before turning back to her father or Harper John.

She had enough to keep her so busy that she crawled exhausted under the wagon at night and, once asleep, slept soundly until the rooster's call at first light. Then she would rise to another day and do it all again.

Tonight as she tucked the quilt around Harper John, she noticed the stillness. She lay back and listened for the owl and the nighttime rustlings of every other night but all was still. Maybe the weather was changing. Her father and her son breathed softly in the silence. She relaxed.

"AHH!" SHE CRIED OUT at the rough bone-grinding crunch in her arm, and the sudden weight of the man on top of her. She felt a vicious grab at her thigh and pulled away but pain punched her whole body. "Father, help me!"

Harper John howled off to her right and a man grunted in her ear. He had her pinned with his body weight and one hand. With the other he yanked up her skirt. She wrenched from left to right trying to kick him. But he was too strong. She heard the rip of her underclothes.

Her nose was pressed against his chest. Sweat. And dirt. She gagged and felt hot tears even as he struggled against her, into her, tearing and ramming against her futile screams, and then sagging limp, a hot putrid weight pushing her into the ground. She sobbed.

The man pulled away and left Lucy lying naked and exposed. She rolled onto her side and into a ball clutching herself as silent tears drenched her face. She heard him a few feet off.

"Your turn."

Gradually she realized what that meant, opened her eyes and, in the dim morning light, saw her rifle. Her fingers closed over the cold metal and found the trigger. She breathed in the dank dawn air and watched the muddied boots come nearer. She saw them bend and knew he was kneeling.

A bearded face poked into view, black eyes squinting in the dimness. Lucy's chest heaved as she yanked the trigger. The wagon lurched and the ground seemed to lift as she and Harper John yelled together.

He fell across her feet. She shoved him off and felt a sticky goo on her hand. The other one was back and pulled at her shoulders from behind.

She had forgotten him. For a moment she relaxed, confused. He had her out from under the wagon now and dragged her to her feet. He thwacked across her mouth and she tasted blood.

"Crazy woman. You'll learn your manners now." He slapped her again, sending her tripping sideways to the ground, where he kicked her ribs then knelt and twisted her hands behind her back. The rope cut into her wrists but she pulled against the pain anyhow, struggling to be free. His boot struck her cheekbone and she went limp, falling.

The salty taste of blood roused her and she pulled at her bound hands, then remembered. All was quiet. She opened one eye. The fire was burning, steady wisps of smoke lifting into the blue. Bacon. She smelled bacon and felt her lips move.

Ouch. Her tongue licked at the blood. She heard only the crackling of the fire. Where was Harper John? Father? She strained to see more and felt a sharp pain in her side but struggled to one elbow anyhow. "Ohhhh." The sound escaped her lips.

"So you're awake, little lady." The man's voice came from behind.

She turned to the sound. "Who are you?"

His lips parted to show a few yellowed teeth punctuated by black gaps. "Don't you remember me, little lady?" He leered at her and she knew. "Oh, yes. You remember, don't you? I knew you and I would meet again but I had a time finding you, I did."

"Where is my father?" Lucy bit off each word.

The man studied her, his eyes following the contours of her body. "Father, is it? I thought he looked too old to have a sweet young thing like you."

"Where is he?"

"Oh, he won't be any more trouble for us."

She gasped and pulled herself up, scanning the campsite. A fresh mound of rocks and clods of earth rose beside the path to the river.

"That's the man you shot in the face, you she-devil." He glared at her. Slowly his hand rose and he pointed off into the trees where a huddled form lay face down in the dirt.

"Father!" She lurched to her feet, groaning, hands still tied, and limped toward her father's body. She knelt and nudged him over with her shoulder. "Oh, Father."

He seemed to stare right at her and her breath caught, but then she realized he would never see again. And they had taken his hair. The horror struck her in great gasping sobs. They had scalped her gentle father. Her sobs turned to gulps of air until she felt anger surge up from her gut. These men had killed him. And then scalped him.

She struggled upright and stared back at the watching murderer. She stomped toward his grinning face, bile filling her mouth. She spat at his feet. "Why? You're not Indian. Why?"

"Why did we kill him or why did we scalp him? You have to be specific, little lady."

Lucy's eyes bored into him. "Both!"

"He was so busy relieving himself, his back to us as we sneaked up, that he never heard a thing. I just reached around nice and easy and slit his throat. Didn't even make a sound. Snake felt left out so he cut a bragging scalp. Looks better without all that hair, don't you think?" He grinned a hairy, gap-toothed leer at her, his eyes open and cruel.

Suddenly she felt her own eyes widen and staggered backwards, away from the man. "My baby. What did you do with my baby?" Screaming, she ran the few steps to the wagon where the night curtains were torn aside but the cradle was empty. Blood spatters covered its sides.

"Harper John. Harper John!" She keened and wailed but heard no answer. Her body ached with sobs as she looked wildly about, beyond the wagon. "What have you done with him?" she screamed and raced toward the man, tripping and falling into him, until he slapped her away.

"Calm down, woman. Calm down. I never saw him. Besides, we're better off without him, don't you think?" He laughed.

But Lucy was beyond caring or even listening, hobbling around the campsite, ranging ever further and further, careening from one place to another, oblivious to her tied hands. "Harper John. Harper John." She wailed and wailed but heard nothing in reply. The trees grabbed her now, lashing against her face as she ran forward, and finally tripped and fell hard into the ground, a sharp jab in her ribs knocking the wind out of her.

She lay on her stomach and tried to breathe but no air came. She pushed onto her back. Eyes wide with pain, she felt she would never breathe again and her hands clenched as she prayed for her lungs to fill, her body screaming for air, her eyes fixing frantically on the patch of blue above, the sharp pain searing her chest and side, sucking the life out of her.

When she felt she would surely die from the airless void inside her, she finally gulped. And choked. And invisible air flooded into her lungs. Coughing and sputtering she lay limp on the ground, the pain in her side easing with every breath, but the pain in her heart still a hungry roar.

Chapter Thirty-Six

August, 1779

SHE JERKED TOWARD THE FAINT SOUND. She strained her ears but now heard nothing. She lurched to her feet. "Harper John!" Imagining his cry she turned toward the sound. There it was, a soft whimpering off to the right. She ran for it.

In a green grassy hollow, partially hidden by huge skunk cabbage leaves, Harper John sucked furiously at his thumb. When he saw her, he let it go and howled. His eyes were red and his cheeks bruised. Red scratches covered his knees and feet. She longed to hold and shush him but her hands were tied. Instead she lay beside him and kissed his wee cheek, murmuring a steady stream of comfort. His sobs stopped but not for long. He was hungry.

"Isn't this a pretty picture?"

She tensed at the familiar voice and the leering eyes. For both of them she forced her fears down and stared at him. "You need to untie me."

"Why should I do that? You'll jist try to run."

Harper John's howl startled them both and she leaned down to kiss him, then fixed her eyes on their captor.

"I won't run. How could I, with a baby?" She watched his eyes open slightly and saw she had made him think. "He's just hungry now. That's why he's crying. Untie me and I'll feed him."

Reaching into a grimy pouch at his waist, the grubby man pulled out a small knife and stepped into the hollow. She watched his eyes as he approached and decided he would not hurt them. She rolled toward Harper John just enough so that her tied hands were exposed to the man.

He stank. She held her breath, felt his hand on hers. She flashed back to the attack under the wagon and struggled against tears, but, suddenly, her hands were free and the smell was gone.

"There. Feed your baby. But don't try to run or I'll kill you both." He glared at her, as she rubbed her wrists. "Your baby first, so's you can watch."

The meanness was back in his eyes and she clutched at Harper John. For a moment, no one moved until, finally, the man turned and stepped out of the hollow.

He walked away, found a tree, fumbled at his britches and turned his back on her. Her face heated up. Shock and then anger seized her, but little Harper John was howling. She closed her eyes and hugged him to her, the familiar tug at her breast no comfort. She tried to forget their captor just a few feet away.

What could she do? Her father was dead. She needed to tend to his body, and bury him, but would the man let her? She opened her eyes to see where he was and squeezed them shut again. A few feet away he leaned against a tree, waiting and watching.

Soiled. She felt dirty and tried not to think of his body over hers but the memory of his rancid smell choked her. Harper John ceased his sucking, blinking his eyes open at her. She patted him until he continued. She had to survive for him. She would figure out a way to escape, or to kill the man as she had his partner. Her body stiffened and her fingers pressed into Harper John.

SHE HAD NO CHANCE TO BE ALONE the rest of the day. When she went off in the woods to relieve herself, the man—Pete, he said his name was—insisted she leave Harper John behind, so that she rushed to get back. She tried to wait until the baby was napping so he would not annoy the hot-tempered Pete. He would shoot her son, and her, with no thought at all, and probably laugh afterwards. He was that ruthless.

Now the evening meal was over and long shadows darkened through the trees. From her spot on the ground she glanced across the fire pit at Pete's still form drowsing against the wagon wheel. All day she had planned and replanned ways to escape but she had come up with nothing. She would take a great risk striking off into the woods alone with Harper John but she had to go. Or find a way to kill her captor.

She glanced again toward the wagon and looked away. He was staring at her, his thoughts all too obvious in his sickening grin.

"There's a chill in the air, little lady." He punched out the last two words and grinned as she looked his way. "Don't worry. I'll warm you, little lady. I'll warm you."

She looked to her rifle on the wagon seat but there was no ammunition in it. She had emptied it on a rabbit yesterday and, with Harper screaming to be fed, had forgotten to reload. She would have to get to the gun and the bullets, load the gun, and aim before she had a chance of shooting him.

Pete moved to stir the fire and she sidled toward the wagon. Maybe when he was sleeping. She crawled under the wagon and laid the sleeping Harper John in his cradle, some part of her noticing how long he had grown. His feet almost touched the end of the wee bed. Soon he would be sleeping on the ground just as she did. She winced as she thought of him near her when the horrid man came to reclaim her body.

As though reading her mind, Pete hollered. "Come out here, little lady."

Her stomach tightened and her heart seemed to beat in her ears. She thought of staying where she was but there was nothing she could do. She had to crawl out into the twilight and face him.

He took her on the ground in the open with only the darkness to hide her despair. She had struggled when first he grabbed her but when he went for the rifle she lost her courage for fear of what he might do to Harper John. Forcing her thoughts away she turned toward the flames, memorizing their shapes as they devoured the dead wood, licking and sniffing around each piece, gradually turning them red hot, then white as death. The logs fell and sparks flew up into the night.

She felt his dead weight upon her and, realizing she was shaking uncontrollably, reached her cold hand toward the fire and the cleansing flames. He pulled away and she breathed fresh air again. She yanked her skirts down. She stood and faced him as he buttoned his trousers.

"I have to go in the woods." Her voice was low and hard.

"Just don't be getting any ideas of running. I'm keeping that baby right here, as a play toy, you know."

She heard his threat as she turned and grabbed the water jug and a cleaning cloth. She needed to bathe.

When she returned Pete sat by the fire, only glancing up as she bent to crawl under the wagon.

"Come here, woman."

Lucy had hoped to avoid the tying up but her captor had other plans. This time he tied her hands in front of her, had her crawl under the wagon, and laced her feet together on a long rope tied to the wheel. She could barely move. He had left her some room to turn over, although certainly no way to escape.

She lay quietly listening to the fire, tuned to every crackle and owl's hoot. If she could get her hands untied, she could easily release her feet. Then she had to kill him. She knew it and was ready to do it. As soon as she could.

He had loaded her rifle today and placed it in the wagon without firing it, watching her the whole time, the threat loud and clear, and he kept it near him wherever he went. If she went for it he would certainly grab it first. He didn't want to kill her—he liked his pleasure—but he would if she gave him any cause. And then what would happen to Harper John?

She felt the tears seep from her eyelids and squeezed them shut in an effort not to cry, bringing her bound hands up to push away the tears. I must be strong. She breathed deeply, felt her chest relax and heard the man shuffling, probably readying the fire for night. Was he coming in here? Her breath caught once more, but eased out as she heard him grunt into place on the ground and settle for the night.

Harper John's gurgles woke her to daylight streaming through the curtains into their shelter under the wagon. The rope cut into her wrists and ankles and she twisted to find a more comfortable position. Pushing the curtain aside she saw the still form by the fire and realized he was sleeping, a blessing in one way, but she needed to get loose. Harper John was becoming insistent. He was hungry.

"Hey." She shouted to wake the man. "Hey. You need to untie me so I can feed the baby." She heard nothing but Harper John's cries beside her. She longed to pick him up but all she could do was reach her bound hands over and rub his belly, a futile gesture which did nothing to end the howls filling the air.

Suddenly the curtains parted and Pete's ugly face appeared. Lucy cringed. He was holding a knife. His eyes were black holes in the mass of hair scraggling over his face as he reached toward Lucy's hands. She flinched.

"Just going to cut you loose, little lady." He grinned and breathed through his mouth and the foul smell made her jerk away. "Hold still."

Finally she was free and alone under the wagon with Harper John hungrily pulling at her breast. She sat against the wheel, her head fallen back, and listened to her captor talking to the animals as he watered them. He did not seem so bad with them or with Harper John.

Only with her did he snarl and shove and laugh when she fell. He delighted in her pain, as if somehow that gave him strength. She stroked Harper John's downy head and felt his hunger. But her glazed eyes were looking right through the wagon, focused on some far off future when this nightmare would be over, when John...

A tear slipped down her cheek.

Chapter Thirty-Seven

August, 1779

THE NIGHT WAS HOT. She had tied back the makeshift curtains to allow a little breeze to waft in on her and Harper John but still she felt drained and lifeless. Her skin crawled with sweat, itching and tickling her, but she barely noticed. On their own her fingers swept across her forehead and came away wet. She felt awash in desperation, but hardly knew what to do.

"You asleep in there, woman?"

She was immediately aware of her short breaths, her stiffened body, and she tried to fake sleep.

"Woman. Come out here."

Her mind raced with possibilities. She thought he didn't want her tonight as he had tied her up without the usual attack on her person, and she had lain here wondering what that could possibly mean. Then her mind had switched to trying to think of a plan to escape and save Harper John and herself. She had been on the verge of an idea when her captor hollered.

"I forgot." His head poked through the open curtains. "You're hogtied, ain't you?" Pushing into the space, he landed on her leg.

"You're hurting me."

"Now, I don't want to do that, do I?"

She felt his sour breath over her, sensed his face pushing down toward hers. She twisted her head away.

"Now you don't want to be that way, little lady. Time you gave me a little kiss. We're getting to be such good friends, ain't we?" His one hand gripped her neck while his other stroked across her cheek and down over her breasts, fondling and squeezing as he explored. "You might get to enjoy this." His hand suddenly tweaked her nipple and she jerked.

"We are never going to be friends." She spat the words at the hated face and felt his furious hands tighten on her neck until she could hardly breathe. She could not move yet the pain seemed to be stretching her neck longer and longer, until her head thumped against the wheel and little stars flashed above her, gone in a second as she felt her eyes bulge and blackness sweep her away.

HARPER JOHN'S HOWLS pulled Lucy back to consciousness and a minute or two passed before she realized what the sound was and reached for his cradle. As she rocked him with her right hand she pulled at her skirt which was up over her stomach. She touched her neck and winced. He had choked her. It all came back now but she struggled to keep calm for Harper John's sake. She was alive. That was something.

Suddenly Lucy's eyes shot open in the blackness. She jerked her hands together and a faint hope kindled inside her. Her hands were loose. He must have cut the rope. For what reason she could not fathom, but her hands were definitely loose.

Harper John had quieted, leaving her free to think. Now was the time. She listened for the man and heard nothing but the odd dropping log and the momentary silence of the crickets and cicadas whirring in the night. When they started up again, she sat and reached for the cords binding her feet but they were as tight as every other night.

She forced herself to see the knots in her mind's eye, feeling where to pull and where to push but the cords kept her imprisoned. She fought her frustration and picked at the knots, her hands dripping in the sweaty night.

She paused to wipe them before trying one more time. Blinking sweat from her eyes, she felt the cords finally loosen. She stifled a cry, paused to wipe her arm over her face, and took a long, quiet breath.

She was free. Sucking damp air into her lungs she leaned toward the curtains and peeked out. A faint glow from the fire showed the outline of Pete's sleeping form but the night was black and bleak. She would have trouble moving around without tripping. Maybe she would wait until the predawn light. The rifle was on the wagon. She would get it and make sure it was loaded. She had the bullets in the box beside the cradle and Pete had never seen the need to move them. If she didn't have the rifle she couldn't use the bullets. She smiled.

Ever so slowly she eased out from under the wagon. Listening to the low snoring she strained to see Pete in the starless night. He was asleep. She stood beside the wagon and felt her way along to the front where she had seen him put the rifle, then reached over the box sides and stretched to find the gun.

Behind her, Pete's snoring deepened. She prayed it would keep going. Where was that gun? On tiptoe, she leaned as far as she could into the wagon. Her fingers closed over the cool barrel.

Pete snored on. Slowly the rifle came to her, like a child to its mother. Her courage rose as she lifted the rifle over the box and held it in her arms. Now she had power. Her breath evened out as she turned toward Pete once more. Back under the wagon she went.

Chapter Thirty-Eight

LUCY JERKED AWAKE. The cold rifle was in her hands. She had fallen asleep. Angry, she listened for the man. She heard the tiny whoosh of Harper John's even breathing. Good. She fingered the curtain aside.

In the wet mist of the late August morning the first glimmers of sunlight in the tops of the trees overhead told her she had little time. She studied the camp site, planning her path. He must not hear her. She had to be absolutely silent until she could aim the gun and fire.

She pulled to her feet, lifted the gun out behind her, and turned toward Pete's body. The grass was wet. She should have put on her shoes. Too late. She felt a morning chill and shivered.

She sucked in, raised the gun and sighted along the barrel. She had to get him on the first shot. Only one chance. The trigger was cold against her finger. She squeezed. A little more, a little more. His chest rose and she imagined his heart spot. She pulled hard but at the same instant, the man moved.

The gun kicked her backwards and she struggled to stay upright, but her feet failed. Down she went, tripping backwards, stumbling, the rifle flying up on its own out of her hands, which flailed back to break her fall.

In a tangled mass of arms and legs she hit the ground but, ignoring the shooting pains of her body, struggled to see the man. Did she get him? She pushed to her feet and grabbed the rifle to reload, all the while watching his still form. Was he moving? She listened for any sound from him but nothing came save a loud screeching, which her subconscious knew to ignore, off to her right. The baby could wait.

Lucy edged closer, saw blood on his neck and down his shoulder. He might still be alive. She stood over him but could not touch him. The sun warmed her left arm and she realized how light the day now was.

She looked back at Pete, at his scraggly beard, his unwashed body, his blood seeping onto the ground and felt...nothing. Nothing but rage. She lowered the gun and backed away. She would have to think what to do next, but not now. First, Harper John.

SITTING IN JOHN'S ROCKER on the other side of the wagon—she hadn't wanted to look at the man—Lucy's fingers swept over her baby's brow, soothing him every time he shuddered, urging him to eat. She had laid the rifle close beside her, her toes touching its smooth metal, while she stared at the trail in the distance, wishing John would come riding toward her. She was alone now. Her father was dead and John was gone, maybe never to return.

A twig snapped. She pulled Harper John from her breast and grabbed the rifle, jerked to her feet, and wrenched around. Nothing moved in the clearing. The hens and rooster pecked in the sand, a bird called in the trees and the oxen shuffled as they grazed nearby.

And the man. He lay as before, still and disgusting, a dark pile of filth marring the summer greens. She could almost smell his stench. She squared her shoulders, lowered the rifle and went back to her babe.

Harper John played under the wagon, away from the dreaded sight of the man while Lucy tied what she could up on top. She had no reason to stay now, and she was anxious to leave behind the memories of this place. Besides, she had to find John. Even though the road was dangerous, staying here was unthinkable. She had to leave, and the sooner the better, as the sun was riding high in the sky. She would not stay another night in this place. Her brow was wet and she paused to catch her breath.

She had the wagon loaded and the oxen almost hitched ready to go. She glanced into the trees to the south, saw her path to the river and wished she could swim but did not dare take the time. Her eyes came back to the camp where the body lay and—he was gone. She reached for the rifle but had left it on the other side of the wagon. She jerked back and forth looking for the man but saw nothing.

"Lookin' for me, little lady?" The voice came from below.

Lucy staggered backwards and almost fell. Pete's menacing black eyes peered out of his filthy face, mocking her, challenging her. His arms were casually wrapped around Harper John. She dropped her empty hands and stared. She was beaten. She knew it and Pete knew it.

A long moment later she sagged to the hard ground, staring at him, her rage turned to despair. She shielded her face from his bitter eyes. She took a deep breath, and watched as he slid toward her from under the wagon, his bloody hands gripping her son. Harper John reached a pudgy hand toward her but didn't make a sound. He turned to grab at the man's beard.

No, dirty. Don't touch him. Rigid she watched the man stand and then stoop to pull up her son—tears blinded her—and she struggled to her own feet just in time to see the upraised arm holding Harper John at length and the other arm smash him across the face.

"Stop! Stop! Please. I'll do anything you want. Just don't hurt him." She lunged for her screaming boy but Pete held him away from her, pushing at her with his free hand. She couldn't reach far enough but kept flailing at Pete's arm anyhow. He dropped the baby to the ground, and punched her across the nose, driving her down as well.

She lay a moment in the grass, blood filling her mouth, staring as Pete stood over her with fists clenched. He was going to kill her. In a mad frenzy, she looked around for something, anything, to stop him. Harper John lay still and silent a few feet away.

She staggered to her feet, dipping and twisting away from Pete's outstretched hands, and ran for the wagon. He panted after her, grabbing from behind. Her fingers closed around the rifle on the seat.

He had her skirt. She felt the pull but fell away in the opposite direction, and heard the cloth rip, her legs suddenly cool. She ran toward the fire pit, chanced a look over her shoulder. He was only two steps away. She veered to the right and jumped clear of the fire pit, too fast for Pete to follow. He stumbled into the rocks and ashes and went down hard against a tree stump where he lay gasping and groaning.

Lucy sighted the rifle on the half-conscious man and pulled the trigger but nothing happened. No sound, no knocking her backwards, nothing. Pete's eyes were open now, his hatred a living thing glinting at her, threatening her.

He tried to stand, fell back, and tried again. She didn't know how he was still alive. Her fingers checked the firing mechanism. Empty. She reached for her pocket but realized her skirt was gone. And he was on his feet again, coming for her, wild and staggering, his eyes wide and terrible.

She bolted for the ammunition box, found it and ran to the other side of the wagon. Her fingers fumbled with the bullets while, over the top of the wagon load, she watched Pete. He staggered and caught himself on the wagon. His eyes were bloody and fearsome. He saw the gun and lumbered toward her.

She jammed the bullet into place just as he tugged on the rifle. She held tight on the trigger. She was angry now and felt freedom close. She yanked again and somehow her strength was a match for his but not enough to free the rifle.

She smelled his sweat and felt his putrid breath in her face, and her hate exploded, giving her strength, pushing her on. With a great powerful fury she smashed her knee upward and his grip dissolved, the gun fired, and smashed against her chest. He fell screaming to the ground, and landed, curled up, half under the wagon, his hands between his legs.

And then, incredibly, he was watching her again, and trying to rise.

She grabbed the rifle, picked a bullet from those strewn on the ground. But the wagon was moving. Before her eyes the wagon wheel cut across the screaming man, the enraged oxen pulling their best. The wagon twisted and seemed to lift in the air and fall back, askew. Her carefully packed possessions tipped onto the ground in a splintering, splitting crash. The oxen, suddenly released from the half-hitched harness, stampeded toward the trees.

"Harper John," she screamed and ran for the hollering, kicking form across the clearing but he had not been in the wagon's path. She scooped him up. "You're safe, Harper John. You're safe." She clutched him to her and wheeled around to check on her attacker.

He lay groaning where the wagon had left him. He was suffering. She didn't care. She put the baby in his cradle and grabbed the rifle. The man was no longer a threat but she rammed the ammunition into the gun, slammed it to her shoulder and sighted along the barrel.

Her eyes burned into his still form. His eyes flickered and filled with fear, but she felt only the cold will to kill. She squeezed the trigger.

SHE HAD CHANGED TO HER OTHER SKIRT and sat gripping Harper John in her arms. Briefly she considered burying the body, but didn't. He wasn't worth the effort. Let the wolves have him. The real problem was the wagon. She had no way to fix the completely shattered wheel.

She had to move on. She had no reason to delay now that her father was dead. Harper John stopped sucking, his eyes frightened. "Shh. Not to worry, little one. You're all right now." She stroked the downy fluff of his head.

Later, as the sun's heat beat on her from above, she packed the winter supplies she had dried into the leather pouch. She added clothing for Harper John, a blanket and the remains of a rabbit from the day before.

The contents of her mother's chest were strewn on the ground and she picked her buttons and silver spoon out of the mess. She tied Harper John into the pack on the side of Frank's horse and, grabbing her rifle, swung up.

She looked around the campsite. All was quiet now, the distant body still. The upended wagon, their life's possessions spilling out, and her father's shallow grave hinted at what had happened here. She sat up straighter in the saddle, snapped the reins, and turned the horse into the trees.

Chapter Thirty-Nine

THE NEXT MORNING, far away from the terrible camp, she held Harper John to her breast, both of them lying cocooned in the blanket against the cool morning air. She had no fire. She feared giving others signs of their whereabouts and she didn't have a tinder box anyhow. It was back in the wagon.

When the baby finished they would be on their way through the trees once more, toward Niagara. How far it was she did not know. The thought terrified her but she pushed it away. Afraid of strangers, she knew she had to risk going back to the trail or she would get lost. She sat up, her hands patting rhythmically, her mind awhirl with the task before her, until Harper John's urgent kicks brought her back to him.

"Time to go, little one. Time to find your father."

Chapter Forty

September, 1779

JOHN YANKED THE BLANKET over his ears and shifted to his other side. Beside him Lucy's red-gold hair curled over her shoulder and her bright laughing eyes were the colour of cornflower in July. As the rooster crowed he reached for her but she rolled away pulling the patchwork quilt with her. He struggled to touch her but couldn't.

A sharp nip of frigid air on his back wakened him. He was alone on the cold wet grass beside the burned-out fire. He wanted to go back to the dream, to avoid the nightmare that was real. He must find Lucy. His hands covered his eyes for just a moment and then he stood, shook the stiffness from his shoulders and folded his blanket.

"Cross."

Hilton's huddled form was small in the grey blanket.

"Cross," he said. The blanket moved. "Time to go, Hilton."

Slowly the older man struggled to his feet, peered at John, and turned to the trees. "Back in a minute."

When he returned he walked straight to John who was packing his blanket on the already saddled Maudie. "I think we should take a good look around this whole area, John, before we move on."

John turned to Hilton's earnest eyes. "You think they might be dead in the woods somewhere?" he croaked.

"No, I don't. But we might find something to help us. We should look in all directions but especially down by the river. Obviously they would have gone there often."

"You're right. She did come here and we have no other clue. All of the animals are gone, but they could have just wandered off. Say. Did you hear a rooster this morning?" John's face brightened.

"No, I don't think I did."

"I am sure I heard that old rooster. Maybe he's close by. And maybe Lucy is, too." He turned back to his horse.

"Wait a minute, John. I need something to eat first."

"Eat some of that dried beef and let's be on our way. We have to find Lucy."

They packed their horses and swung up. He went south to the river and Hilton rode west into the trees. If one of them found anything he would shoot into the air and the other would come. The sun was warm now and burning off the morning mist. He watched Hilton ride away until the grey shadows overlaying the black of the distant trees swallowed him up. He shivered and clucked Maudie on to the river.

He could see a definite path here, and noticed the grass had been trodden even though it was growing back now. Someone had been here. Well, he knew that already. He studied the ground.

"Whoa, Maudie." He slipped off and stooped down to pick up a small rock about the size of his fist. He held it up in the filtering sunlight. It was streaked with brown. He flaked some of the colour off and tasted it. Definitely blood. His hand went limp. He dropped the stone and walked on, Maudie behind him.

The brown trail of blood on the stony ground led to the river's edge. The water rippled steadily away from him, and bright spots of sunlight slanted through the circling trees. Robins sang in the distance. He turned to the sun, closed his eyes and listened.

There was another sound, more strident, raucous even, off down the river bank. He could barely make out crows circling and diving down. Wait a minute. They were too big to be crows.

He tied Maudie to a small maple, grabbed his gun, felt for his knife and struck off through the brush along the riverbank. There was no trail here and the going was rough. Thorny bushes and tall willows dipped to the water's edge but he made steady progress, the bird call leading him on as it grew louder.

A whoosh of sound and flapping startled him. He ducked and flailed his arms at the flurry of black feathers. A smell of rot and carnage—John knew it well from the battlefield—made him gag. He covered his nose and stepped closer.

"Merciful heavens." He shut his eyes for a moment, thinking of the body all those years ago in England, before looking once more. He had to know who this was, or had been. A man. He could see the trousers, ripped and torn though they were. Was it William?

He moved closer but could not identify the man, he was so badly tossed and torn, although he did see black hair and maybe a beard. William was grey. The body was scuffed and lay in a broken heap as though it had been dragged. He stepped back, away from the putrid smell, and the circling birds flew in once more. Should he fire the musket to signal Cross?

Suddenly he heard a shot to the west, turned and thrashed through the brush to his horse, mounted and hurried off in search of Hilton. Maybe he had found Lucy? And Harper John?

His neck was a throbbing knot of tension. He tried to loosen his shoulders by shrugging and turning his head. Maybe they were dead. He threw the thought away, rammed his heels into Maudie and thundered toward the sound.

Hilton was bent over something, John could see, but what he did not know. He caught a glimpse of light-colored cloth on the ground, and kicked to hurry Maudie.

The morning sun had almost cleared the trees by this time. He squinted to make out what Hilton was doing. "Hilton! Hilton!" The man straightened and turned. He raised his arm as John came closer.

"What did you find?" John leapt from his horse.

"I am thinking this is a clout from a baby?" He stepped aside and pointed to a ragged piece of cloth in the dirt, stained brown in spots but still recognizable.

John bent over. "I think you are right. And this might be soiled or," he glanced up at Hilton, "it could be blood, couldn't it?"

"What I thought." Hilton pursed his lips and nodded.

He picked the cloth out of the dirt and held it to his nose. "Can't really tell but I think it's night soil. But what does it mean?"

"Anything. It could mean they just lost it, and maybe didn't even know."

"Or it could be worse." He held the cloth in his hands for a moment before folding it and stuffing it into his pack. "Let's search this area. Something happened back there and we need to figure out what." Quickly he told Hilton about the body but neither could say if it had anything to do with Lucy or not.

"Over here." John stood by a small pine and pointed to the ground. "A hoof print." He looked off in the distance as Hilton approached. "And look. There are more leading this way." He mounted and led off following the trail through the forest, his eyes trained on the ground, his heart thumping in his chest. Maybe she was close by.

They followed the trail easily, winding through the trees, up hills and down slopes, occasionally losing the prints and searching beyond a patch of rock or stony ground until one of them found the trail again and they carried on.

The sun was overhead now and sweat ran down John's back, but he dared not stop. He had to find Lucy. When Hilton called for a halt to eat John handed him some dried meat and turned to the trail once more, gnawing on a piece himself not from hunger but only because he knew he needed it. Eventually their path led them back out of the woods and into the open. The going was easier there and they rode side by side until Hilton gradually dropped back.

John turned in the saddle. "We're heading for the main trail."

"I'll never make it if I don't stop for a bit." Hilton's voice was thin and faint and John reined Maudie in to wait.

"I am sorry, Hilton. I have given no thought to you at all. We'll head for those trees just ahead and step down for a bit. All right?"

"Thank you. Just for a bit."

The two reached the trees and sat drinking water, silent in the afternoon shadows. Hilton leaned against a maple while John held his arms around his drawn-up knees, and jabbed a stick in the dirt. Every few moments he glanced at his friend and sighed. He had to give Hilton a rest. The man had aged ten or fifteen years in the last two, that was a fact. He was breathing heavy now; he knew without looking that Hilton was sleeping but didn't wake him and, although the waiting pained, tried to relax.

He drowsed a few moments before straightening and jumping to his feet, looking off in the distance. He had heard something, he was sure, but saw nothing either way on the trail. The horses were restless, though. He reached down to shake Cross. "Hilton," he whispered.

"Time to go, John?" He shook himself awake and used the tree to get to his feet.

"I thought I heard something. Be careful."

Instantly Cross turned his back and scanned their surroundings. Eyes and ears straining, John felt for his knife and picked up his musket, all the while watching and listening. But there was no sound.

"Mighty quiet."

"Right." John's voice was a whisper. He turned toward the horses a few steps away. Maudie's ears were up and her eyelids pulled back. He stroked her forehead keeping his eyes on the surroundings, then moved to her side. Behind him Hilton was already in the saddle. He swung up and, holding his musket in one hand and the reins in the other, urged Maudie out of the thicket. Cross followed.

The sound exploded behind John, a terrible mix of man and horse and something screaming. Behind him Cross fought off a mass of tawny fur, spotted black, while his horse twisted and thrashed. He had his gun up but couldn't get a clear shot. He came alongside and with his musket pounded at the lynx, trying to release Hilton from its claws.

Suddenly they were all tumbling to the ground as the spooked horses reared and threw them. In the dirt John aimed his musket at the fleeing cat, but missed. As quickly as he had come, the attacker disappeared.

Hilton's head was bloodied and his one eyelid sagged but, other than a few scratches on his arms, he was not seriously hurt. He lay on the ground, his eyes closed and his breathing slow, as John tended his cuts. He kept watch for the cat but also for the horses to come back.

"Are you still feeling poorly, Hilton?"

The man's eyes moved behind his scratched lids but he did not open them.

"Hilton."

Slowly Hilton opened his eyes and looked at John. "I'm fine. Just tired. Need to sleep."

He sat back and waited but Hilton's eyes were shut. He was asleep and John hadn't the heart to wake him. A twig snapped and he jerked his head around. Maudie was coming back along the trail. He whistled softly. She whinnied in reply. He took off the saddle and brushed her down while Hilton slept. They would have to make camp here for the night. Another day lost. He shook his head and began to set up the tent once more.

For hours Hilton lay motionless in the dirt while John tended to the horses—Hilton's was back now, too—and sewed up a rip in his shirt, on guard the whole time. The sun stretched across the sky and dropped behind the western clouds gathering in the distance, another worry in the crowded turmoil of John's mind. Finally he woke his friend, gave him water and got him to his feet.

"I thought I'd look for a rabbit or two, Hilton. Could you keep watch with the gun?"

"Not dead yet, Garner." He stared up, his eyes a watered blue poking through his thinning yellow-grey hair, two sparks of defiance.

John smiled, for the first time in days it seemed, and turned to the hunt. "Light a fire, if you're not too sickly." He tossed the words over his shoulder then turned to grin at Cross, who was already gathering twigs and dead branches.

Much later the two men sat silent and still by the fire as the flames ripped and tore into the deadwood but John saw none of it. Where Lucy might be and when he might find her were mysteries to him. He tried to picture his son but the little face wouldn't come. He almost had it but then it disappeared. He shivered and rubbed his arms and his voice came low. "Going to be cold tonight."

Hilton's face in the firelight showed that he, too, was far away in his thoughts. John hardly knew anything about Hilton's life, let alone his family. The man straightened and his hand swept quickly across his face, wiping something away. He took a deep breath.

"That it is."

"No stars, either."

"Maybe rain come morning."

He nodded and stood, took a final look around, checked the horses were tied securely nearby and stepped into the tent.

Chapter Forty-One

September, 1779

SOMETIME IN THE NIGHT THE RAIN STARTED, coming in sheets which pounded against the flimsy tent until the fabric was soaked and water dripped onto the men below. The fire had been drowned as well, leaving them no option but to try to sleep, shivering, until morning.

As he lay wrapped in his sodden blanket, his eyes vainly closed, he heard the tearing screech of the wind outside, felt its insistent push against the tent, and prayed the horses were safe. He knew he could do nothing to help them. Soon he grew used to the thundering and crashing, pushing the sound and the lightning to the back of his mind while he thought and thought about how to find Lucy.

He could hear Hilton's ragged breathing. At least he was sleeping. John rolled over and pulled the blanket around his head, forced his own breathing to slow and his mind to empty, and slowly fell into a fitful sleep.

He woke to almost complete silence. Above him the tent's roof was bright with dawn's first streaks. He touched the sloping side. Dry. Beside him Hilton snored softly but John knew they had to go.

"Hilton." He sat up to open the tent. "Hilton." The noisy breathing stopped and John looked back to see him rubbing the sleep from half open eyes.

"Time to go." He stepped outside.

Their camp was a washed-out ruin of downed branches, snapped off bushes and water puddles full of leaves and twigs. The fire pit was completely drowned with only a few blackened logs remaining. The rain had prevented their burning. And in this wet there would be no fire today, either. He stepped behind the tent to check the horses.

He ran through the puddles, calling to Hilton behind him. Ahead, a huge pine lay across the two downed animals, their heads just visible through the branches.

"Help me. We've got to get them out."

But Hilton knelt beside Maudie, and touched her neck. "She's gone, John." His hand dropped as he sat back on his heels. "They're both gone."

"My God. I heard nothing."

"Nothing but the storm." Hilton turned to John. "What now? We have no horses."

"I guess we walk. We'll have to stay on the main trail and hope for a ride from someone." He turned back to look at Maudie but said nothing.

"Anyone could be on that trail, John."

"I know. We have no other choice." He stared at Cross and spit out the next words. "Do we?"

Hilton looked away. "No."

The two friends packed what they could into bundles, hoisted them onto their backs and started for the trail. They were still wet, their packs were wet, and the trail was drowned in a series of pools and tiny lakes. They struggled around puddles of water, over fallen trees, and under rain-soaked branches. When they reached an opening in the trees where the sun had dried a large grassy area, John stopped.

"I think we should camp here for the night. Otherwise we have no hope of getting anything dried out."

"Don't need our belongings moldy, do we?" Hilton was already easing his pack to the ground.

They spread their things and built a huge fire. John took his musket and went in search of game while Hilton combed the area for berries or greens. Maybe some mushrooms would be sprouting after the rain.

The night came quickly. Summer was coming to an end. John lay down to sleep, but this time tried to keep his mind off Lucy, to push the hopelessness away. He would not think of it. He would sleep. Beside him Hilton already breathed heavily and John tried to slow his own breathing. Soon he slept.

THE NEXT DAY THE MEN HEADED WEST on the trail, hoping to find some sign of Lucy, but more immediately looking for fresh horses. Yesterday's sun had dried up much of the water, making the walking easier. But the packs were dead weight and the men rested often.

"Now, John, what do you make of that?"

He turned to look. Horses. Many horses with riders. He stood up. "Maybe we can get help."

"I am surely ready for it." Hilton struggled to his feet as well.

He stared at the approaching riders. His hands clenched. "It's Rangers. Maybe it's Colonel Butler." He was not sure if this was good news or bad but had no choice. He had to get a horse.

On came the soldiers as the two men stood watching, their muskets at their sides. In the lead, rode two battle-ready Rangers unknown to John but they were flanking a short, pudgy man on a grey horse. Colonel Butler. John took a quick breath in. His heartbeat seemed to race. What would his reception be this time? Butler had sent him on a mission and he had deserted.

"It's the Colonel." Hilton's voice lifted.

"Yes." He stood his ground. The company came closer. He could see the look of recognition on Butler's face and the swift glower that followed. The horses stopped about ten paces away.

"Name." The sergeant on the left barked the order.

"John Garner. The Colonel knows it well." He stared at the Colonel.

The small eyes peered from the dusty, lined face as the Colonel considered, then nodded curtly to John and turned to Hilton. "Cross." His head moved slowly as he looked from one to the other. "How did you two end up together?"

"It is quite a tale, sir." He stepped forward, Hilton beside him.

"Wait." The Colonel's hand came up. "We don't have time just now. No time. Put your packs on the wagon and march with us. You can explain in camp tonight."

For a second John's head dropped before he remembered to look up and salute his colonel, whose hard eyes burned into him.

"Forward!" Colonel Butler bellowed and urged his horse toward the two men who quickly pulled their packs aside. "Sergeant Warner. Accompany these men."

Soon he and Hilton, their heavy packs loaded, were keeping pace with the other Rangers on foot, a new and grueling struggle for both of them. John fell into the steady step and escaped to his thoughts.

Now he was marching in the wrong direction. How would he find Lucy going this way? He didn't want to desert Butler but his mind raced with plans to escape. Perhaps at night? Would Butler imprison them? Or worse?

Of course Hilton was not a soldier so he was in no danger. John didn't really know exactly what his friend's position was. Spy? Agent? Butler had said very little to him; in fact, he had barely looked at Hilton. All his anger had been for John. Another reason to escape and find Lucy.

"We're stopping."

The voice at his side brought John back to reality. "Yes."

The men all around seemed to be shifting and forming groups to go down an embankment. He and Hilton were swept along with them.

"A river." He could see the blue expanse through the trees.

"That's a mighty big river. More like a lake, I'm thinking. Where are we?"

Even as they stepped closer, the men saw boats all up and down the shore. The soldiers were piling into them.

"We're going for a ride, John, my boy. We're going to ride." Hilton clapped his hands together. "No more walking. I'm a-liking this more all the time." He looked at his face. "You're not, are you?"

John looked from side to side, up and down the water's edge, trying to see a way to escape. The boats would take them so far away that he would never find Lucy. He stepped out of line, ready to run, but Sergeant Warner stepped with him and edged him back. Besides, he had no horse and no pack. How could he survive?

Back in line with Hilton, he made his way down the embankment, into the shallow water and up over the side of the boat, landing with a thud against the rough wood. He righted himself, glanced at Hilton, and sat in the bottom of the small vessel.

Quickly the boats were loaded to more than capacity and put out from shore to catch the current south. He had been pressed into rowing and sat silent, his arms yanking the heavy oar over and over through the water, his mind an empty well of despair.

Chapter Forty-Two

September, 1779

LUCY CLUTCHED THE WHIMPERING HARPER JOHN close to her breast, wishing he might stay quiet. She knew someone was close—she had heard the horses and a low chatter before pulling the freshly cut branches across the opening to her dark cave. Hopefully the voices would disappear as the few others had on this lonely trail in the last five days.

Perhaps the people were friendly but she did not want to take a chance and had tried her best to avoid anyone she saw. Keeping herself and Harper John clean, fed, and warm at night was a constant battle, especially all alone as she was. But the baby gurgled and giggled as he rode in his special pouch, reaching out to pull at her clothing or the horse's tail when he was really rambunctious, and happily exploring his world.

She had stopped often, slowing her pace considerably, but she was making headway. How far to Niagara she could only guess but hoped another week would see her at the fort John had described to her.

"Sh, little one." She pressed the baby closer and breathed the words into his ear, rocking back and forth on the hard ground, holding him tight.

"Look here. A cave."

She tightened her arms around Harper John and held her breath. She heard the rustle. They were pulling her branches away. Light knifed across her outstretched legs and up her body exposing her. She gasped.

"I wondered whose horse we found." The voice was low and gravelly.

She could not see his face, only his outline against the sunlight.

"Don't be afraid. I would not think of hurting you. Come out." He backed out of the small space and motioned for her to follow. She struggled to crawl out with Harper John, now quiet in her arms, and stood up to face the strangers.

Before her, towered a tanned and muscular Indian, bare to the waist, with only a small breech cloth covering the rest of him. He wore a bear claw necklace. A single eagle feather hung at an odd angle from the shiny black hair and framed his angular face. The light caught his white teeth as he spoke.

"What are you doing here, madam?"

She stared at him a moment before answering in the same perfect English. "I am travelling to find my husband."

"All alone? I do not know many white women who would do that with only a horse." He motioned toward the animal grazing close by.

"Who are you?" Her voice sounded loud even to her but she held the man's watching eyes.

"I am of the Seneca tribe." His dark head tipped back and his shoulders straightened. "We are travelling to our village, a day's ride to the south." He reached out to touch Harper John, who tucked his head back into her shoulder. "Where is your husband?"

"He is a soldier. I don't know where he is." She wondered how much to tell. His tribe fought with the British, but so much time had passed since she had heard any current news, the Seneca could have changed sides.

"Ah. I understand. Where are you going?"

"I told you. To find my husband."

"Do not worry. My friends and I will not harm you or your child, madam." He pointed to about fifteen Indians down the steep hill, staring at her. Harper John wailed again.

"I have frightened you, madam." The man reached to comfort Harper John but she pulled back. "As you wish. Come." He turned and led off to the horses. She followed.

"Where are you taking us?"

"Somewhere safe."

"How far is it?"

"Not far. You will have a good place to sleep, and your baby, too," he added, seeing her indecision.

The Indian was as good as his word. Before the sun had set, their little party entered a sizable village of temporary Indian tents, complete with children playing, elders smoking silently together and women stirring pots over makeshift cooking fires. She followed the man to a tent where he dismounted and motioned for her to do the same. He took her reins while she lifted the sleeping Harper John from his pouch and led her to a wizened up old woman dressed in ragged skirts, who sat smoking in the evening sun.

Lucy could not understand the words but she saw the old woman's eyes narrow and her hands take the pipe from her mouth to bark a question. Her rescuer answered in a calm voice and turned to point out Harper John, at which gesture the woman's face relaxed. She nodded, once, her eyes boring into Lucy, scaring her but at the same time somehow reassuring her. Despite her outward appearance this woman seemed straightforward and kind, and she relaxed her grip on Harper John.

Night fell as she moved into the shelter provided by Henry Montour, her rescuer. Following a meal of squash and some kind of delicious meat, she settled Harper John for the night and sat for a moment watching him sleep. She had been given space in a tent with the old woman, who seemed to be alone and glad to share. She spoke no English but, as she sat on the ground a few steps away, avidly watched Harper John sleep. Her one front tooth gaped as she grinned broadly and her eyes widened with every little snuffle the child made. Lucy smiled and nodded her thanks before stretching out beside her baby. For the first time in weeks, she relaxed and slept.

IN THE DAYS THAT FOLLOWED she learned much about her hosts and marveled that in the midst of a shifting of their village—they had been thwarted by the war and forced to camp here temporarily—and the fighting itself between the British and the Continentals, these people were helping strangers, a white woman no less, and her baby. Grateful, she tried to help each day wherever she could, finding berries, roots and nuts, and washing clothing. Today she watched Harper John kick and roll as she worked on a large bowl of peas. She smiled to think how similar this was to her life on the farm.

She stopped shelling peas and felt her eyes hot and wet. Thoughts of John and their lovely little cabin, her stove, John's chair, their tiny bedroom where John had held her under the patchwork quilt were all a wild whirl in her mind. Her head fell forward and her shoulders sagged. A giant sob escaped and her hands flew to her face.

The bowl of peas, half-shelled, tipped into the dirt. Her hands across her chest, she held herself and sobbed out her months of anguish. She felt lost and beaten, with no one left except a helpless baby. Her face wet, she wiped her bare arm across her cheek, leaving red streaks of despair.

As her sobbing eased, her breath evened out, with only the occasional shudder rocking her chest, and she felt again the quiet of the camp around her. A hand barely touched her arm.

The old woman's dark eyes were ink pots of tenderness reaching deep inside Lucy. The rough hands stroked her arm, back and forth, back and forth. She forced a smile.

"Thank you. I am so sorry." A long sob escaped and she blinked her eyes again.

The woman shook her head, withdrew her arm and, smiling, picked up the fallen dish of peas. Lucy reached to help. The strength of the woman lifted her spirits and together they sorted the peas.

....

"What is your name?"

The woman shook her head, puzzled.

She indicated her own chest. "Lucy," she said.

With a wide grin and much nodding of her head, the woman repeated the word. "Lu-cy."

"Yes. Lucy. You are right." She pointed at the woman and raised her eyebrows. "You?"

"Mai-ree." She tapped her breast and Lucy repeated the name.

"Friend." She pointed from herself to her friend until Mairee nodded and smiled. They rose together and went for water to wash the peas.

LATER THAT DAY HENRY MONTOUR caught up as she sat with Harper John on a blanket laughing at the antics of another child nearby. The children so interested her she did not notice Mr. Montour until he spoke, whereupon she immediately turned and stood to receive her visitor.

"Mr. Montour. Good day to you."

"Mrs. Garner. How are you today?" His quiet brown eyes solicited an answer.

"I am well, thank you, but I must speak with you. We, Harper John and I, must continue our journey."

"This is what I came to discuss with you. I am taking a party in the morning to Fort Niagara. We will be travelling quickly and you may not be able to keep up but would you like to try? Would you like to accompany us?"

"Yes!" She almost shouted the words. "Thank you so much. We'll not hold you back, Mr. Montour. Thank you."

He chuckled and leaned over to scoop up Harper John. "Are you ready to travel, little soldier man?" The baby grabbed Montour's nose and pulled.

"Harper John. No!" She grabbed his hand.

"Do not worry, Mrs. Garner. I am used to fine young boys such as this." He handed the giggling baby back. "We leave at first light."

EXCITEMENT TINGLED IN THE CRISP DAWN AIR as the lean and muscled men tied their packs to their horses, their women rushing back and forth to add a water skin or a wrapped bundle of food. Mairee quietly helped with Harper John and insisted on giving Lucy a blanket, flint, a water skin and a sack of food.

"From all." Mairee extended her arm to include the whole camp.

Lucy looked into her shining eyes and, nodding, accepted the gifts. She tied the quiet Harper John into his pouch, tucked his wee jacket snug around him in the cool air and turned to her friend.

"You have been a great help, Mairee. From the bottom of my heart, I thank you." She reached to pat the woman's arm but Mairee took her hand and held it in hers, then released it and stepped back, smiling. Lucy nodded and turned to her horse, mounted, checked Harper John once more and fell into line with the departing Indians.

There were ten of them travelling together, eight Senecas and Lucy and Harper John. They rode quietly, their clothing and their signaling sounds blending into the forest as much as possible. Even Harper John seemed to sense the need for silence, rarely making any noise and, when he did, just cooing softly or giggling at something only he saw or heard. Eventually his head dropped forward against the horse and he slept. Lucy smiled to see him rocking to the rhythm of the dark brown horse, oblivious to the advancing day.

He woke with a startling cry. Henry Montour turned in his saddle, his eyebrows raised at Lucy, who shrugged her shoulders and shook her head. The child needed attention. Mr. Montour whistled ahead and the column stopped. Everyone dismounted, Lucy, too. Before she could grab Harper John, Montour's strong hands had him out of his pouch and into her arms where she stroked and tried to settle him.

"He is hungry. Can we stop while I feed him?" She looked at Montour. "I know I said we would not slow you down but he needs to eat."

"The horses need watering. We can rest a few minutes." He turned and walked away.

Quickly she changed Harper John and held him to her breast. She would eat while they rode.

Back on the trail the small group rode on through endless trees, sunlight, bird song and rushing waters. The excitement of the morning gradually gave way to aching muscles, jarring bones, sweat trickling down and dust caking their wet faces.

She wanted to stop and run cool water over her cheeks but the Indians rode on, pausing only for Harper John's needs—they had all adopted his schedule—until she thought her legs must be red and raw with chafing against the horse.

Harper John was napping again. He seemed to be adjusting well, a good thing, as she shuddered to think what might happen if the Indians had to leave them behind.

The camp that night was simple but adequate. She and Harper John were in the only tent which was pitched in the middle of a circle of Indians wrapped in their blankets on the ground. As the sun settled to the west she snuggled next to her baby and slept.

In the morning they rode northwest toward Fort Niagara where the Senecas had business. She had no idea what, nor did she care.

Midway through the morning she sat against a fallen tree nursing Harper John while the Indians waited patiently, some tending their horses, some off in the bushes, and one stretched full length on the ground a few feet from Lucy and Harper John. His eyes were closed and Lucy watched the slow rise and fall of his chest. She was not the only one exhausted by this ride.

A gunshot exploded and she yelped at the pain in her nipple. Harper John had bitten her. Now he howled, while all around them men ran shouting and screaming. More shots, flashing knives, the clash of metal on metal.

She rolled on top of Harper John to protect him, pushing them both into the forest floor against the tree trunk where she couldn't see anymore. Someone landed on her leg but was gone again before she could even look. She pressed the baby tighter against the fallen tree, oblivious to his screams.

Men's voices shouted, but she could not make out words; only the fire and fury of their fighting came to her. She sensed someone near and looked around. Henry Montour was locked in the grip of an enemy soldier, Henry's grey eyes red and bulging.

Before she could help him, a knife was against his neck, and a thin red line widened into streaming blood. She rolled back against the tree trunk and Henry's body thumped onto her back, almost knocking the wind out of her even as she felt her stomach roil and spew all over Harper John and the ground before her.

She tried to breathe but sucked in dirt and vomit. She choked on the dank smell, pushed against the smothering weight above her, thought of Harper John, strained and twisted again, but could not dislodge the dead body pinning her into the earth. She thought she would die but gave one last wild push to free herself and the still baby beneath her.

Chapter Forty-Three

"WHAT HAVE WE HERE?"

She heard the voice and realized the fighting around her had stopped. The weight of Montour's body lifted off her and she sucked in air before turning to the voice.

"What have we here?" The soldier sneered as he towered over her. "Get up, woman."

She sat against the log, and stroked the whimpering Harper John in her arms, her eyes on the man the whole time. He wore a fringed buckskin shirt, open at the neck, and closely fitting trousers above high leather boots. On his head a brown, brimmed hat, flipped up on one side, showed a medallion of the Continentals. He flung his arm out and up in an impatient gesture. She cringed. But his angry eyes told her to obey. She struggled to her feet and stared at the man.

"You're a white woman." He stepped back and looked at Harper John. "With a white baby." He paused. "What are you doing with those Senecas?"

Her head swam as she tried to think. If he thought she was the enemy they would probably both die immediately. She dropped her eyes, sniffled a couple of times, and spoke.

Elaine Cougler

"Oh, thank you for finding us. Those Indians took the baby and me from our cabin two days ago." She looked into the soldier's green eyes. "I feared for our lives, sir." She sobbed as she rocked the crying Harper John back and forth in her arms, and wondered if he believed her.

"Looked to me like that Injun was trying to protect you, lady."

"I do not know. He was supposed to look after me, I guess."

"Did they, um," he looked away, "hurt you?" He met her eyes again, boring into her, and she knew everything depended on her answer.

"No. They fed us and all, never let us be alone, but they did not hurt us, either of us." She kissed Harper John's head, rocking him back and forth. After a moment she looked up again to see the man nodding his head and looking her over, thinking.

"All right then. Come with me."

As she followed the soldier's tan uniform she saw the devastation left by the attack. Seneca warriors who had a few minutes before been laughing and resting, now lay strewn over the small area, in various awkward positions, bloodied and dead where they had fallen. She held Harper John's head to her bosom blinding him to the horror, averting her own eyes as much as she could. At their horses the soldier turned and spoke.

"Where is your horse? How did you carry the baby?"

"I have a pouch set up on my horse for him." She looked around for her mount. "The horses must have bolted."

"They'll be back before we're ready to leave." He glanced at her. "What's your name?"

She felt her insides knot again. "Lucy. Lucy Smith." She forced herself to look at him.

"Lucy. Nice name." He motioned to a flat rock beside the path. "Sit here and wait for us, Lucy."

She clutched Harper John as she waited for the soldiers. About twenty of them there were, and they were dressed in various uniform and clothing pieces, but all wore Continental Army emblems somewhere on their persons.

The men quickly searched the dead, pocketed what they could, and piled the bodies together in a heap. Lucy turned away but her curiosity and her need to know her captors made her look back at the grisly sight. At least they were not scalping the dead.

Presently the leader stood before her once more, holding the bridle of a horse. "This one yours?" He pointed at the rigged side pouch.

She nodded and stood.

"Time to go." He handed the reins to her.

"I need a few moments in the woods first."

He studied her face. "Leave the kid with me." He reached out his arms and she slowly handed over Harper John.

"I won't be long." She turned and ran into the trees.

TROTTING ALONG ONCE MORE with Harper John settled in his pouch, Lucy drooped her head and felt her shoulders sag. She paid no attention to the baby talking behind her; in fact, she barely heard him she was so sunken within herself.

The trees changed from maple to pine and hemlock and the trail wound up and over the rough terrain with barely a path to follow. The sun shone in back of the party now although they rarely felt it through the dense forest canopy overhead.

They were going east, away from Fort Niagara, away from safety for her and Harper John, away from all hope. Tears slipped down her cheeks, unbidden and unnoticed. She was too tired to fight anymore.

Suddenly the horse ahead stopped and her own halted abruptly. Lucy stirred.

"What are you doing to that kid?"

The voice cut into her thoughts and she opened her eyes wide. Harper John was screaming and she had not even heard him. She reached back to stroke him, but he yelled even louder.

"I have to feed him," she called.

For a long moment he stared, then nodded and called a rest period. In a trice she was off the horse and holding her son. His wails turned to sporadic sobs as she changed him. How could she have ignored him? And not even heard his cries?

She had to take hold of herself, to pay attention, if not for her sake, for Harper John's. She settled him at her breast and gazed into his damp eyes. His little mouth clamped on and sucked. Every few seconds he stopped as a shudder escaped and she soothed him until he settled again.

As Harper John calmed, so did Lucy. She sat on the hard ground beside a huge pine, so close she could smell it. She felt safe as long as these soldiers did not know she was a Loyalist. But they would be asking questions before long and she had no answers. She glanced around.

The soldiers were a respectful distance away taking their leisure until she might be ready to move again, but they were too close for her to even think of escape. And, anyway, she had no idea where she was.

She would have to keep up the charade. Perhaps at night she could manage something. Her Seneca friends—the thought of their fate almost made her gag—had put flint and supplies in her saddlebags. She had to get away from these Continentals although the idea of being alone in the woods again brought shivers to her whole body.

Back on the trail the soldiers hurried to make up for the lost time. She held her head high and watched the countryside open before them as they headed down toward a lush valley below. It was beautiful, bathed in the afternoon sun, with leaves yellowing ever so slightly, and a small lake blinking blue and white in the light.

Suddenly the leader stopped and held up his hand. She strained to see. A wisp of white smoke filtered up from the ground far below them and into the blue above. And another one. Enemies? She hoped not.

Three, maybe four farms nestled prettily together along the small river below. At this distance the fields were green and gold squares of colour, herringboned with split rail fences. As the party crept closer she made out cows lazing in the afternoon sun, horses, and oxen, too—all resting peacefully. Her eyes swam as she thought of her own farm abandoned months ago to an unknown fate.

They were stopping again. Her fingers ached with the constant pull of the reins and her backside must be black and blue. She needed a rest and pulled her horse up to wait. The leader came alongside her, glaring into her eyes.

"Get down."

"What…why do you want me to get down?" Something in his hard eyes made her cringe. She glanced back at the still sleeping Harper John.

"Get down." He grabbed her reins and threw out his other arm, pointing to the ground.

She dismounted and reached for her reins but the soldier held tight.

"You don't need the horse. Take the child."

She clasped the sleeping baby under his little arms and pulled him up and out of the pouch, settling him against her shoulder. He slept on, a heavy weight. She faced the soldier.

"This is as far as you go." He started to pull away.

She cried out, and Harper John stirred. "You can't leave us with nothing."

"Oh, but I can." His scowl gave way to a half smile. "Don't worry, ma'am. We have some work to do and we'll be back. Just wait here." He signaled the others and rode off down the hill.

As the soldiers whooped into the settlement below, tiny figures rushed from the cabins, women and children, men and young boys, all running about as the soldiers set fire to the buildings. One man held a musket to his shoulder, aimed and fired, but the shot went wild and, before he could load again, a soldier rode up and struck him with his bayonet, pausing only long enough to pull the blade out and ride on.

The body slumped to the ground. A woman rushed to the man, knelt and turned him over. Her hands flew in the air and Lucy imagined her screaming although no sound reached her.

She looked away, laid Harper John in the grass, and watched in horrified disbelief as the soldiers went about their work, raiding the cabins, barns, sheds, and gathering the animals on a tether. Through it all the soldiers threw off the pleading women and ignored the defeated men whose hands they had tied together, looping them all in a small circle facing each other.

Her eyes streamed helpless tears as she watched the destruction. A soldier slapped one particularly insistent woman across the face throwing her into the dirt, a sobbing mass of homespun and flying hair. Lucy held her sides and cried. She could do nothing.

Harper John cried, too, as she held him. Together they stood on the hillside watching the soldiers set fire to the golden wheat, the hay stacks, the barns, the corn fields so close to harvest time and, finally, to the cabins. A black plume of smoke rose to block out the fluffy clouds, darkening the sky with a filthy, oily haze which covered the whole settlement.

Out of it all rode the twenty soldiers, a line of stacked wagons and tethered animals snaking behind them. Through the stinking smoke she caught glimpses of the dispossessed settlers watching their lives evaporate. Her stomach churned and she tasted bitter bile which she tried to swallow. Her eyes floated back into her head and she clutched at Harper John as she sank to the ground.

Chapter Forty-Four

September-October, 1779

"GARNER."

He opened his eyes to darkness and wondered if he was dreaming.

"Garner." The low voice spoke, insistent, right outside the tent. He lurched to the opening and peered into the grey dawn. It was the sergeant.

"Get your boots and come with me. Butler wants you."

Now the real punishment, he thought, as he trudged to the command tent, but he was ready. If he could repay his debt to that British soldier back in England, he would. They had set up camp late the night before after spending hours on the lake. His muscles ached from his long stint rowing and he shrugged his shoulders and twisted his neck to loosen them up. On his right he could just make out the water's edge. The sky gradually lightened. This would be a killing day for him with no sleep, no horse, and Butler's wrath.

"Over here." The sergeant pointed to the command tent. "Wait." He stepped inside and John heard his name. Immediately the sergeant came back outside again. "Enter," he barked.

Inside John stood at attention studying the centre pole, waiting to hear the command to rest easy. As the minutes ticked by, his arms and legs tensed. Colonel Butler sat at his table, papers spread before him. Occasionally he turned something over, or back, and then forward again, oblivious to John's presence.

The sergeant cleared his throat but Butler gave no sign of noticing until, finally, he leaned back in his chair, folded his hands over his considerable belly, and slowly raised his eyes to the room before him. He stared at John's boots, his legs, his middle and, finally, looked him in the eyes. John did not dare to return the look but stared at the pole before him.

"Garner. What do you have to say for yourself?" The voice was cold.

"I am sorry, sir. We were attacked by a band of Oneidas. Everyone was killed." He paused. "Except me, that is. Frank…Frank Smyth was killed, too." He stopped and took a breath.

"Why did you not come back to us?"

"I know I should have, sir, but a Mohawk came upon the site as I was cleaning up and took me to his village, sir. To where I was before, when I met Chief Joseph Brant, sir."

"Yes. Go on."

"I made the decision to look for my wife, sir. She is lost somewhere between our farm and Niagara. I am sorry, sir, but I had to go." His voice fell off and he sucked in a quick breath.

"Garner, I do not know what to do with you. Such a good soldier. Good soldier. But I understand why you wanted to look for your wife. God only knows where she is now. God only knows." He shook his head and studied John.

"Yes, sir."

"You will come along with us now to Newtown." He paused. "To Newtown, yes. And we'll see what we can do for you after that."

"Yes, sir." His shoulders ached with the strain of standing rigid all this time but he did not move. The colonel could have been much harder on him.

Colonel Butler's pudgy face twisted as he dropped his eyes to the papers on his desk and began to read. A moment later he waved his arm vaguely. "Dismissed, Garner. Dismissed."

AFTER TWO DAYS OF HARD MARCHING with little food and virtually no rest, John and the other tired and severely weakened Rangers reached Newtown, many of them sick and useless for battle. Word had filtered through that Major General Sullivan was leading a massive enemy army toward the Loyalist settlers.

Colonel Butler had little choice but to establish a defensive line with his weakened Rangers and what assistance he could get from the Indians. He wanted to help as many Loyalists as possible to escape the wrath of the enemy army. But the Indians, too, needed to help their people. With four to six thousand enemy troops advancing on their position, many of the Delawares and other Indians left to move their families and possessions to safety. This left Butler with severely reduced numbers, in total barely six hundred to fight six thousand.

He sent the sick and injured off to safer ground with the baggage wagons and set about fortifying their position on a ridge overlooking the probable route of the coming army. Along the front of this position fresh cut boughs camouflaged a rough log breastwork and several rifle pits. From this position the advantage would certainly be to Butler's men if the enemy approached as expected.

With the other foot soldiers, John spent his energy digging the breastwork in the hot August sun. When that was done, they took up position in the centre of the line with Joseph Brant and a pitifully small number of Indians to the right, and Chief Sangerachta with his warriors to the left. When no one had marched against them by sundown, Butler ordered everyone back to camp.

The next morning they resumed their positions and waited for Sullivan's army. The day grew long and hot with nothing and no one in sight, although scouts reported hearing wood chopping from the direction of the enemy. By nightfall more of Butler's Rangers were sick, so terribly weakened were they from existing for days on only underripe corn cobs. The call came again to fall back for the night.

John trudged the mile back to camp to sleep once more on the cold ground, one of the few soldiers to have a blanket, worn and shredded though it was. As he lay curled up hoping for sleep, his mind tracked back to when he first met Lucy, a lively and bright-haired spitfire, back in Boston. They took some time convincing her father to let her marry him and the man had not given in easily. But the years had changed all that and now William was with Lucy. At least John hoped he was because the alternative could not be borne. He shifted away from a sharp stone under his ribs.

In the morning the Rangers resumed their vigil, waiting in their lines and watching for the enemy to appear. Before the sun was full in the sky the word came down the line that a number of enemy horsemen were approaching. At first he could see nothing, but gradually the tall grasses seemed to move more than normal and metal flashed as the sun caught it. The men approached slowly, with lots of stops and starts. Were they suspicious? His fingers stiffened on the musket until he wondered if they would even bend when the time came. He blinked several times, staring through the grass and trying to concentrate.

Suddenly he saw someone climb a tree, then another the tree beside. They'll surely see us. His stomach tightened. He flexed his musket fingers. With his free hand he found his cartridge box. Colonel Butler moved among his men, keeping his head down before the advancing enemy.

"Are you ready for a fight, Garner?"

"Yes, sir." He kept his eyes on the enemy.

"Remember, after this we'll let you go find your wife. Find your wife."

"Yes, sir."

"But we have to win here first." The colonel touched John's shoulder and moved off down the line.

A lone rifle roared in the distance. Out of the corner of his eye, he saw Butler jump into a place in the line to return fire with his men. In the smoky confusion behind the breastwork the Rangers loaded, took aim and fired, loaded, took aim and fired again. All along the line used paper packets fell to the ground in a frantic flurry of white.

The enemy did not seem to be coming any closer and some part of John's brain wondered about that but he fought on until he saw someone near him fall and heard—or felt, he wasn't sure which—musket shot fly across in front of his face. He dropped to the ground and looked back over his left shoulder.

"Sir, they've moved up behind us."

Butler screamed orders. "Fall back, men! Fall back!" He led the retreat of men and horses through a stand of sheltering trees, back out of the line of fire of those on the far hill. Each man tried to save himself, running and jumping over rocks and into hidden gopher holes, trying not to fall, racing, clutching guns and not even looking behind.

John's legs moved on their own, his breath came in great gasps, and he felt the hot air slice through his sweaty hair as he ran for his life. Gradually he became aware that the only noises he heard were his own ragged breathing and tramping feet. He chanced a glance backward.

He ran alone. He looked ahead to a dense thicket of trees and pushed his spent legs to carry him there. He tripped and fell to the ground, gasped for breath, and rolled over into the undergrowth with his musket in hand.

As his chest heaved in the dank and dark hole under the trees he struggled to calm down and breathe more quietly. His long pulls of air gradually lessened until he swallowed his fright and blinked open his eyes.

Phew. This place smelled. As his eyes focused in the dim light he realized he was in an animal den. Overhead were sheltering branches through which the daylight filtered. He was alone. He lay back to listen. He heard no enemy nor Ranger nor anything.

He needed a plan. He could look for the Rangers—they couldn't be far—and stay with them or he could chance going on his own, hoping to avoid the enemy and find Lucy. Neither option seemed a good idea with all the Patriot soldiers in the area. He might as well try to regroup with his unit and hope for the safety of numbers. Butler had said he would help.

Certainly he could not stay here. He listened for sound outside his lair and, hearing none, wriggled into the open once more. In the silence he checked his musket and started walking, his eyes wide, his ears strained and his step cautious. He must find the Rangers.

He had not walked far when he heard faint sounds behind him. He stopped to listen, his eyes and ears straining for some clue as to what or who was in pursuit, but could not tell.

Thinking enemy soldiers were chasing down stragglers he began to run, his head bobbing from side to side as he looked for somewhere to hide. The area was heavily wooded with old growth pines stretching to the sky but their bare trunks gave no cover on the ground which was a brown expanse of dead pine needles, cushiony soft and slippery.

John struggled to keep his footing as he gulped air. He feared collapse and discovery by the enemy. His mind was a blur of bloody battle images and one thought—escape. His legs pounded the uneven ground, his musket bounced up and down in his right hand and he ran for his very life.

He was down. He tried to rise but great searing pain shot from his ankle. He swallowed a scream and sucked in air, then stayed still in the dirt. He lay in a slight depression beside a fallen pine, hardly enough for cover but he had no choice. His ankle throbbed. He would run no more today. Quickly he burrowed into the bed of needles against the soggy tree, pulled his shirt up over his head enough to cover his face, and lay still trying to slow his ragged breathing. He heard nothing.

As he lay rigid under the pine needles he hoped he was not visible. It was too late now to shift. Whoever was behind him would be approaching and any movement he made would give him away. He felt the musket against his thigh and the metal of the trigger mechanism cutting into his finger. His ankle screamed pain and he longed to stroke it, hoped it was not bleeding. But he lay perfectly still. Long slow breaths. Long slow breaths. He con-centrated on breathing with barely any movement of his chest. Slowly he grew calmer though his ears still listened for the enemy.

Chapter Forty-Five

AS THE MOMENTS PASSED he began to hope he had been wrong about pursuers. The needles itched against his bare skin but he lay still and tried to think of other things, and to ignore the creeping feeling moving along his belly.

He tensed. What was that swooshing sound? And that smell? More than the rotting pine smell, he was sure. Cautiously he pulled his clothing off his face. The smoke hit him and he breathed in fresh fear, quickly rolling over to peer across the log.

In the distance the trees were shrouded in white, the tops spouting orange flames which leaped wildly into the black sky. Fire. He staggered to his feet ignoring the mass of pine needles sticking to him. He stepped on the ankle and gasped but forced himself to hobble as quickly as he could ahead of the fire. Now he saw movement in the woods ahead of him and realized the animals were fleeing. Terrified, he raced to keep up to them.

He could hear screaming, animal or human he didn't know, but the screeches were horrible and he ran full out, the ankle forgotten, his eyes wide and wild. He searched for safety, running, tripping once, springing to his feet again with a quick glance behind at the warm wall of fire. He felt its heat and heard it leap from one treetop to the next, snapping ever closer with an angry roaring which assailed his suffering ear drums.

On his right a flaming animal rushed by. His breath came in huge gulps of hot air burning his throat and, suddenly, he threw off his flaming hat. Now the screaming was louder. He realized it was his own voice struggling to be heard over the monstrous roar of the fire.

He veered left toward the only blue sky he could see and the trees broke open before him. He was in the air falling out of the smoke into he knew not what. Nor did he care. He sucked in a huge gulp of cleansing air before he hit the water, thrashing, trying to hold the musket up—a useless idea—and keep himself afloat. His weight pushed down, down until his feet touched something and he kicked hard, propelling himself back to the surface.

Rising through the water, he saw red flames eating the trees on the cliff above from where, moments before, he had jumped. As his head broke the surface he realized he had company. Wild-eyed squirrels, otters and a beaver flailed in the water as flaming twigs and branches crashed down around them. John ducked to miss an orange-red treetop which hissed into the water beside him.

Gradually his terror lessened and he tried to see a place on the shore of the wide river where he might climb out, but the flying fiery bits had lit everything on the shore and he could see nowhere to go. He wondered how long he could swim and alternated resting on his back with dog paddling slowly while he waited for the fire to subside, all the while holding desperately to his musket.

Aside from the terrified animals, he saw no one and began to wonder how the fire started. Sullivan's army had been laying waste to everything in their path destroying Indian and Loyalist villages alike on their way to Colonel Butler and the battle at Newtown. One of the scorched earth fires must have gotten away from them and crept unnoticed into the forest.

Above him on the shore the flames gave way to clouds of smoke which settled heavily over onto the water and he began to cough and sputter. He could see nothing but smoky ash falling all around him. His legs were tiring and his arms ached with the dead weight of the musket and trying to keep afloat. His body wanted to sink but he fought to keep paddling until a gust of wind blew the killing smoke away and he could breathe again. He drifted far out into the current, letting it carry him where it would as long as he avoided the heavy air.

Suddenly he sputtered and coughed, spitting out the water which had swept into his mouth. Something had created a wave. When he finally breathed again he kicked around for a look but saw nothing. His feet touched a rocky bottom and he gladly put his weight on them, pulling his waterlogged body toward the shore. He was across the river where the fire had not reached and he appeared to be alone. He dragged up onto the grassy riverbank, sniffed the zesty tar of the towering pines, gazed in all directions for danger, and collapsed.

HOURS LATER THE SUN'S RECEDING RAYS had cooled the air over John's sleeping form. He shivered. His exposed back and arms were cold. He rolled over, clutching his sides, and grunted. The rock in his ribs brought him fully awake and he cracked open his eyes, trying to remember. The river was right beside him. He sat up, alert, knowing again the danger all around him.

In the fading light he took off his shirt, grabbed the musket, and dried the ramrod and the barrel until he was satisfied the gun would work again. His paper packets were soggy, and useless until he could get them dry, but he had nothing for a fire, or for food or clothing. He had to find the Rangers.

Dressed and ready again, he surveyed the land. He had to get across the river but he had no boat and did not relish another swim in the dark of night. Besides he would find no food in the fire-ravaged forest. He decided to head north until he could find a crossing. Butler would have moved on by now and had probably counted him dead or escaped again. No one would be looking for him. Except Sullivan's army. His stomach tightened at the thought of being found by the enemy. He started walking, hobbling along with the stick he had found, favoring his swollen ankle.

The river trail was overgrown with witch hazel and grape vine, thorn bushes John had to skirt around, and long reedy grasses which seemed to grab onto him in the dark, and hold him back. He slipped into the water again and again more than once soaking his feet. Nevertheless, he kept going. He had to make time before the sun came up when he would be vulnerable again.

As the first streaks of dawn lit his path he came upon a ghostly homestead with a cabin and a small barn looming dark ahead of him. He knelt in the grass and watched for a few moments but could see no sign of life, not even smoke from the chimney. Of course at this time of year that meant very little. And animals. He saw none. He thought of their rooster's morning cries—his and Lucy's—but pushed it from his mind. He must concentrate.

The cabin door creaked open and an old woman hobbled out, closing the door behind her. She seemed to sniff the air as she peered around the homestead. He crouched lower. The woman reached her hands to her straggly hair and smoothed it back behind her ears, then lumbered off around the corner of the cabin toward a lonely outhouse.

He waited a moment, and watched for any other sign of life but saw nothing. Slowly he inched across the open space toward the barn, slipped the bar, and crept inside. He stood for a moment trying to see in the pitch black. He heard no sound but smelled the musty hay of other years mingled with stale manure. He seemed to be alone. Maybe the animals were outside, he thought, but remembered he had seen none.

Suddenly the door opened wide behind him catching him in the daylight and he spun around to see the old woman's form dark against the bright light of day. He had no time to do anything and stood still, staring at her.

"Who are you?" She held a pitchfork like a weapon.

He stood his ground, his musket at his side.

"Who are you?" The old woman's voice was gravelly and forced as she took another step toward him, pitchfork at the ready.

"I am a settler, ma'am." He waited a second. "And I'm hungry."

"What are you doing in my barn?"

He heard the anger in her voice and watched her jerk the pitchfork at him. "I am sorry, ma'am. I thought the place was deserted." He dropped his head.

The woman stood a moment and then spoke. "Come outside where I can see you." She motioned him by her and out into the new day.

"You look to have run into some trouble."

"Yes, ma'am."

"Are you one of those soldiers?"

"I have been fighting to save my land, ma'am, yes." John looked her in the eye.

"Are you hurt?" She had seen his limp.

"I am fine, ma'am. Just a sore ankle." John could see her eyes soften as she lowered the pitchfork to study him.

"Well, come in, then, and we will see what we can find to feed you." She turned and led him into the cabin.

He blinked in the dark room but could only make out a table and two chairs. The woman pointed to one and he sat waiting for his eyes to adjust in the half light.

The room had a bed in the corner, a small wood stove with its blackened chimney reaching up and out of the roof, and a wooden dry sink cupboard where she stood slicing bacon off a small hunk and slapping the strips into the cast iron frying pan. In moments the aroma of the bacon was almost more than he could stand, not having eaten well for weeks.

"May I wash up, ma'am?"

"Outside. Behind the cabin."

He opened the door and blinked at the bright sunshine. The day was fine, with a clear blue sky and a few white clouds dashing ahead of the breeze. He found the pump and washed using the lye soap piece lying there, and followed the smell of bacon back into the cabin.

"Who are you?" The woman banged a plate to the table before him. She seemed to look right inside him.

He held the fork in mid air. "I'm a soldier…trying to get back to my unit."

"And which unit would that be?" She sat opposite him, still staring.

He didn't know what to say. If she were a Loyalist, all would be well. But if she took the side of the Americans, he didn't know what she might do. "It's a dangerous time to speak of sides, don't you think, ma'am?" He speared a piece of bacon and stuffed it into his mouth, then drank the coffee as quickly as he could. She was still staring at him but she blinked a couple of times and looked away. "What side are you on?" John asked.

She moved to the window and looked out. "Since my husband died, I've just tried to survive out here by myself. I don't think much of sides. But I would like to go back to the way it was. Stop all this fighting." She looked back at him. "Wouldn't you?"

"Yes. And I'd like to have my wife and son, my farm, my friends—all of it back. As long as I can have those things I don't much care whose side wins anymore." John pushed his empty plate away and thanked the woman.

He hurried on his way north along the river bank. The woman had said he could easily cross over down further. For the first time in days he smiled and thought of Lucy. He would find her, he knew he would. And Harper John. He must be getting quite a size. John counted the months since the baby's birth. Eight. He smiled again. Maybe he could even stand up or walk.

His neck hairs prickled. He ducked behind some bushes on the riverbank. Voices. The words were not clear. He inched his head up and saw a small boat coming across from the other side of the river.

Two men were rowing toward him. One wore a dark blue coat faced with red and a tricorn hat. The other had on a brown hunting shirt and a dark brown brimmed hat, one side cocked up and fixed with a brooch of some kind. Continentals, for sure. He crouched down, desperate for a plan should the soldiers land near him.

The voices drifted away. With his whole body he concentrated but the sounds were gone. He sat up to check and dropped back. Not ten feet away the boat had pulled to the shore. He lay low hoping the soldiers would not come near him. He'd shoot one and knife the other. But with the wet powder, would the musket fire? And the sound might alert other soldiers. Surely these two would not be alone.

"Not far now, sir."

The voice stabbed at him, so close it was, almost upon him, and he heard the swishing of the grass. The men were coming toward him. His knife clenched in his sweaty hand, he held his breath and tried to hear over the blood pounding in his ears. He listened for the tell-tale "Aha!" But nothing happened. The sounds were gone. He chanced a look. Two heads, one behind the other, bobbed away from him.

He sank back down and breathed. He was safe but not for long. They would be back. He crawled to the water's edge, to the boat wedged against the rocks. He slipped into the water, nudged the little craft free and rolled over the side into the bottom. He smacked his bruised ankle against the side and stifled a groan.

His hands found the oars and he maneuvered the boat away from shore, making barely a ripple in the placid water, before rowing north in earnest. He kept close to shore out of sight of the two soldiers and all was quiet as he pulled away. In a few minutes he glanced back but saw nothing and no one where he had been. Smiling to himself he lifted the left oar for a couple of strokes to turn the boat out into the current. He pulled two-handed once more toward the far shore and, he hoped, safety.

Chapter Forty-Six

September, 1779

CRYING. She could hear the noise of it in the distant blackness. Her eyes squeezed tighter trying to shut it out but suddenly she started straight up and grabbed for Harper John beside her. She clutched him to her breast, rocking back and forth in the grass. She looked around, shuddering at the horrors she had seen. Coming back to Harper John's need, she stroked his soft curls comforting herself as much as him.

"Are you having a good sleep, woman?"

Lucy had not heard the soldiers' approach.

The leader spoke once again. "Come on, lady. We have no time to wait for you."

His nasty growl brought her to her feet and she plunked Harper John into his pouch and pulled herself up onto her waiting horse. The leader waved the troupe onward. She settled in line behind his horse, wondering how far they would go before the daylight failed. The sun was close to sinking in the west, and Lucy could see the soldier urge his horse on as he surveyed the territory they had come through earlier in the day.

Hours later the man raised his right arm and pulled his horse to a stop. He turned and shouted, "We'll camp here."

She dropped her head on her chest and sighed. They could rest. She dismounted and pulled Harper John out of his pouch and spread her blanket on the ground for him. As she was taking the saddle off, one of the men came to help her and led her horse away to feed with the others.

She sat beside her son and watched the men set up camp for the night. There were no tents, only a large fire, around which the men spread their blankets, each trying to claim just the right spot for sleeping—not too close to the fire, but not too far away either. Someone put a plate of hot sludgy stew into her hands and she gulped it down, sharing a few bits with Harper John.

By the time Lucy had finished, the darkness was complete, broken only by the dying fire. She glanced around needing a trip to the woods by herself but afraid to leave Harper John. She knew the men would not let her take him with her.

"Need some help, ma'am?"

The leader had come up behind her and she struggled to keep her voice even. "Yes. Could you watch the baby again?" She nodded toward the darkness and straightened her shoulders. "I need a few moments." She stood, her back to the fire, to face the man and for the first time all day she saw his features soften into a broad smile.

"Do not take too long, Mrs. Smith." He knelt and picked Harper John from the blanket. "And watch you don't go far. Never know who is out there at night."

She hurried a few paces down the trail and slipped out of sight into the tall grasses. She could see nothing and anxiously relieved herself before hurrying back to the fire and Harper John. The soldier was bouncing her baby on his lap, making him laugh and gurgle, flopping his little arms up and down. When he stopped, Harper John sat still a moment before kicking with his legs to bounce again. She stood a few feet off and watched as the man played with her child, both of them laughing together.

"It is time I settled him for the night, sir." She stood before him and reached for the child.

....

He nodded and stood. "A strapping little boy you have there, Mrs. Smith." He turned and strode to the far side of the fire and she busied herself with calming Harper John for sleep.

In the night Lucy jerked her eyes open in the blackness, listening. There was a moon shining through the trees and she heard the faint rustling of sleeping men shifting on the ground. An owl hooted nearby. Harper John wriggled close against her and she stroked his arm, wrapping the thin blanket tighter around them both. Her eyes slid shut and she slept again.

Hours later she woke to Harper John giggling beside her. She felt his dampness against her drawn up legs and blinked awake to change him. And sat up.

They were alone. Her horse was tethered a few feet away. She scrambled to her feet, saw the cold fire pit, the sunlight glancing off the wet maples and a squirrel scooting up a tree trunk a few feet away. As she knelt to put the last clean clout on her soaking son, she heard birdsong all around her. But still she started at every other noise. And tried to understand why the soldiers had left.

She shrugged and moved to the horse to take stock of what she had. Her pack held the baby's things, her flint and her knife. She still had her rifle with a little ammunition and she had the horse, her blanket, and, of course, Harper John. She should be thankful the soldiers had not hurt them as they had the Senecas.

By this time Harper John was in her arms nuzzling her breast so she nursed him while her mind whirled. She did not know where she was but she knew to head northwest toward Fort Niagara again. She would follow this trail until she found something or someone for directions and food.

She needed to eat. She finished with Harper John and checked the horse. In the ashes of last night's fire a pot had been left with a little stew. Quickly she scooped it up. This would last a day or two if she stretched it, and she could maybe get squash or beans along the way. And, thankfully, the men had left her rifle. She would kill a rabbit or a raccoon if she could.

Free again to head west Lucy packed up her horse, tied the pan to one side and her son to the other and swung her bedraggled skirts up into the saddle. First chance she would take a swim and get clean. In the sunny warmth of the morning her heart lifted as she chucked Frank's horse ahead. She could look for John again. Was he still with Frank? She would have to thank Frank, for sure, and explain to both men all that had happened to their possessions.

She had not gone far before Harper John's head rested against the horse's hide, his eyes closed, his little arms tucked inside the pouch. Good. She hurried on, hoping to find a safe place for the night or at least someone to point her toward Fort Niagara. The horse seemed to sense her excitement and needed no urging to move.

By nightfall she had travelled quite a distance but was ready to sleep. In a little clearing just off the trail she watered the horse, tethered him in the grass, and fed Harper John and herself, before snuggling him into the blanket. She had her rifle beside her, loaded and ready, but she felt so sure that the morning would take her closer to safety, and John, that she immediately drifted off to sleep.

The next day went as well as the first and she made good time travelling a more used trail—she was anxious about the many hoof prints in the softer sections—and mother and son fell into a rhythm of eating, riding, sleeping and laughing together. On one of their rest periods in late afternoon, Lucy sat nursing. A noise in the distance startled them both and she struggled to her feet, still holding Harper John at her breast.

Behind her along the trail, just now coming out of the trees, was a group of riders. As she watched the great cloud of dust looming behind them her arms stiffened and she jerked the baby away. They were coming quickly and had probably already seen her. She put the crying Harper John into his pouch, stood rigid by the side of the trail, rifle at the ready, and watched the group approach. Her fingers were stiff on the trigger. She flexed them once as she fought to breathe evenly and calm her racing heart.

The five men were dressed alike—soldiers probably, but whose? Everyone had different uniforms or none at all and Lucy had no hope of distinguishing them. She watched for some sign as the men slowed and stared at her, a lone woman and a child out in the wilderness.

Suddenly she noticed a brass plate on the hat of one of the men. She thought it looked familiar. She squinted to see its lettering.

"Good day, madam." The lead man gazed at her, his arms across his saddle, as his eyes bored into her.

"Good day." She stood her ground.

"Pardon me, ma'am, but what is a lady such as yourself doing out here alone, in the middle of nowhere? And with a child?" He nodded at Harper John.

"Who are you, sir?" she asked.

The man paused a moment, watching her, his face a mask, until he nodded slightly and spoke. "I am Corporal Peter Wood, ma'am. Who are you?" A slight smile softened his face.

"Where are you going?" She still held the gun ready.

"We are going to Fort Niagara, ma'am. And now, will you tell me who you are?"

"One more thing." She pointed to the hat badge. "What is that?"

The man turned to see where she pointed. "The brass plate? Why that is our Ranger insignia. We are Butler's Rangers, ma'am."

She felt her whole body relax as she lowered the gun and took a step toward the men. "Do you know my husband? John Garner?"

"I believe I have heard the name, ma'am, but I do not know him." He looked around to the others and one nodded.

"Where is he?" She forced herself to be calm.

Corporal Wood stepped down and, motioning the others to stay mounted, had a few whispered words with the soldier who had nodded, before turning back to Lucy. He reached for her hand. "No one has seen him since the Battle at Newtown, ma'am. I am sorry to tell you."

She stared at the corporal. She felt nothing but a huge bottomless crater opening before her and the ground under her feet slipping away. At the last moment she grabbed the corporal's arm and squeaked out the words. "Was he killed?" She dug her hands into the brown shirt of the corporal. "Did you find his body?"

"No, ma'am. We did not."

"Then how do you know he is dead?"

"He did not report after the retreat and no one saw him, or several others." He watched her face. "And the enemy set everything on fire behind us. I am sorry ma'am."

She felt her whole body sag but she stared at the corporal. "Then you have no proof he is dead."

"No, ma'am."

"My name is Lucinda Garner and this is my, our, son, Harper John." Her voice caught. She took a deep breath. "We are trying to get to Fort Niagara, too," she continued. "May we ride with you?"

Sergeant Wood nodded and helped her mount before swinging up himself and moving the small group ahead. She rode beside him and from time to time felt him watching her. He was a kind man, she had seen it in his eyes, but she had no time for him.

She clenched the reins in her hardened brown hands. Her mind was numb, her throat dry. For once the sleeping Harper John was far from her thoughts. She had tried for so long to reach the fort yet now their nearness to it was nothing. She felt her cheeks wither and crack in the searing sun but didn't move to pull up her drooping sun bonnet. She bent forward, lower and lower over the horse, as she accompanied the Rangers to Fort Niagara.

Chapter Forty-Seven

October, 1779

HE HAD ALMOST REACHED THE OTHER SIDE of the wide river when shouts came at him across the choppy water. The two red-faced soldiers jumped and gestured on the far bank, waving him back with their boat. He ducked down as far as he could and pulled on the oars with all his strength. He knew he was not far enough away to avoid getting shot if the men were lucky. Only a few more minutes and he would be into the trees and safe. They couldn't follow him but John wondered if the commotion would raise someone on this side and he scanned the approaching shore.

He reached the water's edge and crept over the side into knee-deep water hiding moss-covered rocks. He slipped and slid to shore, twisted again his weakened ankle, and grabbed an over-hanging branch to steady his pull up the bank into the cover of the trees. He heard nothing, but taking no chances hobbled off to the northwest as fast as he could go through the dense forest.

The fire had not reached this far north. He reveled in the rich forest smells which made him think of home and Lucy. He could never go back there now. He did not even know where Lucy was. His first thought now was to get completely away from Sullivan's punishing army.

He was loyal to the crown and, by this time, knew there was no hope for his kind in this new America. Whether he found Lucy or not, he had to go to the fort at Niagara, as long as it still flew the British flag. His ankle ached with every step he took but he walked on, pushed aside branches, climbed over giant tree trunks and followed the animal paths whenever they went his way.

He had nothing to eat but a few berries, some roots and leaves he knew to be safe. His stomach ached for more but he forced the feeling down and clenched his teeth as he stumbled forward.

He took a long drink from a small stream and refilled his water flask. He chanced a taste of some of the greenery along the shore but spit it out again and rinsed his mouth. He would have to keep looking.

At nightfall he stopped as he could not see his way. He was still in the trees, thankful for their shelter, and burrowed under a pine for the night, hungry and cold.

At first light he set off again, checking his direction with the rising sun, and worrying about the grey clouds in the west. His ankle was even more swollen today but he did not want to think about it. He had to go on.

The pain became so sharp that he could not escape it and all his thoughts were focused on keeping his ankle going and himself heading in the right direction. He thrashed through the underbrush. The branches thwacked against his smoke-streaked face, while his ankle throbbed and throbbed, a huge knob of pain at the end of his leg.

Finally, he had to rest. He slid onto a downed tree and hoisted his foot up on it to have a look. The ankle was red and purple, swollen so large that he knew he had to stop or he might never recover. He glanced at the sun overhead and realized there was not much daylight left. This was as good a place as any.

Sometime in the night John felt the first wet drips of rain and huddled closer to the tree but was soon soaked through. He had no fire, no protection, no food and, finally, no hope. As he lay wait-

....

ing for first light, he began to shiver and shake. His close-wrapped arms were no help.

His mind wandered, first with visions of food and fire and, toward morning, of Lucy and Frank, of his mother—he had not thought of her in years, of the scythe slicing through the hay, of the cabin burning, the animals screaming, a tree falling on Maudie, squashing the life out of her, blood running red all around him, coming closer across the ground as he held back, but he couldn't escape and his whole body turned red and hot as fire. He tried to get away from the heat but walls held him in the flames. The soldier ran with him to the ship, away from the fallen man. He did not feel the rain stop nor see the dawn creep toward him.

The morning drizzle was cold, the first sign of fall. Water drip-dripped from the red-tinged maples. Huge drops clung to the pines until eventually they slid along the branches and fell to the ground soaking the forest floor. They washed away bits of fallen branches and dead grass, weathered pine cones and withered leaves, first in small rivulets and then in a great sweeping torrent as the rain once again poured from the sky.

He lay shivering in a puddle, soaking and sweating, oblivious to the chattering of his teeth and the wet light of day.

The punishing rain continued for hours. John groaned and shook, with barely a coherent thought until, finally, the absence of rain registered in his brain and his eyes slit open to brightness.

He blinked to keep the dripping water from his eyes and tried to stand. He had to go on.

He pulled himself up to sit on the log but barely knew where he was or what he was about. He just knew he had to move and staggered to his feet, cried out at the pain, but lurched off toward the thin strand of sunshine calling him west.

SULLIVAN'S SOLDIERS HAD BEEN STOPPED by the mighty storm as well, and huddled in their flimsy tents under the pounding rain which doused their fires and soaked their food supplies. When finally the sun came out so did the men, anxious to dry off and eat again. The fires were lit and great misty clouds rose from the damp wood until their haphazard camp was a hissing haze of spitting fires and wet smoke. The General decided to stop for another night to dry out before continuing his swath through Loyalist and Indian territory.

In the morning the soldiers marched at first light, the camp already dismantled and the fires extinguished. Sullivan's orders were to wipe out the Indian resistance once and for all, to punish the enemy and end the war as quickly as possible.

He forged ahead through small farms and large forests, burning and destroying the countryside but leaving the people untouched unless they fought back. He had orders to destroy possessions, not people, and he tried his best to follow them. At times, however, his soldiers did not listen.

THE SHOUTING FROM BEHIND assailed the fevered recesses of John's brain. He barely noticed. He lurched from one foot to the other, from one log to the next, from tree to tree, his body such a sea of pain that he couldn't think, tried not to feel, only to stumble on. His mind was numb. But still something told him to keep going. His green eyes were wild and shot with blood, his hair a straggle of matted rope falling over his sooty face streaked by the relentless rain, and his tattered clothing was worn through in some places and completely rent in others.

He tried to outrun the noise but suddenly tripped and fell to the side, landing hard. Tiny stars swirled in the darkness of his brain. Lucy... Rough hands found him, finally, and pulled, but he was gone.

Chapter Forty-Eight

Spring, 1780

LUCY SAT IN THE COMMANDER'S OFFICE where she had first been led after appearing at the fort and demanding to know about her husband. She had been many times since with no luck.

Rangers had straggled in to Fort Niagara throughout the fall of 1779 but no one had brought any news of John. No one had seen him killed or found his body. No one had seen where he had run to when the Rangers had retreated and he had not regrouped with the rest of them after the terrible rout at Newtown.

He seemed to have vanished, but she could not accept that fact. John would do everything to get back to her. He would. She knew he would.

"Now, Mrs. Garner, we have been over this many times. Your husband is listed as missing and presumed dead."

She stared at the officer's hazel eyes, his well-trimmed brown hair. He was concerned for her, but she would not be persuaded.

"I am sorry, sir. I thought…I hoped there might be some news." Her voice came out thin, weak even, but she sat erect in the chair.

"No. There has been nothing, ma'am." He came around the corner of the desk. "I am sorry, Mrs. Garner, but there has been no word. I can do nothing for you."

Elaine Cougler

She felt the familiar sickening in her stomach, the tightening in her chest. Her head dropped. Without a word she eased herself out of the chair and turned to the door. "Thank you," she whispered.

In the corridor she leaned against the cold stone wall a moment, blinking back the tears. She must get back to Harper John. She had left him with Nellie who, with her Ranger husband, allowed her to sleep on a cot in their small cabin while they waited the winter out before crossing to claim land and start a farm safe in British territory.

She wiped her eyes, stood away from the wall, and dragged herself down the steps of the old stone building. She went out the main door, past hurrying Rangers and British soldiers, toward the small huts off to the right. They had been hastily erected to house the steady influx of settlers stopping here on their flight to Canada. Some stayed only a night or two before being ferried across the Niagara River but she had been here all winter and was no closer to finding John than when she arrived.

Near the cabin she barely noticed the new green grass poking into the sunshine or the freshening breeze off the water. She heard Harper John's squeal and saw him standing, by himself, Nellie's outstretched arms ready to catch him if he fell. Her face broke into a smile. He would be walking in no time. She scooped him up and pressed his struggling body close.

"Any news?" Nellie peered at her.

"The commander says John must be dead. I expect he doesn't have time to look for one lost soldier." She set Harper John on the grass and watched as he tried to step out.

"Perhaps you need to decide what to do, Lucinda."

She dropped the baby's hand and straightened up to look at Nellie, her eyes filling again. "I just cannot leave. I cannot. Supposing he should come and I weren't here?" She looked out over the river. "And I do not know what I would do over there by myself with a baby. It's a snowy wasteland. How can I start over? Everything we had is gone. Except for the horse. And a few buttons and Harper John's silver spoon."

"You could consider Mr. Butcher's offer. He needs a wife and you need a husband. Besides he has a wagon full of household goods—more than enough." Nellie put her rough hand on Lucy's arm. "We could all go together, be neighbors. Please think about it, my friend." Nellie gave Lucy's arm a squeeze.

"I just don't know."

Harper John tottered away from her. She grabbed him up and slipped into the cabin.

On the cot she sat and held her son, rocking him back and forth. The hot tears started again. This time they wouldn't stop. Her mind swam with images of what she had lost, the farm, their animals, the lovely little cabin with its stove and its table—John's rocking chair—and her mother's patchwork quilt. Each new thought brought fresh tears and deep sobs.

She cried for the couple she and John had been in their wedding engraving, but were no more. She pictured herself riding beside Mr. Butcher on his loaded wagon but choked at the thought of his arms around her.

Harper John squealed, wriggled and finally wailed. This frightened scream got her attention. She stroked his back and settled him to her breast, gradually stifling her sobs.

As she sat, she realized what she had to do. Impossible as it was, she would cross with Nellie and her husband on the morrow. They had certainly begged her to come. She had to start a new life, hard as it might be. And she would try to think again of Mr. Butcher.

Harper John pulled at her breast. She was glad she had John's child to remind her of where and who she had been. If he were alive he would have come by now. She had to move on. Stroking the baby's cheeks, she ignored a sudden commotion outside.

She dried her eyes and felt calm. A new cold courage to forge a life for herself and her son rose in her. The warm afternoon sun streamed in the open door against her back. Harper John kicked to be let down and she let his little legs hit the floor while she held his chubby fingers to steady him.

A shadow dimmed the room. She turned. Dark, against the bright sun, stood a man. She jumped up and pushed Harper John behind her.

"Yes?" Her voice shook as she spoke. But there was something about the man.

"John!" She grabbed up Harper John and stumbled across the room, crushing herself and the baby against him, laughing, crying, saying his name over and over, in the wonderful warmth of his arms.

They rocked back and forth, John sniffing into her wild curls and Lucy lost in his fierce embrace until Harper John's squirming forced them apart. She smiled into John's wet eyes.

"Lucy." His voice broke.

"You're here. Oh, you're here. I am so happy." Her own tears gone, she stepped back to look at him. "Come. We have much to tell."

They sat at the tiny table, Harper John playing on the floor, and told their stories. John had been found by Seneca Indians fleeing General Sullivan's advance as well, and they had taken him with them, nursing him the whole winter until he was able to push on himself to Fort Niagara. He told her of his despair at not being able to find her and, at last, of the British soldier who had saved him years before, his reason for siding with the King.

She told him about her father's death and her trek to Fort Niagara, and even of her decision to cross the river in the morning with the other Loyalists. She didn't burden him with the whole truth about losing the wagon or of Mr. Butcher's intentions toward her. And she never would.

"You've come just in time, my dear. Now, we can go as a family."

"We can start again in this Canada, can't we?" John's green eyes lit when he spoke. "Of course, I'll still be with the Rangers for some time yet. But the fight is almost over."

She broke in, "We can never go home to our farm, can we?"

"No. We must forget that and move forward now. Start again in Canada." His green eyes lit up. He turned to her.

"Yes," she said. "We three can start a new life." She reached across the table.

He grabbed her outstretched hand. It was worn and rough now, but warm and strong.

Books Consulted By The Author

1. *Mrs. Simcoe's Diary*, Mary Quayle Innis, ed. 1965 MacMillan of Canada, Toronto, St. Martin's Press, New York.

2. *Niagara-on-the-Lake: Its Heritage and Its Festival*, James Lorimer & Company Ltd., Publishers, Toronto.

3. *History of Niagara*, Janet Carnochan, originally published by William Briggs, Toronto, 1914, this edition published by Global Heritage Press, Milton, 2006.

4. *Canada & the American Revolution 1774-1783*, Gustave Lanctot of the Royal Society, Clarke, Irwin & Company, Toronto, 1967.

5. *Eleven Exiles: Account of the American Revolution*, Phyllis R. Blakeley, John N. Grant, ed., Dundurn Press Limited, Toronto, 1982.

6. *The Loyalists: Revolution, Exile, Settlement*, Christopher Moore, Macmillan of Canada, A division of Gage Publishing Limited, Toronto, 1984.

7. *King's Men: The Soldier Founders of Ontario*, Mary Beacock Fryer, Dundurn Press Limited, Toronto, 1980.

8. *Joseph Brant and His World*, James W. Paxton, James Lorimer & Company Ltd., Publishers, Toronto, 2008.

9. *Loyal She Remains: A Pictorial History of Ontario*, published by The United Empire Loyalists' Association of Canada, Toronto, 1984.

10. *Pease Porridge: Beyond the King's Bread*, JoAnn Demler, Old Fort Niagara Association, Inc., Youngstown, New York, 2003.

11. *Much To Be Done: Private Life in Ontario from Victorian Diaries*, Hoffman, Frances, Taylor, Ryan, Natural Heritage / Natural History Inc., Toronto, 1996.

Topics and Questions For Discussion

1. At the time of the American Revolutionary War the term 'loyalist' was used to mark those who disagreed with the upstart idea for the Thirteen Colonies to break away from England and form a new country. What is the significance of the title in relation to the theme of *The Loyalist's Wife*?

2. How are John and Lucy well suited to each other and how are their individual characteristics a trial for them?

3. Is it realistic for the time and place of *The Loyalist's Wife* for this young couple to be so isolated in New York State as the novel opens, or has the author played with fact? What details from the novel or other research support your position?

4. Butler's Rangers were a significant force in the British fight against the Continentals / Americans but they (and the other British forces) were not successful in wiping out the zeal for revolution against the British. What might be some of the reasons for their ultimate losing of the battle to save the Loyalist lands and the Loyalists themselves in this war?

5. Depending on what one reads about the Wyoming Valley battles the Rangers were either despicable and heartless murderers or they were ordinary men caught in extraordinary circumstances fighting alongside Natives with their own agenda. Discuss the reasons why such varied accounts exist from good quality sources.

6. How realistic is it that a man would leave his wife alone to tend their farm in the midst of so unsettled a time? Realizing that the British fully expected to squash the upstart rebels and keep their firm hand on the colonies, why would so many colonists fight against such a formidable foe as Great Britain?

7. How does Lucy's character throughout the novel change and mature? Is her decision not to ever tell John about the rape believable?

8. What is the overall impression readers get about the Iroquois nations, specifically the Mohawks and the Senecas, and is it believable? Point to specific incidents to support your opinions.

9. By having John return at the end of the book, the author has opened the door to another book or more in the series. Was this a satisfying ending or would you have preferred something different? Explain.

COMING SOON!

Book Two in the Loyalist Series

The Loyalist's Luck

by Elaine Cougler

John and Lucy escape the Revolutionary War to the unsettled British territory across the Niagara River with almost nothing. In the untamed wilderness they must fight to survive, he, off on a secret mission for Colonel Butler and she, left behind with her young son and pregnant once again. In the camp full of distrust, hunger, and poverty, word has seeped out that John has gone over to the American side and only two people will associate with Lucy—her friend, Nellie, who delights in telling her all the current gossip, and Sergeant Crawford, who refuses to set the record straight and clear John's name. To make matters worse, the sergeant has made improper advances toward Lucy. With John's reputation besmirched, she must walk a thin line depending as she does on the British army, and Sergeant Crawford, for her family's very survival.